An American Dream Girl

OTHER BOOKS BY JAMES T. FARRELL

STUDS LONIGAN

A trilogy comprising "Young Lonigan," "The Young Manhood of Studs Lonigan," and "Judgment Day"

The Danny O'Neill Tetralogy

A WORLD I NEVER MADE

NO STAR IS LOST

FATHER AND SON

MY DAYS OF ANGER

BERNARD CLARE

THE ROAD BETWEEN

THE SHORT STORIES OF JAMES T. FARRELL

Comprising "Calico Shoes and Other Stories," "Guillotine Party and Other Stories," and "Can All This Grandeur Perish and Other Stories"

THE LIFE ADVENTUROUS

WHEN BOYHOOD DREAMS COME TRUE

TO WHOM IT MAY CONCERN

$1,000 A WEEK

GAS-HOUSE MCGINTY

ELLEN ROGERS

TOMMY GALLAGHER'S CRUSADE

A NOTE ON LITERARY CRITICISM

THE LEAGUE OF FRIGHTENED PHILISTINES

LITERATURE AND MORALITY

An American Dream Girl

BY

JAMES T. FARRELL

THE VANGUARD PRESS, INC.

New York

To

MARGARET DE SILVER

and to the memory of

CARLO TRESCA

Acknowledgments

I wish to express my gratitude to Mr. Stanley Pargellis, Director of the Newberry Library, and to the Board of Directors of that institution for having granted me a fellowship which helped me to complete this book, and which also has aided me in work on an uncompleted novel.

But O, sick children of the world . . .

From "The Song of the Happy Shepherd"
by WILLIAM BUTLER YEATS

Contents

An American Dream Girl

A Misunderstanding

EVEN THOUGH THEY PUT ME HERE in a lunatic asylum, I know that I'm not crazy. I don't think I'm like the inmates. Some of them are pretty far gone. If you look at them or listen to them talk, and then look at me or listen to me talk, you can tell that they are lunatics, and you can see that there is a difference between them and me. Of course, I am a little quiet now and not like I used to be with the boys in the office. But who is there to talk to in a lunatic asylum? The inmates here? We have one inmate who thinks he's Winston Churchill. And another is convinced that an atom bomb is being manufactured to blow up the entire world just so he'll be killed. He says that they are spending billions of dollars just to bump him off. I don't know who he means by *they*, but *they* sound like people who are around here or someplace nearby. And another fellow who never washes, he prays a lot and walks all around the grounds three times a day, taking the same route, making the same faces and motions at the same places, all because he says God told him to do just this so that he can keep evil out of the world.

I feel kind of sorry for these people, but I am not like them, and if you really know the circumstances which led me to do what I did, why, you'll agree with me that I'm no lunatic. In fact, I am sorry I did what I did. I killed my wife. The story was in the papers, on the front pages. I didn't want to cop a plea, as I think the saying goes. I insisted that I was sane. But, anyway, they declared me to be a lunatic. So—here I am. And

3

it looks like I'm going to spend the rest of my life here, meeting Mr. Churchill and Mr. Truman, and listening to a number of people who are very important because billions of dollars are being spent to kill them, and meeting other people who are keeping evil out of the world, and listening to the howling and the raving and the screaming and the cursing. I don't belong here. All I did was to kill Molly. There are other fellows here who killed their wives, and I tried to talk to them to find out why they did it, but I haven't been able to make any contact with them. They're lunatics, too. One of them is Mr. Phillips. Mr. Phillips thinks that he is living with his wife. Every day he walks around by himself, talking, and he thinks that he is talking to her. He doesn't believe that he killed her with a hammer. But he did. I'm not like him. I know I killed Molly.

I tried to tell the court and the jury how and why I did it. And I tried to explain it to the docs here. But what can you tell a doc in a place like this? After trying to tell them, and seeing how I was not getting anywheres near convincing them, I gave it up, and I decided that there are two kinds of lunatics here: those who are put away, and the privileged lunatics who take care of us and have control of the keys to all the doors— the docs. But that is not what I want to talk about. What I want to explain is why I killed my wife.

Molly was a good woman. All our friends thought she was a wonderful wife. I suppose she was. She used to work and work away in the kitchen. She loved to scour the pots. In fact, she'd scour them until I began to feel sorry for the poor pots. I would see her on a hot day, scouring away at one of them with the sweat dripping down her face, and I would feel sorry for her. I would feel that I must be doing something to her to have her work so hard in the kitchen. It wasn't right and would make me feel bad, as if I'd done something rotten.

"Molly, why don't you let that pot alone?" I would say. "It's a hot day, and those pots are clean enough."

But she would scour away, paying no attention to me.

"Molly, you've done enough. Come sit down now and drink

a glass of beer with me—it's hot as hell, and you don't have to be working so hard on them pots."

"I'll have to get that Quick Scour advertised on the radio," she would answer.

Now, that's what I mean when I say that I am not a lunatic because I killed her.

Whatever I would say to her, she would talk about something else. She was always off my beam, and I was never able to get on her beam, if you can get what I mean. I wasn't talking about some new powder for scouring pots. I was telling her to take it easy because life is short and there's no sense in a woman spending an hour scouring a pot when it doesn't need to be scoured at all. She would cook some peas in a pot, and then, after we ate, there she would be, rubbing away at that pot. I don't know how she failed to scour the pots until she scoured off the finish. But it wasn't that, the scouring and the working away the way she did, that bothered me most. It was what she said.

Molly and I didn't quarrel and fight very much, hardly at all. We never had the fights some married folks have. We had our little spats, and sometimes she nagged me and got cranky, but I began to see that this wasn't important, and I used not to mind a spat now and then. I liked everything about Molly but the way she talked.

For instance—I would come home from the office, and I would think that I am going to have a nice quiet evening, and Molly and I would have a talk, and we would relax, and, well, we would enjoy our home and our life together. And so I would come home and give her a kiss, and I would say something like:

"Hello, dear, how are you? Did you have a nice day?"

"I'll have to try a different kind of soap. I don't like this Sudsy-Suds I've been using."

"But did you have a nice day, Molly?"

"There wasn't any mail, dear."

"But I didn't ask you about the mail, Molly, dear. Did you have a nice day?"

"I think there's a new mailman, and he might have made some mistake and put our mail in somebody else's box."

"But, Molly, what kind of a day did you have?"

"Oh!" she would exclaim.

And that is what I mean when I say that I am not a lunatic because I killed Molly.

"Is supper ready?" I would ask her, because I used to have a good appetite, and I liked to eat, but she would be off then, telling me about something else that had nothing to do with the question I asked.

Towards the end, I wasn't eating much, but once I came to this place I found that my appetite was what it used to be. But I can't get enough food here. Of course, it is cooked pretty badly, but not as bad as Molly's cooking. Now, Molly thought she was a good cook. She would start cooking my supper at two or three o'clock in the afternoon. And I would get home at six.

"Is supper ready, Molly?"

"I'm going to try using peanut oil instead of olive oil as a base for my salad dressing," she would say.

Now, why should a man care if his wife uses peanut oil or olive oil as a base for a salad dressing when his wife makes the dressing so that you make a face every time you taste it. So I would go into the parlor and read my newspaper and wait. And Molly would be working away in the kitchen. My God, you would have thought she was a coolie. She would have pans and dishes and pots all over the place and on the floor, and there was hardly room to move in. I remember how one night I was hungry. I had had a hard day at the office, because the boss had been on my tail. I guess maybe his wife must have been on his tail at breakfast that morning and he was getting even with her by hopping on me. Well, I was hungry and tired, fagged out, and I wanted a nice, good, solid meal and a quiet night. And so I sat in the parlor, reading my newspaper, and as the time passed I began to hear my stomach making noises, and I was getting pretty damned hungry. I went out to the kitchen. There was Molly working like a coolie, with pots and pans all over the place—dishes, flour, a biscuit tin greased and buttered and ready for the dough—and she had already been cooking for a couple of hours. So I asked her:

"Molly, do you need all this equipment around to cook me supper?"

"Oh, of course, I was cleaning the pots."

"But couldn't you do that some morning when I am at the office and just cook my supper in the evening?"

"Well, the pots needed to be cleaned, and I had to defrost the refrigerator."

I admit it made me sore. But I didn't say anything. I went back and read my newspaper, and my stomach made noises until I began to feel weak with hunger. In about twenty minutes I went back to the kitchen. She was working just as hard, and she was only just then putting the dough for the biscuits into the pan.

"Molly, I don't want any biscuits for supper. I want to eat."

"Oh, of course. I have to watch that ham so that it doesn't burn."

Well, that night I got my dinner at ten minutes after nine, and Molly's biscuits gave me such an attack of indigestion that I didn't sleep a wink all night.

Molly used to read a lot. She would go to the rental library a block away and get all of the latest books. I like to read a book now and then, and once in a while I would read one of the books she rented. I remember there was one book—I forget the title, but that doesn't matter—that seemed to me to be pretty phony. Well, Molly sat up late at night reading it for two weeks, and every once in a while she would groan and grunt. I was kind of curious about why she seemed to like it so much. I wondered what kind of book it was that was keeping her up and making her sigh and make such a noise when she read. So I read the book myself. I tell you, it was as phony as it could be. I am not a literary critic or a particularly well-educated man or anything like that, but sometimes, if something is phony, I have enough horse sense to know it. So I asked

Molly why she read the book and took so much time reading
it, at that.

"Oh," says Molly. "Remember that book by Bromfield I
read last month? I told you about it. Well, that book was a
strange book."

But what about the book I was talking about? I asked Molly
questions for half an hour, and then, after I worked as if I was
pulling teeth, she tells me that she read this book just because
she read it. Now perhaps you can begin to understand the point
I'm getting at.

I was young, of course, when I met and courted and married
Molly. She was a pretty thing, and I was mighty proud to
think that a girl as sweet and pretty as Molly would fall in
love with me. I was really in the clouds in those days. She
talked just the way she always did, but I was young then,
and she so pretty a girl, so innocent, and I used to think
that she was just like a flower, and I felt that I was kind of
rotten to be picking as beautiful a flower as Molly. And I
loved her and thought that there was nothing that could be
improved in her, not even the way she talked, even her never
answering a question. When we were first married, I liked the
way she talked and the way she took time to cook my dinner,
and I liked it that she would think of spending so much time in
the kitchen cooking for me, not to mention washing pots and
pans and dishes. I used to help her, and now and then I would
think to myself that we could work faster, and I would try to
speed up the domestic work, but Molly always had something
else to do, and always had to do everything I did over again. I
decided that it was a woman's way, and gradually I let her
have her way.

I don't want you to think, furthermore, that I'm complaining. I'm not. But we could have saved some money if Molly
would have helped me. My God, when I think of all the money
she spent on butter and dough and flour, and only a woman
would know what else, to bake me biscuits that I couldn't eat,
and, mind you, to bake them just when the meat was ready
and would get cold while the biscuits were baking! And the

money she spent on salad dressings, getting different bases when the dressings were just not to my taste. She used to tell me, too, that she was cooking all of these fancy things that took so much time because she wanted to attract my palate.

It was worse when we had friends to dinner. Then we were always lucky if we could sit down to eat at ten-thirty. And the meat would always be burned. Once, I remember we had our friends to dinner, the Hoffmans. Well, we finally get seated at ten-thirty, and there's the ham burned on the outside. So I asked Molly, and I was not being sarcastic, but I was only wanting to know, so I asked her:

"Molly, was burning the ham part of the recipe in that new cookbook of yours?"

I forgot to say that she spent a small fortune on cookbooks.

"Oh," says Molly, "that's the oven."

"Maybe we had better tell the landlord to have a man come and look at the oven and fix it up. After all, it doesn't make much sense to have an oven that burns a perfectly good ham."

"Of course," she says, and when she would say "Oh" or "Of course," I would feel kind of foolish, because she would say it as if to say you don't have to say that, because everybody knows it. So this night, with the Hoffmans there, and all of us eating burned ham that took so long to burn that the potatoes were cold when we ate them, why, Molly she says "of course" in just that way, and she says:

"I bought this ham from a new butcher."

"But, dear, I was talking about getting the oven fixed so we won't have our ham burned no matter where we buy it."

"Of course, if you don't want me to go to the new butcher, I'll go back to Mr. Herzog," she says.

Well, it was always the same old story. If I said one thing, Molly said something else. If I asked her questions, she would talk about the answers to questions I didn't ask instead of the ones I did ask. Now, this is a small thing, and, after all, you might say that a man has no right to kill his wife because she won't answer a question. But before you say that, I would say to you that you try and live twenty years with a woman and

not have her ever once answer a question, or say to you something that follows from what you say to her. As I say, when I
first met her, I didn't notice all this because she was so young
and so pretty and I felt so good and proud of myself being
married to a pretty girl and thinking that she loved me more
than I had any right to deserve to be loved. But love kind of
wears off, and you want to be happy and comfortable, and you
only ask for a few things. You work all day, and you want to
have a quiet supper, and, besides loving your wife at night,
you want a little sociableness, and now and then a friend or
two in. But it got so nobody would come to supper because
they didn't know if they were going to get supper or breakfast. And there I was, usually eating only a sandwich in a
hurry for lunch, and then I would have to wait until eight,
nine, ten o'clock for my meal. Now, once I had the boys at
the office to the house. I was mighty proud and told them how
I had a little woman who was a cook, and I meant a cook. And
we talked and kidded for a week about the meal Molly was
going to give the boys. Well, they came, and we have cocktails, and talk, and Molly is in and out and mostly out in the
kitchen, and the time passes. It gets to be seven o'clock. I go
out and ask Molly:

"Will the eats be ready soon?"

"I'm using olive oil as a base for my salad dressing tonight
instead of peanut oil," she answers.

"But what time will we eat?"

"I think that the biscuits are going to be luscious tonight."

And I can't find out what time we eat, and so it gets to be
seven-thirty. The boys are nervous, and then it's eight o'clock,
and they are restless, and I am so embarrassed I don't know
what to say.

"Molly, it's eight o'clock," I say, going out to the kitchen.

"I'm using cinnamon on the apricots for dessert. I know the
boys will like it," she answers.

To make a long story short, we ate at nine-thirty.

"That was *some* meal the missus cooked us last night," says

Clark, one of the boys at the office, when I went to work the next morning.

Well, I kind of wished I could have sunk right through the floor. And the boys kidded me, saying we ate late to put on the dog, as if we thought we were in society or something like that. But, anyway, the boys never came again, and, to tell you the truth, I never had the heart to ask them.

I could go on and tell you more about Molly, but I think you got the idea. Now, I didn't really mean to kill her. That night, I came home with a present for her. It was our twentieth anniversary, and I was thinking how we had pulled together all of these years, and, sure, Molly has her peculiarities, but maybe we all have them, and what if we don't get seated at dinner before eight-thirty or nine, Molly is Molly, and she was just as pretty, just like a flower, as when she was young. So I go home and I have a ring for her. A small diamond ring. I saved up my money for it for a long time, and that is one of the reasons why I ate only sandwiches for lunch. The boys even used to call me a cheap skate and a piker because of the way I ate.

Anyway, I kissed her when I got home and, after making a fuss and being, you know, a little mysterious, I give her the ring.

"I got a new brand of olive oil," she says, looking at the ring.

"Do you know what it is?"

"Last Monday was a scorcher, wasn't it, dear," she says, and that was her way of answering my question by telling me that it was Monday.

I felt sunk, I was so let down. So I told her it was our anniversary, and she told me that the landlord's daughter was engaged to be married.

"Do you like the ring, Molly, old girl?" I asked her.

"The landlord's daughter is getting a diamond engagement ring."

"This is a diamond. Look at the way it shines. Isn't it pretty?"

"I saw the nicest rug today. I was shopping."

"But what do you think of that little sparkler, Molly?"

"Oh, when I was a little girl, I loved sparklers on the Fourth of July."

So it goes on like that.

"Molly, don't you know that you will never answer a question if I ask one?" I said to her.

"Of course," she says in that way of hers, her face looking puzzled. And then I realized that whenever I asked her a question, she looks at me as if she didn't know what I was talking about. I admit I was sunk. It dawned on me that here we are, married twenty years, and I am living with Molly, and, no matter what I say to her, she doesn't know what I am talking about. I don't know her. I don't know what it is she is always thinking about and what the devil is making her tick.

"Molly, if I say it is hot out, you tell me it was cold yesterday. If I ask you a question about the oven, you talk about the butcher."

"Of course, I don't," she says.

"I've been living with you twenty years, and you have never once answered a question of mine. Come to think of it, I remember now when I asked you to marry me you didn't even say 'yes.' You said that when your grandfather proposed to your grandmother she asked your grandaunt to accept the proposal by letter, and that you thought marriage was a fine thing."

"I married you," she says.

Yes, that was true. Anyway, I decided that I was going to make her for once say yes or no, even if Hell froze over. So I told her:

"Molly, answer my question."

"Of course," she says.

"Do you like that ring?"

"I read a book last week, and the story was about how a diamond ring was stolen."

"But what's that got to do with my question?"

"Weren't you talking about diamond rings?"

I lost my head. So I decided on the spur of the moment I was really going to make her say yes or no. I said:

"Molly, I'm going to punch you in the nose, and I want to know if it hurts."

So I hit her, and she fell, and her head hit the floor, and she didn't come to consciousness again. She had a concussion and a hemorrhage of the brain, and she died. I was sorry. I didn't mean to kill her. I only wanted her to say yes or no to me. But when she was dead, I was not really sorry. I wished I hadn't punched her in the nose and killed her. But, still, I just didn't feel anything. Because it had dawned on me I didn't know her, and all of these years it was as if she didn't really exist, because, after all, our talk was like wires that didn't even get crossed. We lived like on different telephone party lines. So that's my story.

I ask you, now, does it prove that I'm a lunatic?

But still they have me here. And, as I say, I know a man here who thinks he is Winston Churchill. I was walking about, because they let me walk around the grounds, and I saw him, and I say to him that it is a fine morning. So he answers me by saying:

"I never go to the House of Commons in the morning."

That was what brought Molly to my mind. I walked around the grounds, and I looked at all of the people here, inmates, and I thought of her, and I thought of them, and I realized that I didn't really belong here. All I did was to try and do the only thing I could think of doing so that I would get Molly, for once, to say yes or no to a question. That's all I wanted when I punched her. It was an accident that her head hit the floor. And that's the story of how I killed my wife. But I do often wonder, now, if she hadn't died, would she have said it hurt when I punched her in the nose?

The Fastest Runner on Sixty-first Street

I

MORTY AIKEN liked to run and to skate. He liked running games and races. He liked running so much that sometimes he'd go over to Washington Park all by himself and run just for the fun of it. He got a kick out of running, and he had raced every kid he could get to run against him. His love of racing and running had even become a joke among many of the boys he knew. But even when they gave him the horse laugh it was done in a good-natured way, because he was a very popular boy. Older fellows liked him, and when they would see him, they'd say, there's a damn good kid and a damned fast runner.

When he passed his fourteenth birthday, Morty was a trifle smaller than most boys of his own age. But he was well known, and, in a way, almost famous in his own neighborhood. He lived at Sixty-first and Eberhardt, but kids in the whole area had heard of him, and many of them would speak of what a runner and what a skater Morty Aiken was.

He won medals in playground tournaments, and, in fact, he was the only lad from his school who had ever won medals in these tournaments. In these events he became the champion in the fifty- and hundred-yard dash, and with this he gained the reputation of being the best runner, for his age, on the South Side of Chicago.

He was as good a skater as he was a runner. In winter,

he was to be seen regularly almost every day on the ice at the
Washington Park lagoon or over on the Midway. He had a
pair of Johnson racers which his father had given him, and he
treasured these more than any other possession. His mother
knitted him red socks and a red stocking cap for skating, and
he had a red-and-white sweater. When he skated, he was like a
streak of red. His form was excellent, and his sense of himself
and of his body on the ice was sure and right. Almost every
day there would be a game of I-Got-It. The skater who was *it*
would skate in a wide circle, chased by the pack until he was
caught. Morty loved to play I-Got-It, and on many a day this
boy in short pants, wearing the red stocking cap, the red-and-
white sweater, and the thick, knitted red woolen socks coming
above the black shoes of his Johnson racers, would lead the
pack, circling around and around and around, his head forward, his upper torso bent forward, his hands behind his back,
his legs working with grace and giving him a speed that sometimes seemed miraculous. And in February, 1919, Morty com-
peted in an ice derby, conducted under the auspices of the
Chicago *Clarion*. He won two gold medals. His picture was
on the first page of the sports section of the Sunday *Clarion*.
All in all, he was a famous and celebrated lad. His father and
mother were proud of him. His teacher and Mrs. Bixby, the
principal of the school, were proud of him. Merchants on
Sixty-first Street were proud of him. There was not a lad in
the neighborhood who was greeted on the street by strangers
as often as Morty.

Although he was outwardly modest, Morty had his dreams.
He was graduated from grammar school in 1919, and was
planning to go to Park High in the fall. He was impatient to
go to high school and to get into high-school track meets. He'd
never been coached, and yet look how good he was! Think of
how good he would be when he had some coaching! He'd be a
streak of lightning, if there ever was one. He dreamed that he
would be called the Human Streak of Lightning. And after
high school there would be college, college track meets, and

the Big Ten championship, and after that he would join an athletic club and run in track meets, and he would win a place on the Olympic team, and somewhere, in Paris or Rome or some European city, he would beat the best runners in the world, and, like Ty Cobb in baseball and Jess Willard in prize fighting, he'd be the world's greatest runner.

And girls would all like him, and the most beautiful girl in the world would marry him. He liked girls, but girls liked him even more than he liked them. In May, a little while before his graduation, the class had a picnic, and they played post office. The post office was behind a clump of bushes in Jackson Park. He was called to the post office more than any other of the boys. There was giggling and talking and teasing, but it hadn't bothered him, especially because he knew that the other fellows liked and kind of envied him. To Morty, this was only natural. He accepted it. He accepted the fact that he was a streak of lightning on his feet and on the ice, and that this made him feel somehow different from other boys and very important. Even Tony Rabuski looked at him in this way, and if any kid would have picked on him, Tony would have piled into that kid. Tony was the toughest boy in school, and he was also considered to be the dumbest. He was also the poorest. He would often come to school wearing a black shirt, because a black shirt didn't show the dirt the way that other shirts did, and his parents couldn't afford to buy him many shirts. One day Tony was walking away from school with Morty, and Tony said:

"Kid, you run de fastest, I fight de best in de whole school. We make a crack-up team. We're pals. Shake, kid, we're pals."

Morty shook Tony's hand. For a fourteen-year-old boy, Tony had very big and strong hands. The other kids sometimes called them "meat hooks."

Morty looked on this handshake as a pledge. He and Tony became friends, and they were often together. Morty had Tony come over to his house to play, and sometimes Tony stayed for a meal. Tony ate voraciously and wolfishly. When Morty's parents spoke of the way Tony ate and of the quantity

of food he ate, Morty would reply by telling them that Tony
was his friend.

Because he was poor and somewhat stupid, a dull and fierce
resentment smoldered in Tony. Other boys out-talked him,
and they were often able to plague and annoy him, and then
outrun him because he was heavy footed. The kids used to
laugh at Tony because they said he had lead, iron, and bricks
in his big feet. After Morty and Tony had shaken hands and
become pals, Morty never would join the other boys in razzing
Tony. And he and Tony doped out a way that would permit
Tony to get even with kids who tried to torment him. If some
of the boys made game of Tony until he was confused and
enraged and went for them, Morty would chase the boys. He
had no difficulty in catching one of them. When he caught
any of the boys who'd been teasing and annoying Tony, he'd
usually manage to hold the boy until Tony would lumber up
and exact his punishment and revenge. Sometimes Tony would
be cruel, and on a couple of occasions when Tony, in a dull
and stupefied rage, was sitting on a hurt, screaming boy and
pounding him, Morty ordered Tony to lay off. Tony did so
instantly. Morty didn't want Tony to be too cruel. He had
come to like Tony and to look on him as a big brother. He'd
always wanted a brother, and sometimes he would imagine
how wonderful it would be if Tony could even come to live at
his house.

The system Morty and Tony worked out, with Morty chasing and catching one of the boys who ragged Tony, worked
out well. Soon the kids stopped ragging Tony. Because of
their fear, and because they liked and respected Morty and
wanted him to play with them, they began to accept Tony.
And Tony began to change. Once accepted, so that he was no
longer the butt of jokes, he looked on all the boys in Morty's
gang as his pals. He would protect them as he would protect
Morty. Tony then stopped scowling and making fierce and
funny faces and acting in many odd little ways. After he became accepted, as a result of being Morty's pal, his behavior
changed, and because he was strong and could fight, the boys

began to admire him. At times he really hoped for strange boys to come around the neighborhood and act like bullies so he could beat them up. He wanted to fight and punch because he could feel powerful and would be praised and admired.

II

Ever since he had been a little fellow, Tony had often been called a "Polack" or a "dirty Polack." After he became one of the gang or group around Morty, some of the boys would tell him that he was a "white Polack." In his slow way, he thought about these words and what they meant. When you were called certain words, you were laughed at, you were looked at as if something were wrong with you. If you were a Polack, many girls didn't want to have anything to do with you. The boys and girls who weren't Polacks had fun together that Polacks couldn't have. Being a Polack and being called a Polack was like being called a sonofabitch. It was a name. When you were called a name like this, you were looked at as a different kind of kid from one who wasn't called a name. Morty Aiken wasn't called names. Tony didn't want to be called names. And if he fought and beat up those who called him names, they would be afraid of him. He wanted that. But he also wanted to have as much fun as the kids had who weren't called these names. And he worked it out that these kids felt better when they called other kids names. He could fight and he could call names, and if he called a kid a name, and that kid got tough, he could beat him up. He began to call names. And there was a name even worse than Polack—"nigger." If Tony didn't like a kid, he called him a "nigger." And he talked about the "niggers." He felt as good as he guessed these other kids did when he talked about the "niggers." And they could be beat up. They weren't supposed to go to Washington Park because that was a park for the whites. That was what he had often heard.

He heard it said so much that he believed it. He sometimes

got a gang of the boys together and they would roam Washington Park, looking for colored boys to beat up. Morty went with them. He didn't particularly like to beat up anyone, but when they saw a colored kid and chased him, he would always be at the head, and he would be the one who caught the colored boy. He could grab or tackle him, and by that time the others would catch up. He worked the same plan that he and Tony had worked against the other boys. And after they caught and beat up a colored boy, they would all talk and shout and brag about what they had done, and talk about how they had each gotten in their licks and punches and kicks, and how fast Morty had run to catch that shine, and what a sock Tony had given him, and, talking all together and strutting and bragging, they felt good and proud of themselves, and they talked about how the Sixty-first Street boys would see to it that Washington Park would stay a white man's park.

And this became more and more important to Tony. There were those names, "Polack," "dirty Polack," "white Polack." If you could be called a "Polack," you weren't considered white. Well, when he beat them up, was he or wasn't he white? They knew. After the way he clouted these black ones, how could the other kids not say that Tony Rabuski wasn't white? That showed them all. That showed he was a hero. He was a hero as much as Morty Aiken was.

III

Morty was a proud boy on the night he graduated from grammar school in June, 1919. When he received his diploma, there was more applause in the auditorium than there was for any other member of the class. He felt good when he heard this clapping, but, then, he expected it. He lived in a world where he was somebody, and he was going into a bigger world where he would still be somebody. He was a fine, clean-looking lad, with dark hair, frank blue eyes, regular and friendly features. He was thin but strong. He wore a blue serge suit with short trousers and a belted jacket, and a white shirt with a white bow tie. His class colors, orange and black ribbons, were pinned on the lapel of his coat. He was scrubbed and washed and combed. And he was in the midst of an atmosphere of gaiety and friendliness. The teachers were happy. There were proud and happy parents and aunts and uncles and older sisters. The local alderman made a speech, praising everybody, and speaking of the graduating boys and girls as fine future Americans. And he declared that in their midst there were many promising lads and lassies who would live to enjoy great esteem and success. He also said that among this group there was also one who not only promised to become a stellar athlete but who had already won gold medals and honors.

And on that night, Morty's father and mother were very happy. They kept beaming with proud smiles. Morty was their only son. Mr. Aiken was a carpenter. He worked steadily, and he had saved his money so that the house he owned was now paid for. He and his wife were quiet-living people who minded their own business. Mr. Aiken was tall and rugged, with swarthy skin, a rough-hewn face, and the look and manner of a workman. He was a gentle but firm man, and was inarticulate with his son. He believed that a boy should have a good time in sports, should fight his own battles, and that boyhood —the best time of one's life—should be filled with happy memories.

The mother was faded and maternal. She usually had little to say; her life was dedicated to caring for her son and her husband and to keeping their home clean and orderly. She was especially happy to know that Morty liked running and skating, because these were not dangerous.

After the graduation ceremonies, the father and mother took Morty home where they had cake and ice cream. The three of them sat together, eating these refreshments, quiet but happy. The two parents were deeply moved. They were filled with gratification because of the applause given their son when he had walked forward on the stage to receive his diploma. They were raising a fine boy, and they could look people in the neighborhood in the eye and know that they had done their duty as parents. The father was putting money by for Morty's college education and hoped that, besides becoming a famous runner, Morty would become a professional man. He talked of this to the son and the mother over their ice cream and cake, and the boy seemed to accept his father's plans. And as the father gazed shyly at Morty he thought of his own boyhood on a Wisconsin farm, and of long summer days there. Morty had the whole summer before him. He would play and grow and enjoy himself. He was not a bad boy, he had never gotten into trouble, he wasn't the kind of boy who caused worry. It was fine. In August there would be his vacation, and they would all go to Wisconsin, and he would go fishing with the boy.

That evening Morty's parents went to bed feeling that this was the happiest day of their lives.

And Morty went to bed, a happy, light-hearted boy, thinking of the summer vacation which had now begun.

IV

The days passed. Some days were better than others. Some days there was little to do, and on other days there was a lot to do. Morty guessed that this was turning out to be as good as any summer he could remember.

Tony Rabuski was working, delivering flowers for a flower merchant, but he sometimes came around after supper, and the kids sat talking or playing on the steps of Morty's house or of another house in the neighborhood. Morty liked to play Run, Sheep, Run, because it gave him a chance to run, and he also liked hiding and searching and hearing the signals called out, and the excitement and tingling and fun when he'd be hiding, perhaps under some porch, and the other side would be near, maybe even passing right by, and he, and the other kids with him, would have to be so still, and he'd even try to hold his breath, and then finally, the signal for which he had been waiting—Run, Sheep, Run—and the race, setting off, tearing away along sidewalks and across streets, running like hell and like a streak of lightning, and feeling your speed in your legs and muscles and getting to the goal first.

The summer was going by, and it was fun. There wasn't anything to worry about, and there were dreams. Edna Purcell, who had been in his class, seemed sweet on him, and she was a wonderful girl. One night she and some other girls came around, and they sat on the steps of Morty's house and played Tin-Tin. Morty had to kiss her. He did, with the kids laughing, and it seemed that something happened to him. He hadn't been shy when he was with girls, but now, when Edna was around, he would be shy. She was wonderful. She was more than wonderful. When he did have the courage to talk to her, he talked about running and ice skating. She told him she knew what a runner and skater he was. A fast skater, such as he was, wouldn't want to think of skating with someone like her. He said that he would, and that next winter he would teach her to skate better. Immediately, he found himself wishing it were next winter already, and he would imagine himself skating with her, and he could see them walking over to the Washington Park lagoon and coming home again. He would carry her skates, and when they breathed they would be able to see their breaths, and the weather would be cold and sharp and would make her red cheeks redder, and they would be alone, walking home, with the snow packed on the park, alone, the two of them walking in the park, with it quiet, so quiet that you would hear nothing, and it would be like they were in another world, and then, there in the quiet park, with white snow all over it, he would kiss Edna Purcell. He had kissed Edna when they'd played Tin-Tin, and Post Office, but he looked forward to the day that he got from her the kiss that would mean that she was his girl, his sweetheart, and the girl who would one day be his wife just like his mother was his father's wife. Everything he dreamed of doing, all the honors

he would get, all the medals and cups he dreamed of winning
—now all of this would be for Edna. And she was also going to
Park High. He would walk to school with her, eat lunch with
her, walk her home from school. When he ran in high-school
track meets for Park High, Edna would be in the stands. He
would give her his medals. He wanted to give her one of his
gold skating medals, but he didn't know how to go about
asking her to accept it.

No matter what Morty thought about, he thought about
Edna at the same time. He thought about her every time he
dreamed. When he walked on streets in the neighborhood, he
thought of her. When he went to Washington Park or swimming, he thought of Edna. Edna, just to think of her, Edna
made everything in the world wonderfully wonderful.

And thus the summer of 1919 was passing for Morty.

v

Morty sat on the curb with a group of boys, and they were
bored and restless. They couldn't agree about what game to
play, where to go, what to do to amuse themselves. A couple
of them started to play Knife but gave it up. Morty suggested
a race, but no one would race him. They couldn't agree on
playing ball. One boy suggested swimming, but no one would
go with him. Several of the boys wrestled, and a fight almost
started. Morty sat by himself and thought about Edna. He
guessed that he'd rather be with her than with the kids. He
didn't know where she was. If he knew that she'd gone swimming, he'd go swimming. He didn't know what to do with
himself. If he only could find Edna and if they would do
something together, or go somewhere, like Jackson Park Beach,
just the two of them, why, then, he knew that today
would be the day that he would find a way of giving her one
of his *Clarion* gold medals. But he didn't know where she was.

Tony Rabuski came around with four tough-looking kids.

Tony had lost his job, and he said that the niggers had jumped him when he was delivering flowers down around Forty-seventh Street, and he wanted his pals to stick by him. He told them what had happened, but they didn't get it, because Tony couldn't tell a story straight. Tony asked them didn't they know what was happening? There were race riots, and the beaches and Washington Park and the whole South Side were full of dark clouds, and over on Wentworth Avenue the big guys were fighting, and the dark clouds were out after whites. They didn't believe Tony. But Morty said it was in the newspapers, and that there were race riots. The bored boys became excited. They bragged about what they would do if the jigs came over to their neighborhood. Tony said they had to get some before they got this far. When asked where they were, Tony said all over. Finally, they went over to Washington Park, picking up sticks and clubs and rocks on the way. The park was calm. A few adults were walking and strolling about. A lad of eighteen or nineteen lay under a tree with his head in the lap of a girl who was stroking his hair. Some of the kids smirked and leered as they passed the couple. Morty thought of Edna and wished he could take her to Washington Park and kiss her. There were seven or eight rowboats on the lagoon, but all of the occupants were white. The park sheep were grazing. Tony threw a rock at them, frightening the sheep, and they all ran, but no cop was around to shag them. They passed the boathouse, talking and bragging. They now believed the rumors which they themselves had made up. White girls and women were in danger, and anything might happen. A tall lad sat in the grass with a nursemaid. A baby carriage was near them. The lad called them over and asked them what they were doing with their clubs and rocks. Tony said they were looking for niggers. The lad said that he'd seen two near the goldfish pond and urged the boys to go and get the sonsofbitches. Screaming and shouting, they ran to the goldfish pond. Suddenly, Tony shouted:

"Dark clouds."

VI

They ran. Two Negro boys, near the goldfish pond, heard Tony's cry, and then the others' cry, and they ran. The mob of boys chased them. Morty was in the lead. Running at the head of the screaming, angry pack of boys, he forgot everything except how well and how fast he was running, and images of Edna flashed in and out of his mind. If she could see him running! He was running beautifully. He'd catch them. He was gaining. The colored boys ran in a northwest direction. They crossed the drive which flanked the southern end of the Washington Park ball field. Morty was stopped by a funeral procession. The other boys caught up with him. When the funeral procession passed, it was too late to try and catch the colored boys they had been chasing. Angry, bragging, they crossed over to the ball field and marched across it, shouting and yelling. They picked up about eight boys of their own age and three older lads of seventeen or eighteen. The older lads said they knew where they'd find some shines. Now was the time to teach them their place once and for all. Led by the older boys, they emerged from the north end of Washington Park and marched down Grand Boulevard, still picking up men and boys as they went along. One of the men who joined them had a gun. They screamed, looked in doorways for Negroes, believed everything anyone said about Negroes, and kept boasting about what they would do when they found some.

"Dark clouds," Tony boomed.

The mob let out. They crossed to the other side of Grand Boulevard and ran cursing and shouting after a Negro. Morty was in the lead. He was outrunning the men and the older fellows. He heard them shouting behind him. He was running. He was running like the playground hundred-yard champion of the South Side of Chicago. He was running like

the future Olympic champion. He was running like he'd run
for Edna. He was tearing along, pivoting out of the way of
shocked, surprised pedestrians, running, really running. He
was running like a streak of lightning.

The Negro turned east on Forty-eighth Street. He had a
start of a block. But Morty would catch him. He turned into
Forty-eighth Street. He tore along the center of the street. He
began to breathe heavily. But he couldn't stop running now.
He was outdistancing the gang, and he was racing his own
gang and the Negro he was chasing. Down the center of the
street and about half a block ahead of him, the Negro was
tearing away for dear life. But Morty was gaining on him.
Gaining. He was now about a half a block ahead of his own
gang. They screamed murderously behind him. And they encouraged him. He heard shouts of encouragement.

"Catch 'em, Morty boy!"

"Thata boy, Morty boy!"

He heard Tony's voice. He ran.

The Negro turned into an alley just east of Forestville.
Morty ran. He turned into the alley just in time to see the
fleeing Negro spurt into a yard in the center of the block. He'd
gained more. He was way ahead of the white mob. Somewhere behind him they were coming and yelling. He tore on.
He had gained his second wind. He felt himself running, felt
the movement of his legs and muscles, felt his arms, felt the
sensation of his whole body as he raced down the alley. Never
had he run so swiftly. Suddenly Negroes jumped out of yards.
He was caught and pinioned. His only thought was one of
surprise. Before he even realized what had happened, his
throat was slashed. He fell, bleeding. Feebly, he mumbled just
once:

"Mother!"

The Negroes disappeared.

He lay bleeding in the center of the dirty alley, and when
the gang of whites caught up with him they found him dead
in dirt and his own blood in the center of the alley. No Negroes were in sight. The whites surrounded his body. The boys

trembled with fear. Some of them cried. One wet his pants. Then they became maddened. And they stood in impotent rage around the bleeding, limp body of Morty Aiken, the fastest runner on Sixty-first Street.

Summer Tryout

I

THE DAY WAS LOVELY, the bay was calm; the water glittered in the sunlight; there were spots which shone like diamonds, patches of unearthly blue, and large stretches of soft, gray water. Sailboats passed gracefully in the distance. It was quiet, very quiet in Flowerdale.

Gazing at the bay, Bill Danning sat with his thoughts in a haze. He had looked up at the substanceless blue of the sky and watched the wandering, pure white clouds. He had day-dreamed of success and of the future, and his thoughts and dreams had vanished into a pleasing and almost imageless blur. Then he lit a cigarette, and he tried to assure himself that there was no reason in the world why he should be worried. He should relax. This scene should fill him with calm and with an artist's feeling for beauty. But he could relax for only short intervals, and then his mind would wheel around in the same endless circle of doubts and anxieties. There was so much at stake for him. He might have a Broadway hit on his hands. If this tryout were successful, then Gilman Allenby would bring his play to Broadway in the fall. Yes, he had reason to be nervous and worried. He threw away his cigarette, looked down at the bay from the small hill-like knob near the Flowerdale Playhouse, and with a welling-up of sympathy for himself he wished his ordeal were over. How could he really enjoy himself here? How could he let the calm of the Sound and the sky enter his spirit? He had this heavy worry about his play, *The Human Equation*.

28

The cast for the summer tryout had arrived, and immediately there had been distressing blowups. If these continued, how could the cast do its best? Without harmony, the production could be ruined. Only a week ago in New York, he'd been patting himself on the back about the cast. Now he had grave reason to be seriously concerned. He had always been of the opinion that the theater depended on the writer. Without writers, there could be no theater. Actors and actresses were necessary but not so important as the dramatist. And, being of lesser importance, they were more temperamental. Why, the members of this cast had no sooner arrived than there was trouble. They didn't like their temporary living arrangements, as though that were a major issue. They didn't like the food, either. Practically every member of the cast had been temperamental about something or other. And the first rehearsal was called for this afternoon. Would they be calmed down by then?

If everything went perfectly, he could still be optimistic. And, of course, the play wouldn't open here at Flowerdale until Tuesday night. There was all this afternoon and this evening for rehearsals, tomorrow for more, tomorrow night for dress rehearsal, and, if necessary, they had Tuesday, too, in which to fix up minor details. But, even so, that was very little time, and his entire future depended on how his play went. So many things could go wrong. But, God, why did he have to worry about all this pettiness? It was almost unbearable.

He lit a fresh cigarette and told himself he ought to forget about these problems. But how could he? Forget the most important event of his life? Yes, he had to watch everything, supervise everything. He had to attend to every little detail himself. If he didn't, there might be a disaster. He knew his play was damned good. Why, there wasn't the slightest doubt that it could be a smash hit if the actors would only do their best. He'd become the new voice for which the American theater had been waiting so long. And Broadway needed a new voice that was clear and honest and new. Critics would

hear that voice in the author of *The Human Equation*. He
imagined himself reading rave reviews of his play. He became
elated. Then he told himself, with meaningless resolution and
with hope, that everything just had to go off right.

Bill was thirty-one. He was tall, well built, large boned,
and soft and fleshy around the abdomen. His face was long,
with large jawbones. It was not a sensitive face. Born in
Chicago, he had spent his youth largely on the streets, and it
had been typical of the early years of many a poor boy. He
often enjoyed talking of it, and when he did, he liked to
boast of how some of his boyhood playmates had become
gangsters. He had hoboed all over America, had been employed at many odd and miscellaneous jobs, and had worked
his way through one year of college. During his hobo days he
had begun to develop literary ambitions. At that time he
had read Jack London, and also Maxim Gorky's *My University Days*. He had come to regard himself as the American
Maxim Gorky. He looked back on his days as a hobo with
great pride. He thought of himself as a young writer who
had lifted himself out of the gutter, who had risen above an
environment where the dregs of human life were to be found.
Transcending himself, he had not been destroyed by this vile
capitalistic system. Now he was here in Flowerdale, on the
eve of his public self-vindication.

Smoking, he looked out at the calm waters of Long Island
Sound, thinking of these things. He was momentarily calm
and assured. He told himself that it was a lovely sight. And,
realizing he was an artist, he believed that he was specially able
to appreciate it. This was Beauty. Beauty was the real aim of
the artist. And now he was an artist, gazing upon this scene of
Beauty, and he was appreciating it. He looked long at the
sunny bay. His weak eyes watered in the strong glare of the
sun. He puffed on his cigarette and gazed at the bay through
his tears, still trying to absorb this beauty to the full. He
thought, too, that this was a terrible world. But nevertheless
he was a rising star; his own future was promising.

Then he cursed, rose, and paced the beach. His calm was

gone. The actors had done this to him. Why must actors be so temperamental? If they understood more, if they had any social consciousness, they would readily see it was capitalism that was responsible for the bad accommodations with which they had to put up. And was this more important than his play, which was a work of social consciousness, a devastating criticism of capitalism. And besides its social significance it promised much to the cast. It would make money for them, honest money. They would get along, and they would contribute to a powerful artistic protest against the system. Yes, wasn't all this more important than bad accommodations? Why couldn't they understand this? Why couldn't they consider this?

Frustrated, he flung away his cigarette. His legs twitching nervously, his eyes blinking as he looked at the bay again, he stood still, and he was moved by his own thoughts and feelings.

—The play must go on, he told himself.

Then he decided to have a bottle of beer and went in to the bar.

II

The Flowerdale Playhouse, facing the bay at Flowerdale, Long Island, was a low, rambling structure. Its fresh white paint emphasized the newness of its construction. At the same time, it somehow looked just temporary. The bar and restaurant were in the same building and next to the theater. The restaurant was partly enclosed by glass; it was light and cheerful. It looked out on the waters of the bay. Now the restaurant was filling up.

Rehearsal broke up at five o'clock, and some of the members of the cast sat at tables near the bar. Other actors, students from the local school of the Flowerdale Playhouse, and a few people who looked like tourists were at other tables. Bill sat talking seriously with Gilman Allenby, the producer. Gilman was drinking Scotch and soda; Bill was having beer.

Gilman Allenby was proud to be descended from an old American family that dated back to the colonial period. He was a very good-looking, if plump, young man, but he was soft, and his face suggested weakness. He held himself rigidly aloof from most people. While talking with others, he would regularly take out a comb and run it through his hair. His manners were effeminate, but at times he seemed imposing largely because of his habit of not talking, or else of talking and saying nothing in such a way as to suggest that the situation did not merit any comment from him. He had the air of being a young man of authority and position, and this was strengthened by a recent marriage to a very rich girl. Her wealth really provided the secure basis of his position. He had been in the theater for a number of years, but he had never made a name for himself. He was important without having any achievements to his credit. He had frequently planned to put on plays which he had then decided not to produce. He had, however, put on a number of summer plays, but never with any distinction. He had produced two flops, and one Ibsen revival with a star which had made money. He was now producing and directing *The Human Equation*. It was his first serious effort at directing, and if it clicked on Broadway it would constitute his first real success.

"Bill, don't worry," Gilman said with a sudden suggestion of sympathetic understanding in his voice.

"I'm not worried," Bill quickly answered. "Gil, I'm merely anxious to see that everything goes right."

"Yes," Gilman said profoundly. After a pause, during which he sipped Scotch, he went on: "I know just how you feel. The play is your baby. You know, when one of my dogs is ill, I become so frightened that I suffer from an acute case of the jitters. Why, I simply can't begin to describe how upset I become when anything happens to one of my dogs. So I understand how you feel."

Bill didn't answer immediately. He looked off at a black-haired student actress who sat smoking a cigarette as though she were acting in a play. He turned back to Gilman and said:

"Catherine isn't playing the love scenes with passion, with enough passion. She doesn't get the passion into it, don't you know."

Gilman pursed his lips as if deep in thought. He fiddled with his glass. He scratched his upper lip with his left hand and then said:

"I'm not disturbed about that."

"But we open in a couple of days and . . ."

"Yes, Bill," Gilman interrupted, and he waited to give Bill a chance to hang onto his words before he continued. "Yes, Bill, but she's good. She's a coming actress. I'm not disturbed about her. She'll have passion on opening night."

"Oh, I'm not really worried. Of course she will. No, I'm not worried."

"Bill, you've written a dandy play, a swell play."

Bill's face broke into a smile of almost childish gratitude, and he blushed modestly.

"The cast, now, it's satisfactory, Gilman, it's good. But it hasn't gotten into the right tempo yet, the right tempo. Something isn't just right yet—don't you know?"

As usual, Gilman delayed a moment before replying. Then he said:

"In general, Bill, I'd say the rehearsals are coming along well. It's just a question of details."

"Yes, it's just the details, don't you know," Bill agreed, but in the voice of one seeking confirmation.

III

Catherine Silvio had dinner with Albert Wright in the luncheon wagon on the main street of Flowerdale. She was bright, lively, and very pretty. She seemed very fresh and young and spunky, and had clear, light-blue eyes which

seemed to suggest a frankness of nature. Her hair was fluffy
and curly, and she had a wide, high forehead. She always
looked as if she had just washed, and she was slightly freckled.
Albert was an instructor in a university in New York City
and had just completed teaching the first half of the summer
term. He was staying with Catherine in Flowerdale. He had
had a difficult year and was rather fatigued. He looked forward
to the week as one of rest and relaxation. He was about
thirty, youngish-looking, dark, attractive.

"You don't know how awful the play is, darling," Catherine said to him while they were finishing their blue-plate
specials.

"Then why are you playing in it?" he asked.

She smiled, fixed her bright eyes on him tenderly, and
answered:

"I took it because I thought the play was so awful it might
be a hit. But I'm beginning to have my doubts."

"How many times do I have to see it?" Albert asked.

"Only once. I wouldn't ask my worst enemy to have to
sit through this play every night in the week."

"Well," he began, paused, and then went on, "is Allenby
doing anything to improve it?"

"That boy improve anything?" She laughed sarcastically.
"That boy is supercilious. He doesn't know the first thing
about directing or acting. He's just bewildered and stage
struck."

"Danning seems to be a decent enough chap," Albert said.

"I can't make him out, except to say that he isn't overly
endowed," Catherine said.

"He's ignorant, but then I presume it isn't his fault," Albert went on.

"That might be true. He's had a hard time trying to come
up. But, then, should that justify his conceit?"

"He buttonholed me this afternoon," Albert said. "I said
I hadn't read his play and thought it would be better for
me to wait and see it. And—oh, yes, he asked me to speak
to you."

"About what?"

With a gleam in his eyes he told her:

"He said you're going to be swell in your part. Swell, you're going to be just swell—but he wondered if I couldn't get you to put more passion in the love scenes."

"So that's what he wants?" She laughed. "He's a poor fool. You can't honestly read his passionate lines. They don't speak. When I give them, I feel as if I were a sputtering fool. The situation is this. I'm pregnant."

"I'm glad it is only so in the play," he cut in.

"I wouldn't mind it if it were true in real life. But, darling, don't interrupt me. I'm pregnant, and at the same time I'm supposed to be having a love affair with my brother-in-law. It is supposed to be burning passion, mind you, and I say to my lover—'Be my master. Step on me. Bite your love into me. Bite your love into my life.' He thinks those lines are gems, gems that only he could write. It's simply horrendous. . . . But, then, darling, it's a job, a lousy job. It's worth more than fifty dollars a week for me to make a fool out of myself in a part like this. So what can I do?"

"You shouldn't have taken it."

"If I wait until I take what I want, I'll wait and wait, and then I'll wait."

"I guess so. Doesn't the contradiction ever strike you?"

"What?"

"Why—having to take stupid parts in stupid plays. Having to earn your living by participating in the degradation of what you consider to be art."

She looked at him with irritation.

"Yes—but what can I do?"

"Yes, I know. You have no alternative, my dear." He glanced at his watch. "Say, it's time for you to be getting back to rehearsal."

"I wonder what the Master Minds have cooked up for us since we broke up for dinner," she said wearily and sarcastically.

He paid the bill. Outside, they got into his Ford, and he drove her back to the Playhouse.

                                                        •

IV

The rehearsal was in progress. Albert Wright sat by the bay. He puffed on a cigarette. He would have been utterly relaxed and content were it not for the mosquitoes. He slapped at his arms and his face. He tried to ignore the insects. He was bitten. His face and arms itched with bites. He went inside to the bar and ordered a beer.

"Are you in show business?" the bartender asked.

"No. No, I'm only distantly related to this company," he answered dryly.

The bartender looked at him quizzically.

"My girl's in the play that opens on Tuesday," Albert said.

"I used to be in show business. Yeh, I was in show business. But show business isn't what it used to be. Take me, now. I played all over America. I used to sing in vaudeville, played the Orpheum circuit. But I got out of it. No, sir, show business isn't what it used to be."

"No, I guess it isn't. Can I have another beer?" Albert said.

The bartender served him another bottle.

"How's business?" Albert asked casually.

The bartender shook his head as if he were making a profound observation and then told Albert:

"We do pretty good here. Yes, we do pretty good. We get a lot of summer people because of the plays. The summer people like to see light stuff. Comedies. They're not going to like this new play. You see, most of the summer people who come out this way are Irish Catholics from Brooklyn."

Albert nodded as though in agreement. Bill came out of the theater, swung onto a chair beside Albert, and lit a cigarette.

"A bottle of beer," he ordered.

He turned and gazed at the moonlit bay through the glass behind him. His face was clouded.

"Goddamn it, everything's going wrong," Bill said angrily.

Albert turned to look at Bill and waited for him to go on.

"You're not a playwright, so you can't really know what I mean. Everything's going wrong. Now, take my lines. . . . I worked over them very carefully. They don't need to be changed. They're just right. And then I sit and listen to the cast giving them back to me, and they aren't right. Of course, I don't mean Catherine," he added hastily. "She's swell. Swell. I don't mean her."

"I often noticed, Mr. Danning," the bartender interrupted, "I often noticed—if a rehearsal goes too well, then the play doesn't come off so good. That's been my experience out here. And, then, I've been in show business myself."

"Yes, yes, that's true," Bill said instantly, as if to impress the bartender with his own knowledge of show business. He went on, "Yes, I know that. But don't you know, things aren't going right, just right. Of course, they will be. Yes, we'll whip everything into shape by Tuesday night. But they aren't right, and it's a strain, a nervous strain. We've got to work at it— hard. Hard. That's all. But it's a nervous strain, don't you know. I've got to watch everything."

He gulped down his beer and, without waiting for either Albert or the bartender to answer him, he went back to the theater.

Albert yawned. It was dull and boring out here. And, thanks to the mosquitoes, he couldn't even stay outside. His choices were limited to sitting in his hotel room, sitting here at the bar, or going inside to watch the rehearsal. The bar was the least depressing. The rehearsal would be too much to sit through, even though missing it meant foregoing the pleasure of watching Catherine on the stage, looking at her move, listening to her voice, sitting enthralled and thinking with such pride that she, that voice and that body, was all his. All his. He glowed with pride at the recurrence of this thought.

V

Mrs. Jackson came out to the restaurant accompanied by Milton Shuler, Gilman's business manager.

"I simply don't understand this company," she exclaimed in a voice of self-pity.

"Neither do I," Milton Shuler answered as they moved on to a table.

Albert had met Milton already, and, looking at his half-finished glass of beer, he thought that Milton's main asset was his winningly pathetic but evasive smile. Earlier today, when members of the cast had complained about the food prices they had to pay at the restaurant run by the Flowerdale Playhouse, Milton had answered them with this smile. And Mrs. Jackson. She had gray hair but a rather young face without a line in it. Her features were regular and pleasing. She was well dressed, in informal clothes, and moved about this establishment, which she managed with her husband, with the air of a lady. She was also an agent, and Bill Danning was her client.

"We've never had trouble with actors before. This is the first company that has ever protested and caused trouble for us," Albert heard her say to Shuler with an air of injured innocence, almost of bewilderment.

Albert casually listened to their conversation. They talked about Mr. Schulz, who managed the restaurant and had been rude to and officious with some members of the cast shortly after their arrival. He had bluntly told them they would have to pay twelve dollars a week for food at the Flowerdale Playhouse restaurant, and that they'd have to eat at the tables in the rear. They couldn't sit in front with the regular trade. And he had bullishly and rudely given them specified hours at which to eat. Breakfast before nine-thirty, luncheon from twelve to one, dinner from five-thirty to six-thirty. If they ate at any other time they would have to pay the full rates charged for tourists. Also, they'd have no choice of food but would

have to eat what they were given. The moment he had been
questioned, he had answered that they had to abide by the rules
he set for running the restaurant. They had stormed and had
even held an impromptu protest meeting. And then they had
complained about the poor quality of the food and cooking
and had declared they would not eat in the restaurant. This
meant a financial loss to Mr. and Mrs. Jackson. Albert watched
her as she talked with great suaveness.

"It's all arranged now. They'll eat where they want to," he
heard her telling Shuler.

"I think your arrangements are satisfactory—that is, personally. But, then, I'm not an actor. I'm only a business
manager," he said to Mrs. Jackson.

"Mr. Shuler, I've met show people before. I know them. I
know they're temperamental. But this is incomprehensible.
Maybe it's because they're Italian. Perhaps they're too temperamental. But, still, I don't understand, for the life of me,
why they should have made such a rumpus. And I put in a
store of supplies. Now, here I am—left high and dry."

"I can't make them eat where they don't want to, Mrs. Jackson," Shuler replied, his tone as suave as hers. "I tried my best
to explain the situation and circumstances to them."

She noticed Albert. Catherine had been one of those who had
complained most volubly. She rose from the table and walked
over to him.

"How are you, Mr. Wright?" she said with exaggerated
geniality.

"Very well, thank you."

"Mr. Wright, I was just explaining to Mr. Shuler here that I
simply can't understand these protests."

"Of course, I know nothing about it."

"Our French cook is one of the best in America."

"I don't have anything to do with it. I'm not a member of
the company."

"I know, I know, but I just wanted to explain my side to
you, Mr. Wright. Why, my husband and I—we're nonplussed.
And the actors complained just when we were rushed, serving

our Sunday dinner. Nothing, absolutely nothing like that has ever happened here before. Everyone who knows me, everyone who knows about our place here, they all think it's the best run summer theater on Long Island."

"Maybe the cast is nervous," Albert said casually and to avoid further discussion. "You know, they were working very hard in New York before coming out here. As a play approaches the opening, the cast becomes tense."

"Don't tell me," she responded with a knowing smile. "I've been associated with show business for years."

"Oh, Mrs. Jackson," Shuler called from his table.

"Excuse me, Mr. Wright," she said ingratiatingly, and she went back to see Shuler. They spoke in low voices.

"No, my friend, show business isn't what it was in my time," the bartender exclaimed nostalgically.

VI

A group of the actors were eating breakfast in a room partitioned off from the remainder of the Pullman car diner on the main street of Flowerdale. The Carlucci family sat together —father, mother, and the two daughters—at one of the tables. Pietro Carlucci was a gray-haired, red-faced, paternal, and jolly-looking man of about sixty; he was medium-sized and rotund. His appearance suggested a calm and kindly man. In the play, he had the role of an Italian fruit pedlar, who was also the head of the family. It was the first opportunity he had had to make a Broadway appearance in more than two decades, and the entire Carlucci family radiated hope. He had been an actor since his early boyhood, but he had appeared mainly in the Italian theater.

Mrs. Carlucci was a buxom woman, dumpy, gray haired, and maternal; she had been his leading lady for years. The two daughters resembled their parents in physical make-up; they, too, were rather dumpy. Marie, the youngest, was attractive, with a round face, olive skin, lustrous black hair, and deep, dark eyes; she was a blooming, virginal girl. Her older sister, Teresa, looked prissy. She was plain, she dressed plainly, and her black hair lacked the fine texture and lustrous quality of her sister's. She wore glasses and seemed very earnest and serious. Marie had a bit part in the play; Teresa had been hired by Gilman Allenby to serve as a technical adviser. Her husband, Milton Stein, was a stodgy, bald-headed young man, and he sat with the family at the breakfast table.

"Papa and I are never separated," Mrs. Carlucci said in a quietly triumphant tone of voice.

"I've never seen such a wonderful family," declared Henry Por, one of the actors.

"Yes," Catherine remarked without interest.

"Papa has me go to the radio station with him every day," Mrs. Carlucci said.

"He sells macaroni," Catherine whispered to Albert.

"Such lovebirds," Mrs. Carlucci said, noticing Catherine whisper as she gazed at her and Albert.

"I'm worried about the play," Teresa cut in seriously.

"Why worry? And about such a play?" Catherine retorted.

"But that's not the right way to look at it," Teresa came back in her dull but earnest voice. "Of course, the play has faults. I know that. But they aren't being corrected by the direction."

"I haven't seen it yet. I'll see the dress rehearsal tonight," Milton remarked.

"We have to get together and save the play," Teresa said tensely.

"It's bad enough to be in it without having to talk about it over breakfast," Catherine said.

"But we have to iron out the flaws," Teresa said, agitated.

"Ah, I like these ham and eggs," Papa Carlucci said.

"Oh, Papa is so wonderful," Teresa said.

"You played with Duse?" Catherine asked, looking over at Papa Carlucci.

"Ah, she was my friend," the old man answered, his eyes lighting up, his tone that of a ham actor.

"Tell me something about her," Catherine continued.

"She was my friend," Papa Carlucci answered with melo-dramatic quaverings in his voice.

"What was she like?" asked Catherine.

"Ah, she was magnificent."

"But I'm very serious. We have to do something about the play," Teresa cut in, speaking with anxiety as well as serious-ness.

Catherine threw a swift look of contempt at her.

"What can we do?" asked Antonio Musseli, one of the actors.

"That's what I'm studying and thinking about. I'm going to take notes tonight," Teresa answered.

"Do you think that the genius who wrote the play, or the Master Mind directing it, will deign to listen to you?" Cath-erine curtly asked Teresa.

"Yes. Because I'm going to talk until they do listen to me. The play is the thing," Teresa said.

"Bill Danning will listen to you as long as you talk about him and his work," Albert said. "But that's all he'll do—listen."

"When I go out in the second act and I say—'Do I feel like an ice cream soda?'—how can I put passion into that line? What do you think, Teresa?" Catherine asked ironically.

"Yes, that ought to be changed," Teresa said, unsure of her-self.

"What ought to be changed?" asked Catherine.

"The line."

"So you want to break Danning's heart," Catherine sneered.

"Papa isn't getting direction," Mama Carlucci interrupted. "He has to do everything himself."

"Oh, I'm sick of the play. Let's talk about Flowerdale," Catherine said.

VII

Bill Danning entered the restaurant, and the group became suddenly and embarrassingly silent.

"How's everybody this morning?" Bill asked awkwardly.

Most of those present said they were all right, their voices showing no interest.

"Well, we still have lots of work to do," he said.

"That's just what I was saying," Teresa said ingratiatingly.

"Teresa, how do you think it's going?" Bill asked.

Catherine and Antonio Musseli looked knowingly at each other.

"All right. On the whole, good," she said with measured words. "But, of course, some things have to be changed."

"Yes, of course. It isn't perfect. It can be better if we work together," Bill said eagerly.

"Bill, we can't attain perfection in a day, can we?" Albert said with false naïveté.

"No, we can't," Bill said. He paused. "No, that's very true, don't you know? But we'll whip it into the right spirit, the play. What we need is more passion, passion." Bill's face became intense. He spoke with concentrated feeling, but he looked directly at no one. "That reminds me, Catherine, about your love scene in the second act. Don't you know, you're in love, you're in love with this man. You have to make the audience know it, feel it. That's what I mean. Of course, you're improving, and you're going to be swell, but you're not yet getting quite enough passion into your lines."

"But there are too many lines. The scene drags. It doesn't really play right. Can't you cut it down?"

"Oh, no—you're wrong. I thought a long time about every word I wrote. Not one word could come out of that scene without hurting it. You see that's the word scene, the scene with poetry, fantasy. We can't cut it . . . it's poetry."

Catherine sank back in her chair, silent.

"At our dress rehearsal tonight, you'll all see what I mean. Won't they, Albert?" Bill said.

Albert nodded slightly at Bill.

"But, Bill, there are some serious points I want to talk about," Teresa said.

"Well, I always welcome criticism. I'm not the kind of playwright who doesn't welcome criticism. You know me that well now."

"Now, you know when Papa walks across the stage in the second act," Teresa said.

Bill's eyes lit up, as they always did when anyone spoke of his work.

"There ought to be a line. Papa needs a line there."

"Teresa, dear, I think it's all right now," Papa Carlucci said.

"Well, I'll have to think about that," Bill said abstractedly.

"What time do we rehearse today?" asked Antonio Musseli.

"Ten-thirty, and I hope everybody is on time. We have so much to iron out," Bill said.

"If we work all day, and then more than half the night on the dress rehearsal, we're going to be dead tired," Catherine said.

"I'll be just as tired as you'll be," Bill said.

"Catherine, I really think the play needs more work," Teresa said.

"Well, I've got to get back to my hotel now," Catherine said.

She and Albert rose. So did Antonio. He was a dark, handsome, quiet lad. The Carlucci family started haggling over the exact amount which each of them owed for breakfast, and in the midst of it Papa Carlucci said:

"I haven't enough for my bill."

"Why, Papa, I gave you a dollar last night," Mama Carlucci answered him in an injured voice.

"I know. But, Mama, I ate after rehearsal."

With a grudging look, she dug into her pocketbook and handed him a half dollar. Then everyone but Bill left. He ate alone, his face softened in meditation.

VIII

The dress rehearsal had gone badly. The cast was weary because of endless rehearsals during which neither Allenby nor

Danning could make up his mind as to what he wanted done.
Everyone was kept doing everything differently. Allenby had
not given one bit of intelligent direction. Most important of
all, the pacing and timing were off. Again and again, cues
were being picked up much too slowly. And the actors found
difficulty in rendering many of the lines. They just couldn't
speak them. As casts went in summer plays, this was a good
one. But it was confused and demoralized by the incompetence
and willfulness of Gilman Allenby.

And the play itself put almost insuperable obstacles in their
way. *The Human Equation* was a crude piece of work, written
in the naturalistic manner but without any real feeling or insight. It attempted to represent the life of a Chicago Italian
family. The plot hinged on a phony and badly motivated love
affair between a girl and her brother-in-law, who was a small-
time gangster, being played by Antonio Musseli. The relations
between the characters were revealed in a needlessly ugly
manner, and they didn't seem real or true. As a so-called realistic play, *The Human Equation* was neither real nor human.
The sons in it spoke to their mother as if she were a girl they
were trying to pick up on a street corner. And, in the name of
humor, their disrespect for their father went to the point where
they tried to rip his fly open several times. He, in turn, amused
himself by clutching at their flies. The sons enjoyed themselves
most when they goosed one another, especially in their mother's
presence. Also, the play seemed to embody just about every
corny trick of worn-out melodrama.

Bill Danning himself was of Jewish extraction, rather than
Italian, and the dialogue was full of revealing little words and
phrases which might possibly be heard in a Jewish household
but not in an Italian one. The writing was heavy, dull and
clumsy; at every point at which there was a need for action, the
action slowed down, clogged by words. The cast had sweated
over it in New York, as they were now doing at Flowerdale.
They had given their best. But it went slowly, and neither
Gilman nor Bill knew what the matter was. The real source of

the difficulties was in the script itself, but Gilman and Bill couldn't know how bad it was.

And now the actors sat on the stage, bored and listless. Bill and Allenby stood below stage, whispering.

"It's dead," Catherine said in a quiet voice; she sat on a chair to the right.

"Well," Antonio replied, also in a low voice, "you must remember, darling—the play's the thing."

"Nothing can be funny about it," she said wearily.

"The play's the thing. It must go on," Antonio said, amused.

"Even when there isn't a play," Henry Por said.

"All right. Attention, everybody!" Gilman called officiously, clapping his hands rather briskly.

He girlishly climbed up onto the stage and went to the center. The cast waited for him.

He turned to Andrucci, who played the role of one of the sons. He was medium-sized, darkish, a harum-scarum-looking young actor of twenty-one.

"Andrucci," Gilman said contemptuously. "There's no use directing you or even talking to you. Talking to you is like pouring water into a bucket without any bottom."

Andrucci stared at Gilman and, genuinely disturbed, asked:

"But tell me—tell me, what's wrong with my performance?"

"Don't talk back to me," Gilman snapped, "don't talk back! I'm speaking, and I say there's no use in talking to you."

"Oh, Gil," Bill called.

"Yes, Bill," Gilman replied in a calmer tone, swinging around to Bill, who was seated in a front-row orchestra seat.

"We ought to settle that question, too—about the stove in the second act."

"Yes, we'll do that now."

"But, listen, Mr. Gilman," Andrucci said.

"I'm busy," Gilman replied without turning to face Andrucci.

Bill leaped up onto the stage. He and Gilman examined the stove in the center. They discussed it in low voices, calculating,

guessing, speculating on how much coal should be put into it.
The cast waited, weary, bored, and half asleep. Andrucci sat
alone in a corner, speechless, moody, looking crushed.

After twenty minutes, the coal question seemed settled, and
then Bill said rather loudly:

"Gil, there's that clothesline in the third act."

"Gracious, yes. I almost forgot about it. Yes, the clothesline."

"We'll have to straighten it out," Bill said.

"Yes, Bill." Gilman looked around the stage, glancing at one
after another of the actors, and said curtly: "Everything went
wrong tonight."

He then turned to Marguerita Ferra. She was a motion picture character actress, a slender, well-preserved woman, with
soft brown hair that was almost amber, and a youthful face.
She played the role of mother of the family. The entire play
revolved around her.

"Marguerita," Gilman said; he spoke more respectfully to
her than to the other members of the cast.

"Yes," she answered, coming forward, her movements slow
but graceful.

"You know the scene in the third act where you talk with
Catherine, and at the same time you set up the clothesline and
hang up clothes?"

She nodded, her face becoming alive with interest.

"Well, I think it's too slow."

"What should I do?" she asked, bewildered.

Gilman meditated. Then, with an accompaniment of various
girlish gestures, he set out to show her. Speaking her lines, he
set up the line and hung up the clothes, pinning them on the
line with clothespins. It was a boring performance on his part,
and it seemed intolerably long. When he finished, he turned to
Bill, who was now standing by the front row of seats.

"Do you think we could shorten this? There are seven pieces
of clothing to hang up here. Now, couldn't there be just six?"

"Don't you know—I thought a lot about just that. No, I

don't see how we can have any other number of pieces but
seven," Bill said.

Gilman jumped off the stage, and he and Bill whispered in a
huddle.

"Well, let's see," Bill was heard to say.

Gilman and Bill continued whispering. Waiting, Marguerita
seemed very nervous. Catherine walked noisily up and down at
the back. Andrucci sulked in a corner. The others sat around,
woebegone.

Gilman suddenly nodded. He turned to Marguerita.

"Marguerita, will you try the scene now?"

Her face dropped, but she picked up the basket, took off
the line the clothes that Gilman had just pinned on, and then
she did the scene, hanging up the clothes as she spoke her lines.
The scene still went very slowly. It couldn't go any other way
because of the amount of business in it and the difficulty of
speaking the wordy lines.

Finishing, she stood at the corner of the stage and waited.
Gilman went back and forth a couple of times, and then, turning to her and shaking his head from side to side, he said:
"It's still too slow. I'm sorry, but we'll have to try it again and
see if it can't go faster."

She began taking down the clothes from the line again.

"Gil," Bill called.

"Just a minute, Marguerita," Gilman said, and he turned to
look down toward Bill.

"I've been thinking about it. We have just got to have seven
pieces of clothing. Don't you know, she's doing the family
washing, hanging it up to dry."

"Yes, yes, I understand," Gilman interrupted.

"Well, I'm glad you see it. You see, it's a big family, and
there's a lot of washing."

Catherine stopped pacing and looked at both of them with
contempt. She shrugged her shoulders and sat down in a chair
in a corner.

"We'll have to try again and make it move faster," Gilman
told Marguerita.

She went through the scene again. She was an uninspired actress, and the scene was particularly heavy. Catherine, who was in the scene, was forced to go through it with Marguerita. She did it, utterly fatigued, with no spirit or concern as to what she was doing.

After she and Marguerita had done the scene this time, Gilman still shook his head. He clucked his lips. He said:

"No, it's still too slow. We'll have to work on it in the morning."

He and Bill again spoke in whispers. Then Bill remarked for all to hear:

"Yes, that's a good idea."

"All right, cast dismissed, all except Catherine and Antonio," Gilman said briskly.

Catherine and Antonio exchanged glances of disgust, while the rest of the cast dropped off the stage.

Gilman motioned to Catherine and Antonio. When they came slowly up to him he said:

"Now that we've settled the question of how much coal to put into the stove in your love scene, I want to try it again."

Catherine looked at him blankly. Antonio gave him a shallow smile. Bill joined them and said:

"Yes, now, Catherine, you're swell. But it's the biggest moment in my play. The big love scene, and try to make it more passionate."

"How can I now? I'm dead tired. My voice is going. I can't do a thing now," she said.

"What do you mean?" Bill asked anxiously.

"Exactly what I said. I'm not a truck horse. I'm dead on my feet. I can't act it out now."

"But, Catherine, you don't have to get excited," Bill said conciliatingly. "We're just trying to make everything the best we can, and I'm trying to help you."

"Just a minute, Bill," Gilman interrupted. He turned to Catherine. "Catherine, I merely want you to run through it in order to be sure the coal business is straightened out."

She shrugged her shoulders, as if to say all right, and wearily

went through the scene. Bill sat with a sulky look on his face,
listening, watching, and scribbling down notes.

IX

"Marguerita gives Papa nothing. What can he do? What
can we do?" Teresa asked on Tuesday morning over the breakfast table at the diner.

"Teresa, child, now you must not worry," Papa Carlucci
said in a somewhat embarrassed voice, keeping his eyes on his
plate of ham and eggs as he spoke.

"Papa, don't you worry. But it's true. Just because you're so
wonderful you don't see it's true. You're too good to see that.
But Marguerita is taking advantage of you, giving you
nothing."

"Here she comes," Mama Carlucci said sharply as she saw
Marguerita through the window of the diner; Marguerita
wore an attractive red and white peasant dress.

She came in, smiled, said good morning, and sat down at the
only vacant place, which was opposite Mama Carlucci. In contrast to Mama Carlucci, Marguerita looked youthful.

"Hello, Maggy," Mama said in a sugary but insinuating tone
of voice.

Marguerita looked up with anger concentrated in her dark
eyes; she said with quiet anger:

"Marguerita is my name."

"But we've known you so long that we can't help thinking
of you as little Maggy. Don't you remember when I was
Papa's leading lady and you were in the chorus?"

"Yes," Marguerita answered, stressing the word and then
going on, "yes, that was a long time ago. And now, now I am
his leading lady. But I don't think we are doing too well. Last
night's dress rehearsal was terrible. Terrible."

"But you were very good, Marguerita," Teresa said nervously.

"You really think so?" asked Marguerita uncertainly.

"Yes. I mean it," Teresa said, watching her mother from the corner of her eye.

"Yes, Marguerita, you were fine, very good. Tonight you will perform in the great tradition," Papa Carlucci said.

"Ah," sighed Mama Carlucci, "ah, the great tradition. When I was Papa's leading lady, there was a tradition in the theater."

"Mama, you and Papa mustn't take it so much to heart— what's happened to the Italian theater," Teresa said.

"Yes, Teresa, my chick. I don't. I am growing gracefully old. I have done my trouping and I am growing gracefully old." She turned and looked sidewise at Marguerita and said in a soft voice: "Yes, I am growing gracefully old and am not ashamed to admit my age."

"Yes. When I was a little girl, I remember that you had been an actress then for quite some time," Marguerita said, also in a quiet voice.

The Carlucci girls became tense.

"Oh, I am worried about tonight's performance," Teresa said.

"We'll try to do our best," Antonio said.

"If we're not rehearsed into a coma before tonight," Catherine added bitterly.

"I just hope everything goes right tonight," Teresa said. "You know, I sat up until three-thirty last night, arguing and talking with Danning about the play. But I think it was worth it. He agreed with me. I am sure I made an impression on him. He promised to make some changes in Papa's lines."

"He will!" Catherine said decisively. "He'll substitute three 'Ahs' for three 'Ohs,' and then he'll be convinced that this brilliant idea of improving the play is all due to his own inspiration."

"What do you think of the play, Al?" Teresa asked.

He smiled at her enigmatically.

"Of course, the play has faults," she said with earnestness. "I know it. But we've got to do something about it." Her voice now became urgent, charged with notes of suppressed

hysteria. "We've got to do something to improve it. We've got
to help Danning, even though we do it by force."

Bill Danning slouched into the diner. He said hello in an
abstracted voice, pulled over a chair, sat down, and asked how
everyone felt.

"Bill, everyone here has called a halt to discussing the play at
breakfast," Albert said.

"Say, that's a good idea," Bill answered.

Five minutes later, he was again talking about his play.

                              x

Backstage, everyone was nervous. The members of the company were dressing and getting ready for the opening. The
dressing rooms consisted of little wooden partitions, with cur-
tains across the openings. A hum of conversation could be
heard passing from behind the curtained-off partitions. Albert
came out of Catherine's partition and knocked on the board of
Papa Carlucci's, which was next to hers.

"Come in."

Papa Carlucci sat in woolen underwear, necessary for his
part, and he was putting paint on his face.

"I merely wanted to wish you luck," Albert said.

Papa rose, faced Albert, and said with pomposity:

"I promise you that I will give everything that is in me. I
will give myself tonight."

"I know it, and good luck," Albert said, struggling to conceal the fact that Papa embarrassed him.

He wished good luck to the others in the company who had
already arrived. Then Bill Danning came around and knocked
on the wood beside the curtain of Catherine's dressing room.

"Come in," she said.

"Now, listen, Catherine, I'm with you on the boards tonight. I'm with you, don't you know, and you just remember
that and remember what I said—more passion, passion, don't
you know, and you'll be a knockout."

"Please let me alone. I want to dress," she answered in an agitated voice.

"Don't get excited," he said awkwardly.

"Bill, don't you know a company's always on edge on an opening night? Please get out of here and stop bothering me."

He retreated in embarrassment. But then she heard him giving advice to Papa Carlucci, and Papa Carlucci answered with the same pompousness with which he'd just spoken to Albert.

XI

Teresa left her father's little partition, where a group of friends, Italian intellectuals and actors, were gathered. They had driven to Flowerdale to see him, and now there was noisy talk in English and Italian. She sat on a bench looking out at the bay, and her husband joined her.

"I'm worried," she said wistfully, agitated.

"Don't worry."

"It's Papa," she said. "He's so nervous. And Marguerita gives him nothing. Oh, God, God," she went on, her voice throbbing. "God, if this only comes out right. If Marguerita only gives him the least chance."

She wrung her hands.

"The play's no good. It's phony," her husband said.

"I know it, I know it. But we can't merely stand aside and criticize. We can't let it be a flop. If Papa only gets going tonight. Poor Papa, he's so nervous, and he must come through such obstacles. But then he will. Yes, he will. Papa's a trouper, an old trouper."

"Let's hope—for Papa."

"I don't like the attitude of the company. They don't act like troupers. Something has happened to the theater. It doesn't beget troupers any more, troupers like Papa. The theater just isn't in their blood. It's in Papa's blood, and it's in our blood. Oh, I hope, I hope, I hope."

"Well, Teresa, I hope it comes out very well. And, dear, please don't overexcite yourself."

"I'm not. But how can I stand by calmly when Papa's reputation, his future, is hanging in the balance. Papa can be a star on Broadway. It's what he needs, and he deserves it, too. He's so depressed about the state of the Italian theater, the way it's gone down. Oh, poor Papa!"

"We'd better get back to our friends," he said.

But she was in tears, and he had to lead her away from the bench to someplace where she could calm down without being observed.

XII

The curtain went up late. The play was slow, badly paced, and badly directed, although it wasn't so slow as it had been in the last rehearsals. The cast was very nervous and conveyed this agitation to the audience, which sweltered as it watched. Cues weren't picked up quickly, and each act dragged and dragged. The weakness of *The Human Equation*, its lack of characterization, of insight and sensibility, were exposed in sharp focus. After the play crawled stupidly and pointlessly along for the first five minutes, a ruddy man with Celtic features stood up in the rear of the theater and loudly began to dispute with a group of his friends.

"This is dirty, filthy," he yelled, incensed.

The actors struggled valiantly to go on, ignoring this disturbance.

"I want to stay," a girl, the man's youngest daughter, whispered, but she was heard by those around her.

"Silence," someone called to them.

At this point, and according to the direction, the male members of the cast were playing and pulling at one another's flies, and in the midst of this Papa Carlucci, again according to direction, was goosed on stage. The irate man noisily demanded that his family and friends leave. Sullenly, they followed him out of the theater. In the foyer, he stamped his feet and shouted as he demanded his money back; he could be heard inside.

"You must understand we're not responsible for what's in this play," Mrs. Jackson told him, trying to soothe him; her voice was persuasive and ingratiating.

"The police should close it down," the man shouted back, and his face became almost apoplectically purple.

"This isn't our company," Mrs. Jackson said in a pleading voice. "This theater was leased by Mr. Allenby. I'm very sorry. I'm even a little mortified, and if I had only known what kind of play this was, then I'd never, never have signed the contract with Mr. Allenby. But now my hands are tied."

"You ought to know what you let go on. You ought to know your business."

The two daughters, girls in their late teens, stood nearby, blushing.

"I know, I know I should. I was so busy, I had so much to do. I can't tell you, words can't express how I regret this. I assure you, this will never happen again in Flowerdale," Mrs. Jackson said.

"Well, I say—whoever is responsible for such a loathsome, disgusting play will be behind bars in short order. Flowerdale will not tolerate such brazen filth, even if New York does."

Having gotten his money back, he led his party out of the foyer.

Inside, the play went on, boring part of the audience, entrancing another portion of it.

Papa Carlucci was on stage during most of the play, and he hammed every minute. He constantly had his eyes focused on the audience, talked to it in disregard of the other players, mugged, rolled his eyes, coyly flirted, almost like a woman, and, in fact, acted as if he were making love to everyone sitting in the darkness beyond the footlights. And still the play dragged on, from scene to slow scene, from act to act. It lasted over two and a half hours, and after the last curtain call, stimulated by friends of the cast, who were doing their duty of friendship, a frazzled audience left the theater, talking, discussing, protesting, and attacking the play.

XIII

"Did you like it?" Bill Danning asked Albert in the foyer as the crowd filed out.

"Oh, yes," Albert answered, glancing off as he spoke.

"It didn't go so badly, did it?" Bill asked eagerly. Without waiting for Albert to answer him, he went on, "What did you think of the reaction of the audience?"

"It seemed divided," Albert said.

"Well, it was a hick audience. It wasn't a Broadway audience."

Albert merely shook his head.

"Well, I knew you'd like the play," Bill said, and he moved off to talk to some Broadway agent.

Albert went outside. He watched the crowd leaving. He saw groups getting into automobiles. He watched the cars driving off. He wandered over to a bench and sat down, staring at the dark, quiet bay. He thought of the play. Here was the group, working so hard, giving whatever they had, struggling to make a success of this dreary play, which revealed not one spark of talent on the part of the author. If it succeeded, they would all profit in varying degrees. It all seemed so worthless, senseless, so stupid. Catherine, acting in a play she detested, would join him soon. If she didn't have the part, someone else would. Had she acted well or not tonight? He wasn't really able to decide. He had loved her on the stage because he loved her. But he had winced at some of the lines she'd had to say. He got up, lit a cigarette, and walked up and down, because the mosquitoes were not quite as bothersome when he walked.

He saw Allenby and Bill in a huddle in front of the building. He continued to walk up and down, looking out at the bay. He turned back and saw the two of them still talking.

These two talentless young men. Did the future, as far as success and esteem went, belong to chaps like these? In some twisted, narcissistic manner they seemed to believe in what they were doing. Or was it that they were so shallow emotionally that belief was meaningless?

Catherine joined him. He kissed her.

"Gosh, you're serious, and in such moonlight," she said.

"Forgive me. I guess seriousness is something to apologize for," he said.

"If I took this play seriously, where would I be?" she asked.

"And yet you have to," he said.

"That's why I'm so tired," she said, squeezing his elbow. They strolled slowly on.

"Danning and Gilman really think they have a hit and are going to make a mint out of this," she said.

"They might, too."

"Yes, that's just it, they might," she said ironically. "After all, Danning has inflicted greatness on himself."

"Mediocrity is an infliction," he added.

"If the shoe business were run as ignorantly and as incompetently as Broadway people like Gilman are trying to run the theater, this country would go barefooted," Catherine said.

Albert agreed. He kissed her, took her arm, and they walked slowly on toward the diner.

The Girls at the Sphinx

I HAD HAD DINNER with Sorel. Although I was very poor, Sorel usually managed to borrow money from me, and it was difficult to get him to repay these loans. But on this night he was in an expansive and Christian mood. He had taken me to dinner in a restaurant on the Boulevard Montparnasse, and he'd tried to cheer me up. Our newborn baby had died, and my wife was still in the hospital. It was close to Christmas, and the shock of the baby's death had left me in a state of depression.

My thoughts went back to Chicago. I recalled past Christmas times, but I dwelt on dissatisfactions and disappointments rather than joyful memories. And my own circumstances were very precarious. Our money was running out. It was impossible to get work in Paris, or even to get a *carte de travail* that would give me the legal right to find work. What would the future hold for me? How would we get along? When she came out of the hospital, my wife would be in a weakened condition. How could she be built up and regain her strength? Where would we get the money so that we could go on? How could I continue with my writing? Could I remain hopeful, as I had these last seven months in Paris? Now I was alone and struggling to restore that sense of hope.

But Sorel was not the person to cheer up anyone. He deeply resented the world and was intensely absorbed in himself. He was a gifted and well-educated Frenchman of my own age— I was then twenty-seven. His hatreds were deeply fixed in his

character, and he lacked any sense of responsibility. Though I
often disagreed with him, I was taken by his brilliance, for at
that time I was somewhat naïve. At times I would try to disagree with him, to state attitudes counter to his, and to point
out what I considered the unreasonableness of his views and
declamations. My naïveté consisted of my speaking and acting
on the assumption that everyone—including Sorel—was concerned with trying to discover the truth and with trying to
reason logically. But Sorel had the saving grace of wit, a wit
that was bound up with his own feeling of pity for himself
and with the pathos that marked all his thinking.

It had been a good dinner. The restaurant was small, and
the customers and waiters had been friendly. The place had
been almost filled, and I had been the only American eating
there. All around me there had been unknown Frenchmen,
talking and enjoying their food. Sorel had talked steadily, and
he had been in good form. Not one known figure in contemporary French literature had escaped his scorn or condemnation. He had imitated and parodied his employers, the
Dubuisson brothers, who were famous publishers, and this had
been very entertaining. He had regaled me with anecdotes
about what went on in the Dubuisson offices, and these were
most amusing. I should add, however, that Sorel made himself
the center of every story, and he would usually conclude his
anecdotes by quoting one of his *bons mots,* which he properly
appreciated. Also, his conversation was sprinkled with ugly
descriptions of the physical and moral traits of the men he
talked about. They were all pigs and dogs and lice. And he
lamented the state of France and of the world. His was not
particularly cheerful conversation, nor was it stimulating.

After eating, he remarked that he could not stand the sight
of crowds of people, of human *merde,* and he said he would
take me to a quiet place, instead of to a café like the Select or
the Dôme, where I often went in the evening.

He took me to the Sphinx, on the Boulevard Edgar-Quinet,
and as we were walking there, he remarked that it was a
famous brothel, but that it would be quiet and we could sit

there and have a drink. I became excited. I even thought that
a girl might make me forget, and that I had a need to forget.
But Sorel and I both agreed we didn't want to go with any
of the girls, that we wanted only a quiet place in which we
could sit and talk.

The inside looked like a café. It was lit dimly. A fat, middle-
aged woman in a dark evening dress greeted us, and Sorel
spoke French with her, telling her that we merely wanted a
drink. We took seats along a wall in a corner, and immediately
four girls crowded around us. Sorel ordered an *apéritif*, and I
ordered a beer. He also ordered drinks for the girls.

They were buxom, country girls. Three of them were plump
and dark, and one was tall and slenderer than the others, and
she had blonde hair. They were all clad in lacy step-ins, and
they immediately invited us upstairs, speaking rapidly in
French and telling us what pleasures they would provide us.
Sorel translated for me, telling me what a pity it was that I
couldn't understand them and their argot.

"It's as good as your Chicago argot," he added.

He told them I was an American, and with this information
their interest in me increased. The girl next to me was fleshy,
and she had soft, dark eyes and dark, bobbed hair. She reminded me in a vague way of a girl I had once known but
whose name I couldn't remember. Then I remembered that
she reminded me of a girl from a small town in Texas whom
I had met at a party in my fourth year of high school, and
whom I had asked for a date. I hadn't gotten the date. I looked
at this dark-eyed, plump, French prostitute in deshabille, a
French country girl, and thought of the girl from Texas.

In the meantime, she and the other girls had kept up their
rapid, saucy chatter. Sorel told them that he and I both had
"femmes fidèles." They laughed at us contemptuously and also
with bewilderment. They couldn't understand why *"femmes fidèles"* should interfere with our going upstairs with them.
They didn't believe us, and continued to urge us, Sorel trans-
lating what they said. If we didn't want to go upstairs with
them, then there was something wrong with us. The girl be-

side me asked Sorel about me. He said I was a writer and used the word *"talent."* The dark-eyed girl looked at me, wide eyed for a moment, and then she laughed sarcastically. She winked at me suggestively. The other girls talked to me rapidly, but as they used an argot I couldn't possibly make out what they were saying, and yet, at the same time, I knew. They wanted me to take one of them upstairs. They were promising me satisfaction. And they were taunting me, insulting me, and laughing at me.

This went on for about ten more minutes, and we all sat drinking. Then the girls became convinced that we weren't customers. But they remained sitting with us because there were no other customers or prospective customers in the establishment. But at least they were getting drinks and smoking our cigarettes. They asked if I didn't have American cigarettes, but I said I'd come to like *Gaulloise Bleu* and only smoked those. This pleased Sorel, whose French chauvinism carried down to the smallest detail.

The girls sang for us. I listened to them moodily, wondering what the words of the songs meant and why they seemed to me to be so gay and spirited, so attractive. I liked the way they tossed their heads, the smiles that came and went on their faces, and their fresh and inviting appearance.

"Do you know what they're singing?" Sorel asked me.

I didn't. He told me. It was a song in which they wished that I were ordure floating on the Seine. Then they launched into new torrents of insults. They all spoke at once, cut in on one another, talked rapidly, and to me there were mingled notes of gaiety and self-pity in their voices. I listened and watched them and liked them. Had I been alone, I should have been more than tempted to go upstairs. To be close to one of them promised an experience that might be very human. I might touch the pulse of a fellow creature, although she now understood me as little as I could understand her. They were cynical and young, and yet, as they rambled on, they seemed like simple girls, like children. They were having fun, and undoubtedly were enjoying themselves more by talking to

me, insulting me, calling me names—since I didn't understand
what they were saying—singing songs about me in an argot,
than they should have had by going upstairs with me. They
found some release in these forms of expression, perhaps as
much as I often found in writing. I had something to forget,
a hurt feeling to let sink out of my consciousness. The death
of our little boy, only five days after his birth, had left me
with such a feeling of helplessness and powerlessness. It had
forced into my mind moody reflections on the ultimate powerlessness of man. And these reflections came back as I sat in a
corner of the Sphinx with Sorel and these girls. It was clear
that they looked on me with contempt. I, watching them,
sipping beer and smoking, thought of them as little girls, as
children. Paris sophistication in sin, so-called, was no different
from what sophistication in sin was in Chicago or in New
York. And I couldn't help but believe that the cynicism of
these girls was merely skin deep. I even envied them this shallow cynicism.

They continued to speak in torrents of abuse. The girl beside me laughed. Then she said something, and the others
laughed. Another of the girls looked at me and patted her
breast. The dark-eyed girl beside me took my hand and laid
it on her round thigh. The desires I had felt a few moments
before were gone. I took my hand away and patted her head,
as though she were a small girl. Then the conversation went
flat. We just sat, all of us silent. I happened casually to take
an old but shiny cigarette case out of my pocket. I had bought
it for ten cents in New York. It worked badly. When the
dark-eyed girl beside me saw it, she was fascinated with it.
Her face and eyes lit up with childlike wonder. She looked at
it as a child would at a bright new toy.

"*Vous le désirez?*" I asked her.

She nodded her head eagerly.

I handed her the cigarette case. She clutched it, stared at it,
stared at me with suspicion, and said something in French.

"She wants to know if she can have it."

"*Oui,*" I told her.

Her face broke into a wide and grateful smile. Then she looked with pride at the other girls. She spoke to them, to me, to Sorel.

"She's saying that she curses you and sings insulting songs about you, and then you give her a present. She doesn't understand you. She wants to know if all Americans are like you."

Now the girls became friendlier. I talked about America, and Sorel translated my remarks. They listened and no longer urged us to go upstairs with them. And when we left, they asked us to come back. The dark-eyed girl clutched the tawdry ten-cent cigarette case, looked at me with simplicity on her round and pretty face, and said:

"*Merci, merci bien, m'sieur.*"

Digging Our Own Graves

I AM NOW on one of the ditch-digging details. Here, in this particular camp for politicals, digging ditches is the major task assigned us. We march out early in the morning and dig. There are two guards for each of us. They march beside us at a distance of five feet, with their guns pointed at us. For some reason or other, they also have fixed bayonets. I do not believe this is necessary, because we have no chance to escape, nor any place to which to escape in the event that one of us, in some miraculous manner, should get away. But it is policy to guard us with fixed bayonets, and nowadays policy is all wise.

Why do we dig ditches? Nobody has ever offered a valid explanation for this custom. Professor Marvin Morganstern did begin to answer the question when he was here. He started by explaining the cultural significance of the graves dug in ancient Assyria, and he had gone on down to grave-digging in Ireland in the eighth century. He was twelve centuries away from the answer to this question when he suddenly was assigned to the grave-digging detail. When you are put on the grave-digging detail, you march the same as you do every day, but you don't come back at night. After you dig the grave, they put you in it, and the next day a detail is assigned to fill up the grave. Such is life here in this camp.

As I say, I am still digging ditches. I don't know when they will shift me to the grave-digging detail. The number of gravediggers varies from day to day. We go along, and

only small details go out to work in the big graveyard beyond
the hill on the other side of the stream in our camp. And,
then, there is a competition between the camps. The Leader
offers a star of the Order of the Leader to the camp which
shows the greatest proficiency in crushing the enemies of the
people, and there is a big to-do in camp. There are meetings
and speeches, and the camp leader sets a plan and establishes
a big quota of graves. Each camp leader puts in an order for
more shovels, and he vows to fulfill his quota of graves. Then
there is excitement and activity at the camp. The grave-
digging details are bigger, and ditch-digging lags for a while
until new batches of politicals are arrested.

The supply of politicals seems to be endless. Our country
is the greatest and happiest in the world, but the enemies of
the people are many. These indirect aggressors are daily plot-
ting to assassinate our great and good Leader, to destroy our
democratic liberties, and to ruin the country. Of course, there
were the radicals, but nearly all the radicals are gone now.
After the radicals were brought here they dug ditches and
then were put on the grave-digging detail; then there were
the novelists and poets, the literary critics, the journalists, the
college professors, and the scientists. They came in batches,
but they, too, are now gone. Later there was a new competition, and Democrats by the dozens were dragged here in
chains. Our camp won that competition, and we have more
Democratic Party graves over the hill and by the stream than
any other camp in this great, free country.

But now all is quiet again. Every morning three, four, or
five of the prisoners get summonses. They march along the
corridor of their particular cell block and are brought into
the office of the Leader of this building. Four guards with
guns and fixed bayonets accompany each prisoner into the
office so there are no assassinations. The Building Leader sits
at his desk and smokes a pipe. All the other leaders smoke
pipes because the Great Leader in Washington smokes a pipe.
The Building Leader then offers each prisoner congratulations
in the name of the Leader of the Country. The prisoners are

then called upon to do their duty to their Leader and their country by disappearing from the face of the earth. After this patriotic ceremony, they are marched out of the office. They don't eat breakfast that morning because they will need no more food. If they drop from hunger, they are laid by the side of the detail and shot lying down. Their comrades dig the graves of those who pass out, and the unfortunate traitor who can't summon the strength to dig his own grave is additionally condemned as an enemy of the Leader and a Betrayer of his Country.

Right after our camp won the national competition for shooting Democrats, it was discovered that a group of radicals in my building had been forgotten. They had been kept here for one year digging ditches. One morning, a guard walked along the corridor, looked into the cells, and began asking the prisoners their names. When they told him, he shook his head, blinked his eyes, stared at prisoner after prisoner with incredulity, scratched his head, and then he told the prisoners that they were lying, in violation of the Leader's new democratic constitution, because, according to the official records, they were all dead, and he had the records to prove it. He hurried off to the offices and reported his discovery, but he was shot for believing in ghosts. An investigation was held, and a squad of the best security agents in the country came to our camp. They questioned everybody, examined the records, and even put these records through the new Super Truth-Finding machine which detects a lie when it is written on paper. But our officials, of course, are all imbued with the spirit of the great weapon of the dialectics, which tells you when yes means no and when no means yes. Now, the machine showed that all the records registered true, not false. But in this instance the dialectics proved that the camp records were all false. Then there was a gala day, and all the officials of the camp were put in striped clothes and assigned to the grave-digging detail. A new set of officials came to run our camp. All the prisoners were reclassified, and then new records were made and put into the files. It was after this reorganization, which was a triumph of the People's Vigilance, that these forgotten radicals were assigned to the grave-digging detail. Something happened somewhere, and I wasn't called to join them that morning, and so I am still waiting for my day of honor. But I was working nearby, digging a big ditch. This ditch had been dug and filled in five times in the last four years, but it wasn't dug according to plan. We have a new Five Year Plan of Ditch-Digging here. A group of plotters disrupted our last ditch-digging plan, and so every ditch in our entire camp had to be filled in and dug all over again. I was working on the biggest ditch to be dug in the new plan. Perhaps that was why I wasn't put in with the gravediggers. But I heard them talking as they dug their own graves.

I might remark that since they have gone our building is less noisy. We are beginning to get in batches of Republicans. Instead of discussing politics, they curse and gripe about a Mr. Roosevelt, who used to be president, and they play cards whenever they have a chance. It seems that many of them had the suppressed desire to become postmasters, and they claim they were frustrated by this Mr. Roosevelt and never became postmasters. They often play postmaster in their cells, and others play political conventions and pretend they were made president. This is a game called ancient history, because a long time ago, about six years back in the hoary past, we used to have a fascist constitution and elect presidents. Now, with the Leader, we have a democratic constitution and do not hold antidemocratic elections to choose a president. As I say, the Republicans don't make as much noise as their predecessors. The Democrats used to fight all the time and were a pretty noisy crowd. But the noisiest of all were the radicals.

It was a fine spring day, and I was digging and sweating away. But I have now dug so many ditches for my Leader and my country that I can work right along with the best of them and not think about what I am doing. So there I was, shoveling away in this big new ditch, and the radicals were a little distance off, digging their own graves.

They had had a big political discussion the night before. Some one of them had proposed a united front, and they had had a united-front meeting. There were fifteen revolutionary parties represented, not to mention six other parties which claimed to be socialist but were for a peaceful evolution. And then there were a few independents.

One little fat fellow with gray hair—they were all old and gray-haired and had spent their lives in politics—opened the meeting with a resolution. He said that this was the best resolution he had ever written, and that it was the crowning achievement of his political career. He had written about a thousand resolutions, and he was proud of them. He used to tell the prisoners that if the Chinese implemented a resolution he had sent them from New York, they would have won the Chinese Revolution. But there was a journalist in the camp at the time who said the Chinese had never gotten his resolution on the implementation of the Chinese victory. The little fat fellow couldn't understand why the Chinese had never read his resolution, but he was proud of it nonetheless. His resolution for a new orientation was his masterpiece. It contained seventy-five thousand words and was divided into fifteen sections. The first section was short—only two thousand words. It analyzed the historic causes of the defeat of the Movement. The fat fellow began to read his resolution, and then things began to happen.

A tall, thin, gray-haired man, who was a Social Democrat, interrupted and said that Leninism was Stalinism, and that Lenin was responsible for the predicament in which they now found themselves. The little fat fellow said this was a vicious argument, and someone jumped up and said there was a Menshevik in the house. The tall, thin political who had protested said he was a democrat and that if the Bolsheviks under Lenin hadn't viciously attacked the Mensheviks in 1903 —but at this point he was interrupted by a fellow with glasses who said that Lenin and the Mensheviks and the Bolsheviks were all state capitalists and therefore were bourgeois, and that his party was the only true Marxist party, and as soon as the workers agreed with him they would make the socialist revolution by voting for it. Then a Socialist got up and said the Communists were immoral. Well, when he started talking, another man got up, and everybody said he would have been the Lenin of America if he hadn't drunk so much whisky. And he said he represented the true party of Joseph Stalin, and that the American Communist party of Browder and Foster had betrayed Joseph Stalin and corrupted Stalin's party and that was why they were all in this jail and why they needed a new orientation, and he said he had this new orientation.

But before he could offer his orientation, someone else jumped up and said his party had proven that Russia was not a degenerate worker's state but, rather, an imperialistic, bureaucratic collectivism, and that this was the scientific interpretation, and that events had confirmed all the prognostications of his party. An old man, who was called America's Number One Socialist, then took the floor and said the last speaker was a petty bourgeois and half-democratic reactionary whom he had thrown out of his party. And that when the Revolution had been in its greatest hour of need and the imperialists had attacked the Soviet Union, he and his party alone had correctly defended the workers' state. And that his party was the only party and his comrades the only moral people, and that history would remember them because they had held the correct position and had had principles and integrity, and that he had built a party of one thousand true Bolsheviks, but that Stalin had betrayed the Revolution. Then a Communist took the floor and said everyone else was a Trotskyite, and that a Trotskyite was an American imperialist, and an imperialist was a Hitlerite, and a Hitlerite was a fascist, and a fascist was an enemy of the human race. He asked that a resolution be passed calling for war to the death against all Trotskyite-American-imperialist-Hitlerite fascists, and long live the memory of Stalin, the Mountain and the Sun of the Universe. Then a former Yale man started to talk about a moral revolution, but he stuttered, and before he could get going, someone else angrily proclaimed that Noske had betrayed the German Revolution in 1918.

Well, that led back to something about Lenin calling some Menshevik a name in 1903, and someone else said that at the Party Congress in London in 1903 Lenin had been Robespierre. So someone else said something about Robespierre, and then a bitter argument about Robespierre ensued. The little fat fellow then shouted that he had put everything in his resolution, and if they would only listen to it they would learn the correct analysis, which was that what had happened in our country was describable as an unforeseen historical variant. Someone else shouted that the little fat fellow couldn't give the correct analysis because he wasn't a dialectical materialist. Then a professor got up and said the first question was to decide whether or not Engels's nature-dialectic was true or false. And someone said Engels had exposed Dühring's bourgeois philosophical errors. So another professor said the question was whether or not the correspondence theory of knowledge explained more than the pragmatic theory, but before he could say what he thought there was an argument about the theory of surplus value. Then an anarchist jumped up and said the law of the falling rate of profit was false and that they all had to start the sexual revolution right away, because the sexual revolution would merge into the social revolution.

Well, by this time it was dawn. The guards came along and broke up the meeting. The radicals were lined up, and they were marched out by three regiments of soldiers with drawn guns and fixed bayonets. They all received the congratulations of the Great Leader, who was permitting them, at last, to be obliterated from the face of the earth. And then they were marched over the hill to the graveyard by the stream. I had bread and water for breakfast and was busy digging the biggest ditch in the new Five Year Plan of Ditch-Digging, and as I was digging away, with the sun streaming down on me, I heard the politics still talking as they dug their own graves.

"A Bolshevik is the best soldier in the army, the best worker in the factory," one old man said. "I am a Bolshevik. I am the best grave-digger in this detail."

He dug away, throwing up shovelsful of dirt so fast that you would have thought he was digging a foxhole in ten seconds flat in order to get into it before an enemy army advanced.

"You know," mused the little fat fellow who had written his greatest resolution the night before, "I would have said that theoretically this could never have happened to us."

"You never understood," someone else called out, "that this is still capitalism."

"But what state of capitalism is it?"

"It's a new form of society, a historical miscegenation," someone said.

"Marx said—" one of the gray-haired radicals said.

"Trotsky said—" another interrupted.

"Luxembourg said—"

"But De Leon said—"

"Stalin said—"

Then they began to shout so boisterously that they woke up the captain of the guards, who had been sleeping in the shade of an old apple tree nearby, and he came over and ordered the soldiers to prod them with bayonets so they would stop making so much noise.

It was quiet then. Far off, I heard birds singing. Every day I went on digging the biggest ditch for our Great Leader.

That spring day passed, and, of course, the day's grave-digging detail didn't return. That night the Republicans played postmaster, and one old fat fellow with a bald head said that if only there hadn't been Mr. Roosevelt he would have become the greatest postmaster since Will Hays.

Our jail is becoming exciting again because there is to be a new competition. They are bringing in more Republicans by the truckload. We are fulfilling our Five Year Plan of ditches ahead of schedule, and tomorrow there is to be a ceremony to dedicate our new ditch. We have dug the biggest ditch yet dug. So I expect I will be told the good news that our Leader has decided to give me the honor of digging my own grave and disappearing from the earth, too, all for his honor and glory.

The Wake of Patsy McLaughlin

PATSY MCLAUGHLIN always said to himself and to others that he wanted to die in harness with his boots on. This was but one of the many reasons why the sunny day in June, 1929, when he retired as Superintendent of the Vehicle Department of the Continental Express Company, was one of the saddest of his life. His doctor had insisted on his retirement. Besides a cardiac condition, he had high blood pressure. He was sixty-two, and he knew that he wasn't the man he used to be. Driven around to the depots every day, he would puff and grow tired, and when he got home at night he would feel dull and weary. Even the White Sox ball games, which he had always enjoyed so fully, fatigued him. He had become a weary, heavy, white-haired man, whose rough and wrinkled ruddy face was blotched with darkening clusters of broken blood vessels. His manner had always been gruff, but in his dealings with the men under his supervision he'd been direct. He valued his word highly, and he had never broken it. He had bawled out many a teamster and chauffeur, given lay-offs and fired men, but most of the men on the wagon loved and respected as well as feared him. Around the garages, stables, and depots he was called "Patsy," "Old Patsy," and "The Old Man." On his last day, many of the wagon men were sad and regretful. The old-timers, especially, knew that they were going to miss him. He had once been one of them, and when he'd gone up the ladder he hadn't changed. In his heart he was still an old-time teamster. He always remem-

bered the men when he'd run across them, and he would call
them by their first names and would ask some of them about
their families. They forgot the times he had been harsh and
thought only of when he'd been lenient and given a man a
break.

The dispatchers and route inspectors, too, felt much as the
vehicle men did. Like Patsy, with very few exceptions they
had once been on the wagons. They, as well as he, could remember how they'd once felt, getting a load of fish, working
long hours during the Christmas rush, or being out on icy
days in winter. Many of them had changed more than he
after their promotions. He would call them in on the carpet
and give them tongue-lashings the way they did their drivers
and helpers. But on the day of his retirement such matters
were forgotten. Work went on, and they were in the depots
as early as usual, getting out the wagon loads. They were conscious that this was Patsy's last day. They had thought of
growing old themselves, of retiring, and of one day dying, but
somehow they hadn't thought of the day Patsy would go. In
relationship to the Old Man they were like children who can-
not clearly think of their father dying. On Patsy's last day
they were a nervous, jumpy, saddened group of men. Many of
them had strange, sad, and dark feelings they could not clearly
describe to themselves—the kind of feelings and moods that
caused them to think or remark that they needed to change
their luck. And Patsy's retirement was full of forebodings
for them. With Patsy over them, they had been secure. Most
of them, at least, couldn't think of Patsy firing them. He'd
been their boss for years now. They had a settled feeling
about their jobs and the Company. Now and then, big
muckety-mucks from the Main Office, and even from the
East, and Efficiency Experts, too, had introduced or tried to
introduce changes in the casual and inefficient way in which
the Department functioned, but their new-fangled schemes
had never really taken hold. Patsy could have changed no
more than they. Tough as he occasionally had been, Patsy
nevertheless had been anything but a really hard boss. They

felt that he understood them and that he also had been a shield for them against the muckety-mucks. And they took pride in him. He knew the big-shot politicians, important police officials, dignitaries of the Church—the kind of men they would like to mingle with and would know if they got as far up the ladder as Old Patsy had.

They were a bit lost on this day. Cooper, who had been Superintendent of the Depot Department, was coming in to fill Patsy's shoes. They all knew that Cooper could never take Patsy's place. Some of them privately had called the new boss Gumshoe Cooper, and they were fearful as to how they'd fare under him. There would be shifts, and no one knew where he would end up. A couple of the Dispatchers and Route Inspectors even feared they might be sent packing back on the wagons or trucks, and that would be raw. Working all these years, they had come to feel at home on the job, and the Company had seemed less big and impersonal than it really was. Much as they now and then loafed and complained, they had come to like their work, and to see Old John Continental as something friendly and accessible. Sometimes when they referred to the Company as Old John Continental, they would even think of Patsy. And now the Old Man was retiring. They felt themselves to be less than they had been a week ago, as though they had shrunk in height.

Patsy had become part of their life, of their memories. His Ford coupé, sliding in and out of the depots, his grunts and coughs in his office, his gruff voice, his gentle, gray eyes, his heavy-footed walk, his slightly slouched shoulders—all this was so familiar. They had begun to feel the weight of time in their own lives, but now that that weight had fallen on Old Patsy, they felt it more heavily. They were very, very lonely on Patsy McLaughlin's last day.

Patsy himself seemed gradually to have accustomed himself to the idea of his retirement. Besides his pension, he had enough savings and investments to assure his security. As the time of his retirement approached, he had many moments when he thought this would be a good thing for him, and

he looked forward to spending his last years in ease, free of
all the strains and tensions of responsibility. He fancied how
he and Mrs. McLaughlin would do some traveling, and would
spend the remaining winters of their life in Florida or California. There would be ball games and friends, and he could
take up gardening. Time would pass in quiet happiness until
he was called. But he never could fully believe in his own plans
and dreams. And on his last day he had to force back a flow
of feelings which frightened him. He didn't want to retire.
He didn't want to accept the fact that all his years, all his life
as an expressman had come to an end. So much was gone, so
much he had taken for granted. During all these years he had
never wanted to have long vacations, and many times on a
Sunday he'd run down to his office or around the depots just
to be doing something. Now he would have nothing to do.
He was retiring in order to try and enjoy the grace and quiet
of a happy death. He felt weak and even powerless. The
authority he had had would end with this day. He would
walk out of his office for the last time, and then he would be
respected and liked, but he wouldn't have authority and
responsibility. Instead of being a Superintendent, he would
merely be an old man. What he said or did on this last day
wouldn't mean much because it could be undone in the
morning. He had never really thought of how much his job
meant to him, and on his last day he didn't think clearly about
this or reason out what his retirement meant. But it was clear to
him that his job had, as it were, become part of himself, and
that he and his job as Superintendent of the Vehicle Department of the Continental Express Company had seemed to be
inseparable. His job and his Department and the Company
itself had all become part of his life.

Now part of his life was to be taken away, severed. This
was like a foretaste of death. Retirement was a form of dying.
He looked at the large office, saw Route Inspectors and Dispatchers, dictated a few letters, accepted and listened to
greetings, congratulations, and expressions of good wishes, but
all of this only left him with the feeling that he wasn't quite

understood. And his pride was hurt. He had to retire because he wasn't the man he once was. Father Time had taken hold of him. And this was almost as though he had lost a vital part of his manhood. He concealed all this and tried to act like the same Patsy McLaughlin he'd always been. He talked of plans with Wade Norris, his Chief Clerk, and with some of the inspectors. He talked for a while with Joe Leonard, one of his assistant superintendents, telling Joe that he would go up to one of the Wisconsin lakes this summer and get in a lot of fishing. He thanked everyone for the gifts he had received. But he felt as though he might even be dreaming. All this didn't seem to be quite true, quite real. It was too soon to realize what was happening, that after today he wouldn't be here any more. It would take him time to get used to his retirement. He had been a superintendent for over twenty years. Days and months and years had passed, his hair had turned white, he had gained a little weight, and his old ticker had started skipping a beat here and there, and this all seemed to have happened in such a short time. He had gone on acting as though he'd be the boss here forever. And now he was leaving. He didn't know how to say what he felt. He couldn't even say it clearly to himself.

And when the day passed, he left his office for the last time. He said good night to Wade Norris for the last time. He walked out of the office for the last time. He was driven home in the Company's Ford coupé for the last time. And he was very sad and very lonely.

II

Patsy died in September. The summer had passed slowly for him, and he had been bored and irritable. He hadn't known what to do with himself. He and his wife had spent a month in Wisconsin, and he had enjoyed the fishing. That had been the best part of his short life in retirement. At home, he had had nothing to do. He had sat for hours, reading news-

papers, listening to the radio, or merely sitting, with his mind
vague, recalling at random incidents from his years as an expressman, thinking of the days when he had driven a single
wagon, of men who had passed away, like his cousin, Jim
O'Neill, and others. He had been saddened to be old and
childless, and had imagined himself with sons and daughters
who would now be married and have made him a grandfather. He'd puttered about the house. Over and over again
he had announced that he would take up gardening, but he
never had. He often had sat on the back porch in the shade
and fallen asleep. He had come to want sleep, but he'd slept
badly at night, and he came to dread each night. He had
suspected old friends of thinking he wasn't the man he'd once
been, and he had begun to lose interest in them. He had had
nothing to do and had become very irritable because of his
boredom.

Patsy died peacefully after having suffered severely from a
heart attack. The doctor had thought that he had a good
chance to survive the attack, but just as he seemed to be on
the way to recovery, he passed away in his sleep.

Patsy was waked for three nights. He had had many friends,
and the house, on a quiet North Side street near Evanston,
was filled each night. Politicians, policemen, friends, express
company officials, supervisors from his old department, and
wagon men all came and paid their last respects. When the
men from the Vehicle Department came, they looked at his
corpse with awe and with regretful eyes, knelt down to say
a few prayers for the repose of his soul, and hurried out to
sit in the kitchen in the rear of the house. The kitchen was
large and on the last night of the wake it was almost filled
with expressmen. They sat there as though they wanted to
huddle together, and a number of them seemed to be uncomfortable in their Sunday clothes. The Route Inspectors
saw one another every day, and many of the wagon men
present also saw one another almost daily. In their encounters
at work, they were usually talkative; they needled and
ragged and insulted one another. Here, they were shy and dif-

fident, and some of them were even a little solemn. Even dead, Patsy awed them. The sense of their difference from him remained even though his corpse lay in the casket surrounded by flowers in the front of the house. They sat on camp chairs and stood in corners, and now and then someone would say something about death, or about how Patsy had gone fast. A distant cousin of Patsy's passed cigars, and everyone took one, as though it were a ritual. Then Gashouse McGinty nudged Mike Mulroney and said that Willie Collins had snatched three cigars, but Mike hadn't picked up the joke. And no one picked up Willie's retaliatory jibe about how McGinty had long since beaten all comers in the contest to become champion cigar-snatcher at wakes. There were small flurries of talk, but they seemed to die out quickly, and the men sat in solemn silence.

While in the back of the McLaughlin home, most of these supervisors and wagon men were thinking, at one moment or another, that their day, too, would come, just as Patsy's had. His death spanned the working lives of most of their lives. He had been the man who had taken McGinty, Collins, Father Bryan, Heinie Mueller, and many of the others off the wagons and made them dispatchers and inspectors. He had singled them out from among hundreds of others, and he had kept them in their present jobs. Their lives had been changed because of his decisions. For years, day after day in their work, they had thought of him and had gone along thinking they were doing things for him, and that if they fell down on their jobs they would be letting Patsy down. They had gone on in the same way under his successor, Gumshoe Cooper, but it hadn't been the same. They hadn't become used to Cooper, as they had been to Patsy. Just as they had felt hurt and lost when Patsy had retired, so now did they feel hurt and lost, only their feelings were sadder, and they all repressed their own fright and fear. Smoking, talking, tapping their feet, and making many little nervous movements, these men all were troubled with thoughts and fears and memories they dared not express. There were thoughts as to who would go next, who would live longest. They thought of past wakes, and of endless little episodes in their lives in which Patsy was involved. Willie Collins confessed that he might go down to work tomorrow and even think the Old Man was still in the front office, and said that Patsy had always stood by him. McGinty said that Patsy had always been fair and had stood by any man who kept his eyes on the ball. Heinie Mueller declared that Patsy had been as square a man as anyone he ever knew. Mike Mulroney said no man could ever have had a better friend. The talk would break out like this, and then there would be moments of silences, and the men would quietly watch one another. Tomorrow, and for many days and years to come, they would talk and kid about this wake, but now, while attending it, they were strangely quiet. It meant something to them, something very tragic which they did not clearly put into words. It meant that a long period of their lives, the best period, had come to an end. It meant that one of the props for their feeling of belonging to the Continental had been destroyed. It brought them sadly back to the days when, as teamsters, they had been young and strong. Now they were middle-aged or old. Some were fat. Some had their hair beginning to gray, or even white hair. They felt a personal loss. They felt strangely uneasy to think that the Old Man was gone and that they were actually sitting in his kitchen and paying their last respects to him. One by one, or in small groups, they left, taking a last look at their dead boss, saying a last prayer, a last word of condolence to his gray-haired widow. Most of them would have cried had they dared to. Patsy was the man they would like to have been. He was gone. They would never be able to sit in his shoes, and no one who ever did sit in his shoes would be quite the same. The Company wouldn't be the same, either, or at least not for a long, long time. Burying him was like burying John Continental himself. It was like burying years of their work for the Company. They all went back to their homes saddened, and they went to work the next day, still saddened. They had lost something, something of themselves and of their own lives.

Candy from Fairyland

A TALL MAN, wearing a very fine suit of clothes, walked through a destroyed village. He came upon two small boys and a little girl who were sitting in the ruins of what had once been a stone house. The two small boys and the little girl were thin, and their sallow faces looked old and sad. Near them was a gray-haired woman, her back bent from work, and with a worn, lined face. She was digging in the ruins.

"Who is that man?" the little girl asked.

The old woman, on seeing the man and hearing the little girl's question, hurried over to join the children. The tall man glanced down at the children with a pained but kindly expression on his face.

"That man comes from America," the old woman said.

The children looked at the old woman, and then they stared mutely up at the tall man and at his very fine suit of clothes.

"What is America?" asked the blond boy.

"I never heard of America," the little girl said.

"You never heard of America?" asked the tall man.

The three little heads moved gravely from side to side.

"You little ones know America," the old woman said.

Again the three little heads moved gravely from side to side. And their stares became suspicious and curious.

"What is America?" asked the little girl.

"Where is America?" the blond boy asked.

"Is America a man or a country?" asked the other little boy.

"I want to know about America," the little girl said.

81

The tall man looked down at the children, smiling, but with an expression of sorrow on his face. He said nothing.

"America is where toys come from," the old lady said.

"That's not America," the little girl said with childlike assurance.

"Toys don't come from America," the blond boy said.

"I know where toys come from," the little girl said.

"Where?" asked the tall man.

His question was met with silent suspicion.

"It's not America," the little girl said.

"What is not America?" the tall man asked.

"The place where toys come from," the little girl said.

"Where is it?" asked the man.

"Where is what?" the little girl asked.

"The place where toys come from?" asked the man.

"Fairyland," the little girl said.

"That's America," the old woman said.

"We call it Fairyland," the little girl said gravely.

"Do you come from America?" asked one of the little boys.

The tall man slowly and sadly nodded his head in affirmation.

"He comes from Fairyland," the little girl said.

"Is he a prince?" asked the blond boy.

"Where are your toys?" asked the other little boy.

"I know all about Fairyland," the little girl said proudly.

"Tell me," the man said.

"What?" asked the little girl.

"Tell me what you know about Fairyland," the tall man said.

The little girl looked at him, still suspicious.

"I know," the blond boy said.

"I know, too," the other little boy added.

"Sometimes I play Fairyland. I like to play Christmas in Fairyland," the little girl said.

"Nobody ever goes to Fairyland. Fairyland is pretending," the blond boy said.

"What happens in Fairyland?" asked the tall man.

"Oh, in Fairyland there are lots of toys—more toys than you can count," the little girl said.

"And candy," the blond boy said.

"I know what children have in Fairyland," said the little girl.

"What?" asked the man.

"I know, but I won't tell," the little girl said.

"Tell," the blond boy said.

"I'll give you these if you tell," the other little boy said, pulling out two rusty nails from his pocket and offering them to the little girl.

"In Fairyland children have fathers and mommies," the little girl said, taking the nails.

"How do you know they do?" the other boy asked.

"Because children have fun in Fairyland. I know something else about Fairyland," the little girl said.

"What else do you know?" the tall man asked.

"Fairyland is Fairyland just for children. When Christmas comes in Fairyland every boy and girl has a tree with lights and candy, and his father and mommy play with him. That's what happens in Fairyland on Christmas."

"Is that true, Mr. Fairy Prince?" the blond boy asked, looking up at the tall man.

The tall man shook his head, but he didn't speak. His face showed strain.

"Why can't we go to Fairyland?" asked the blond boy.

"Of course, we can't go," the little girl said.

"Why?" the boy asked.

"Because we can't," the girl said.

"Why can't Fairyland be here?" the other boy asked.

"Because it is someplace else," the girl said.

"Where?" asked the blond boy.

The girl pointed up toward the blue, sunny sky.

They all looked up.

"No," the other boy said, shaking his head. "Only airplanes are there."

"And that's where Fairyland is."

"I don't believe in Fairyland," the blond boy said.

The tall man took out three sticks of colored peppermint candy and gave them to the children. They stared at the candy as though bewitched.

"This comes from Fairyland," the blond boy said.

The children immediately and greedily began to suck the candy sticks. The tall man watched them, visibly moved.

"Give me something else from Fairyland," the girl said, extending a thin, bony, dirty hand.

The tall man shook his head and said:

"That's all I have."

He patted the three children and walked slowly on, past more rubble, more ruins, where other children sat or played, and where others, old and young, dug and hunted.

The three children silently sat sucking their candy with expressions of absorption and joy on their faces. When they had all finished, they licked their sticky hands.

"Let's play Fairyland," the little girl said.

"I don't believe in Fairyland," the blond boy said.

"Let's be brothers and sisters and play Christmas in Fairyland," the girl said.

"Where are my toys?" the blond boy said.

"Pretend they are there," the girl said, pointing to some pebbles and crushed pieces of white stone.

"We wake up early in the morning," the little girl said.

She rose and put her finger to her lips.

"Shssh," she whispered.

The two boys rose.

"It's dark now, and don't make any noise," she whispered with an air of maternal command.

They walked, single file, on tiptoe, for a yard or so, and then the girl turned to them and said:

"There's the tree."

"I don't like to pretend," the blond boy said, shaking his head.

"It's green. Oh, look at all the pretty lights on the tree. See the candles and the candy."

Reaching up, she pretended to take something off the imaginary tree.

"I'm eating Fairyland Christmas candy," she said, pretending to suck on a piece of candy.

"So am I," the second boy said.

"And, oh, look at the toys," she said, bending down. She picked up a rock. "This is my new pretty doll."

She rocked the stone in her arm as though it were a doll.

"And I have an airplane," the blond boy said, holding his hand up as though he had a toy airplane in it. He made noises to imitate the sounds of an airplane.

The other boy sat in the dust.

"I have a train," he said.

"Good morning, Mommy," the girl said.

She looked up and held out her arms.

"My Mommy kissed me, and so did my Father," she said.

"Mine did, too. She gave me a Christmas kiss," said the boy who was sitting in the dust, still playing with his imaginary train.

"And now my Mommy has breakfast for all of us. Sit down."

She pointed out places for them to sit in the dirt, and they sat down.

"Now we will eat and drink milk. In Fairyland boys and girls can drink all the milk they want." She looked sternly at one of the little boys. "You drink your milk."

They pretended to eat and drink.

"I don't like this game," the blond boy said, getting up and walking off.

"Now, here is your candy," the little girl said to the other boy, handing him a handful of dust.

He put it in his mouth, spat it out, and started to cry.

"I want real candy," he said.

The three children lost all interest in their game. They sat in the dirt, staring off at the ruins, with dreamy expressions on their emaciated little faces.

Have I Got Sun in My Eyes?

NOW, DON'T GET ME WRONG, I like New York. It's a wonderful city. Before I came here from Peoria, Illinois, and got my job as a salesman for Thomas and Thomas, selling candy and chewing gum, I knew I was going to like New York.

Well, I'm still young and unattached, and, of course, when I was coming to New York, I thought about the girls. Now, you take the girls back home in Peoria. I like the girls in Peoria. But, then, I told myself that the girls in Peoria wouldn't be a match for the big-city girls in New York. And I am not ashamed to admit it, I was sure looking forward to the girls in New York.

Well, I guess I am still looking forward to the girls in New York. I'm getting along fine and dandy as a salesman. I'm not exactly a hotshot, but I sell enough. I get along. And I managed to get me a nice apartment down in Greenwich Village, because I thought that was where I would find the real big-city girls. When I first came here, I went out to the Thomas and Thomas factory, and I was watching the girls out there in the candy factory. Some of them were pretty. I watched them pulling candy, plunk, plunk, getting their hands all sticky, and some of them looked mighty pretty. But I told myself these girls were like the girls in Peoria, and now in the city I'm going to get me some of these chic, sophisticated, smart, experienced big-city girls.

Well, I didn't see any girls like that during my first days here. But I knew I was going to, and I kept looking the girls

86

over as I went about my business, and I knew that sooner or later I was going to meet these big-city girls. But now that I have been here for over a year, I don't know. I don't know what to say. There is something I don't understand. I don't understand the girls in New York any more than I understand Closebuyer.

I call him Closebuyer, although that isn't his real name. He's one of my customers. Well, every time I go in to see him, he takes a sample stick of gum from me and he weighs it. Then, after he weighs it, he puts it into his mouth for a while and chews all the sugar out of it. Then, after he has done that, he weighs it again in order to find out how much sugar Thomas and Thomas put in their chewing gum. Then he tells me a lot of jokes. Now, there is one joke he always tells me, and I don't get it. You see, I don't go much for politics. If one man is President, that's okay by me. If another man is President, that's okay by me. But Closebuyer, he's different. I guess he doesn't even know that Mr. Roosevelt is dead. So every time I come in, he tells me jokes, and after he weighs the chewing gum to find out how much sugar is in it, he tells me his same old joke. He begins by telling me something about miracles that happened a long time ago, then he goes on to a long list of miracles, and I try not to listen to it, but I put a smile on my face, because I've got to sell candy and chewing gum, even to Closebuyer. So then, after he's told me all about these miracles, he asks me:

"Joe, you know the greatest miracle of all?"

And, as I say, I'm trying to sell him, so I ask him what is the biggest miracle of all.

"The greatest miracle of all is that they took a horse's ass, put a smile on his face, and made him President of the United States."

Well, about the sixth time he told me that joke, I said to him:

"I missed that one. I had the sun in my eyes."

I guess I still got the sun in my eyes. I told you about Closebuyer because I can no more understand the girls of New York than I can understand him.

Now, the girls of New York, they are beautiful. I like to look at them. I never go out in the street but what I look at them. I look at their figures, their clothes, their legs, their faces. And I think how chic they are and how well they dress. Well, I've been looking at these girls for a long time, and I like to do more than look at them. Well, I'm not going to tell you all the things I thought about these girls before I met some of them.

Because, as I say, New York is wonderful, but New York hasn't been as wonderful as I thought it was going to be. And it's all Freud. He wrote heavy books. I don't read heavy books. I might read a light, funny book once in a while, but a heavy book is something for the long-hairs they got down in the Village, where I live. But that's not my style. If I tried to read those heavy books, I sure would have sun in my eyes all the time. And that's the thing I discovered about the girls in New York. It seems as though they all read this Freud.

Now, you take Marian. Marian lived down in the Village. Marian is a singer. Actually, of course, she is a waitress, but she wants to be a singer, and she has a pretty good voice. And some day, who knows, she might be a famous singer. Well, I got to talking to her because I used to eat in the restaurant where she worked, and I kept watching her. I left good tips, and finally I dated her up. She's dark eyed, and she has fine, dark hair. You look at Marian and you think you are looking at passion itself. And, seeing her, you tell yourself she knows a trick or two. That's the way she looks. Beautiful and experienced, she looks just like passion itself. And, seeing her, you can't help but believe that if you could only take her out and pet her you'd feel mighty good, and she'd feel mighty good. Well, that's what I thought about Marian.

So I got a date with Marian. Well, when I met her she had a book by Freud under her arm. I didn't pay any attention to it. We went for a walk, and we had a few drinks and talked, and she liked my jokes. Of course, when she talked, I didn't get all

she had to say, because some of it was deep. Marian comes from
Iowa, but she's been here about five years, and now she is a
New Yorker and knows her way around. She doesn't talk like
the girls from Iowa, at least not if the girls from Iowa talk
like the girls in Peoria, Illinois.

As I said, her talk was deep, but then, from the way she
talked, I got the feeling that Marian was sure the kind of a
girl who would say yes. She let me take her arm, and she
laughed at my jokes and seemed mighty pleasant. As I sat
looking at her across the table at that bar, she got prettier and
prettier by the second. I talked my best, because I didn't want
her to think that I was just another Joe but that I was a special
Joe. And I confess I was hopeful. But I didn't want to go too
fast, because back home, whenever I tried to go too fast, I
wasn't as successful. So, the first time, I merely said good night
to her and made a second date. The second night I kissed her
good night. After that she let me hug her in taxis and in the
doorway, and I got to be mighty fond of her. She was free, and
I was free, and I began to think we might even set up house-
keeping. And as I was making enough money selling candy
and chewing gum, she might stop working at the restaurant. I
even began to dream that I might help her become a singer.
I didn't exactly think about marrying her, but then, who
knows? She was the first girl in New York I had really met,
and having a girl makes you feel better. It does something
good to you. I went out to work in the morning full of pep
and snap, thinking I'd see Marian that night, and not even
Closebuyer could faze me.

And so Marian invited me up to her place. We sat down side
by side on the couch. We had a drink and a smoke, and talked
about one thing and another, and she got into some deep talk
about Freud, who wrote the book she was reading. Well, I
listened and made out that I understood, and then I took her
in my arms. I'm not a rough guy. I was gentle. I didn't go too
fast, and I didn't go too slow. I went just right, kissing her,
petting her, trying to give her time for her feelings to grow,
and everything was just right. And I was getting excited, and

she seemed to be excited, too. Then she pulled herself out of
my arms, and she sits up straight and says to me:

"I can't. I can't do it. If I did it with you, it would be an
escape."

Now, suppose you were me, would you understand what she
meant? I didn't.

"Escape?"

I shrugged my shoulders. I confess I felt that I had a lot of
sun in my eyes. I just didn't get it. So then Marian says:

"It would be an escape from life and from yourself. It isn't
good to escape, Joe. I tried to escape, and I didn't."

Well, I still didn't understand her, and I don't think I do
to this day. But I tried talking soft, turtledove-like. But
Marian interrupts me:

"You're frustrated, Joe."

Well, at that moment I guess I was frustrated. I wanted
Marian. I took her in my arms quick, and I kissed her hard and
long, and I thought to myself, perhaps Marian has only been
sparring with me, and what she wanted was for me to show
her I was determined. So I kissed her with all of the determination I could. She seemed to like it. She kissed me back. Now,
something was bound to happen. But once again Marian pulled
herself out of my arms. She looks at me, and it was a kind of
funny look. I can't describe it. She said:

"No, Joe, don't." She shakes her head. "It would be an escape. It is just frustration."

As I said above, it was frustration, all right. Why, even now,
when I think of that night—and it was over a year ago—I
still feel frustrated. I just didn't get the point of this escape
and this frustration business. I asked her what she meant. She
explained it to me. I listened very carefully, and I tried to
understand. But I just have to confess that I couldn't make
head or tail of what she was telling me. It was something about
how you were frustrated because of sex. Now, that I understand. But then you tried to escape from yourself and your
frustration, and sex is an escape. Well, when she started explaining that, using all those big words, she had me coming

and going. I was a little dizzy when I left that night, and all I got were these dizzy words. She let me kiss her again, and when I left I put my arms around her and I kissed her hard again, hoping that this time she'd give in. But she kissed me, and then she says to me again:

"I can't, Joe; it would be an escape."

Well, I know when I am licked. I was turning to go when she suddenly says:

"Maybe I ought to escape myself."

I turned around fast. That set me up high. So I started trying again, but still it was no use. No matter what I said or did, Marian would come back to say that it was an escape. She kept telling me I was escaping from life because I was frustrated.

I saw Marian a few times after that night, but it was the same story. I gave up seeing her. It all still doesn't make sense to me. Now, if Marian didn't like me, I'd understand. If she'd been insulted when I took her in my arms and kissed her, I'd understand. There are girls like that. But she wasn't. It was this Freud.

Well, Marian wasn't the only girl in New York. New York is full of them. Didn't I tell you, when I looked at them on the street, it hurt? They were so pretty. And I always liked them pretty. The girls I went for were always the pretty ones. Anyway, I kept on working and forgot about Marian. Josephine helped me forget about her. Josephine was a redhead. She was a little pale, but she was a beauty. She had the neatest blue eyes you ever saw. And her little mouth was so cute you want to kiss it the minute you see her. Josephine worked in an advertising agency and had a good job. She was a very chic dresser. Taking her out made me feel good, because I knew that a lot of fellows would turn and look after me and envy me. That's how good looking she was.

But with Josephine there was this Freud again. She was going to a psychoanalyst. I don't know why. She had everything a girl could want, and she had it in abundance. She was gay, she was jolly, and she was fun, and merely being with her and talking to her was fun. It was exciting even to talk about the weather with her. She'd laugh easy, and she had a soft and insinuating way of laughing that went right to your spine. You wanted to be with Josephine and you wanted her. I did.

Well, after I had dated her a couple of times, I began to be glad, mighty glad, that she was my girl instead of Marian. I would begin to remember little things that Marian had said, and I would compare them with what Josephine said. And when I compared Marian and Josephine, Josephine had it all over Marian. And then as I looked back on how Marian used to say that everything was an escape, that kissing was an escape, that petting was an escape, and her singing was an escape, it seemed a bit screwy to me. I remembered how when we'd be taking a drink, and I'd lift my glass, and she'd lift her glass and we'd have a toast, then she'd say something about this escape. She was always talking about enjoying life and escaping, and it didn't quite click with me, because I didn't see how you could have a good time that way. So, I was glad it wasn't Marian I was dating.

Yes, by comparison, Josephine looked like my real dish of tea. And it wasn't long before I was getting anxious to have my tea. I thought I was going to have it, and I was convinced I was going to like it. But then, once again I didn't pay attention to the little things. When I was with Josephine, I remembered the little things about Marian, but that was all over. Josephine began to ask me a lot of questions about my mother. That pleased me. I always thought my mother was pretty much all right, a good sport and a good mother. I still do. I send her money, and I'm always sending her presents. I was glad to tell Josephine about my mother, about what a wonderful woman she is. And I must have been dizzy, because I thought that this meant that she was interested in me. Of course, I reached the stage of cuddling with Josephine pretty quick. That's the best stage. You and she both want to talk, you tell her about yourself, and she tells you about herself. You begin to believe that here is real understanding, here is the goods. And that's how it seemed to be with me and Josephine. And after she asked me questions about my mother, and I told

her, she told me that my mother must have been better than
her mother, but that she didn't envy me, because maybe it
was best for you if you didn't have too good a mother. She
used to tell me that if her mother had understood her better,
perhaps she would never have come to New York and become
what she had become. Then she told me that her divorced husband had had a good mother. It was good news to know that
she had been married and divorced. That made me feel that it
was going to be easy. She wasn't inexperienced. She told me
that her husband used to talk about his good mother, about
how good a cook she was, and how clean she kept the house,
and how his mother had thought only of her children, and so
on. She said she had gotten fed up listening to him talk about
his mother. Well, I decided I wouldn't talk about my mother.
But she kept asking me questions, and I answered them, because I only wanted to please, and I knew that if I pleased
Josephine she was going to please me. But still, as I look back
at it now, what she said didn't click with me. Then, of course,
I wasn't worried about what was clicking and what was not
clicking. I had Josephine on my mind. She was wonderful.

Well, I don't want to say more here, except that Josephine and I didn't hit it off either, and it wasn't my fault.
I was very careful, and I was very tender with her. She seemed
to like me when I kissed her. She was soft and warm and loving, and it looked like now it was tea time for me and Josephine. But suddenly she sits up and she says:

"No, no, Joe, I can't."

She goes on and says she wants to, but she can't, because I
have something called an Oedipus complex. That means that I
have a mother fixation, and that if she let me I would think
that she was my mother, and that wouldn't be good, because
there was some kind of a state of violent confusion about my
mother in my libidinal cathexis. Dope that out if you can. I
couldn't. It got me groggy. The sun was sure in my eyes then.
Even though it was Josephine, I would rather have been talking to Closebuyer, I was that dizzy.

Picture me. Here I am, nervous, anxious. After all, I am

young and human. And there she is beside me, and just a minute ago she has been so loving and so passionate in my arms, and then suddenly she is telling me this. Now, after all, I'm like everybody else, like every other man. Girls affect me. And if a girl lets me hold her and kiss her and pet her, then I feel a certain way, and I want something. Then, to be let down like that, I tell you, it makes you feel mighty uncomfortable. I don't have to tell you about what they call physiology. You know the way I felt. And I really didn't think Josephine was my mother. I know my mother. But Josephine just couldn't get it out of her head. I didn't want her to act like my mother; I just wanted her to make love to me. Gosh, if I thought of her as like my mother, I wouldn't have touched her. I'm not that kind of a guy.

Well, that's the way it is. I like girls, and I don't think it's bad to like them. But I think I'm a decent fellow, all things considered, and if what Josephine was trying to tell me was true—no, no, I still can't get it. It doesn't make sense. But try and convince Josephine I don't think she's my mother. You just try. And then there was something else she said that wasn't at all clear to me. She said that I thought she was something like a mother surrogate. That sounded legal. I don't know what it means, but I know surrogate is a legal word. Now, that's something I never expected to happen to me. There I was with Josephine beside me. A minute ago, like I said, I had my arms around her, and she was warm and close to me and I was kissing her. And, now, there we were, side by side, and she was telling me about this surrogate stuff.

Well, I guess Josephine wasn't my dish of tea. At least, I didn't have the tea. And after Josephine I got to thinking times just must have changed, and I began to wonder if the girls in New York were peculiar. Well, I told myself that the girls in New York weren't what I'd expected them to be. Because Josephine was a bigger surprise to me than Marian. After Josephine, Marian seemed simple. All Marian had said, in effect, was that I was frustrated. Well, I was. But what Josephine said was—I didn't get it. I still don't get it. I don't know what it means. And would you get it? You take a girl like Josephine, and you kiss her, and is there anything else in your head? And then she talks to you this way. She tells you about this Freud. Why, I didn't even know I had a libidinal cathexis. But Josephine did. And when she got finished telling me about it, I was hanging on the ropes.

Now, I could tell you about some more of my experiences with girls in New York, but I think maybe it will make you feel the way I felt. But I do want to tell you about Annabelle. Annabelle was a hat-check girl, blonde and beautiful. Back home in Peoria when the boys saw a girl like Annabelle, they used to say that she had capacity for action. Well, she did. I won't go into how we got worked up, but we did get worked up, and then Annabelle springs something on me. And this is Freud, too. It must be. It couldn't be anybody else. Annabelle told me that when I wanted to pet her I had neurotic drives. Maybe she was right. I had plenty of drives, all right. I was pretty crazy for her. You would have been yourself if you saw her. Well, this time I didn't wait for the full explanation. I couldn't take any more explanation from Freud.

And so, here I am. I still look at the girls in New York, and I think of how beautiful they are. I can't help it. I look at them, and I want to pet them. But so far the girls in New York are so smart, and they know so much, and they all seem to know me like a book, they tell me what I need, all except that one thing that any young fellow like myself kind of thinks he needs. And by now I guess they're right. I guess I am a little frustrated, just as they told me. Then I wonder. Who wouldn't be after meeting girls like Marian and Josephine and Annabelle and a few more of these girls in New York? So, as I say, while I like New York and the girls in New York, I've got to say that the girls in New York are not like the girls in Peoria. The girls in Peoria just never talk that way. And I was thinking of this the other day when I was back out in the factory and watching the girls out there, pulling at the candy, plunk, plunk, plunk, plunk, getting their hands in the goo, and I looked at a couple of pretty ones, and I thought

maybe I'd like to take them out. But I was wondering had they
read this Freud? And I noticed that when some of them were
going out at the end of the day they had books. One of the
prettiest ones had a book, and that made me kind of afraid.
And then yesterday I was thinking about all this, and I went
to see Closebuyer, and what did he do but weigh the gum
again and tell me that same joke about miracles. Then I was
walking around the streets, and I was looking at the girls, and
I was thinking about them, and they were awfully pretty. And
I was thinking about the girls in Peoria, and I was wondering
when am I going to find a girl in New York who hasn't read
this Freud? Because that's just what I want. If I could only
find a girl that is pretty as Marian or Josephine or Annabelle,
and smart in the way I want them to be smart but more like
the girls in Peoria than the girls who read this Freud. As I say,
I still like New York. Don't get me wrong. It's wonderful.
But the girls in New York—when they talk to me, I really
have sun in my eyes.

Slouch

IT WAS A PLEASANT NIGHT many years ago, and I was wandering about aimlessly in Jackson Park when I ran into Slouch
opposite the entrance to the beach lockers.

He was a narrow-shouldered little fellow who used to hang
around Louisa Nolan's at Sixty-third and Stony Island when
I was going to high school. He always walked with what I
used to style a don't-care gait; he had a long face, thin lips,
an almost toothpick neck, and small, suspicious eyes. Most
of the time he would seem to be sneering, but suddenly I
would be uncertain as to whether it was a sneer or a look
of sadness and self-pity on his face. I guessed he felt down
at the world because of his size. When he wasn't dancing,
he sometimes appeared to be almost not living in the present
at all; he seemed to be only half awake. He was always togged
out in the nobbiest clothes. No lad around the corner of
Sixty-third and Stony Island had wider bell-bottom trousers
than he; no one wore louder ties; none of the boys could
have used more Vaseline or brilliantine on his hair than Slouch
did.

I often watched him dance. The popular girls who went
to Nolan's would rarely give dances to anyone but the regu-
lars. Slouch was a regular, and, despite his size, he nearly
always got a dance. No one at Nolan's could have expressed
greater vanity than Slouch when he danced. He always held
his head rigidly at an angle, and his face always beamed with
gratification and self-esteem. Judging from the gravity of

his expression, dancing seemed a serious matter to him. Often dancing with a girl as tall or taller than himself, he never so much as gave a sign of recognition to anyone who might catch his eye on the dance floor or from the sidelines. He was one of the best dancers around Nolan's, and nearly everyone who hung out there was a good dancer. He used to be soused very regularly, and, like most of the other lads, he would brag of how drunk he'd been and how he had drunk so much moon that he had vomited or passed out. When drunk, he would seem even sadder than when he was sober.

On the night I met Slouch, he was in shirt sleeves. A cigarette hung from the corner of his mouth, and he looked no different than he had when I used to see him back around 1923 and 1924. As usual, he seemed to be looking at nothing, and it might have been that he was thinking of nothing. First he saw me. Then there was a slow dawning of recognition upon his face. Then he slowly took the cigarette from between his lips, inhaled with a jerk of his head, and smiled.

"Well, hello. How are you?"

When he spoke to me in the old days, there had been an embittered and self-pitying tone to his voice, and his greeting sounded to me as if he had not changed any.

"Oh, pretty good. How are you, Slouch, and what's new with you?" I answered.

He said he was out of work but that he and another fellow were running a bus between the beach and Sixty-third and Stony. There wasn't much business, and he wasn't making much dough. And then he gazed off at nothing and remarked:

"Noel Merton's in town. I mean he was. I was out with him."

"Does he still talk the way he used to?" I asked.

"No, he's grown up. Since he lived so long in the South he talks like a nigger."

I waited for him to go on.

"And, say, can he eat! Holy Jesus, I was gonna pay the check, just for old times' sake, but when I saw the way he was wolfing, no, sir. I decided I'm not breaking my arm paying for his check, old times or no auld lang syne. Boy, can he eat!"

He said this in a tone that suggested contempt for Noel, with whom he'd been friendly in the old days.

There was a pause in our talk.

"His mother died," Slouch said, looking off again, but in another direction. "It was pretty tough. But, then, it didn't hurt his appetite none. I was afraid he'd start chewing the tablecloth. He left nothing on his plate—and I mean nothing."

"What's new around the corner of Sixty-third and Stony?" I asked.

He didn't answer immediately. He took his time lighting a cigarette but didn't offer me one. He let the cigarette droop from his lips and then said:

"Oh, nothin'."

He gazed vacantly at the sky. Then he went on:

"Marty still ain't married. He'll have to marry her out of pity. He's been going around with the dame so long she lost all of her boy friends, and so she's alone, and he'll have to marry her out of pity."

"I suppose so."

"I almost got married. Almost," he said with a bitter laugh.

"Well, congratulations on your escape," I said flippantly.

"Yes, almost," he said again just as bitterly.

"How did it happen?" I asked, guessing he'd like me to.

"It's a pretty long story," he said, flicking off some ashes. He looked off again. "I used to go around with my friend Val. Val Lexington. Did you know him?"

"No, I didn't."

"I thought he was my buddy. I used to see him all the time. We'd go around, you know, Val and his wife and me, and drink beer and have parties, and it was all on him, that is, on his wife. I was with him the night he met her. Christ, he was a lucky sonofabitch, and I saw her first, too."

"What's she like?"

"Well, yes, she's plenty hot. He and I went to White City Ballroom one night to dance, thinking maybe we'll dance and

pick up two Polacks. And there she is. This blonde, her name
is Irene. Well, I see her first. She looks hot, and was she
dressed to kill! She looks too classy to be in this place, but
there she is."

He paused. Then he went on, his voice becoming intensely
bitter. "How little I know."

"Why?"

"Everything! Everything! She's rich. She's got dough. Now,
here I was, imagining all of my life how I'm going to go out
stepping some night, and I'm going to meet a dame with
dough, and she's going to fall head over heels for me and go
boom. And that's going to settle all my problems. I knew I
was going to meet a dame like that. A dame with everything,
looks, build, a willing disposition, and the dough. And I did.
But what good did it do me?"

"Your buddy took her away from you? Is that the story?"

"I didn't think so—then. I just thought—the fortunes of
war. But now I know he did. Because when I saw her, she
gave me the eye. I was walking just about a foot ahead of
Val, and she gives us the eye, and I know now she was giving
me the eye. But he makes a beeline for her. So I figure the
next dance is mine. I watch them dance, and there he is
giving her a line, and she's clinging to him, and so I figure,
Val, now, he's got something. So I get myself something. A
Polack. She's as hot as this blonde, Irene, that's her name,
but she isn't rich. So there you are. Just my luck. She has
dough. I mean dough. And she falls for Val. Hell, he has
nothing I ain't got, and if it was not because of my luck, I'd
'a had her. Come to think of it, I knew what kind of a guy
he was even then. But you know me. I never play a buddy a
dirty trick. And that's what I get for it. That's why I'm
here now, running a goddamn half-broken-down bus for
pennies."

"That's tough."

"I called him up to go to White City with me that night,
too. Now, if I had gone alone, I'd be living sweet and nice
in New York City like that bastard is this minute, not lifting

his finger. Val Lexington." He paused, and then, in contempt
and bitterness, added: "My buddy."

"Well, that's tough, isn't it, Slouch?"

"My buddy," Slouch repeated.

I waited for him to go on.

"Anyway, Irene fell for him, and so they got married.
And so, when I was down on my uppers, Val asks me to
stay with them. He has a layout! You should have seen it,
in Flamingo, looking right out on the lake, and, Christ, he's
living like a king, and, think of it, I could have had that all
for myself. And this wife of his, does she love him? Christ,
he was pooped all of the time. She worked him for what she
gave him, but, then, I guess it was worth it. Only she wouldn't
have pooped me like she did Val. I never met the girl who
could poop me. But, then, you never can tell what's going to
get inside of her head."

"Yes, Slouch," I said, making conversation.

"Well, we had parties and drinks. Boy, we had drinks!
And so there was a party at their house, and she has a girl
friend there, a girl from someplace in Ohio; and so I meet
this girl friend at a party, and when we go out I am asked
by Val's wife to take out the girl friend, and it's no dough
out of my pocket, because Val's wife, Irene, she pays the
bills. And so we, the girl friend and I, we start going together. I was workin' at the steel mills then, and Val, he was
livin' just like what he was—a gigolo. But I was makin' good
jack at the time and spendin' it on the girl friend, and I
thought I was makin' enough, so one night I popped the
question on the girl friend. Well, we become engaged."

He spat, lit another cigarette, let it hang from the corner
of his mouth, and went on. "Everything went along jake
for a while. I liked her, and she seems to like me. And so
one night I have a date with her. It's Saturday night. I was
workin' the three-to-eleven shift, and I was supposed to get
her after work. I go to pick her up, and they tell me she's
at a party. I was sort of puzzled, and, sucker that I was, I
didn't kick her in the teeth then and there. But that's the

way it is. I'm always too damn softhearted and don't like
to believe people are as lousy as they are. That's me, and so,
there you are. So I see her, and she tells me she hadda go
with some friends. So I believed her and thought nothin' of
it. And it happens again, except this time I'm to call for
her at the party, and I do, and there she is with some friends,
all of them poops, and not my kind at all. One of 'em was
some loogin who has a wife, but the wife's gone away somewhere. Well, they was drinkin' beer. And I didn't think
nothin' of it, and that time we went out to the Palm Tree.
Well, the same thing happens the next week when I was
working on the eleven shift, and, you know, there I was
thinkin' she has dough because Val's wife has, but she hasn't
a sou of her own. Why, she soaks me for fifty bucks I was
savin' up for the wedding bells. You see, she came up here,
she says, to help out a sister, and the sister has got a baby
and is gonna have another, and Val's wife, she could help
out but she doesn't. And there I am, paying for somebody
else's baby, or so I believe, and my dame, Barbara, she's supposed to be helping out the married sister. And then her
parents get sick, and she hasn't got the railroad fare back
to Ohio, and does Val's wife shell out? Not on your life. I
do. And it all comes out of my nest egg. Fifty bucks more.
Good-by," and as he said this he blew off a kiss. "Good-by."
He blew another kiss. "Well, she is out of town, so she tells
me, and then she comes back, and I see her, and we go out
to the North Side one night. She has to stop off to help a girl
darn something or other. Well, the train passes her station,
and so I ask about it, and she says she'll ride to Belmont with
me and then go back. I leave her at Belmont and grab a
Jackson Park train and come back. And she does what? She
takes the next Jackson Park train right back. And then what
happens? My kid brother, he happens to stop off at Val's.
And in walks my girl. And after her there's two friends, and
one of them was that married loogin whose wife's gone away.
They didn't think nobody was gonna be at Val's, and they
was going to have a party there. Well, after that, I checked

out, and I says, 'No, sir, that's not for me, not me.' But it's funny, me, me taken for a ride by a girl from someplace in Ohio. Why, I can't even remember the jerk town she came from. So I thought after that no girl from Ohio's playin' me for a chump. And so there you are. Val, that bastard, he draws the rich blonde out of the deck, and, once she sees him, she wouldn't look at no one else, but I draw this girl friend of hers from someplace in Ohio. Now, can you beat that for luck?"

"It was pretty tough, all right," I said. "Particularly when somebody's been around the way you have, Slouch."

He agreed with me.

We stood there. He looked at his watch. It wasn't time yet for his next trip, and we talked casually, and I asked him:

"How's Louisa Nolan these days?"

"Oh, she's getting on; you know, she has a place on Sixty-third down past Woodlawn. She charges two bits a dance now, unless you can get in with one of the dames she has workin' there, and if you do, you can get a free dance now and then."

"That's high, isn't it?"

"I suppose so. But a lot of the old lads go back to her place. But the broads up there—" he made a face. "I was up there one night last week dancing with a redhead. She—a dancer? I said to her—'Are you an instructor?' And she looks at me, puzzled, and wants to know why I ask a question like that. And so I tell her—'You and the floor don't get along, because you're always keeping your feet on my shoes instead of the floor.' Call that dancing?"

I nodded.

"Well, where are you living now?" I asked.

"I'm livin' with my sister. I was livin' at home, but no, sir. One house ain't big enough for me and my older brother. We're like cats and dogs. You see, at home there's us four brothers and the old man, and all of us wear the same size clothes. Now, my older brother, he's a real estate salesman, and he changes shirts, including my shirts, several times a day. He wears one shirt to play golf in in the mornin', and one shirt to work in in the afternoon, and another one in the evenin'. And my kid brother bought a tie four months ago, but he ain't seen it since, and my turn to wear the tie didn't come around when I went to live with my sister a week or so ago. Or like this, I went to buy an overcoat last winter when I was still workin' at the steel mills before I was laid off, and I took my kid brother along. So they show me one of those coats, what you call 'em, Johnny Walker? No, Jimmie Walker's, that's it—you know, a tight fit with the velvet collars? Well, we go to see a guy my kid brother knows, and they bring me out one of them, and they want six bits in dollars for it. So I told them—'That's too rich for my blood. Yes, sir, that's too rich for my blood.' So I bought my kid brother's old coat for ten bucks. We all wear the same size clothes, and they wore mine all of the time. So I'm livin' with my sister."

"Isn't this new business of yours any good at all?" I asked.

"When you've got seven Chicago Motor Coaches competing against you, and every day you have a run-in with another car, or a flat tire or something, what business is there? I don't make no dough. Something always goes wrong with the car, and something always goes wrong with me. Like Val getting the rich dame when I spotted her first."

"Well, I'm going to drift on," I said.

"Wait a minute. Want a ride back to the corner?"

"No, thanks, I'm not going that way," I said.

"Say, I saw Studebaker the other night."

"How is he?" I asked.

"Him and his bunch, they're thumbs down as far as I'm concerned. They're tight. I mean tight. Why, every time you go out on a party with 'em, they come around to see you the next day with a pencil and a notebook and tell you you owe 'em fifty-nine cents, and if they knew fractions they'd even tell you what fraction of a cent you owed them. You got to be a financial wizard to go out with Studebaker and his pals. All of 'em is penny-squeezers except Frank, remember him?"

"Oh, yes, how is he?"

"Frank, he's all right. You gotta give him credit, the way he takes care of his mother. You won't find many lads like him doin' that, taking their mother out to a show two or three times a week. You gotta give him credit. Yes, I like to see Frank and go out with him. We go out and we spend money, and then we don't do no penny-squeezin' arithmetic about who spent a penny more than the other, like Two-bits Jerry Rooney, and Half-a-buck Studebaker and the rest of that crowd. And Rooney, he always comes around and tells me how he's a knockout with some new dame, and every damn time he meets a dame, what does she do? She makes a damn fool out of him. Yes, they all give me a pain, except, of course, Frank. He's like me. He'll take care of his mother. Like when I was workin' at the mills before I got laid off. I had a chance to go and work in Calcutta, India, and could have taken a leave of absence to go, but I wouldn't. I wouldn't leave my mother and be so far away from her, because I know I won't always have her. And Calcutta is too far away. I like my three squares a day close to home."

"Yes, in this country you can always get back home, but when an ocean separates you," I said, yawning.

"I like my three squares a day," Slouch went on. "And, say, I saw Morrison the other day. He looks like a hobo with his heels all run down. His suit was unpressed, and he had on a dirty shirt, and he even needed a shave. Ain't that a come-down, him lookin' like a hobo?"

"That's too bad."

"Yeh, he looked just like a hobo."

"Too bad," I said.

"Now, me, I like the idea of workin', having my own dough. But Morrison, he looked just like a hobo. And then, before I was workin' at the steel mills, I was tending bar in a flat, and Benny—remember him?—he used to come up with his wife, and is she something? She's got a hatchet face, and she's never sober. No, Benny, now, he didn't do so good, either. But, then, it takes all kinds of people to make a world."

He looked at his watch. He had to go. There were a few bathers in his truck. He said so-long to me and told me to drop around the corner of Sixty-third and Stony Island sometime to see him. He was usually there. I watched him drive off the old truck with four paying customers in it, and then I wandered on in Jackson Park.

I never saw Slouch again after our chance encounter and talk that night fifteen years ago in Jackson Park. He was reported Missing in Action in the South Pacific.

A Coincidence

AT THE AGE OF THIRTY-FIVE, Harry Ansel was getting bald; he was an unprepossessing-looking man, tall, bony, undistinguished. Vain about himself and his appearance, he always dressed with great care and spent as much money on clothes as his means would allow. He had married his college sweetheart.

Jean Ansel was of medium height, blonde and bovine. She was a conventionally good wife, and she managed her home as if it were a well-run delicatessen store, keeping it clean and orderly. She was thrifty, positive, assertive, unsentimental, and she dominated her husband. She helped Harry in his work —he was an editor on a trade journal—and he always discussed his problems and business affairs with her and acted on her advice. He believed that it was due to her prodding of him that he had received a raise and a promotion that would permit them both to realize their ambition: to leave Chicago and settle in New York. Harry was being sent there to open and run an office of the journal.

The Ansels had one child, a pretty baby girl whom they were bringing up in the modern way, without sentimentality. Just as Jean had taken her home and husband in hand, so had she also taken this little girl Marion in hand.

The thought of moving to New York was very exciting to Harry. He saw a whole new life ahead of him. He was gratified with himself and believed this promotion had stamped him as a successful man. He would meet new friends and live a better life than he had in Chicago. Not that he was so dissatisfied with his life in Chicago, although it had begun to pall on him. He needed Jean and would have been lost without her, robbed of his power of making decisions, deprived of further chances of getting on. He had become so dependent on her that she was like a part of himself, that part of his being usually described by the word "will." He had been married to Jean for ten years. He needed her, and he feared her. At times he indulged in sexual fantasies, imagining himself having affairs with other and younger girls. He would think of young girls, girls in their teens and early twenties, their bodies white and slender and warm and mysterious. He didn't want his marriage with Jean to be broken up, he merely hoped for some passing liaisons in which he would be gratified but which would be without dangerous consequences or responsibilities.

He looked forward to his trip to New York with the hope of finding some girls. He would be free for a month or so, living by himself. Jean did not force him to tell her everything, to report to her, as it were. He did it out of fear, compulsion, inner necessity. And he balked at what he did, and he often silently would condemn himself for lacking independence. In such moods he would resent Jean and want, all the more, to prove his virility in bed with a young girl. After all, he was only in his middle thirties, and while he was content with his wife most of the time, now and then he had his moments of depression. Time seemed to have passed so rapidly. Much that he had wanted to do had never been done. The years pass, and soon a man will be forty. And from forty on, the prospect was one of decline. He had never caroused in his youth like some of his college companions, and he had looked down with moral disapproval on those who had. Yet he wanted to do that of which he disapproved, and the desire to do so kept recurring. For years now a whole succession of silent dissatisfactions with Jean had grown within him. He often wished he could recapture the feelings he had experienced in their first days. Now he could no longer find them, he could not feel about her sexually as he had once. And they had no other deep and gratifying bonds. Their home was established on the unspoken idea of possessing things, possessing things that were always clean and in their place. There was nothing unconventional in it. And the gratification that can be found in things is limited. It was for Harry.

New York loomed more and more in his mind as a place where he could have a fling before he settled his affairs, found a place for his family, and brought them on to a new life. He was eager and hopeful. He thought and dreamed of how he would have some discreet liaisons. He yearned for the time when he would leave Chicago, when he would be in New York alone. He wanted to be alone. It would give him time to think. He felt the need to have such time. A man reaching thirty-five needed to settle his emotional accounts with himself. He had to think of what he had been and done, and of what he was to be and was to do. He had more and more gotten into the mood where the past and future were the regions in which he found contentment. Nostalgia for the past, hope for the future, kept drowning out his enjoyment of the present. The present spun past one too fast; too much of it was lost in banalities, details, petty details that had to be taken care of.

At last, and with Jean's instructions drummed properly into his head, he left. He had hoped he would meet some unattached girl on the train, but he had not. He registered at a good hotel in the Herald Square region, attended to his business affairs, and got in touch with some real estate agents about an apartment. There was much for him to do, much to attend to. His colleagues invited him to their homes socially once or twice, and he was pleased, but, of course, he could not have his fling with their wives, their friends, or with anyone they knew.

He was eager, expectant, and during his first days—he had been there several times on business trips and was somewhat familiar with the city—he now and then felt impulses that reminded him of his youth. He felt free, and this feeling of

freedom was all the more glorious because it was only temporary. It was like a vacation, a moral holiday. He would have
dreaded being free for all the rest of his life. New York
was full of women, beautiful, chic, sophisticated. He saw them
every day on the streets, every evening at dinner, and when
he walked around, went to motion picture theaters or to plays
on Broadway. And he feasted on them with begging eyes.
Every morning he woke up hoping, expecting to meet one
and to spend the night with her. He put off trying during his
first days because he had so many engagements. And he didn't
know how to go about it. Being vain, he feared being re-
pulsed. Being married and holding down a new and responsible
position, he dreaded a scandal. At times he even grappled with
the moral aspect of the problem: It would be disloyal to Jean;
it would be unfair. He needed Jean; she had helped him,
helped him so much. And yet other men who loved their
wives philandered now and then and got away with it. Man
was different from woman. He was not made for just one
woman. He even would sink into fits when he would be
sorry for himself thinking he had to spend all the rest of
his potent life sleeping with his wife. Things were wrong. A
man should be allowed more freedom. A man should be allowed to have a mistress, as long as he was discreet. And he
was afraid. His moral problems arose from fear, rather than
from any sense of good and bad, of loyalty and disloyalty.

Here he was, free! But what was he doing? He eyed, almost
ogled, women on the street, and then he would suddenly try
to seem casual and would walk on, shamed and disturbed. He
went to the theater and let his imagination wallow in the
sight of half-dressed girls. Actresses, chorus girls, movie stars,
they could be so gratifying to a man. In particular, he wanted
a dancer. A girl who danced would know how to do so much
with her body. His mind fastened on the ways some woman
would act, her movements, cries, words, the way she would
describe the act after it had been consummated. He longed
to find out. He longed merely for the sensations of sex. He did
nothing but want, yearn, fill his mind with sexual fantasies and

look at women on the street and in theaters. He avidly read the gossip columns, thinking of the lives of celebrities, of those who were reported heated and superheated with one another, and so on. And yet he disapproved of this and of his own desires. But disapproval of the flesh does not quiet urges rising out of that flesh.

Harry became very lonely. He wanted his family with him, but he wanted a fling before they came. And he often asked himself—then why didn't he take that fling? But he held back in fear.

He was not enjoying his new success, for he was finding no way of expressing it. Thus, though he knew he would have better things in his home, he knew, too, that in time he would become bored with them. He wanted to make some kind of demonstration to the world that he was a success. What could he do? He wanted a woman, a new woman, one who would be glamorous and young. Several times he went alone to the night clubs and restaurants mentioned in the gossip columns, but when he was there he would sit brooding over drinks, watching and looking and listening to whatever he could overhear, thinking every woman he saw was an actress, a Hollywood star, a celebrity, a society woman. And he grew more and more lonely. He was sorry for himself, a man temporarily doomed to live in a hotel room, to eat alone, to spend many evenings by himself. The corridor of his hotel floor was long, dreary, and rather dark. On either side it was flanked by boxlike rooms with only numbers on them, temporary lodgings in which one did not live but merely existed in transition. If he heard a laugh from one of the rooms, it seemed false. And the lobby seemed to him filled with lonely men, sitting, gazing, gaping. In New York there was a sharp contrast between this loneliness and the city's activity. There were so many theaters, so many night clubs, cabarets, restaurants, where people gathered and where there was loud and gay talk. He saw so many men with glamorously dressed women, and he was alone in his frustration.

Finally, Harry made up his mind. He was determined to get

a woman, and he became grim, as if this decision involved his very life. He asked a taxi driver about a prostitute. The hackie put him in touch with a call house. He bought prophylactics at a drugstore as if he were committing a crime against the government, a murder. He slunk out of the drugstore and walked three blocks in one direction and two in another, and then he took a cab. He met the girl on a corner. She was not what he had expected. He had wanted someone tall and dark and just a trifle plump. The girl was short, with red hair. But she looked sweet, even innocent. She was neatly dressed and carried a little valise in her hand.

"Mr. Smith?" she said.

He answered yes, and smiled. He felt possessive. His entire way of life asserted itself at this moment. He was used to buying things and to doing what he wanted with what he bought. He was buying this girl's body, and it would be his to use. She couldn't say no, and she wouldn't. He was paying her fifty dollars to say yes, and for fifty bucks she was going to do with and to him whatever he wanted.

"I'm Diana Sweeny," she said.

"Well, well, hello, Diana."

"Hello, Mr. Smith," she said in a rather matter-of-fact tone. He stood with her a moment.

"Shall we go?" she asked.

He nodded.

She led him toward a hotel. After taking a few steps, he thought to take her bag and asked for it. She handed it to him. He hoped she would observe this and note that he was a gentleman and didn't look down on her. He was nervous about registering at a hotel but tried to calm himself and conceal his nervousness. The clerk was casual, hardened, a cynical-looking bald-headed man, who wanted the money in advance, asked if they wanted the room for one night, and then called a bellboy. With his eyes lowered, Harry hastened to the elevator. He was glad for its obscurity. Suppose he had been seen? Jean knew some people in New York. Suppose one of them had seen him entering the hotel? But they hadn't.

Nobody would ever know of this. And he was actually going to get what he wanted, what he had wanted for so long. It was better this way. Pay for it, with no consequences.

They were let into the room. The bellboy fussed with the shades, light, and bedspread, opened the bureau drawers noisily, turned on the bathroom faucet, pointed to the shower and ruffled the shower curtain for Harry to hear him, pointed to the telephone, drew a "Not To Be Disturbed" sign from a bureau drawer, and then, looking coldly at Harry, asked if there was anything he needed. Harry was unnerved and gave him a dollar tip.

He was alone with the girl.

She opened her suitcase and casually pulled out a black lace nightgown and asked him if he wanted her to wear it. He shook his head. He was so inflamed he couldn't speak.

He went to her and embraced her. She was pliant and practiced in his arms. She strained herself to him, held her lips and body to his as long as he wished.

"Let me take your clothes off," he said in a gulp.

"Yes, dearie."

He fumbled.

"Mr. Smith, could I have the money first?" she asked.

"Of course, of course," he said.

A passing feeling of disappointment crushed him. After all, this was being bought. Bought love, a bought body. But he wanted it. He had put the money in a vest pocket, and he pulled it out in a lump and handed it to her.

She calmly counted it while he waited, his blood pounding in his head.

"All right. I hope I give satisfaction," she said.

She put the money in her little valise, put the bag in a drawer, and then, assuming a demure smile, came to him with open arms.

Just before leaving, he clutched her, wanting a last, long kiss. She turned away quickly. Her entire manner changed. She was distant now, almost as if she were evading him. She seemed to become removed and unapproachable.

They had coffee and doughnuts in a restaurant near Times Square, and she didn't seem to want to talk much to him. He talked about himself as a businessman. She wasn't interested. She eyed the clock. It was late. The restaurant was almost deserted.

Harry was weary. But he wanted more. He wanted to talk now. He wanted to talk about her, himself, about what they had done together.

"Tell me, Diana. What does it feel like to have thrills?"

"Oh, it's just thrills. You know, you have thrills."

"Do you like your work?"

"Oh, I make good money. The woman I work for, she's nice. We keep half of what we make, and she gets half, and I don't mind it."

He pried her. She answered rather cursorily. He saw that she wanted to leave. She had given him the commodity he had bought. He had had his use of her. Now she was retiring into a shell. That body of hers he had wanted, it was her own again, not his. If he wanted it again, it would be for another time, for another fifty dollars.

She rose. She had to go. She said good-by. She left the restaurant with him and went to the curb for a taxicab.

"Don't I get a kiss good night?"

She held her forehead to him, said she thought she'd see him again, and was gone.

It was very late. The night was cool and hazy. He walked back to his hotel, thinking. Now all of his wanting of this— it was like ashes. Her coldness, her sudden unapproachability now made him bitter. And if any of his friends knew he had spent fifty dollars just to get a whore, they'd laugh at him mercilessly. Think of what he had spent! No, it wasn't worth the money.

He walked along. The street was dark. The buildings towered up on either side, mysterious, suddenly menacing in the night. He heard night sounds off in the distance. The sidewalk was scattered with papers. A man passed him. He was lonely. He suddenly became fearful. Suppose, in addition to the cost, he should have contracted a disease? He rushed on to his hotel to apply a prophylactic, thinking that in his folly he had spent fifty dollars and risked ruining his life. Hurrying on, he saw his entire life crumbling into ruins.

II

In time, everything was ready, and Harry's wife and child came to New York. They had a pleasant, roomy apartment in the east Eighties, and they lived the same kind of life they had in Chicago. They made new friends, who were much like their old friends in Chicago, except that their new friends had more money, just as they did. They played bridge, went to the theater, and now and then to a night club. They summered in Connecticut and thought of buying a house. Harry sank back into his old role of the husband who was dominated, directed, guided by his wife. He was often bored, but he managed to go on as he had in Chicago, doing nothing about it. At the same time he was proud of his possessions, and he was devoted to his growing and mischievous child as long as the child didn't occupy too much of his time. His night with the prostitute disappeared into the past, and it was only now and then that he thought of it. Sometimes, when it came to mind, he would wince at the amount of money he had spent on a mere whore. At other times he would wish he had seen her once more. If he had, the second time she would have been used to him, she would have known him, and then it would have been an experience. At still other times he was proud of that night as one of the big adventures of his life. It had been a daring thing to do, hadn't it?

He was slowly growing older. Soon he would be forty. He did not suffer deeply, and not even boredom caused him to suffer. His suffering was keyed to his temperament. He was a man who knew neither great happiness nor great sorrow. He

was dully dissatisfied, but he smothered his dissatisfaction in
his work, in his home, in amusements, and in sleeping. He
slept as much as he could.

After Pearl Harbor, the maid situation became bad in New
York. They needed someone to take care of the child, for the
child, the housework, and her social life were too much for
Jean. They had some unpleasant experiences with maids, and
one of them stole some of Jean's clothes. Then they had to
advertise all over again. Most of those who applied were unsatisfactory: old women, subnormal creatures, the abandoned
of our society. Others, or almost all others, were getting better
kinds of work.

One gloomy Sunday they were interviewing applicants at
their home. It was boring, and they were anxious to get it
settled. A woebegone-looking girl, pale, with circles under her
eyes, came in. She was thin and shabbily dressed. When she
entered, Harry was sitting rather pompously in the living
room, smoking a cigarette in an ivory holder. When this girl
entered, he saw that she wouldn't do. She was dirty. Her face
seemed vaguely familiar, but he couldn't place her. She said
she had been sick, but was now recovered.

"What was the matter with you?" Jean asked.

The girl hesitated, and then said, with an eagerness and
desire to convince that roused the suspicions of both Harry
and Jean:

"It was my teeth. My teeth bothered me. I had some of
them pulled, but I am better now."

"Teeth are troublesome, I know," Jean said, eyeing her.

"What kind of experience have you had?" Harry asked,
and he became disturbed because she was eyeing him in such a
singular way.

"Oh, I worked—I worked at all kinds of jobs. In restaurants."

"What were you—a waitress?"

"Oh, no, I was—a cashier."

Yes, where had he heard the voice? Where had he seen this
creature?

"What restaurants?"

"It wasn't here. It was in—Columbus."

"Are you from Columbus?"

"Yes."

He had made a couple of business trips to Columbus, Ohio, and on asking her casual questions he could see that she was lying. He was annoyed. She was wasting their time. And she was lying to him. But there was something familiar about her, and a more vague sense of annoyance with the girl troubled him. Jean also questioned her. The girl became very confused and couldn't give a clear story about her past. It suddenly occurred to Harry that she must be a prostitute. He turned pale, but fortunately Jean was talking with the girl and didn't notice him. He watched the girl from the corner of his eye. He wasn't sure.

She seemed to want the job and kept on talking.

"I took care of my brothers and sisters. I get along well with little ones."

Jean said that she didn't think it would work. The girl finally left, casting a last curious look at Harry.

He turned away. Yes, it must be the one he'd had that night in the hotel. What had she said her name was? He couldn't remember the name. This troubled him.

Jean went to the door with the girl. He was pale and trembling and went to the bathroom, so Jean wouldn't notice.

He came out, more composed, but ill at ease.

"She's a prostitute," Jean said.

"How do you know?"

"What else could she be? Look at her. She looks filthy. She can't tell what jobs she has had. Why, she was even making eyes at you right here, and if you weren't so unobserving you'd have noticed it."

"I rather thought she was a whore," Harry said.

"I'll bet my last nickel she is. The idea of it, too, a whore coming to live in a decent home, and to take care of a child."

"Yes, it is nerve."

Jean spoke about it for a few moments, denouncing the girl.

"Yes, we're lucky we didn't take her."

"There was no danger of that," Jean said with emphasis.

The bell rang. Jean answered it. Harry sank back in his chair and sighed with relief. It had been a narrow escape, and now he was convinced that it had been the girl to whom he had paid the fifty dollars for that night. His relief vanished quickly. She might have recognized him. She might blackmail him.

Another applicant came. She was an old woman and was unsatisfactory. Jean questioned her. Harry seemed pale and concerned with something. When the woman had gone, Jean came to him and said:

"Is there something wrong?"

"Yes, I feel rotten. I guess it must be something I ate."

"You better lie down, and I'll tend to things."

He went to his bed, lay down, and worried. She might blackmail him, ruin his life. His folly might catch up with him. He tossed and reasoned with himself, but he couldn't erase his fear. He would deny it. But he had signed a hotel register. They could trap him. Of course, it wasn't his name. But it was his handwriting. He thought all this was improbable, but it worried him nonetheless. He was almost paralyzed with dread.

"Feel any better?" Jean called in.

"No, I feel rotten."

"You better take a bicarbonate."

"Yes, I better," he said, relieved at continuing the pretense.

III

The girl who had applied for the job with the Ansels walked listlessly in the rain toward Fifth Avenue. She didn't know where to go, what to do. Her shoes needed to be soled, and her feet were wet. These last people she had seen, they hadn't been nice. And the man had seemed familiar. Had he ever come to her?

She tried to remember, but she had been with so many men on business that she couldn't remember. It hadn't been a bad life, and she wished she were back at it now. But she couldn't go back.

She had just been released from the hospital, ruined in health. What could she do?

Hungry and depressed, not knowing what to do, she walked along Fifth Avenue, feeling she had no right to be on this street.

Yes, that man had seemed familiar. Had he ever come to her?

She walked on, hungry and wet, and wondered what to do.

The Martyr

I

AFTER joylessly celebrating his fortieth birthday, Leonard Luckman returned to New York in the fall of 1945. He had spent six years in Hollywood working as a scenarist.

Leonard was tall and slender, and his hair had begun to turn gray. During the first days following his arrival in New York, Leonard and Anne, his wife, saw old friends, re-familiarized themselves with old sights, went to restaurants at which they had eaten during their days of courtship back in 1935, took in shows on Broadway, and went to night clubs. But Leonard didn't really enjoy himself. He kept thinking that he was no longer a youth, no longer a promising young writer. He couldn't recapture a convincing sense of the hope he had felt in New York during the 1930's. He was changed. New York was changed. The world was changed. He had hoped that once he was back in New York, his confidence in himself as an artist would return, that he would experience a new and purifying flood of feelings, and he would see his wonderful native city as though for the first time. But his impressions were commonplace, and he was unable to articulate his feelings and his moods clearly, even to himself. He had vowed to himself that he would write a novel before he went back to work in a studio on the Coast, and he had counted on the excitement of New York to serve as a new stimulation. But he wasn't stimulated. To the contrary, he was depressed, confused, and at times almost overwhelmed.

New York was crowded and dirty. When he wasn't moving

in familiar Party, literary, and Broadway circles, he became uneasy. People on the street seemed like utter strangers to him. He would stare at them and wonder what they would think if they knew that he had been working in a studio at a salary of twenty-five hundred dollars a week. When he visited his parents in the Bronx and moodily wandered about the streets of his boyhood and youth, these streets and sights appeared unreal. The crowds on the East Side and along Fourteenth Street seemed equally unreal. He rode on subways and busses, when he could have used taxicabs, merely to try to regain a lost sense of closeness to ordinary people. But he couldn't banish his sense of separation.

And Leonard was oppressed by the changes he found in New York. When he saw old friends and acquaintances, he waited with unexpressed eagerness for them to remark that he was the same as he'd always been. He wanted them to think that he hadn't gone Hollywood, that he hadn't been corrupted. He met with recurrent disappointments. Words couldn't exorcise the fact that years had gone by, years that had made history.

Above all else, Leonard had looked forward to finding stimulation, assurance, and respect in the literary circles around the Party. He had grown increasingly dissatisfied with the Party people and sympathizers on the Coast. This was bound up with his dissatisfaction with Hollywood. He had missed the literary conversations he used to have in New York. Despite his picture credits, despite the efforts he and other writers had made to assert that scenario writing was an art, he had been unable to believe this. He had constantly feared he was wasting valuable years of his life. He had been 4F in the draft because of a punctured eardrum, and he had remained in Hollywood under Party instructions. In the eyes of the Party, he had done a fine job and had made a contribution to the Cause. Over and over again he had been described in Party publications as one of the most progressive writers in Hollywood. He had written patriotic scenarios that had been used for highly praised box-office hits. He had worked with others in trying to deepen the

influence of the Party in the industry. On the surface, he had
lived in a world of comradeship and understanding. But underneath this surface there had been rivalry, jealousy, and suspicion. On the Coast, writers who had never written a novel, or
even a short story, had been his equals. He had to compete
and keep pace with them in a medium that he didn't fully
respect. The Party leaders on the Coast praised him for his
scenarios, but they seemed to have forgotten his four novels.
He had written these novels with greater belief than he had
had when writing for pictures. Some of his pictures, thanks to
the war alliance of the United States and the Soviet Union, had
had more political importance in the eyes of the Party than his
novels had had. And in this he had seen ground for his old
complaint. The Party political leaders looked on art merely in
a tactical sense.

He had hoped to find a different atmosphere in New York.
Immediately after his arrival, he had gone to see Moses Kallisch.
Moses had worked on *Mass Action* all through the War. He
had been one of the American writers and poets who had
joined the Party back in the Depression, and he had remained
loyal through all the years. And unlike many of the other
Party literary men, Moses had never gone out to make the big
money. He was a tall, soft, plump man with a weak, kindly
face. His voice and manners were insinuatingly gentle. He had
always loved literature, and, more than anything else, he had
wanted to be a poet and a novelist. But he had swallowed his
ambitions and desires again and again, and he had capitulated
to the Party politicians. He had condemned writers he admired because they refused to follow the Party line, and then
he had even stopped reading them in secret. He had lauded
as artists other writers he didn't respect, merely because they
supported the Party line. In order to carry out Party literary
assignments, he had postponed working on a novel which he
had dreamed of writing for years. And now Leonard found
Moses middle aged and gray, friendly but disturbed. Moses
and Leonard believed they understood each other, and Moses

was almost childishly happy to see his old friend after the passing of years.

Both Leonard and Moses had joined the Party back in 1932. They had shared hopes of seeing a great proletarian culture arise in America and had believed that they would grow with this culture and that they would achieve a status in America similar to Gorky's in the Soviet Union. They had loyally accepted Party directives in the cultural field, and they had tried to create works of art which at the same time would celebrate the Party line. They had burdened themselves with guilty doubts, and they had often blamed themselves when they had failed to create art within the confines of the Party line. They had willingly carried out Party assignments— Leonard in Hollywood, and Moses as a Party hack—when they had wanted to devote their time to their own work. In their youth, they both had been filled with soft, sensitive, and hurt feelings about life, and they had often taken long walks all over New York, talking of it as their city, sentimentally loving the poor people of its East Side, discussing poets and novelists they admired, and speaking of the books they wanted to write. They had accepted and defended the zigzags and changes of the Party line with strain and uncertainty, sacrificing their feelings and perceptions for the Cause. They had broken with friends who had refused to do as they had done. They had deferred their own judgments to that of the political leaders, who, as they well knew, did not possess the love of literature which they felt they themselves had. On more than one occasion the Party had sacrificed their work because of changes of the line. And back in 1932, when they had both joined the Party, they had both believed that they were embarking on a course of danger, dedication, and sacrifice. They had believed they were bravely risking their dreamed-of chances of success. They had fancied themselves bold artists of the future.

And when Leonard and Moses sat at lunch in a restaurant in Greenwich Village, all that was common in their past lurked behind every word they spoke. They felt a warm bond of friendship and understanding which they could not express clearly in words. Moses was almost inarticulate as he kept telling Leonard how glad he was that Leonard had come back East. Leonard, aware that he was so much richer than Moses, wanted to say that he knew Moses could help him rediscover himself as an artist. Together, they wanted to pick up where they had been in the early 1930's and to go forward now as the writers they had dreamed of becoming. The books they had written were almost forgotten, except in Party circles. Sitting across from each other in the dim booth, their graying hair obscured, they even had passing illusions that they were still young. These illusions were brief but vivid, and they served only to add to the mood of wistful nostalgia which saddened them both.

Leonard and Moses didn't really talk until after they had eaten, had drunk several glasses of red wine, and were sitting over their coffee. It was not merely their own feelings that had stood in the way of their talking as they wanted to; there was also the Party situation. From top to bottom, the Party ranks had been thrown into convulsion. Eldridge, the Beloved Leader of all these years and zigzags in the Party line, had been expelled after a clear if indirect repudiation from Moscow. Other leaders feared expulsion, and they had vied with one another in confessing their political mistakes and denouncing Eldridge. The word "Eldridgism" had been coined as a term of political abuse and condemnation, and it was being used synonymously with the words "Trotskyism" and "Fascism." Only a few months ago, Moses had written a panegyric of Eldridge the Leader, and had even described him as a great American stylist. At *Mass Action* there was confusion and great suspicion. Moses himself was under a cloud. The same situation prevailed on the Coast, but there people were more removed, and they had been waiting for clarifications from New York. Leonard was distressed by this development, especially since it had come precisely at the time when he wanted to eschew politics and to put forth the major effort he felt he must make if he were to achieve his ambition of adding a really lasting contribution to

American literature. And since he had left the Coast he had become doubly unsure of himself. He had scarcely landed at La Guardia Field when he began to feel New York was no longer his city. He was afraid that now, at forty, he lacked the moral stamina to launch out on his own, to trust his own judgments and risk independent political thought. He had never done much political thinking, but, rather, had gone along accepting the Party line. Now, with the War over, he was confused. He feared the onset of another depression. At times he trembled at the prospect of a rise of fascism in America. Even though successful in Hollywood, he had been insecure out there. He detested the rulers of the motion picture industry. He could see no basis of support for himself anywhere but in the Party. He was afraid to stand alone.

"We're in a transition period here, Lennie. Nothing is jelling," Moses finally said in an apologetic manner.

Leonard knew what Moses meant. He was glad Moses was hinting at the subject of the Party situation, but at the same time he was tense. He and Moses ought to trust each other. Yet he was familiar with so many examples of a violated trust among friends and comrades. His own experiences during the last fifteen years included so many instances of broken friendships and betrayals, of friendships turning into hatreds. He knew that all this was necessitated by political considerations, and that in some cases these ruptures had been unavoidable. But at the same time he wished politics could be different and that there could be more trust and tolerance in the world. Sometimes violent polemics had disturbed and frightened him. And the new turn in the Party was producing violent and ugly denunciations. He wanted to remain loyal to the Party, but at the same time he wanted to write without fear of political deviation. And with the War over, he thought that now was the time for a more liberal policy in the Left-wing cultural movement. Would the expulsion of Eldridge lead to this? He feared not. Eldridge had been called a Menshevik, a liquidator, a class collaborator, and an ally of Wall Street. He was apprehensive lest there be attacks on writers. And if this happened, he feared the results might even be tragic.

Leonard asked Moses how things were shaping up among writers and artists, and whether or not they had become involved in the Party situation yet.

"Lennie, I don't know what is going to happen," Moses said dispiritedly. "Situations like the present are very unfortunate. The Leftists and sectarians always make capital out of them."

"Leftism in culture would be tragic now," Leonard said.

They were both silent for several moments. Then Moses asked Leonard if he had read Moses' article on Henry James in *Mass Action*. Leonard said he had liked it, and that, in fact, Moses' article suggested the critical approach to novels that ought to be applied in the Movement. Moses beamed with satisfaction and thanked Leonard for his praise.

"I was attacked for my essay. Didn't you see Mark Silver's letter raking me over the coals? It was printed about three weeks ago."

"I missed it. What did Mark have to say?"

"Mark hasn't changed. I remember years ago in the old days, Mark wrote an attack on Dostoievsky because White Guard officers admire *The Brothers Karamazov*. He corrected my so-called mistake in admiring James as an artist because the Trotskyites admire James. They've stolen him the way they steal everything. Mark would give James to the Trotskyites, just as years ago he'd give Dostoievsky to the White Guards. My point is that great writers like James and Dostoievsky should belong to us, and only to us."

"I had begun to hope that we'd outgrown all that," Leonard said, pained.

"You know, Lennie, how some of our journalists and political leaders have always shown a feeling of hostility to our writers."

"Moses, I can tell you this. I couldn't tell it to everyone. The Movement is too hard on writers. All these years, I've been hoping for a change. I understand why there was so much sectarianism in the early thirties. But now we're in the middle of the 1940's."

They were both moodily silent, and they thought about the fact that it was already the fall of 1945.

"I was just thinking of the May Day parade of 1935. I think it was 1935. Remember how big it was? It was such a sunny day. And we had such a big turnout of writers and intellectuals. I remember one of our slogans—*'Hitler burns books—We write books.'* "

"Hitler burns books—We write books," Moses repeated reflectively.

"And Hitler is dead," Leonard said.

"I hope so."

"Don't you believe he's dead?" Leonard asked.

"Yes. I think so. And Mussolini is dead, too."

Again they sat in moody silence.

"And Trotsky is dead," Moses said.

They both became nervous at the very mention of Trotsky's name.

"He fooled many American writers and intellectuals. He ruined them. Think of the number of writers and intellectuals who marched with us in 1935 and who were seduced and poisoned by Trotsky and Trotskyism."

"Yes, Moses, I feel as though you and I were an old guard."

"We have a newer group, Lennie. They don't understand that."

"Are they against us?"

"No, I wouldn't say that. . . . They aren't precisely against us, but they don't understand. Lennie, they don't understand the sacrifices we made, the times we stuck through thick and thin when we were isolated and the whole bourgeois literary world tried to laugh at us. Lennie, things aren't the same as they were in the old days. It isn't the same."

They reminisced for a while. Then they spoke of books they liked. Both of them shyly confessed to having some admiration for writers who had politically criticized the Party and the policies of Stalin.

"Moses, you know me. You know that when I say an anti-Soviet writer has written a good book, I'm not anti-Soviet. You understand me, don't you?"

"Marx admired Balzac, didn't he?" Moses asked.

"That's just my point."

"A new clarification has to come. There's a false pressure on us. I'm working on another novel. There isn't a thing I plan in it that will hurt the Party. Still I feel the pressure."

"So do I. It's blocking me from writing."

"I was thinking, Lennie. Discussion is going on in the Party. I can get clearance on a good discussion article in *Mass Action*."

"You're closer to the situation than I am, Moses."

"I'm too close to it. And, then, I'm an editor of *M.A.* If I wrote it, it would be taken as official. You've been away from New York. You can see with fresh eyes. And you have a good reputation in the Party. Your loyalty has never been questioned. You're outside of any New York cliques or groups. Lennie, you know, you could do a great service if you would write a clarifying discussion article."

Leonard didn't want to commit himself. And yet he thought that if he did write such an article, he would make a contribution. Such an article might have a lasting significance in American literature. And clarification was needed now. Wasn't this lack of clarification blocking him?

"Well, Lennie, old man, I have to get back to the office. But you think about it, and I'll propose our idea at the editorial conference tomorrow."

Leonard promised to think about writing such an article, but he remained in a state of uncertainty. He didn't want to commit himself definitely.

II

Leonard was perplexed and indecisive after his long luncheon and talk with Moses. Walking back to his hotel off Washington Square, he thought about the proposed article, about writing, and about himself and his career. He really believed he was now ready to write a great novel. But how could he square this novel with the Party? He wanted to do an autobiographical novel, and to describe in it honestly his doubts and fears, and to try and create people outside of or against the Movement as human beings. What he planned would not be against the Movement. It would do no harm to the Party. He'd show, for instance, how those who had left and betrayed the Movement had suffered. Suffering as the cost of betrayal and renegacy would be a main theme of his novel. But would this be understood? He silently argued, explained, and pleaded with an imaginary Party leader that a novel such as he was beginning to project would in no way be anti-Party.

The day was warm and sunny, and when he reached Washington Square, Leonard decided to sit on a bench and think. He found one vacant on the east side of the Square, and sat pondering, with a cigarette in his mouth. He looked melancholy, and, judging from the sight of him, a stranger might have imagined that he was lovelorn. When young, Leonard had often sat in the Square here and dreamed of his future as a writer. He had imagined himself writing novels and stories that would be soft and sad and beautiful and deep, novels and stories that would move America almost to tears. He had been poor then. Suddenly he sat up with a startled look on his face and silently told himself:

—I'm rich.

Leonard slumped back on the bench. His eyes traveled idly over the dying grass, and then he gazed at the clean-looking red brick buildings on the north edge of the Square. Students from New York University passed, and he watched the girls. Some of them seemed to be so young, like children. The sight of them, the sight of the lads, deepened his sadness. He yearned for his own youth back in the 1920's. And now he had begun to turn gray. So much of his life seemed to have been wasted. Was all the time he had spent working in Hollywood worth it? Had the time he had spent on the Coast at political meet-

ings been spent in a worth-while way? Might he have done
differently? He watched a bright-eyed, pert, pretty girl in a
brown suit pass. She was slim, and her features were delicate.
To be young again, and in love with a girl like that, to make
love to her and dream of the future. . . . He watched her walk
on and wished he had talked with her. But what would have
been the use? Yes, in his youth he had been idealistic and romantic. Life had taken the edge off his ideals and his sense of
romance. Again he sadly thought that he had begun to turn
gray.

All he could look forward to in life was art, was to create a
living and lasting work of art. And if he did, what would his
status be in the Movement? In times like these how could the
individual stand alone? All the old ideas of the artist standing
alone as an individual had disappeared in this century. Art,
like everything else good, was dying in this modern capitalist
jungle, and its survival depended on the survival of the Soviet
Union. Outside of the Movement one was divorced from the
Soviet Union. And what could one expect then?

He thought of Hollywood. One Sunday he had walked
around Beverly Hills, telling himself over and over again:

—I'm earning twenty-five hundred dollars a week.

And yet he had been unhappy because he had known he
wasn't really functioning as the artist he wanted to be. He
remembered so many experiences in the studio that had clearly
indicated he had no liberty to create. When he'd worked for
Kling, he had been with a bright, liberal-minded producer.
Kling was even sympathetic to the Party. But in every case of
a difference of opinion over a story or an idea, who had had the
final say? No matter how well he had been paid, there had
always been a boss over him who had decided. Scenario writing
was well-paid slavery. And look at what the movies had done
to the printed word, to the novel! The novel was a dying art
in America. But in the Soviet Union it was different. Soviet
writers, unless they tried to be political oppositionists, had a
future. There, they were respected. And they had subjects to

write about, the building of a whole new world, the mass heroism of a nation of millions in war.

He had to write a novel.

Leonard lit another cigarette and wished he had spoken to that girl in the brown suit, talked to her, gotten to know her. He became excited. Youth like hers would have such a restorative effect on him. Why couldn't he find some beautiful young girl, talk to her, make love to her? He thought of Anne. Perhaps Anne would understand. She was so understanding. She had done so much for him, and meant so much to him, and she still did. But he felt stale and unsure of himself.

But didn't he know that personal experience wasn't the answer? In a world like this modern world, how could personal experience be the answer? He let his eyes rove about the Square again, seeing the sun on the fading grass and the dying leaves, looking at the red of the buildings flanking the Square, watching the movement of people and of automobiles. He watched a mother wheeling a baby carriage and wondered if she were frightened because of the terrors of this atomic age.

This scene was so peaceful. Looking at people and buildings and leaves and trees and grass and black iron railings and stone, it was damned difficult for him to believe that the world was torn, disorganized, and tragic. How often had he not wanted to believe that the Hollywood movie dreams were realities? He wanted to believe now, to believe in peace and softness and love, and he wanted to think that men could have peace and love and, yes, softness in their lives, without so much endless bitter fighting.

Why couldn't it all be different?

He reminded himself that the war was over, that victory had been won. He recalled having heard that one of the literary renegades had recently written that the war had ended in the "gloom of victory." Several of his comrades in Hollywood had spent fifteen or twenty minutes analyzing and denouncing this phrase as Trotskyite sabotage and hatred revealing a conspiratorial lack of faith in the United Nations. Now, this phrase haunted him.

Noting the time, Leonard rose to go back to his hotel. Anne
ought to be home now, and he wanted to discuss the projected
Mass Action article with her. Sitting here in Washington
Square, he had forgotten about it.

III

Anne Luckman was three years older than Leonard, and she
was also several inches taller than he. She was a handsome
woman, brisk and decisive. She spoke in a husky voice that
usually impressed people, and she gave the impression of being
both definite in her opinions and intelligent. She brooked no
disagreement, and whenever she met with opposition she would
become sharp and even insulting. Anne had an almost uncanny
ability to sense the weaknesses of others and to make cutting
remarks that would hurt them. In her youth, she had been a
very active Party worker, had been on picket lines, and had
been arrested several times on disorderly-conduct charges.
Once she had even been sentenced to five days after having
been arrested in a demonstration that had been broken up by
the police. She had also written several stories characterized, in
their time, as proletarian, and she had been involved in organizing Party front organizations. She was highly respected by
important Party functionaries. Leonard was her third husband,
and he was guided by her in almost all his decisions. She discussed his books with him, read them and proposed changes,
helped him with his scenario writings, and resolved all the
recurring doubts and questions he had about the Party. Since
Leonard had started making big money in Hollywood, she
dressed stunningly. Unlike him, she seemed to have no qualms
or twinges of guilt because of their money. They contributed
liberally to the Movement, and at times she had been very
active in Party work on the Coast. She had participated in
political campaigns, had helped to organize benefits and other
affairs, had won over writers and others to a sympathetic interest in the Movement, and had smoothed the way and ar-

ranged for meetings between visiting Party emissaries and important key people in the motion picture industry who were being worked on. There were many people in and out of the Movement who considered her a remarkable woman.

Anne was ambitious for Leonard, and she had encouraged him not to renew his contract in the picture industry. She wanted him to write a novel, and she believed he could win a reputation for himself as one of the leading contemporary American writers, if he completed the autobiographical novel he had talked of writing for so long. His boyhood in the Bronx, his shyness, his sense of alienation, his fears of other boys, and of life, his lonely days in college, the dawning of an ambition to write, his discovery of modern writers, his poverty and struggles in the Depression, his discovery of the Party—all this should be good material for the Great American Novel. The life of a writer in the Party, the successive desertions from the Party and Movement by renegades, and then Hollywood and the War—all this represented the experience of a generation. Both Leonard and she believed that a novel, shaping and ordering these experiences, would not only result in a powerful work of literature but would also constitute a service to the Movement. It would glorify the Movement and demonstrate that it was something natural and normal in American life. Anne personally despised many of Leonard's fellow writers, and their political loyalties in no way affected these personal feelings, even though she would work with them and treat them in a civil manner. At times she would criticize their work on the grounds of style and art. On other occasions she would criticize it politically. And in her presence they became confused. When she and Leonard discussed these comrade writers, she would give vent to feelings of anger and sharply condemn them and their work. But at the same time she was gentle and tactful in her criticism of Leonard's own work.

Riding up in the elevator, Leonard had been painfully anxious lest Anne not be at home. Finding her in, he was relieved, but at the same time he felt guilty because of his thoughts about the girl in the brown suit. He consoled himself with the realization that these had been merely thoughts, and that no one, especially Anne, knew of them. Nothing had happened. He had done nothing but think idly and fleetingly. Still, his relief at finding Anne home was of short duration. He quickly lapsed into a pessimistic mood.

Anne fixed cocktails, and he rather gloomily recounted his conversation with Moses. He wanted to ask Anne point blank whether or not he should write the article for *Mass Action*, but he kept putting it off. Anne was noncommittal, and Leonard, burdened with his own uneasiness, went on talking from sheer necessity.

"I don't see anything wrong with the article you want to write," Anne said then. "All you plan to do, darling, is to restate the position the Party has always taken on literature, isn't it?"

"Yes, yes, that's so," Leonard said eagerly. Then he added as an afterthought, "Of course, I want to do something more than merely restate or rehash. I want . . . I want to give the comrades a sense of the artist's feeling for writing."

"I don't see anything wrong with the idea. Moses doesn't, does he?"

"No."

"He knows the internal setup here, and he'd know if it would be safe for you to do the article now."

"He'll have to get clearance on the article, and, of course, if he gets clearance, then the article won't become a political football. The internal situation here is fluid. Politically, I can see that there is some sense in a hard line. Eldridge didn't see that and didn't move fast enough. But, even so, we can't go back to the early 1930's on the cultural front. I can't see the Movement going back to that, not culturally."

"Yes, darling." She paused for several moments. Then she spoke with great assurance. "That won't happen."

Leonard's vague apprehensions seemed to be allayed. Finishing his cocktail, he thought of how he would win respect with his article, and would stand out almost as a literary leader. He could be the man who saved a dangerous cultural situation for the Movement, and whose article would, he hoped, end much of the confusion and dissatisfaction that existed here in New York as well as on the Coast.

IV

Once he started writing his discussion article, Leonard became the prey of many moods. He did a little reading, jotted down some random notes, and made several starts which he discarded. He knew he was right. He felt this deeply. He had to write this article because it seemed to him that he had come to a turning point in his own career. He would remain confused until he sat down and wrote out a clarification for himself. When he read novels, he would find himself becoming tense because he would try to reconcile what he liked and what moved him with what Party-line critics usually wrote or might possibly write about such a book. There was the case of Henry James. He had recently read *The Figure on the Carpet,* and had been tremendously impressed by James's artistry. But Mark Silver and some of the other Party writers said that you couldn't admire James, because the Trotskyites now admired him. And it was worse when he tried to write, because then he would imagine a barrage of invective being hurled at him. It was painful to think that literary criticism should be reduced to such invective. Often when he read the book reviews in *Mass Action,* he would be dismayed, for so many of the novels praised in the Party press were so inferior. They were praised because they were *kosher*. If this continued, the whole cultural movement would be in danger, and the renegade and Trotskyite writers would gain the influence the Movement should wield. After all, he could speak on this subject with some authority. He was a writer, and even though he had still to write his best book, he had contributed to the literature inspired by the Party and the Movement. He was respected as an artist in the Movement.

If he himself had to face these problems, if he were confused and blocked, if a political emphasis on literature were having this bad effect on him, this was a symptom. Yes, he could accept the conclusion that he ought to write this article, because not only he, personally, but the Movement itself had reached a state of dangerous cultural crisis.

And yet he couldn't write the article. He was afraid. He was recurrently tempted to give up this project. Why must he, an artist, take onto his shoulders a task that belonged to the critics? Why should he risk being a fall guy? Some ineradicable doubt and fear remained with him, despite the plausible and convincing arguments he thought justified the position he wanted to take.

For years now he had tried to prove to the Party that there were writers and intellectuals who could be relied on. Hadn't he proven this again and again? Had he retreated in 1939 and 1940? Hadn't he stood firm when renegades had tried to use the Moscow trials to foment hatred of the Soviet Union? And after working so many years in Hollywood, had he sold out and changed his loyalties? He kept framing questions like these in his mind and developing arguments of self-justification which he would express to himself, but it was all in the manner of a man on trial and answering the charges of a prosecutor. And in these interior monologues he would explain his position and justify himself to Party critics and political leaders. Almost despairingly, he would ask himself why couldn't they understand?

But by thought, reflection, and secret pleading, he couldn't break the spell of years of pressure. Ever since he had been drawn to the Movement back in 1930, he had faced hostility and distrust. How many times had he not been told that the intellectual couldn't be trusted, that the writer wasn't reliable? How many times and in how many ways had he not been impressed with the fact that in the Movement writers and intellectuals did not have the same respect and prestige as the political leaders? How many times had he not been told that Lenin himself had warned against trusting intellectuals?

And in the face of all this he had tried to prove that he could be trusted. This hostility had had an effect on him. Struggle with himself as he might, he could not read a book, express an opinion as a writer, or try to write or to think without becoming confused because of worry or fear of being misunderstood, suspected, and deemed unreliable. He sadly asked himself, wasn't all this unnecessary? Wasn't it the result of an effort to treat art and human emotions from the standpoint of tactics?

On and off for years, Leonard had been thinking in this vein. He remembered many of the controversies among writers in the Movement back in the 1930's, and he had always secretly sympathized with the writers who had resisted politicalization of their work, even though he had never taken an open stand with any of them. He was glad he hadn't taken any position that would have resulted in his breaking with the Movement, because the Movement had to come first. One had to belong to it because one couldn't stand alone. If he had learned anything in Hollywood, he had learned that lesson. He had worked as part of a system and had come to see how powerful that system was, and how little the individual counted. Alone in Hollywood, writers were nothing. Organized, they had gained some rights, and they had hopes. And Hollywood pointed the way of the future: the isolated individual writer didn't and never could have a future. The writer had to belong to something powerful. He saw nothing to which he could belong except to the Movement. He didn't want to write an article that could possibly risk separation from the Movement. But the impulse to write such an article remained. He was torn with indecision.

Moses phoned to say that he had gotten clearance for the discussion article, and he seemed elated. He suggested that Leonard drop around to the office to discuss it further. Leonard was heartened.

Mass Action was housed in a reconverted brownstone house on West Tenth Street, and on entering its premises for his appointment with the editors Leonard thought of the old

days when the *M.A.* offices were in an old building and
everything was shabby, dirty, and disordered. Now, things
were different. *M.A.* had offices as neat and impressive and
up-to-date as any bourgeois liberal magazine. There was
bright and attractive modernistic furniture in the anteroom,
and the walls were hung with pictures of Stalin, Roosevelt,
and American Party leaders. But he noticed that Eldridge's
picture, which formerly had hung in a prominent place, had
been taken down. This observation pained him, not so much
because of Eldridge, whom he had often praised but didn't
know well, but because of all the bitterness and anger gen-
erated by political disputes and differences. Other pictures
had once hung in the office of *Mass Action,* but these, too, had
been removed. Other writers had come to its offices to discuss
important articles with the editors, and they no longer came.
Other editors had sat in these and earlier *Mass Action* offices,
and they no longer sat here. It was as though they were now
living in the world of the dead, outside of the Movement.
One forgot about them for long periods, and then one had
fleeting memories of them, heard their names mentioned, read
of them, and a whole past threatened to well up in one's mind.
There was a past now in the American Movement. To Leonard it was now beginning to seem like a long past.

He met the editors in a long, clean room on the second
floor, and they sat around a table in a relaxed and informal
manner and talked. They were all friendly and excited, and
their enthusiasm about printing his article was reassuring to
Leonard. Moses spoke first, paying tribute to Leonard, re-
marking that the time had come to open up a comradely discussion on the literary question and adding that no one was
more qualified to do this than Leonard. Discussion and clarification, he went on, were essential now to the health of the
progressive cultural movement in America, because for a number of years they had all been misled by the Marxist revision-
ism of Eldridge. Now they had been put back on the right
road politically, but they had to find cultural clarification on
their own because, as everyone well knew, the Party was

neutral as to which tendencies within the framework of the progressive cultural movement were the correct ones. This decision had to be made by progressive cultural workers themselves.

Moses spoke rather slowly, but naturally. Leonard noted this because he had been under a strain himself, and, as he watched Moses across the table and listened to him, he wondered how much of an inner strain Moses felt. But Moses seemed no different than he had ever been. He spoke in a meek and ingratiating manner. He seemed sincere, warm, and friendly. As he offered further comments, Moses explained that he didn't want to sound as if he were merely complaining or denying the great cultural contributions to the Movement. These had been made in the face of the whole farce of bourgeois monopoly culture. But Eldridge had endangered these accomplishments by his deviationist pro-Wall Street, collaborationist, Menshevik, Trotskyite line of personal aggrandizement and retreat, and his policies had been as damaging to culture as to politics.

"Yes, comrades, we all have to admit it. We made mistakes. We were misled by Eldridgism," Don Jones then said.

Leonard hadn't seen Don in about seven years. Don was now fat, and his hair was gray. He vaguely remembered Don in 1930, a slim, young, deferential, quiet lad. Now Don talked with authority, and his very tone of voice was frightening. For years Don had been the editor of *M.A.* responsible to the Ninth Floor, and Leonard knew that whatever Don said would express the position of the Party leaders on the questions involved.

"We have to confess, comrades, we haven't been Marxists," Don said.

Don's remark served as a cue. Moses immediately admitted his deviations from Marxism. Then Ellison admitted his mistakes. Ellison was tall and thin. He had a face like a bird of prey, and he talked with nervousness, arrogance, and aggressiveness. In recent years he had become the leading literary critic in the Party. Leonard didn't know him well, but he had always been uneasy in his presence. Ellison's mistake, he thought, was that of approaching literature from the standpoint of tactics.

After confessing to deviations, Ellison then said:

"Look at the progress our comrades have made in France. If we had followed the correct tactics, we could have matched their progress."

"Comrade Ellison has posed the question clearly," Don Jones said.

Leonard looked to Moses. His reassurance was gone. Jones and Ellison had never been really sympathetic to writers, and their remarks led Leonard to fear that their attitudes would prevail at this meeting. He didn't know how to answer them in speech now because he had no talent for politics, and they did.

"Yes, in a sense, I agree with you. We have to find the right cultural tactics now," Moses said.

"Of course, I'm just a journalist and an editor. I can't solve that problem for you writers. All I can do is to lay out my idea of the general theoretical perspective. Lennie and Ellison, Moses and Bill Plunk and the rest of you will have to do that."

Leonard looked at Bill Plunk. He was now the outstanding young novelist in the Movement, but secretly Leonard had no respect for his writing. Plunk looked very young, even younger than his years. He was tall, blond, precise, and rigid. He had tight lips, small eyes, nervous long hands, and he spoke with an almost offensive cockiness. Leonard was afraid of him, but he didn't know precisely why. Bill started to talk, but Don politely asked him to wait, and Don went on.

"There are certain directives which we can follow as guideposts, and all I'm qualified to do at meetings like this is to state these general directives."

Leonard listened eagerly but with apprehension now, because what Don said about directives would indicate to him how amenable the Party really was to a more liberal attitude on culture.

"The Party doesn't interfere with the form or content of

art. It couldn't do this because, if it did, it would be un-Marxist, and the Party couldn't be un-Marxist. That's why the renegade Eldridge was expelled. But now we have a leadership in which we can have faith . . ."

Leonard remembered how often he had heard Don Jones speak of faith in the Party leadership on other occasions in the past. He recalled one winter afternoon about ten years ago—yes, it must have been ten years ago, he decided—that he'd dropped by the offices of *M.A.* and had heard Don unexpectedly remark that the executions following the assassination of Kirov had been disturbing to read about, and that it was almost unbelievable to think that so many years after the Revolution there could still be a White Guard plot to murder the leaders of the Russian Party.

—But I have faith in the leaders of the Soviet Union, Don had said.

Leonard recalled that it had been around this time that Don had had to take a vacation, and that there had been some fear he might have ulcers of the stomach.

Don was explaining that on the literary question the Party had only one concern—orientation.

"If the writer doesn't have elements of a reactionary, capitalist, fascist, social-democratic, Trotskyite orientation, then what you write is okay with us, okay with the Party. We guard our orientation like the precious jewel that it is. But discussion, differences, different styles and contents, we've always said that's okay."

"That expresses the situation in the well-known nutshell," Ellison joined in.

Don went on talking. He kept reiterating the fact that he was not an artist but only a journalist, and each time he said this he added that he had great respect for art, for genuine progressive art. He knew the Party was disappointed because the writers close to it hadn't produced better works of art for the workers, and for the progressive movement of mankind as a whole. And he felt the same way the Party did on this score.

"The Party says—and I'd say, too—writers must write."

This was wounding to Leonard. He hadn't been writing. He wanted to cut in to tell them that the Party had approved his spending all these last years in Hollywood, and that the Party press had praised the pictures on which he'd worked.

But Don went on talking. Now, he said, was the time for a clarification and reorientation.

"Yes, that's what I think. Of course, I agree with what Don says. The orientation of a writer is important. But what I think is that literature has its own laws," Leonard said hesitantly.

"Didn't Engels say that?" Ellison asked.

"Yes, yes, that's what I meant. And since literature has its own laws, we can't see literature from . . . from a purely tactical standpoint," Leonard added in a cautious manner.

"Lennie, we see eye to eye," Don said.

They talked for a long time. It was decided that Leonard would write the discussion article.

"And, Lennie, no holds barred. Don't pull any punches," Don told him as they were leaving. "Our enemies spread the lie that we don't allow criticism. We'll nail this lie once and for all. From the standpoint of our orientation, you put the case down. We want stiff but comradely discussion."

Leonard was now encouraged, and he was glad he was going to write the article. He wanted to make it an important article —in fact, an historic one.

v

Leonard worked hard on the article, and he worried even more than he worked. He talked it over with Anne many times, and he looked through back copies of *Mass Action* and some of the letters of Marx and Engels. At times he felt he ought to read more before writing the piece, but he began to feel the pressure of urgency, and he was under an increasing tension that he knew couldn't be eased until the article was finished. He saw Moses several times, and they discussed the article and also the situation in the Party. Party leaders were still confessing their errors and pledging their loyalty to the new leadership. They were all promising to dedicate themselves to a re-study of all questions, of the sources of their Movement, of the works of Marx, Engels, Lenin, and Stalin.

"This is a period of study for the Party," Moses said to Leonard at lunch one day.

"I see it's a new course. That's clear," Leonard said.

There was also much private if cautious grumbling. The ritual of confessing and admitting to errors could not wash away the fact that the deposed and expelled leader had been praised, lauded, and followed. Leonard knew he had often said the same things Eldridge had said. He had accepted the position of the Party during the war years, and he secretly hoped this position could be maintained. But at the same time he had hoped for changes, changes that would help the cultural movement. He reasoned himself out of some of his worries by contending that one must apply dialectics to politics and culture. The political line was becoming harder. But wouldn't this, or, at least, couldn't this mean that there would be more interest in quality in writing? He tested Moses with this conclusion, and Moses agreed with him. So did Anne.

He finished his article. While writing his second and final draft, he grew bolder. His piece was a plea for liberalization of attitudes toward literature, and he cited the opinions of Marx and Engels on Balzac, and Lenin on Tolstoy, as support for his plea. And, bulwarking his criticisms with flattery and with acceptance of the Party line, past, present, and future, he then complained about and criticized the narrow imposition of the Party line on the writer, and about the way critics had interpreted works of literature in terms of narrow conceptions of the same Party line. While dissociating himself from the political views of writers the Party denounced as renegades, Leonard did pay some tribute to their talents. He concluded by asking that Party literary critics and political leaders permit writers to try and write lasting works of literature instead of tactical documents, and that, in addition, they

forego making crude political judgments of writers, and of the
literary creations of writers.

Leonard immediately took his manuscript to Moses. He was
nervously eager for his reaction to it. Moses read the manuscript immediately and in Leonard's presence. Leonard had to
use his will to restrain himself from making comments and
asking questions while Moses read. He sat by the side of Moses'
desk, watching impatiently. He thought this was the best article he had ever written, and he sat on the edge of his chair,
craving praise. He watched Moses' face, too, for every little
sign of satisfaction. Moses was interested, and as he read he
kept making sounds of approval. Leonard was sure Moses
would agree that this was the best article he'd ever written.
And not only Moses but others would perceive that he was
one writer who hadn't been ruined by Hollywood and pictures.

Leonard also thought of this little scene as going down in
American literary history, and he suddenly and sadly reflected
that he didn't keep a diary. He ought to, beginning today
and starting with an account of this scene, and of how he felt
and what he thought about sitting here while Moses read his
article. He studied Moses in order to get a clearer sense of the
appearance of this shaggy man with graying hair and a lined
face which suggested kindliness and simplicity. He thought
of him as good old Moses, and only regretted that he couldn't
like or respect Moses' talent as much as he liked and respected
Moses as a person. But, after all, Moses did appreciate good
writing and art. He could tell the difference between good
and bad writing with much greater discernment than Ellison.
And Moses was also playing an important role in the Movement by working here on *M.A.*

Slapping down the manuscript on his cluttered and disorderly desk, Moses said:

"It's damned good."

Leonard was speechlessly happy.

Moses went on to say that he agreed with Leonard basically,
and that this article was precisely what was needed now as a

means of opening up a clarifying and constructive discussion.

"It's clear, isn't it, that I'm not against the Party, that I'm only writing friendly and comradely criticism?" Leonard asked.

Moses assured him on this point. He said that there were some minor details which would have to be gone over.

"Of course, of course," Leonard said.

"But you've done a damned fine and a damned valuable piece. This is first-rate criticism, Lennie, and it's just what we need."

"I tried to make it that. I tried to be fair and sincere."

"Old man, you succeeded."

A sudden mood of sadness and regret threatened to overwhelm Leonard. He reminded himself that he was forty. He saw so much lost time behind him. Now his years in Hollywood looked like so much waste. He could have done so much that he hadn't done. He could have developed so much more than he had, and his literary reputation could have become so much bigger than it was. And wouldn't this have been better for him, better than all the money he had in the bank and the house he owned on the Coast? And, yes, he believed he had more talent than Moses, but Moses had stuck here, worked like a real Jimmie Higgins, done a job on *M.A.*, even though many called him a hack, and he was still doing this job. Moses wasn't rich. Now they were both struggling to write the same kind of novel. Was Moses in a better position to write this than he was? If he hadn't gone to Hollywood, perhaps his novel would already have been written, published, and acclaimed. He was half forgotten, and if he hadn't chucked working in Hollywood, he would soon have become the forgotten man of American letters. Leonard felt sorry for himself. But, then, wasn't he starting to make up for lost time now? He listened to more soothing words of praise from Moses, and his elation returned. He felt just about as good as he had years ago when his first novel had been accepted for publication. Talking with Moses now, he felt as if he were launching himself on his literary career all over again.

VI

Leonard waited for the publication of his article with the same eagerness and expectancy he felt when he had a book coming out. And it had been so long since he had seen any of his work published. It had been years now since any of his own stuff had been printed. He felt wonderful. It was so different waiting for this article to come out from what it was waiting for the release of a picture on which he'd worked. He remembered how, half in shame, half in vanity, he had felt about forthcoming pictures with his name on the credit list that would be flashed before the eyes of millions of people. And, recalling this, he was abashed by many of the thoughts and feelings he had had in Hollywood. He had been pleased and proud out there to meet people with names, even though he hadn't respected them. He had not always been as independent as he might have been. He had been proud of his success in pictures, proud of the money he had made, the parties he'd gone to, the meals eaten at places like the Brown Derby. All those reactions had been so different from his feelings back in New York in the early 1930's, when he'd been a young revolutionary writer. He wanted to regard his *M.A.* article as a kind of purging of his Hollywood experience. He hoped this essay would be the beginning of a new course for himself, personally, as well as for the Left-wing cultural movement.

But underneath all his other thoughts and feelings about the article, there was apprehension. Waiting for it to appear, he found himself still blocked and paralyzed on the novel he wanted to write. And he heard stories, rumors, and remarks which suggested that the feeling of many people in the Party was almost convulsive. Confessions, admissions of errors, and denunciations continued, and there were constant signs suggesting that the new political line would be rigidly Leftist. All this was painful, and he reasoned with himself to prove that art couldn't be created in an atmosphere of such confusion. How could one write or think when such things were going on?

It was in this mood that he met Boris Karen, with whom he had been acquainted years ago. Karen was a rather short fellow with a homely face and suspicious eyes, and back in the early 1930's he had been a hanger-on whom no one had taken seriously. Leonard disliked him and had no respect for him. But he had become a leading Party journalist. Karen had been working on a biography of Eldridge when the Leader was disavowed by Moscow, and yet he had written the most vituperative of all the denunciations of the deposed Leader published in the Party press. He and Leonard had coffee in a Fourteenth Street cafeteria. Leonard would have enjoyed this with almost anyone but Karen. For cafeterias on and around Fourteenth Street brought back to him precious, nostalgic memories. But he was afraid of Karen. Karen denounced Eldridge over the coffee, never mentioning that he had once written eulogies of the Leader and that he had half completed a book eulogizing him as the heir of every great or outstanding man in American history.

Leonard was glad to get away from Karen and walked back to his hotel, brooding and disconsolate. He couldn't cope with people like Karen.

And the news from Russia deepened Leonard's apprehensiveness. Shostakovitch and Eisenstein were both being denounced in the Russian press. Leonard admired both these men as outstanding artists, and it was painful to him to read of the denunciation of their work. Every time one thought about art in the Party atmosphere, it became painful, very painful. All this only proved to him the more that his own position was correct. But would it be supported? And if it didn't win support, what would he do?

This was the question Leonard was avoiding in his own thoughts. The sense of support and solidarity he had gained by association with the Party had been important to him all of these years. At forty, could he stand alone? And what about Anne? When he had spoken to her of the possibility of rejection of his position on literature, she had scoffed at the idea. But about a half hour later she had remarked that a correct literary position wasn't so important in the face of the world crisis.

Leonard became increasingly unsure of himself as he waited for his article to appear.

VII

When Leonard tore the wrapper off *Mass Action,* read his name on the cover, and opened the magazine to his article, he was so moved that he almost cried. He sat down and immediately read the article, but he was in such a state of emotion that he didn't know what he was reading. He was so drunk with his own emotions that even his own sentences didn't click in his mind. He was deeply moved, but he couldn't decide on the merits of his piece or on its style.

And now the die was cast and the Rubicon was crossed. He was committed. Would they, would enough important people in the Party and the Movement understand? Would they see that what he asked for could only help them? Would they understand that, while he had written in general terms, he was also speaking about his own problems as a writer, and about the problems of other writers, who, like himself, were both loyal to the Movement and imbued with the desire to be artists? Would they understand?

He gave the copy of *Mass Action* to Anne and nervously paced about the hotel room while she read it.

"It's fine, darling, fine."

"I don't see how they can disagree with me."

She thought for a moment.

"I don't think they will."

He was buoyed up.

VIII

Leonard was hurt and bewildered. Almost daily, *The Workers Fist*, which was, in reality, a Party organ, had carried attacks on him, and for three successive issues there had been answers to his article in *Mass Action*. On his desk there were about forty letter agreeing with him. But not one word of agreement had been printed in the Party press. Only letters attacking him had been printed. For a week now, he had been in despondent moods, and he had tried to search out his own thoughts. Was he really a "liquidator," a "Menshevik," an "Eldridgite," and was he trying to make concessions to "Trotskyism"? Was he endangering the entire progressive cultural movement? He didn't honestly believe these charges were true. And he privately nourished dreams of immortality he wouldn't dare admit to anyone, not even to Anne. Was this bourgeois? Would these dreams lead him into the camp of the enemy?

Here was his problem. Were art and politics compatible?

All he wanted was some support from the Movement, some freedom in it to try to be an artist, that was all. If he had remained in Hollywood, he couldn't have become the artist he dreamed of being. As it was, too many years of his life were gone. More than half his life was over. He dreaded the idea of dying without really believing he had written a lasting book. On the plane, flying to New York from California, he had had such intense fears. Although he had not mentioned this to Anne, he had been in constant fear that the plane might crash and that he might die without having achieved his artistic ambitions.

And why couldn't they see this? Why was this a danger to the Movement? Why, when he had been so reasonable, had he been attacked with such violence and vehemence? He wasn't a renegade, and yet most of the attacks treated him as though he were.

But Leonard's brooding and the questions he kept asking himself in his almost despondent moods took on the character of self-indulgence. For he was aware of the fact that he had expected just this reaction to his article. And he was equally aware that he could expect no mercy from the Party unless he surrendered, and that surrender now could well mean the death of his artistic ambitions. He saw that his best alternative would be to fight, to return blow for blow, even though this meant ostracism.

But if he fought back, he would have to stand alone. His friends wouldn't speak to him when he met them on the streets. If he went back to Hollywood, he would be ostracized there, too, by many of his fellow writers. The whole machinery of the Movement could be used to discredit him. Where would he find support? Among renegades? Among reactionaries? How could he face that?

He paced his hotel room, wishing he hadn't written the article and wondering why he had done it. Why couldn't he have settled down to work on his novel, and if he'd had to face these attacks, face them because of his novel rather than because of this article? He wasn't a critic in the formal sense, and he wasn't a theoretician. If he got deep into theory, he'd be lost, and then he well might make a fool of himself. Critics like Ellison, and, of course, the Party leaders, could confuse him on matters of theory. Even so, he knew he was right. But did that mean so much when he was being attacked and denounced as an enemy?

How could he do anything now but fight back?

He didn't want to get into this kind of fight. It would be too painful. And how could he win? How could he win against the Party?

He sat down in a comfortable chair, trying to think. He couldn't think. He kept telling himself that he didn't deserve the kind of treatment he was receiving. What had he done to merit it? Where had he called for the liquidation of the progressive cultural movement? Where had he asked for association with renegades? When and where had he said he wanted writers close to the Movement to be palsy-walsy with the Trotskyites? All this was false. Leonard wanted to brand all these and similarly fantastic charges as lies. He hesitated and drew back from using the word "lies" even in his own thoughts. He didn't want to fight. He wanted them to let him be an artist. And yet he had to fight.

He imagined himself fighting back and winning. All over the country young writers and intellectuals, students and others, would be talking about him, taking sides for or against him. And many were on his side. The letters he had already received proved this. He had reason to be hopeful and to have confidence. And wasn't it flattering to have your name become an issue? After all those prosperous but barren years of life in Hollywood, he was the center of a literary controversy. What he needed to do was to carry on. He was even in a position of leadership. The healthiest and most creative forces in the Movement were supporting him. He must fight back. He could write an answer to the attacks, and he could even make a lecture tour. He imagined himself speaking to the new generation of writers on the campuses of big universities, receiving support and applause. He imagined an article, written, perhaps, by Moses, defending and supporting his position. He fancied himself winning over leading Party spokesmen, and he thought of his name becoming important in the Soviet Union and in every country where the Movement and the Party were strong. He slouched back in his chair and happily indulged in dreamy visions of Leonard Luckman as the writer who had fathered a great progressive, Left-wing cultural upswing in America which would lift the cultural movement here to the level it had attained in France.

And, he told himself, all this could come to pass, if only the Party leaders would see that he, and not his critics, was on the right track.

IX

"I can't believe it. I can't understand it," Anne said, as she and Leonard discussed the articles which so vehemently attacked him.

"I don't understand why they want to do this to me."

"They're envious."

"I don't deserve it. Anne, dearest, you know I'm not a renegade or a wrecker, don't you? I'm not an enemy of the Movement."

He waited for her answer. But she was silent and thoughtful. He feared that she, too, was against him, and that he was alone. All his dreams of a few moments ago now seemed to have been stupid, preposterous, foolish.

"Of course, Leonard, you don't deserve it," Anne said after having sat quietly for about two minutes. "That's not what I'm worried about."

"Don't worry. Don't worry, Anne. Everything will be straightened out in time."

"I'm not really worried," she said quickly. "That was only an expression. What I was thinking about was why you had to be attacked."

She was thinking that if this controversy went too far, Leonard could only face ostracism. This, she was certain, would be bad, both for him and for herself. In the last week she had seen a number of friends in the Movement and had talked with two members of the Central Committee. They had regarded her highly, and she knew she had the respect of the Party leaders. Concerning Eldridge, it had been sufficient for her to tell them that she agreed with the Party decision to expel him. It had been explained to her that this was a period of one of the worst crises the Party had faced. Eldridge, renegade and despicable traitor that he was, was causing trouble. He was sending lying documents out broadside to the Party's rank and file, confusing them, bitterly attacking the new leadership, and creating the danger of a real split. His reactionary revisionist leadership had brought the Party close to bankruptcy. Morale was at a very low ebb. There was danger that Party discipline and loyalty might be damaged severely, and that the blows the Party was suffering from Eldridge, and from the support Eldridge was receiving from the bourgeois press, would set it back for years. In the light of these facts and in the face of this crisis, any danger to Party unity was serious. Now, they all had to stand together, firm and implacable, with Leninist hardness.

It hadn't been necessary to relate this specifically to Leonard and to Leonard's article. Anne had made this connection herself. She was troubled, and that was why she had been silent and thoughtful a few moments ago. It was also why she had referred to the needs of the Movement.

She frequently treated Leonard like a child and withheld from him both information and frank statements about her own thoughts. She was convinced that she acted this way for his own good. Now, as she sat with him, she was thinking not only of the needs of the Movement and of the dangers faced by the Party in its present crisis, but also of his future. She was certain that expulsion and ostracism would only destroy Leonard's career. She knew him well enough, or at least believed she did, to be aware of his need for support. Alone, unsupported, he wouldn't be able to write. And at the same time Leonard's expulsion, the loneliness and ostracism they would have to face, alarmed her. The position she had acquired on the Coast was due to association with the Party as much as to Leonard's success. She was not merely a wife; she was a person with authority, a woman of energy, and respected in her own right. She was even feared. Whatever she had learned, whatever she had become, was all linked with the Party. To be separated from it was inconceivable to her.

Furthermore, the Party crisis was an opportunity for her, and, as she saw the situation, an opportunity for Leonard. By helping to heal the present breech, by contributing toward a rebuilding of broken fences, they could win a stronger position

for themselves with the new leadership. The need for firm-
ness, for building a wall-like front before the world and the
bourgeoisie was a political task, not a cultural one. And if
Leonard's cultural position damaged this wall, if it interfered
with political needs, it would have to be sacrificed. Once this
crisis was surmounted, conditions for work would be easier for
writers. Leonard could write. Because she didn't want him to
break with the Party, she didn't want him to fight back. He
was more right than those who were attacking him, and when
she read their attacks she burned with cold hatred. But she
thought it would be politically unwise to answer them. She
believed that if she prevented him from making an open and
intransigent fight, she would be helping him in the long run.
It didn't matter to her that he might think it important to
say in public that he found merit in works written by those
whom the Party denounced as renegades. If such books helped
Leonard as a writer, let him read them and say nothing. And
as for his own writing, let him just go on with it, and when
the time came they could go over it with more intelligent
Party leaders and iron out any causes for trouble.

"What I don't like is the advantage our enemies will take
of this controversy," Anne remarked.

"But I didn't give them any ammunition," Leonard answered quickly but without conviction.

Anne hesitated long enough before speaking so that Leonard began to fear he might have given such ammunition to
the enemies of the Movement, and a burning sense of guilt
began to flame within him. Stung and seared by this guilt,
Leonard talked rapidly, explaining to Anne that he had
pointed out very explicitly that he had not attacked or criticized the political line of the Party, and that though he had
indicated he thought there were renegades who had written
good novels, he did not approve of their politics.

"Yes, angel, but the trouble is that the renegades are using
this controversy. That's the trouble."

"I won't go over to them," he burst out.

Anne was surprised, and her immediate reaction to Leon-

ard's statement was one of alarm. Then she saw she would
have no trouble in guiding Leonard along the course she de-
sired, and she was almost exultant.

They talked about the attacks but reached no definite conclusion other than the decision that Leonard shouldn't rush
any reply to those who were denouncing him.

x

Leonard was a tormented person during those days. He had
moments when he felt intensely alone, and he would sink into
moods of darkest despair. He was almost terrorized by nameless dreads. The world, and life itself, became an impending
threat for him, a nameless dread. He woke up in the morning
filled with this tormenting dread. It waited for him on the
streets. It lurked in the night when he went to bed. It became even more depressing and frightening than thoughts of
the fact that one day he would die. Writing his article, he
had been so convinced he was right, and he had nourished so
many hopes concerning the salutary effects the article would
have! He had had so many dreams of the position and new
importance he would win with the publication of this article.
And the response shocked and surprised him, and left him
afraid, unnerved. The injustice of the attacks hurt. It was
painful to read them, and yet he read them over and over.

And there was such a contrast between the printed articles
about him and about his piece in the Party press and the letters
he received from all over the country. So many of these were
letters of congratulation, in which the writers expressed their
agreement with him. Correspondents unknown to him, who
said they were young writers, thanked him. They lauded his
courage. They told him he had cleared the air. Actually, most
of the letters received at *Mass Action* favored his position, yet
the attacks continued. The correspondence column of *Mass
Action*, and also of *The Fist*, printed additional attacks. This
hurt. It hurt because he knew that, although he had been

right, he couldn't help himself because of his many feelings of guilt. He was self-persecuted because he had the conviction that he had been in the wrong. The leaders of the Party were revolutionists, revolutionists in a sense that he was not, and never could be. In reflection, his days in Hollywood now troubled him. His bank account was a source of guilt. He felt guilty about his expensive clothes, about Anne's clothes, about his home and car out on the Coast, about the hotel at which he was staying, and the restaurants in which he was eating. And at the same time his experience in Hollywood had sapped the last shreds of his faith in writing. He consoled himself about his fears of standing alone by assuring himself that no writer could stand alone. He kept thinking that writing, the art of the novel, even the printed word, was dying. To be a lonely and isolated writer dependent upon the printed word and the bourgeois book market was to fight a losing battle. His books had never sold well. Would they ever sell? Could he even support himself and Anne if he broke with the Movement and went it alone? He thought of the renegades. But it only seemed that they stood alone. In the last analysis, and on all decisive questions, they were with the enemy, and the only alternatives he saw were surrender or going over to the enemy camp.

He thought again and again of his early dreams and ideals. The dream of being a writer had mingled and become one with the dream of changing the world. Back in the early 1930's, he often had been both proud and frightened when he had read his own name in print on pieces in which he was described as a revolutionary writer. And he recalled his own awe and respect for the leaders of the Party, and for Party organizers who went out into the field. He had been attracted and impressed by their bravery and self-sacrifice. He had wanted to be brave. On many occasions he had thought of giving up writing and of becoming an organizer. Shyly, he remembered some of his heroic dreams, of the times he had imagined himself leading strikes, organizing workers, taking risks by doing secret, underground work for the Party. The contrast between these dreams and some of the realities of his life now came back to pain him. Yes, he had dreamed of heroism, self-sacrifice, and adventure. And he had gone to parties in Hollywood, sometimes serving the Movement by paying twenty-five or fifty dollars a plate at banquets in the swankiest and most expensive hotels in Hollywood and Beverly Hills. And he had served the Cause, too, by attending parties and going to meetings at showy and expensive homes. He had not been one of those who had suffered for the Movement. Look at the contrast between his life and career and that of Moses. He had never been really tested. He had never found an opportunity for testing his own bravery. Could he, then, really speak with the authority which not only had been written into the lines of his article but was also implied in it? Could he fight? Had he the right to fight?

He received advice from all sides. He was told to fight, and he was told not to fight. One day at lunch he had a long, heart-to-heart talk with Moses. Moses was discouraged. He had contributed one article to the controversy. It had been noncommittal. Moses had not attacked Leonard, but neither had he defended him. When they met for lunch on the corner of Eighth Street and Fifth Avenue, Moses had greeted him with a meek and apologetic smile. Moses, too, felt a need to explain himself and his article. He privately told Leonard that he agreed with Leonard and was very distressed by the attacks on him. But he couldn't state this in public because his own position was not solid enough, and because he was afraid of being denounced for Eldridgism. He added that he frankly didn't believe that the comrades who were attacking and denouncing Leonard really meant what they wrote in any literal sense. In fact, they all liked him personally and admired him as an artist. But they were writing as they did because of the crisis and the fight over Eldridgism. Now, Moses explained, he could see that Leonard's article had been badly timed. Too many comrades were panicky. It was all distressing, very distressing.

Moses also explained that he had now no authority on *Mass*

Action. Again smiling meekly and apologetically, Moses said:

"I went to bat for you, Leonard, at the last editorial meeting."

Leonard surged with emotion when Moses told him this. Moses was loyal and was sticking by his guns, too. He was eager and hopeful, and he leaned across the table a little as Moses told him of the editorial meeting. Moses had tried to explain that Leonard hadn't meant to do anything that would be disruptive, and that the very last thing he had on his mind was the liquidation of the progressive cultural movement.

Leonard interrupted Moses at this point to say that, of course, this was true.

"Where would I be, and where would you be, Moses, if the progressive cultural movement were to be liquidated?"

"That was just my point, Lennie," Moses told him.

But Moses was sorely dispirited, and he looked forlorn. His remarks had not had much effect. Don Jones had done most of the talking at the meeting, and he had said over and over again that the attitude expressed in Leonard's article was very dangerous, very dangerous. Moses repeated this phrase, and then weakly said:

"Hell, Lennie, that piece of yours isn't dangerous. I tried to explain that to them. But, Lennie, they just wouldn't be convinced."

Moses gave a full account of the meeting. Don Jones had told them they all had made a mistake, and that they would have to recognize it. And Ellison, who at that time already had written three attacks in *The Fist* on Leonard, had launched into another at the editorial board meeting.

"What did he say?" Leonard asked quickly, in impulsive fright.

"Oh, Lennie, he said the same damned thing he always says."

Moses then went on to talk about Ellison. He had no sensitivity, no feeling for literature, and he almost always took a sectarian line. In the presence of important people in the Party he acted like a suck-hole, and he would talk then as though he were speaking in their name. A weary, hurt smile crossed Moses' face.

"From the way he talked, you might have thought that he was Stalin."

They both drew feeble consolation from Moses' remark about Ellison.

But Ellison was one of those setting the tone of the attacks on Leonard. He was dominating the controversy. And Moses explained why Ellison was doing this. The controversy gave him his chance. Six, eight, ten, and twelve years ago, a literary critic like Ellison was of no account in the cultural movement. Even as a sectarian he hadn't been of any importance. But as many of the writers and critics close to the Movement had drifted away from it, or had gone on to do other things, as Leonard had gone out to Hollywood, Ellison had come forward. Now he was using this controversy as a means of winning personal authority for himself. He was a careerist. He was really going beyond the bounds. Don Jones was different. Don had been very close to Eldridge, and he was worried. A couple of weeks ago it had even looked as if Don would lose out as an editor on *Mass Action*, and Don didn't make any real pretensions to being a literary man. He was a journalist and an editor. Don's attack on Leonard's article had been political, and Don wasn't doing this for the same reasons as Ellison. Ellison was really being *kosher* and orthodox.

"He has to be because he's so stupid," Moses added, again smiling wearily and helplessly.

All this hurt and frightened Leonard, but he listened eagerly to everything Moses had to say about the meeting. Moses also made it clear that a real fight was useless. They couldn't win.

They both began to feel sorry for themselves, for the Movement, and for American culture. As they sank into this mood of despair, thoughts and questions arose which they dared not express even to each other. What would the literary world say of this controversy? Leonard had thought of this question before. He wanted outsiders to respect his attitude and like his

article, and at the same time he wanted them to know that he
was not surrendering his Left-wing convictions. Face-to-face
with the literary world, he was ashamed for comrades like
Ellison. Yet he did gain a certain pleasure and pride in knowing
that Ellison and those like him could frighten the bourgeois
literary world. He had seen this happen in the past, back in
the 1930's when he himself had been treated with respect and
fear merely because he was introduced as a Left-wing writer.

Leonard's despair deepened. And, he reflected, the liberal
journals and literary sheets hadn't paid much attention to this
controversy. They didn't consider it important. His hopes of
raising questions that would help to orient American culture
and writing as a whole, as well in the Movement, were dashed.
The lack of interest in the controversy on the part of those
outside the Movement only served to deepen his sense of loneliness.

And Moses couldn't stand by him in any solid and effective
manner. Moses couldn't write a real defense of him. No one
was publicly defending him. He was exposed to those virulent
attacks, and he did not have one defender of importance.

They talked despairingly, and when they parted Leonard
walked off like a beaten man.

XI

A couple of days after his lunch with Moses, Leonard was
asked to attend an editorial board meeting of *Mass Action*. He
went to it nervous and troubled. The cordiality with which he
was received bewildered him. Don Jones shook hands with him,
and spoke as though Leonard had never written his article.
Even Ellison was polite. The mood among all those present reminded Leonard of old times before the War and before he had
gone to Hollywood. The atmosphere was one of comradeliness.
Leonard lost his feeling of being alone and almost excluded.
He regretted having written his article, regretted the fact that
this entire controversy had been started. And he sat around

with the editors, chatting cordially about small matters. No one seemed inclined to mention what was on all their minds. Leonard grew inwardly tense. He became anxious, because he had no confidence in his ability to defend himself face-to-face with these editors and comrades if they attacked his article here as they had in print. He hoped the subject wouldn't come up. But he knew it must be mentioned. He waited for some-one else to broach it, for he was incapable of doing this. He didn't want to argue. He didn't want to fight. He didn't want to do anything that would result in hard feelings. And he tried to convince himself that, in spite of the way he had been attacked, he wouldn't hold anything against anyone.

Leonard was exceedingly nervous by the time Don Jones said to him:

"You know, Lennie, none of us have any personal feelings against you."

They all became tense. Leonard couldn't answer immediately, and then he said to Don:

"I know that, Don, and I can say the same thing myself."

"It's an objective question," Ellison said.

"It's that, and it's more. Lennie, we're interested in you and we don't want to lose you," Don went on.

"Why, I never even thought of that question," Leonard told them, hurt and disturbed to think that they should have even imagined he would break with or betray the Movement.

"That's why the question is objective. Engels told us, didn't he, that men will one thing in history but that what they will doesn't happen the way they willed it?"

Leonard tried to comment on what Ellison had just said, but before he could get started Ellison was off on a long explanation of dialectical materialism. When Ellison stopped talking, Leonard was confused. Then Don talked and told Leonard how much they all respected him as an artist, and how they only regretted that any difficulties had arisen. They were all concerned, very concerned, that this controversy had taken a heated turn, and they were concerned about Leonard. In particular, the leaders of the Party were concerned. They respected Leonard. They didn't want to see him go astray. That was why Don had called this meeting.

Leonard remained bewildered. But he was silently grateful that they weren't attacking him to his face.

"I want to say I appreciate this—I appreciate it deeply," Leonard told them; he was sparring for time because he didn't know what to say. He spoke slowly, as an overwhelming rush of feeling welled up in him. "I have no hard feelings, fellows, and I have never in my life thought of myself as outside of the Movement. I thought that my article made that clear."

Ellison opened his mouth to speak, but Don Jones silenced him with a look, and Don talked.

"I believe you, Lennie. But that's . . . yes, that's the subjective side. The objective angle to the question is another thing. That's what all the shouting is about." A mournful look came over Don's face. "I can see now, Lennie, you made a mistake, and there are dangerous deviationist and liquidationist tendencies in your article."

Ellison looked at Leonard like a fierce bird of prey. Leonard couldn't face him, and then, turning toward Don, who sat across the table from him, he looked past Don.

"I haven't been aware of them, of any such tendencies," Leonard said weakly.

Don smirked. He gazed at Leonard as if he pitied him.

"Don," Moses said, "I know Lennie, and I know that he isn't out to do us any harm. There's no Trotskyism in his make-up, and Lennie was away from us here in the worst days of Eldridgism, so it couldn't have infected him as much as it infected some of us. I don't think that what's been said reveals a correct appreciation of Lennie's attitude, or of his position."

Leonard was very grateful to Moses. But Moses spoke weakly, and as he talked he kept smiling at Don and the others appeasingly.

They talked for a long time. Don kept telling Leonard that he was in the wrong, and that if he would only see that he was, he could correct himself. He spoke in the name of the Movement, and of the good of the Movement. Supported by the others, he stressed the point that whatever was for the good of the Movement was for the good of American culture. It couldn't be otherwise. Leonard tried to explain himself, but when he did they showed him letters and two essays from friends and fellow writers of his on the Coast, denouncing his article. He felt whipped, and at the end of the meeting he walked out, beaten and hurt.

XII

Leonard had a long talk with Anne, and she spoke as Don had. He had another meeting with the board of *Mass Action*. And in the meantime the campaign against him mounted. Then he had lunch with Moses. Moses joined Anne in advising him to retreat. He agreed.

Painfully, he wrote an article in which he retracted all he had said in his previous piece. He agreed with everything his critics had said of him, and thanked those who had been the most severe and denunciatory. He confessed he had been wrong, and he publicly asked everyone who had agreed with him to accept what his critics had said against his position. When he turned this retraction in to Moses, he felt released. He had no burdens now. He didn't feel alone. But he couldn't write. He painfully tried to work on his novel but gave up and went back to the Coast and resumed work at a studio. He was hailed in the Party press as a great writer, and as an honest and progressive Left-wing artist who had the courage to recognize and admit his mistakes. But he was inwardly humiliated and ashamed of himself. He knew he had sacrificed what he wanted to believe in, and, even more, that he had sacrificed his dreams of writing.

Literary Love

MARTHA was approaching forty, and she was trying to find a new life. After having gotten her divorce from a well-known Broadway and Hollywood director, she had taken a cure for alcoholism. While she believed she no longer loved her ex-husband and accepted the fact that their life together was ended, she thought of him constantly and continued to live emotionally in the days when they had been together. She lived in dreams of the past and in thoughts of him as much as she did in her efforts to find a new life. She believed he would be proud if he knew of the struggle she was going through. She was very lonely, and she had nothing to do but think of herself. Thanks to her alimony, she could live in more than comfort. She entertained often, seeing old friends she had known when she had first married, people to whom she had been introduced through Tommy. But they were not the type who could fill her life. Most of them were getting old; the world had passed them by. They were in financial straits, they drank a lot, and they, too, lived too much in the past. When she had these old friends to dinner, she served them excellent meals on the finest china, and they would talk endlessly of the old days, of parties in the twenties, of all-night drinking bouts, speakeasies, the unconventional things they had done to shock a world that had not paid too much attention to them. Their conversation was almost totally of the past.

Martha drew on all her energy to hold herself together, and

this she did quite successfully. She didn't dare take a drink, but she was always able to muster up the will power needed to resist this temptation. She inclined toward those whose lives were ordered on a pattern similar to her own and she liked to be with people who did the things she had once done. In their presence, watching them lose the self-control she now so precariously retained, she gained greater self-confidence. And in this way she constantly strengthened her personal morale.

Martha found a group of friends who lived on the periphery of literary New York, and who used literature and talk about books and plays and pictures as incidental to, and connected with, seductions. Several of the girls in this group, either by inclination or else as a kind of gesture of self-assertion, liked to go to Harlem, seeking colored men, preferably married ones. The members of this loosely knit clique were always having scenes, emotional upsets, troubles, and someone was usually stealing a friend's lover. When this happened there would be a big row, but then everything would be patched up and they would all continue to see one another. And these people sought to add new members to their group with a zeal that bordered on the missionary. They were always on the lookout for someone to bring into their circle, and then they would try to arrange it so that the newcomers would go to bed with someone in the clique.

Martha was introduced to these people by Millicent, a tall, slender, beautiful, and madly carefree girl. Millicent was a nymphomaniac: sleeping with married men was an obsession with her. She had had affairs with more well-known writers, critics, radicals, and others of the New York literary world than she could remember. Despite her many conquests, however, she had not broken up many homes. It was a speculative point as to whether or not she was disappointed by this fact. Millicent not only liked to sleep with as many men as she could find, she wanted everyone else to do likewise. She was almost without jealousy in her attitude toward men, and often she would willingly arrange for one of her own lovers to have an affair with someone else. There were only twenty-four hours in the day, and the world was so full of new masculine bodies for her to sample that she didn't have the time to be possessive and proprietary. If one man was not available, there was always another to take his place.

Millicent took a fancy to Martha and thought it was a pity that Martha didn't have a man. She decided to rectify this and began a campaign to bring Martha and Carl Waller together.

Carl Waller was an almost forgotten legend in New York literary circles. About eleven years earlier, with his first book of poems, he had been recognized as one of the most promising of the younger American poets. And now, because he had sliced several years off his real age, he had been accepted as a member of the younger generation. He had written with a strange and neurotic power, and he had impressed some critics and the more discerning of the literary minded. But he had gradually written in a more and more obscure manner, until his work had disintegrated into a chaos of strange and fantastic words, into a kind of frenzied and solipsistic verbal fantasy that barred others from gaining understanding or sustenance from it. He was a bitterly disappointed writer, and a bitter man inclined to violent anger. He seemed to be obsessed by the necessity to destroy all his relationships. And he had become one of the leading figures in this curious little clique of free Bohemians, although at one time he had expressed only the most violent detestation for people who lived such a life. Suffering from ulcers, he did not dare to drink or smoke, and he had to eat in the most austere manner. Indulgence in tobacco, in gourmandizing, in alcohol, seemed to him to be crude and vulgar, and he developed a moral attitude toward abstinence. Concerning sex, he felt differently. His entire life had been a series of affairs, attempted affairs, violent quarrels over his failures, and humorous incidents with women. He had had many mistresses and several wives, each usually for only a short while. Now he was showing the signs of age. His face was becoming flaccid. His eyes were receding.

He was getting gray at the temples, and was also growing bald. Once he had associated with the best-known liberal and radical writers and intellectuals in New York. Now whenever any of his old time friends or acquaintances saw him, they usually looked the other way, avoided him, hastily crossed the street. They didn't want to see him. Talks with him generally ended in scenes in which he bored them with violent insults, fantastic charges that were more or less character assassinations, and with a general unpleasantness. He had been forced downward into a Bohemian life and was impelled to try to find ever new circles of admirers and disciples among those who had not written, and who probably never would write. But these people used their lack of talent as a kind of moral badge of honor. They were failures because they were too sensitive for this vulgar world.

As Carl went through life, fighting, insulting, threatening a violence he never carried out, he became more and more lonely. His sexual obsessions intensified and tended to become almost the entire content of his life. He continually needed new girls and women in order to gain a sense of personality and fulfillment. And Millicent's clique promised him this. Out of perverse necessity, he managed to remain a member of it for a long time. He retained these people as friends longer than he had almost anyone else.

Carl and Millicent had started out hating and insulting each other. He would call her "a cheap bitch," and she had sneered at him as a poseur. In time, and through mutual hatreds, however, they had become good friends, although they always made it a point to assure people that their friendship was platonic. Millicent, who had once detested Carl's work as much as his personality, had changed her mind. She now considered him a genius. And she was always describing his genius, his charm, his culture to women she met. After she had seen Martha two or three times, she began telling her about Carl. Although unrecognized by his inferiors, he was America's greatest writer, and his work would live in posterity. He was a new American Melville. He was cultured, charming, intelli-

gent, and she wanted Martha to meet him. Martha welcomed
the opportunity to meet a man of this caliber. Millicent's
description of Carl was almost a description of Martha's dream
of Tommy. She could never love anyone but Tommy, and
yet, if she met the ideal she had wanted Tommy to be, who
knows? At least, she would meet him. She would find a friend
here, and she wanted friends. And perhaps . . .

After Millicent had given Martha an account of Carl, her
doorbell rang one dull and rainy evening. A tall man with fine
but torn and intense features stood in the doorway, and he
announced in an overcultivated voice:

"I am Carl Waller."

Martha was pleased and invited him to come in. She had
been lonely and wondering what she would do with herself.

He apologized for not having telephoned and said he had
just been passing, and that since Millicent had spoken so much
of her, he had felt as though he already knew her.

"I'm glad you came. Millicent has told me about you, too."

"She's a very sensitive girl," he said.

"I like her. Can I get you a drink?"

"No, thanks, but have one yourself."

The tone in which he said this puzzled her momentarily,
and then she let it drop out of her thoughts. He talked well
and was very charming. He stayed a half hour, and left, bid-
ding her a gracious good-by. She was glad he had come. However, he had not excited her, even though he had seemed
sensitive, intelligent, and well-mannered.

About four days later, he suddenly appeared at her door
with one of his books. It was raining. He said he hoped he was
not intruding, but he had come only to bring her the book.
He had written a flattering inscription to Martha on the flyleaf
of the book. She invited him in. He seemed tense and nervous.
Unlike the first time he had come, he sat beside her on the
couch instead of in the chair facing her.

"It was very kind of you to come, and in the rain, too, to
bring me your book. I'm looking forward to reading it."

"I know you'll like it. I wouldn't have given it to you if I didn't think you were a sensitive person."

"You don't know me yet. Perhaps you'll change your mind, once you know me."

"I know I shan't."

"I wouldn't bet on that."

"I'm an artist. An artist's impressions of genuinely sensitive people are unerring."

He edged a few inches closer to her. They talked of books. He described his own book he'd just given her as a work of genius. Therefore, he stated, he was proud to tell her it had sold only three hundred and fifty copies. He also asserted that no book that had a large sale could be a work of art. She demurred, and he was mildly annoyed.

"I know more about this than you do, Martha. I wish you wouldn't try to contradict me. You're too sensitive and intelligent to make such statements."

He slid closer to her, but she pretended not to notice. She was, however, genuinely uneasy. He seemed so tense and spoke with a kind of concentrated passion. He frightened her. She wasn't at all sure of herself.

"I saw Millicent. I told her that her description of you was not at all incorrect. I complimented her on knowing a woman as sensitive and as cultivated as you."

"If you were Irish, I'd say you had kissed the Blarney stone."

"Please—I am serious. I strongly object to levity about serious subjects."

"But am I a serious subject of conversation? It's the first time I've ever been considered that."

"I don't lie."

"I know that. I'm certain of that. But I'm afraid you think too highly of me."

"I am an artist. I do not make mistakes."

He edged closer to her on the couch.

"It's a pleasure to be here, if I may say so," he said.

"Thank you."

"Your home is furnished in such good taste," he said.

"Do you think so?"

"Yes, I do," he said meaningfully, as he casually rested his hand on her thigh.

She calmly removed his hand, saying:

"I wanted it to be comfortable and pleasing to the eye."

She didn't want him to make advances to her. But she was no longer frightened; in fact, she was even confident he would be discreet in his approach. But he was beginning to seem a little preposterous to her.

"One of the tests of a woman's sensibility is to be found in her home. If one doesn't live amid things of beauty, how can one's soul be beautiful?" he asked.

Martha now wanted to laugh. She asked herself, how can this man be an artist, how can he be any kind of approximation to what Millicent said he was, if he tried to make love to her in such banal terms?

"Of course, we live now in a time of chain-store culture, when most people think and feel like a herd of animals. To have any sensitivity is to walk about with a stigmata. Feeling, impulse, naturalness—you will never get cigar-store certificates of culture if you possess those traits. One is lonely, and that is why I admire your place. It is you. It is an oasis in a world of cigar-store culture," he said, and again his hand slid gently, caressingly, along her thigh.

"Please don't do that," she said, removing his hand.

"Why?" he asked.

"Frankly, I like you, but I don't want to sleep with you."

"Martha, your nature is too fine for you to speak so crudely," he said, as though her remarks had pained him deeply.

"But isn't that what it means when you caress my legs?"

"It means much more."

"What?"

"You are woman, and I am man," he said in a solemn tone of voice.

She edged away. He edged toward her.

"Why should we not act as man and woman? It is beautiful, it is natural. It is the crowning moment of unity between two sensitive natures. It is not to be crudely described as sleeping together. It is a kind of union that is a work of the art of living, and it is the basis of all other art. Sensitive man, sensitive woman, this is the basis for a work of art in action."

"Please, I don't want to."

"Martha, I plead with you—don't make a mistake," he said in a soothing voice.

"What do you mean?" she asked, removing his hand from her thigh for the third time.

"Rejecting me! Rejecting yourself! Rejecting the beauty that is possible between us."

"I told you—I admire your intelligence, and I like you. But I feel no desire for you."

"But let me induce you to feel sensitive desires," he said persuasively, putting his arm around her shoulder.

"No!" she answered decisively.

"I don't want you to make a mistake. Listen to me!"

"I'm not making a mistake. I don't care to feel sensitive desires toward you."

"But why? You can't live a virginal life. That's stupid. And you are not a stupid woman. Do you think I'd be here if I thought you were stupid?"

"But can't you understand? I don't feel that way toward you."

"Are you not a woman?"

"Please, let's not discuss it."

He sat back.

"You were speaking about Melville when you were here before," she began, hoping she had successfully warded him off and wanting to put him at his ease.

"Melville! But am I sure that you understand Melville?" he said.

"I know I don't. But you might help me. Tell me about him."

"Are you worthy?"

"I don't understand you."

"Not everyone is worthy of reading Melville. I must find out if you are," he said, leaning forward, kissing her.

She drew back.

"I told you. I don't feel that way about you!"

"You don't want to be worthy, even to understand Melville," he said in an angry tone of voice.

"What do you mean?"

He grabbed her, and they tussled on the couch. He sought her lips.

"Let me go," she cried.

He tried to press his weight on top of her.

"Let me go!"

"I will make you worthy of understanding Melville. Kiss me," he said, breathing jerkily.

"Let me go!"

He bore down on her, kissed her again.

She turned aside, and he kissed her cheek.

"Let me go."

"Let me make you worthy."

"Get off me."

"Don't make a serious mistake. Let me . . ."

"I'll bite you. Let me go. Let me go."

She managed to squirm free. She jumped up. Her hair was disheveled, and there was a bruise on her arm.

"Please leave my home."

"You reject my proposal?"

"I ask you, please leave my home."

"Do you know what you are doing?"

"For the last time, please leave my home!"

"With pride! You are crude and insensitive. Don't you dare ever use the name of Melville. You commit a sacrilege if you dare even to mutter his name."

"Now I won't. I'll never read him. You've cured me of him."

"Look at your apartment! This chromium monstrosity! I

have never seen a more vulgar, pretentious living room. It looks like a chromium bordello."

"There's not one bit of chromium in it."

"It looks like a Greyhound Bus station. If I had made the mistake of giving my soul to you here, I'm afraid that in the middle of the act I'd hear a bus announcer shrieking out information about the time of departure of busses for Hollywood."

"Well, I've spared you that embarrassment."

"Give me back my book."

"Gladly," she said in anger.

She stared at him with blazing eyes. Then she moved around a table, each of her steps decisive. She picked up the book, and, speechless, with her lips pressed tight in anger, she handed it to him.

He didn't move.

She waited.

"Well, are you going?"

"I was getting a last look at this miserable pile of junk."

"I am not interested in what you say."

He sneered. He gazed at her, wild eyed. He grabbed her, held her in a viselike grip.

She felt his arms crushing her. He struggled to get his head in position and then kissed her. He took her by such surprise that her lips opened. He held her.

"Let me go!"

"It's too late. You have to. The woman in you cries out."

Again he kissed her.

"Let go or I'll bite your tongue."

"Don't repress the woman in you," he mumbled madly, again kissing her.

"I warn you!"

"I will fulfill you."

"I warn you."

He kissed her again, and in desperation she bit his tongue. He let her go, moaned with pain, and then tried to talk. His features were contorted with pain. He looked old and weak and pathetic. He faced her in pain, blood oozing from his mouth. She drew away, horrified. He pointed an accusing finger at her, opened his mouth to speak, winced with pain.

"I'm sorry. But I warned you."

His shoulders slumped. He looked like a ghoulish old man. She turned away as he found his handkerchief and wiped his mouth. He picked up his book and his belongings, and rushed out of the apartment.

She ran to the door and called to him to come back, saying she would get him a doctor. He walked on, his shoulders hunched.

She closed the door, shrugged her shoulders, sat down, got up and restlessly paced the room, trying to justify her action. She was sorry. She lit a cigarette, took a few puffs, then threw it away. Then she lit a fresh one. Finally her eyes lit on a decanter of wine. She looked at it nervously and fearfully. She tapped her foot on the floor. She slowly went to the table and gazed at the wine. She lifted it, put it down, and then, in a mood of desperation, poured some into a glass. She lifted the glass, but suddenly flung it against the wall. She thrilled with the noise of the breaking glass and said:

"Oh, what the hell!"

Then she looked at the mess she had made and regretted her action. But, despite her regrets, she thrilled with the belief that she had proven something important to herself.

She sat down again. She thought of Carl Waller and was filled with pity for him. But, still, she asked herself, what else could she have done?

And she thought of Tommy, her ex-husband. Had Tommy felt about her as she felt about Carl Waller? The question troubled her. She knew she had reached a turning point. She knew that now she would go out and find some useful work. She looked at the broken glass again and at the wine stains on her walls and rug. To her, these were symbols of something dead within her, symbols of a part of her life that she had buried.

Love Affair in Paris

LESTER BAUMBERG went to Paris late one spring after the break-up of his marriage. He was twenty-four, dark haired, tall, well built, and almost handsome. He had a gentle manner, and he spoke softly. In Paris he lived modestly on money he had saved, and, except when he was in moody periods, he would practice daily for long hours on the piano.

Lester often went to the Club for American students on the Boulevard Raspail. Occupying the first floor of an old building, the Club consisted of a large room with a piano, and every day in the late afternoon there would be tea and dancing. Sometimes Lester played the piano, but he only consented to do this when there was no one else who could.

When he was twenty-one Lester had married Mildred Rosenbaum, who had at that time been a talented dancer of twenty-six. With Mildred, he had found happiness and security. She had been a complete world for him. He had lost interest in his friends, and he had not wanted to go out or to be with them. He had regarded their love and marriage as the rare romantic love of two artists, and he had constantly imagined a future when they would both be famous, she as a dancer and he as a pianist, who would also be her accompanist. He imagined that they would share everything with each other for the whole of their lives. But at moments he would moodily react from these romantic feelings. He would be abashed and secretly guilty. In the fits of depression that would follow then, he would play

Chopin. Mildred had little taste for Chopin, for this music produced a vague uneasiness in her. She would say nothing to Lester, but she would be silently critical.

Mildred was sandy-haired, small, compactly built, and striking in appearance. Despite the fact that she was a dancer, she was a very matter-of-fact person, shrewd, calculating, and possessed of will, determination, and great ambition. Her schedule was rigorous. She taught classes to make money, took lessons herself from an outstanding dancer, kept house, was politically active in the developing Left-wing cultural movement, and tried to find time for reading. She had planned her future carefully and intelligently. At first she tolerated Lester's wistful and dreamy romanticism, but then it became irritating. She was too busy, too preoccupied with her own struggle for the career she thought she deserved, to have time for Lester's moods. Mildred made decisions quickly and confidently; her judgments were sharp and definite. Lester, on the contrary, resisted making small decisions. He became increasingly dependent on her. In time, this situation became exasperating for her. She didn't want him to be so dependent upon her, and she tried to change their relationship to make him less so. But Lester reacted to these efforts with moodiness and silence. Their marriage became impossible. Early in 1930 Mildred left him.

Lester was shaken. For days he couldn't concentrate. He had no one to whom he could talk. His moods had even approached the suicidal. Finally, he had decided to go to Europe to try to forget and to get a new grip on himself.

Lester was lonely during his first days in Paris. Having studied French in college, he quickly developed the ability to speak the language, and he soon found a room in the Montparnasse area with a piano he could use. But he couldn't settle down immediately. He was wounded emotionally. His memories of Mildred remained painfully vivid. Paris seemed unreal; at times it was like a strange and somewhat frightening dream world. Frequently he'd have overpowering illusions that he was back in New York with Mildred. He tried to soothe him-

self by reading Proust's *The Remembrance of Things Past*. He
was deeply stirred by the account of Swann in love, and he
even imagined himself an American Swann. And Proust's por-
trayal of Swann helped him justify to himself his own feelings.
While reading these portions of Proust's work, he would remain in his room for hours, alternately brooding and reading.
Then he would nurse fantasies of a reconciliation with Mildred. He wrote her long letters which he tore up. Daily he
waited and hoped for a letter from her, which he knew he
would not receive. When his moods would threaten to become
unbearable, he'd go to his piano, and as he played he would
imagine he was accompanying her in her first Paris concert,
when she would become a world-famous dancer, the American
Pavlova.

Lester often would tell himself that there was no place in
the world where he belonged. Back in New York, he had never
really belonged. It had not been his world. He had never in his
life been truly sure of himself. Even as a boy he had been more
sensitive than others. And though he had played with children
like a normal boy, he'd been inwardly torn. Only for a short
period with Mildred had he felt that he belonged. And he
didn't belong in Paris, either. Yes, he was an outsider in life.
In his most depressed moments he would tell himself he had
been an expatriate all his life. He even thought of himself as
expatriated not only from New York and America but from
the entire world. Sometimes there was consolation in playing
Chopin. At other times he would visit Notre Dame or Saint-
Germain-des-Prés, and in these dark and magnificent old edi-
fices he would temporarily gain the conviction that he belonged somewhere. But then he'd grow shy and guilty. He'd
fear his own feelings. His sense of irreconcilable alienation
would return. Paris didn't seem to help him get a grip on himself. It looked as if there were no escape.

After meeting Joan Whitfield, Lester suddenly changed.

Joan was twenty-two, friendly, healthy, American, and a
virgin. She looked not only physically but psychologically
healthy. She was well built and plump. She had a convention-

ally pretty face and silky black hair that she did up simply, parted in the center.

Joan was from Madison, Wisconsin. She had graduated from the University there and had come to Paris to study at the Sorbonne. She was an outgoing girl, intelligent, naïve, and kindly disposed toward people. She had Cinderella dreams, spoke French well, and was open with everyone she met.

Joan noticed Lester one afternoon at the Club before he had become aware of her. She was touched by his quiet manner, his shyness, and the brooding sadness she sensed in him. Almost on sight she regarded him as handsome. And his long, slender, soft hands held her attention. They indicated to her that he must be highly sensitive. She assumed instantly that, unlike so many of the young Americans in Montparnasse, he was truly an artist. His dark, sad eyes, his dark hair, his shy and gentle air also attracted her.

II

After Joan and Lester became aware of each other, they both became shy. Lester came to the Club several afternoons and watched Joan without daring to speak to her. And she, bustling about, dancing, laughing, popular with everyone, was aware of him. When she saw him enter the Club, she felt a flutter of excitement. Then one day they looked each other in the eyes, and they both smiled simultaneously. Joan knew instantly that for her, Lester was special. And he hoped, without confidence of success, that she would care for him. They sat together, talked casually, and danced. But he was too shy to say much. Yet he didn't need to. She knew, as if by instinct, that he was interested in her. She asked him questions about himself, his interests, and his work. She quickly sensed that he was sad and hurt, and she was filled with sympathy for him.

They went to dinner at an inexpensive little restaurant on a side street off the Boulevard Saint-Germain, and they prided themselves on being the only Americans in the place. Lester, who had not been eating well because of his state of depression, suddenly discovered he had a big appetite. They liked everything about the restaurant, the sloppy, sad-faced *patron* with a drooping mustache, the middle-aged waitresses in black dresses, the politeness of the *patron* and the waitresses, the food, the French people who dined and talked rather steadily and with a seeming interest in what they had to say, and, above all else, they liked each other.

Before they had finished eating, Lester began to tell Joan the story of his life. She listened with sympathy. Then they went to the Café des Deux Magots for coffee and sat outside, close to the warm brazier. They sat sipping coffee and gazing at the Place Saint-Germain-des-Prés in the cold, dark night, and across at the dark outlines of the Abbey of Saint-Germain-des-Prés. Pedestrians hurried by in the cold. But there was both warmth and light around them, and Lester felt as if the warmth of the brazier and the lights of the café were but a sign or a mirror of the warmth and light he felt within himself. As the minutes passed—warm, rich minutes—Joan seemed to grow more beautiful in his eyes. He began to feel that she would understand him, and that she was a better type of girl for him than Mildred had been. Her youth was as fresh as a flower, and yet she had within her all the traits a woman should have. Womanliness was more important than art. Joan would be womanly.

Unexpectedly, he thought about getting a divorce. He was certain that, if he wanted one, Mildred would consent. The matter could be arranged without any rancor. And why shouldn't he get a divorce? His life with Mildred was over. She had left him shaken and hurt. Might not Joan help heal his wounded feelings? He gazed at her hesitantly as she sat staring out at the street. Yes, she was lovely. And she was good. She would be good for him. Perhaps he needed her doubly because she was a Gentile, for she might be able to help him overcome his introspectiveness and his constant fear that he could never belong anywhere in this world. For she belonged. Even here in France, a foreign country, she acted like one who belonged.

And with a girl like Joan to love, to help and understand him, wouldn't he really settle down to his own career? Might not his real life, his true development, begin?

If he dared, he would ask her now. But he didn't dare.

They sat in the café for a long while. Joan's face was so alive, and her eyes were so very bright. But she also seemed composed and at ease. Her manner was deceptive. Actually, she was frightened. Lester's story of his life had moved her. She wanted to help this boy, to do something to make him feel good and be happy. And she also found herself wanting him to hold her tightly, to kiss her, to look into her eyes with those dark eyes of his, eyes which she thought of as Oriental. He was strange to her. She imagined that there were deep and tender and sensitive and unusual feelings in him which she had never known, but which she would know if he loved her. And somehow she knew that he did love her.

She was afraid she wanted to love him as well as to help him. But he was married. And though she did not criticize others for what they did, she could not see herself in love with a married man. What would her father and mother think back in Madison, Wisconsin, if she were to fall in love with a married man? What would be said in Madison if this should happen, and if friends of hers and of her family should hear of it? But, of course, they didn't have to know. She was free, and she could do what she wanted to. This had been true ever since she had been in Paris, but she had just not happened to think of it in this way before tonight. Now it was a problem. It both frightened and excited her. She feared that she might not be able to control herself, there were such feelings welling up in her. She couldn't talk, and she feared Lester might sense all this.

And, in addition, she was troubled and afraid because she didn't know, she didn't know what love meant and what love felt like. Suddenly she told herself that she had always been afraid of just this—of love, and of the moment when she would know that she might have to say yes or no because it was love. Now that moment was approaching.

Joan laughed strangely, in a state of mild hysteria. Lester quickly turned, disturbed because he thought she might be laughing at him. Her laugh calmed down her feelings. But then she was afraid Lester would understand her laugh, and she hastened to tell him that she had laughed because she had been thinking of how unusual it seemed to her to be sitting here in a café in Paris. And that then she had thought of how wonderful it could be to fall in love in Paris.

Joan quietly watched Lester. Both of them were now speechless, mutually embarrassed. Neither of them could even think of anything to say. They were both troubled by the new and sudden feelings that had welled up within them. Lester smiled at her meekly and shyly. She returned his smile. Joan began to make a remark about the weather. It sounded silly even to her own ears. She lapsed into silence. Lester eagerly asked what she had said. She told him it was nothing. They fell back into an embarrassed silence.

They left the café late and walked slowly back to her hotel. She said nothing when he took her arm. On the dark, narrow streets, hearing the echo of their own footsteps, they were no longer embarrassed by the silence between them.

They stood silent and awkward in front of the hotel on the Rue Délambre. Lester wanted to kiss her. Joan wanted to be kissed. Lester took her hand and shook it, and Joan, speaking with a note of suppressed nervous strain, thanked him for having given her such an enjoyable evening. She turned and hurried inside the hotel.

Lester walked off slowly. He became unsure of himself. He was overwhelmed with the fear that Joan would look down at him, that she might even pity him. He shouldn't have exposed his feelings to her as much as he had. She would think him weak. How could a girl love or respect a man who had been cast aside by another? Yes, he'd made a fool of himself.

It was late and dark and cold. He looked across the street at the lights of the Café du Dôme and thought of going over and sitting there alone to think. He walked on, crossing to the Boulevard Raspail. A few Frenchmen passed him. Paris was now asleep. He was alone in Paris, and the city seemed cold and unfriendly, and he told himself he would never find comfort and ease with himself here in this city. Perhaps he should go back to New York. Didn't he, after all, belong there? In leaving America, hadn't he run away, run away from himself?

He walked on, filled with self-doubts.

III

The next time Lester took Joan out, he kissed her, and she responded to his embraces. Afterward, she was surprised at the boldness of her desires. All her training, all she had been told of sin vanished in that one embrace, and she took the initiative and invited Lester up to her room. She was no longer shy or afraid. And afterward she was happy, utterly happy. She caressed and mussed his hair, petted and kissed him. A calm and deeply contented feeling flowed through her. She knew that she had given happiness to this sad boy. In giving herself to him, she had brought him joy and contentment. The strain and worry were gone from his handsome face. There was gratitude in his dark eyes. And she had helped him to feel strong. He had crushed her in his arms until she had felt his strength and had known that she loved this. All her life had been only a preparation for the joy and the contentment she now felt. These moments with him here in her bed had been the fulfillment of her own life.

They were very happy together. They began to see Paris differently, and they observed things they had never observed before. For both of them, it seemed as though they were seeing the world for the first time. They took walks and looked at streets and people, at buildings and statues and churches as though all these wonders were for their eyes alone. Their vision was clear and sharp. And they were sufficient unto each other. They liked to be alone together. They liked the same things, liked the restaurants they discovered, and began to imagine that they saw and felt alike, and that the bonds of understanding between them were deep and could never be broken. But they didn't speak of marrying or of Lester getting a divorce. They both avoided this question, and they also avoided talking about the future. Each day was sufficient unto itself. They silently and tacitly accepted a view of a permanent and unchanging present.

Lester became more confident of himself. It was as though there were some power within him that had been locked up until he had met Joan, and it had now been released. He decided that he had never really lived before he had met Joan. The past now seemed to him doubly and inexpressibly sad because the present was so happy.

For Joan and Lester, Paris seemed to have become transformed. This was especially so for Lester. Except in very rare moments, the charm of Paris had been veiled off, separated from him. He had looked upon all this beauty from a psychological distance. He had seen pictures in the Louvre, he had visited famous churches, and he had watched people on the streets in moods of utter and barren strangeness. Here were beauty and charm and traditional culture and life, but it had not been for him. It could have little meaning in his own life. When he had found serenity in the cathedrals, it had been merely for short moments, and then he had become guilty and had felt more alone than ever. He had experienced only a cold beauty. He had perceived the creations of others, but at best, they had only saddened him. He had often felt most singularly lonely, and he had seen himself as an outcast in those unexpected moments when he had come upon some sudden revelation or recognition of the beauty of Paris.

But then, when he had come to know Joan and to know that she loved him, all this had changed. His own life in Paris acquired meaning. He now had a reason for seeing and for feeling. He could share his feelings with Joan. He could look at cathedrals and monuments and parks and pictures, and he

could wander on the streets and know that there was someone
who cared and who was glad that he was seeing, feeling, being
touched and moved. He and Joan could talk and hold hands
and kiss, and he knew that later they could go to his or to her
hotel and lie together, and he could sense the beauties he had
visited feeding his own feelings about Joan's beauty and the
beauty of his relationship with her. His eyes had been opened
onto the world. In this mood, they visited the tomb of Abélard
and Héloïse at Père-Lachaise, and to them the cemetery became a scene of joy.

He realized that Mildred had never opened his eyes onto the
world as Joan had. With Mildred he had wanted to feel warmth
and comfort and protection. Most often he had wanted to stay
home with her and sink his head in her lap or against her
breasts, and to forget all the world that was outside their
home. But with Joan it was different; he wanted to go out
with her, hand in hand, exploring the world. He thought that
Joan was the genuine love of his life.

IV

Joan was pliant with Lester. She almost always conceded
to his wishes. She catered to his moods or caressingly tried to
change them. She rarely opposed her own wishes and desires to
his. At times she would sit for long periods listening while he
practiced. She sought out little chores she could perform for
him. And at first he responded to this treatment. In his own
eyes he seemed utterly different from what he had been before
meeting Joan.

During these first months, Lester constantly told himself
that Joan was better, sweeter, more simple than Mildred. And
yet he also had doubts. At odd moments he would become
vaguely uneasy. An atmosphere of chill, like a cold wind that
rises to destroy the warm effects of the sun on an April day,
sometimes swept over him. These moods were like warning
signals, but Lester didn't heed them. He repressed and dis-

missed them, reassuring himself about his new-found happiness.

One mild evening, after leaving Joan, he took a long walk over to the Right Bank. He drifted along the deserted boulevards, seeking some thought lost in himself. And as he prowled and strolled the streets, he grew afraid of himself. His old sense of alienation returned. In this mood of loneliness he began to fear his happiness with Joan couldn't last. He tried to reason with himself. Happiness was not a state of utopianism, of perfection. Just as a healthy man had moments of pain and even of weakness, so did a happy man know periods when he would feel low and depressed. But this reasoning did not calm him. It did not dissipate his apprehension. Then he started to doubt that he had the right to be as happy as he was with Joan.

Following this night, these moods and thoughts would often recur after he had said good night to Joan. Lester also thought frequently of Mildred. He would often compare Paris time with New York time to guess what she might be doing at various moments. And he'd guess what her reactions would be about Joan and him if she should ever hear of his new life. He imagine returning to America with Joan as his wife, and arranging a meeting between Joan and Mildred. He'd be well on his way to fame as a pianist. He'd be most gracious toward Mildred, but nonetheless he would make her clearly understand that he was not broken because she'd rejected him. And Joan's sweetness would hurt Mildred. But all this seemed silly to him and only disturbed him.

One day Lester impulsively wrote a long letter to a mutual friend of his and Mildred's, describing Joan and his own feelings toward her, and hoping his friend would show the letter to Mildred. Then he carried the letter around in his pocket for three days, ashamed, fearing he'd only make a fool of himself if he were to mail it. Then, one morning, he impulsively mailed the letter.

That evening, he and Joan went to a small restaurant off the Boulevard Saint-Michel which they especially liked. It had been one of their discoveries. A number of students patronized it, and they were usually spirited, gay, and noisy. The waiters were White Russians. Joan believed one of them had been a Russian nobleman before the Russian Revolution. He was a tall, blond man who spoke in a gentle voice. It was exciting to be served by him; they felt as if they were achieving some special contact with history when this exiled Russian waited on them.

But during the meal Lester was glum. A group of gay students was sitting next to them. Lester listened to the students with envy. They were young, and he imagined them full of the hopes of youth. And now he felt hopeless. He had never known the gaiety of these students. He never would know it. He scarcely spoke. He was almost overcome with an intense longing for Mildred. It seemed to him that he had really been in love with Mildred all during these recent weeks when he had been carrying on this love affair with Joan. He respected Joan. She was a girl of genuine goodness. But he wanted Mildred. He still loved Mildred. He would always love Mildred. He was incapable of loving anyone but Mildred.

Joan perceived that Lester was troubled. She wanted to say or do something to comfort him. She even guessed what it was that troubled him, and for the first time she began to wonder about her relationship with Lester. Perhaps it couldn't be a permanent one. But she did not dwell on this. Rather, she tried to cheer up Lester. But Lester listened with a tired smile on his face. His thoughts wandered. He was fatigued by his own emotions.

After dinner, they went to Joan's hotel. Lester kissed and hugged her fiercely in an effort really to love her, to forget Mildred. But while he kissed and petted her, he imagined, against his will, that she was Mildred.

v

Joan realized there was something wrong between Lester and herself, and his moodiness began to affect her. She often blamed herself, wondering if there were anything about her that was inadequate. She believed she was deeply in love with Lester, and that he, in spite of his unhappiness, loved and needed her. And she needed him. On those rare days when she didn't see him, she fretted. She was beginning to neglect her studies. Her life was narrowing down to a concentration of feeling and attention upon Lester. She began to dread the possibility that he might reject her. She began to fear that she was losing him. She gradually grew jealous of Mildred. Now and then she would even wish Lester had never known Mildred, and she'd think Lester had come to her only after he had loved and lost another girl. She also began to compare herself unfavorably with Mildred. Unlike Mildred, she did not have an artistic temperament. She could not look forward to a career of fame. Perhaps she wasn't as passionate as Mildred. Perhaps there was something lacking in her.

Joan tried to control herself, to maintain a sweetness and evenness of disposition. But she paid for this effort. She began to brood, and she became forgetful. She was less attentive to others. She skipped classes at the Sorbonne, and when she did attend, her thoughts would often wander, and she would hear almost nothing of the lectures. Lester's attitudes began to act on her like an infection. She wondered if there were not some inescapable sadness in love. Perhaps she and Lester would become the tragic victims of this sadness.

And it was becoming increasingly difficult to talk to him. They were uncomfortable with each other. Joan lost her sense of what to say to Lester, and of how to treat him. She usually blamed herself for this, and she began to ask herself if there were not something wrong with her. If he were unhappy, wasn't this her fault? For the first time in her life, she began to regard living as being really sad.

All winter they had been waiting for the spring to come. As February and March wore away, they became increasingly eager, hoping that the coming of spring would somehow magically restore their love and return them to their first feelings toward each other. They knew how shining and glowing Paris would be, and they continually talked of the coming

spring. And then, when spring came, they were still ill at ease
with each other. They took many walks. They strolled in the
Tuileries, and in the Jardin de Luxembourg. One morning
they crossed over to the Right Bank and sat holding hands and
looking wistfully about in the Parc Monceau. The charm and
orderliness of this little park touched them both. They saw in it
a symbol of their lost happiness. They wanted to cry. Why
couldn't they find and hold onto their happiness here in Paris
in the springtime? In this park, in the other parks, and on the
lively Parisian streets, they could find such a wonderful back-
ground for romance. As they sat holding hands in the Parc
Monceau, looking at so much fresh and wonderful greenness,
seeing two small French children play in a quiet manner,
watching a young French couple gaze passionately into each
other's eyes, they were like bewildered children. There was an
irksome dissatisfaction in them both.

They left the park, walking slowly, not talking. They knew
their love affair was over, but they were afraid to admit this,
even to themselves.

VI

Lester began to think of death, even to wish that the time
for his own death had come. One day he watched a funeral
cortege pass on the Rue des Rennes. The casket was in a black
carriage, draped in black, and drawn by two fine, big brown
horses that were also draped in funereal black. The horses
moved slowly, and men and women walked behind the hearse
in a slow, solemn procession. Men on the sidewalk took off their
hats. Lester did likewise. Such sights were common in Paris.
But before this time he had never really noticed them. He had
forgotten about death for a while in Paris. Now he was conscious of it again.

He walked on, filled with a strange sense of the hollowness
of life. And the trees were so green. The chestnut trees were
glorious. All Paris was green now, so green. He had never in
his life seen a greenness quite like this greenness of Paris in the

springtime. The leaves on the chestnut trees were young and fragile; their color was both light and rich. The color was like the music he dreamed of playing. And people on the streets seemed so happy. There was so much strange and yet familiar life going on. The life of the present and of the past, symbolized in the old buildings and in the cathedrals, was so grand and so tragically full. There was bustle and movement on the streets of Paris, with the rumble of busses, the clutter of tramways, the honking taxicab horns. And the people. On the streets and in the cafés, they gave him the impression they were at home in this city, and that they were never troubled with the feeling that they didn't belong anywhere. He envied them. Life seemed so rich for others but so hollow for him.

That same day he went to the Louvre. He was overwhelmed by the sheer number of the paintings. He left and found a chair in the Tuileries, paying an old woman for it. In the sunlight the green was almost blinding. An old woman in black sat opposite him, contentedly knitting. On his right another old woman was watching a little boy of about three, who half stumbled near her chair. Two lovers passed, pausing in front of him for a passionate kiss. The old woman watched the lovers and cackled. He envied the French boy and girl. They were knowing and feeling something he had never known and never could know. He imagined there was some quality of experience and pleasure in the love and kisses of the young French couple that there had never been in even his most passionate moments with Mildred and Joan. He asked himself if he were incapable of love. Restless, he got up and went to wander in the cemetery of Père-Lachaise. But for some unknown reason he was afraid to go near the tomb of Héloïse and Abélard.

Lester became increasingly nostalgic for the past. He slipped into recurrent moods of homesickness. Even though he spoke French, he did not feel he knew the French people or that he could ever know them. He saw that most of his relationships in France were superficial, and he realized that he was just marking time. It now seemed to him that he was living on an island and that he was suspended in time. The past was unreal to him, and the future was unclear, lost in clouds and fog. He was drifting. He had lost all sense of purpose in life, all ambition. Again the beauty of Paris was lost to him, and it was once more a cold beauty, removed from his own life. He began frequently and with feeling to quote a line of Baudelaire to himself:

Le froid majesté de la femme sterile.

This line seemed to express all his own hurt feelings. And it served as a means of describing how he now felt about Paris. Often, when he thought about the city, he would tell himself that Paris was beautiful only if one were in love, and if, in addition, one were loved. And then he would berate himself with the question—why wasn't he able to be in love? He knew, however, that he was in love with Mildred. He tried to convince himself that if he and Mildred had come to Paris together immediately after their marriage it would all have turned out differently. He knew this was not true, but he didn't want to face intimate truths about himself. And he was often ashamed of his own thoughts and feelings. Still, he persisted in them. And he persisted, against his will, in brooding about his broken marriage.

At the same time, Lester began to pity Joan. He felt guilty because she loved him, and he feared he might even be wrecking her life. He became deferential to her, and, at times, even apologetic. And she was becoming increasingly bewildered. She was more bewildered than hurt. She was not given to analysis and did not articulate many of her feelings or impressions, even to herself. But her impressions and her sense of people and situations were clear. She knew what was troubling Lester, but when she tried to lift his spirits she failed. Then one morning she woke up with the realization that she was not really in love with him. And she knew that when their relationship was broken up, the wound would not be deep. She liked Lester; she sympathized with him; she was glad she had met him; she did not regret having done what she had, but she did not love him. And when she told herself all this, she felt strange. It was strange to her that she could sit in bed in her nightgown and see the spring sun through her hotel window and think of her first love affair in this way. She had been with Lester last night. Afterward she had felt good. She had been calm and had softly hummed as she had fallen asleep. And now she had waked up and had discovered just what she felt about Lester. It shouldn't be this way. A girl—but was she still a girl or was she now a woman?—should not think so coldly, so reasonably, about her lover. And this was not the way love should be, was it? One should love with wild, romantic passion, and then, if love ended, one should be hurt, and sad, and tormented. But she wasn't. Lester was tormented, but not because of her. Shouldn't she at least be angry or jealous? Or, at any rate, shouldn't she pretend she was? What would Lester think of her?

Her pretty round face became very thoughtful. She asked herself:

—What does he think of me?

She wasn't certain she could answer the question. And as the thoughtful expression remained on her face, she wondered if she would or could ever know what he thought of her. She was seeing Lester again tonight. But if she didn't see him, she knew she wouldn't be disappointed. She wouldn't suffer. She had given all of herself to Lester, and now she knew that he couldn't hurt her, hurt her as his wife had hurt him.

She remained in bed because she was so comfortable lying there and seeing the sun flood through the window. It was going to be another beautiful day. And she loved these spring days in Paris. Besides, she seemed to gain some satisfaction by lying here and thinking about herself and Lester and Mildred.

Mildred? Did Mildred know about her? What was Mildred really like? Joan smiled. If she were a different kind of girl, she would have become angry when Lester had talked about Mildred. Some girls would be insulted. Lester thought more of Mildred than he did of her. He thought Mildred was more beautiful than she was. He looked on Mildred as an artist, but he didn't think she was even particularly smart or that there

was anything special about her. She knew that was the way
he felt about her, and yet she wasn't hurt. She didn't want
to be anybody but herself. She wouldn't want to be Mildred.
And she knew she was pretty and attractive and did not have
to think about this. In fact, she never gave a great deal of
thought to herself. Lester thought about himself much more
than she did about herself. She was different from Lester, and,
she guessed, different from Mildred.

But Mildred! She felt that there was a common bond between Mildred and herself. Even if Mildred were more beautiful than she, and gifted in a way that she wasn't, Mildred
must still be a woman. And Lester? He was a boy, and so
moody and introspective that at times you just didn't know
what to say to him, because you were just about certain that
no matter what you did say, it would do no good. He would
be hurt and sad anyway, and you just couldn't take away
his sadness. She realized now that she had been living under
a burden, and suddenly the burden was lifted. She had waked
up more free than when she had gone to bed. A weight had
been lifted from her.

But still, she wondered, what about Lester? Her face puck-
ered up. How would he take it if she were to tell him what
she had been thinking about this morning? But, then, he
didn't love her. Poor boy, he had really loved her, but she
guessed he didn't know how to love. But wasn't that a queer
thought?

Joan got out of bed and began to dress. She knew that today
at the Sorbonne she would pay close attention to the lectures.

VII

When Lester kissed her on the street, she remembered her
thoughts of the morning. She didn't want to be kissed. She
told him she didn't want to go with him. He was taken aback
and asked her why. She didn't reason with him or explain.
She merely told him that she didn't want to. He stared at her,

speechless, looking very troubled. He then asked her what he had done. Joan smiled sweetly. She felt so much older than Lester. She told him he knew. Their eyes met in an instant of recognition. And because of that look in his eyes she knew with even greater certainty that she was right. His expression told her how correct she was. But then he became silent and dejected. They walked along the Boulevard Saint-Germain, silent. Several times Lester started to talk but halted. They walked on toward the Seine.

They stopped on the Pont Royal and looked down at the dark waters. Lester thought of plunging in and imagined that the waters would be icy. But he knew this was merely a daydream and that he wouldn't do it. He knew what he would do. He knew that he was going back to Mildred. She might not take him, but he was going back. There was nothing else for him to do.

Hesitantly, he told Joan that he might have to go to America. He waited for her reaction. She showed no surprise. Then he asked her if she thought he ought to go back. She answered that he ought to decide for himself. He asked her to tell him what she thought. Tenderly, she took his head in her hands and kissed him on the forehead, maternally. Lester was relieved instantly. He confessed to her that he had written to Mildred and asked to be taken back, and he believed she wanted him to come. He asked Joan to forgive him. She said there was nothing to be forgiven for. He told her that he suddenly wanted to play. She went with him and sat listening while he played. The music stirred and saddened her, and she thought him handsome and gentle as he sat at the piano. It was sad, very sad, that he couldn't love her and that she couldn't love him. For a moment she was on the verge of tears. And then she was smiling, and her mood of the morning returned.

Lester finished playing and took her to her hotel. She kissed him for the last time and went up to bed. Lester turned and walked deserted streets, thinking of Mildred.

Two weeks later, he received a letter from her, telling him to come back to New York. He booked passage immediately. And Joan had almost vanished from his memory. When he bade her farewell at the Gare Saint-Lazare, it was as though he were speaking to a stranger.

Milly and the Porker

"ADAM 'N EVE on a raft. Wreck 'em . . . an' a Combina-shun!" Milly, the shapely waitress, shouted in a coarse voice.

She crossed the crowded restaurant on West Madison Street, carrying a stack of dirty dishes. Almost all the customers were men, and many of them watched her with eyes of desire.

Jack "Porky" Mulroy, Billy O'Brien, Mike Mulroney, Jim McHeegan, and Gunner Carlson, all route inspectors at the Continental Express Company, sat together at one table watching Milly cross the restaurant. Porky, a fat man, said:

"You know, fellows, Milly's a gal who could sneeze down my lungs every day in the week." He nervously ran a pudgy hand over his shortly clipped hair and took a wolfish bite of his ham sandwich. "Fellows, a girl with a toilet like Milly's could sneeze right down my lungs whenever she damned well wanted to. Say, listen, if you ask me, why, even the sweat off the feet of a girl like that is perfume . . . good French perfume, at that."

"Listen, Porky, if I'd tell Flo what you just said, she'd brain you with a rollin' pin when you squeezed through the door-way tonight," Billy O'Brien said.

"I wear the pants in my house," Porky said in a husky, un-convincing tone of voice.

"Crap!" sneered Mike Mulroney, looking up from his pork chop.

Billy O'Brien laughed merrily.

Mike eyed Milly closely as she passed near him, carrying several orders.

"But, anyway, Billy boy, don't you think that Milly could keep a sailor from freezin' on a cold and wintry night in the month of January?" Porky asked conciliatingly.

"I'm a respectable married man," Billy answered.

"But, no kiddin', Billy boy, what do you think of her?" Porky asked, his voice and face both hangdog.

Billy concentrated on his veal cutlet. Porky finished his ham sandwich, drank the last of his coffee, and then nervously began to chew his fingernails. His soiled shirt cuff showed when he lifted his arm. He rubbed his broad, ruddy face and then fingered his shirt collar. His finger caught in a rip of the shirt near the collar, and there was a tearing noise.

"My wife sews my shirts. And she washes them, too," Porky said. Mike and Billy laughed at him.

Porky looked hurt but said nothing.

"Listen, Porky, you're too goddamned fat to get in the saddle with a jane like Milly," Mike said cruelly.

"Yeah!" Porky exclaimed, his face reddening.

"I had a heavy load of deliveries today," Gunner Carlson said as he stabbed the last piece of his pork chop.

Billy O'Brien threw his hands up in a despairing, get-away-with-that-stuff gesture.

"Say, Bad News," Billy said. "This is feedin' time, and now work will ruin my digestion, play hell with my liver, and give me a big ache in the bowels. So, please!"

"Well, all I wanted to say was that I had a tough morning of it," Gunner said.

Porky chewed his fingernails again and followed Milly out of the corner of his eye as she was serving coffee to a customer. He noticed that she bent down, and he told himself that if she bent over near his table he could see her breastworks.

"Say, Gunner, what did you give that Call Department gascar you got for mornin' deliveries this mornin'?" asked Jim McHeegan after he finished eating his roast beef.

"That Wiesenberg car? I had to sock it heavy . . ." Gunner answered.

"Listen, Gunner, you better be careful or McGinty is liable

to lose his temper and hang one on you," kidded Billy O'Brien.

"McGinty," Porky sneered, "why, that overblown, balloon-bellied sonofabitch couldn't hit the blind side of a barn with a sling shot. Say, if he ever got in a fight with anybody at all, he wouldn't have the chances of a fart in a windstorm."

Porky's face reddened and began to bulge.

"Listen, Porky, the big Gas-house has your number. I gotta say that much for him," Billy O'Brien said.

"That barrel, uh. . . ." growled Porky.

"Never mind blowin' off. You know goddamn well he's got your number. He may be nothin' but a measly foul ball, but he's got your number," said Billy.

"Well, who ever told you that fairytale?" Porky blusteringly asked.

"Why, everybody knows it. Mac's told everybody in the company how he's always been able to buffalo you," Mike exclaimed.

"He buffaloes me? He buffaloes me? HE BUFFALOES ME? When? How? Where? HE BUFFALOES ME?" said Porky, who, while he talked loudly, alternated between pounding the table and chewing his fingernails.

"Save the dishes," said McHeegan, and they laughed.

"Porky, he's got the jinx sign on you, the same way Eddie Cicotte had a jinx sign on Babe Ruth," said Mike.

Porky raved until Milly paused by their table, and, stooping over so Mike could see her breasts, asked what they had fed Mr. Mulroy.

"Milly, they been tryin' to tell me that that big fathead McGinty has me buffaloed," Porky said, as he looked at her, confident that she would give him moral support.

"Why, I always thought that Mr. Mulroy and Mr. McGinty sat on each other's laps," Milly said.

They guffawed. Porky reddened and looked even more hangdog than before.

Milly took their orders for dessert. Porky didn't order. Mike watched Milly closely. Then she walked away from their table. They all continued to watch her.

"Say, Jim, where are you going on your vacation?" Billy O'Brien asked Jim McHeegan.

Before McHeegan answered, Milly came over again. They could smell the stale perfume on her as she stood near, smiling professionally. She asked Porky a second time whether he wanted any dessert.

"Mr. Mulroy is reducin'," Billy answered for Porky.

Porky smiled like a confused schoolboy.

Milly scrutinized him and said:

"Why, Mr. Mulroy isn't so fat."

"No! You ought to see the baby elephant at Lincoln Park Zoo. . . . Ha! Ha!" exploded Mike Mulroney.

They laughed. Milly smiled, winking at Mike.

"Milly, these guys think they're kidders, but they can't get my goat," Porky said.

"No, Milly, his goat smells too bad to get and keep," said Billy, and they exploded with more laughter.

"Naughty?" said Milly, giving them an inviting smile.

"Say, Milly, I'll take some java," Porky said to change the course of conversation.

"Don't break yourself," Mike said.

Milly left again. They looked after her. Then Jim McHeegan said:

"You was talkin' about vacations, wasn't yuh, Billy?"

"Yeh, Jim."

"Well, I been thinkin' of goin' up to Madison, Wisconsin. Got a cousin up there, and I might as well go up there. He's been askin' me to go for the last five years, so I decided maybe we'll hike up that way this year. It'll save us a little jack, and with that savin' and that back pay we're gettin' in October, I'll be able to get a little ahead of the game."

Looking wistful, his sad eyes belying his boastful words and rough, hearty expression, Porky said:

"Hell, you know, I don't go for this goin' away on vacations. That's why I stayed right at home and put my feet on a box on the back porch and read my *Whizz Bangs* and cowboy stories. I got a book at the library about a guy named Hopalong Cassidy, and, say, he was a two-gun man that makes Bill Hart, Tom Mix, and Bronco Billy look like they was minor leaguers. No, fellows, this goin'-away business ain't for little Jack Mulroy."

Milly returned and set the desserts and coffee down before them. Each cup of coffee had some of its brownish contents spilled sloppily onto the saucers. As Milly bent down, they could see the line of her fulsome breasts again.

"You know, it takes money to live," Jim McHeegan said after Milly had left again. "Things are damn dear. If a fellow wants to live in any kind of decent place at all—you know, a quiet homelike place, one on a nice, quiet, decent street, like the one I live on in Lake View, the kind of a neighborhood where you can bring your kids up and know that they are in a wholesome atmosphere and that they breathe good air and play with kids who aren't goin' to be future murderers or anything like that—well, it takes all the kick out of a guy's kick. It means you gotta shell out a tidy sum for your rent. And then there's all the other livin' expenses a family man has to carry— the kids at school, shoemakers' bills, my lunches, carfare, and cigarette money, insurance, clothes. . . . Me and my wife, well, we have never let a pay day go by since we been married that we didn't put something by for a rainy day, even if it was only fifty cents or a dollar. Yes, fellows, I ain't cryin' at all that we get that back pay next October. It's gonna mean a lot to guys like us."

"Brother, jus' wait till I get my back pay," Porky bragged.

"Say, listen, Porky!" Billy said, "If you ever dared to open your pay envelope, Flo would break every dish in your house on that coconut of yours . . ."

"Yeah! Well, that's all you know about it. Lemme tell you . . ."

Porky was ignored. Jim McHeegan said:

"That back pay is like rain to a farmer in a drought area. You know, it's damn expensive if you try to live at all decently these days."

"Brother, you tell 'em, I stutter. But there just ain't nothin' about the high cost of livin' that Billy O'Brien ain't familiar with, first hand."

"Me, too," chimed in Porky self-consciously.

Nervous under their critical gaze, he chewed his finger-nails and rubbed them on the shiny sleeve of his worn, blue serge coat. He gulped the last of his second cup of coffee. He got up, picked up the punched check Milly had left at the side of his cup, and said he had to leave. Billy got up and said he was going, too, because he had to see Leonard, his boss. Gunner then rose and left the restaurant.

Mike Mulroney and Jim McHeegan lit cigars and leaned back in their chairs. Mike opened his vest, loosened his belt a notch, and said: "Jim, I wouldn't want to be that poor sonofa-bitch Mulroy."

"No, just think, the poor sonofabitch has to carry all that fat around with him," Jim answered. "And he takes kiddin' aw-fully to heart when anyone tells him what a fathead he is. He gets sore as blazes, and you can see that it hurts his feelings like it hurts a woman's feelings to tell her she's getting wrinkles. But, hell, a guy can't resist, because, after all, he's so fat he's funny, and he has got a belly like a German zeppelin."

"He's the world's biggest chump," said Mike.

"Well, the poor bastard must be gettin' it in the neck from his old lady," McHeegan exclaimed philosophically, his voice betraying sympathy for Porky.

"That's why he's so noisy at work and acts so hard boiled with his drivers. They all hate his guts. You know, the way he bawls them out, it's a shame, and I don't see how he ever gets any work out of them. And you watch, one of these days a driver is goin' to jump down off the wagon and punch him full of holes, and he'll have it comin' to him, too," said Mike with a complacent laugh.

"What's his wife like?"

"Flo—she's just like a cow, only worse. She's fatter than he is. She's almost big enough to get a job in a freak show. She looks something like three or four beer barrels if they were tied together, with a piece of calico skirt draped over them."

Mike haw-hawed.

"And she's always pullin' that cute little baby-doll stunt on him, and he, the poor jackass, falls for it. She's got him thinkin' she's weak and sick and nervous, and, you know, some days the poor bastard comes down to work so worried about her that he can't keep his noodle on what's doin'. And, I tell you, she's just one of these skirts that's no goddamn good."

Mike haw-hawed again.

"And, Jim, she makes him bring her her breakfast in bed on Sunday mornin's, and she lays in bed half the mornin', eatin' chocolates and readin' cheap goddamn love stories in magazines about tall, nice young men who save the cherries of poor girls from the villain with a mustache. Goddamn it, nearly every mornin' she's sick or faint. Imagine an elephant as big as she is, faint. She certainly gives that bastard a grand joyride, but he's damn fool enough to take it all and not even whimper. He can't say boo around her. And, say, you know if that poor bastard ever opened his pay envelope, Christ, she'd throw so many fits that they'd both die of apoplexy, and she'd try and get him put in Alimony Row for nonsupport. I tell you, Jim, that fat cow makes that poor sonofabitch Mulroy lead one hell of a dog's life."

They laughed.

"You know, she sometimes even makes him wash her drawers. One day two years back, when him and me both had our vacation the same ten days, I dropped out to see him, and I found him in the kitchen with an apron on, washin' her dirty underdrawers, and, lemme tell you, they were like dirty rags," Mike said.

They laughed again.

"You know, I'd like to peep through the keyhole and see 'em in the saddle," McHeegan then said.

"She makes him sleep on the cot by himself. That's why he's always chewing his fingernails. You know, I think he still uses his hands," Mike said, and he haw-hawed merrily.

"Well, it's time to be going up to the Department," Jim
said, getting up.

They put tips down, Mike leaving a quarter, and Jim a
dime. He lagged behind a moment and talked with Milly.
He joined Jim outside and said boastfully:

"I dated her up. Wait till I tell that to the Pork."

Walking along West Madison Street with Billy O'Brien,
Porky was quiet. They passed some bums, and Billy said:

"Look at them bastards. They don't work. They don't seem
like men."

"Maybe they're happy," Porky said sadly.

Billy looked at Porky, perplexed, but said nothing. They
walked on for a while without speaking, and then Porky
started talking in a sincere, nervous, and self-pitying tone of
voice.

"Jesus Christ, Billy boy, I feel like hell. Jesus Christ, Billy,
you don't know what I go through with my wife. Of course,
I know she's got a nervous disposition, and she hasn't been
well, but, Jesus Christ, you don't know what I go through.
You know, Billy boy, I don't know what to do. I can't go
on like this. Christ, ever since I been married, I had that
damn brother-in-law and mother-in-law of mine on my neck.
You know, that isn't right, and a man can't go on supporting
them like that year in and year out. Christ, with them in
there, my house isn't my own. I'm not even treated as well as
if I was a boarder. Why, Flo never even has my supper ready
for me when I come home from a hard day's work. She's always sick or something so that I never get a decent meal, and
she's nervous, you know how it is. But do you think that
damn mother of hers would give a helping hand? Not on your
life. Not that bitch! Why, she just went and planked her big
ass down in my house, and she's kept it there. And that no-
good brother-in-law of mine, say, he's worn out five fannies
just sitting. That mother of Flo's, do you know she's so
goddamn lazy that she never moves anything but her tongue.
And all of them, they been living off me ever since I married
Flo."

"Why don't you throw 'em out and then give Flo a punch in the teeth?"

Porky looked at Billy in fright.

"But, Christ, Billy, I couldn't do that. Why, I don't know what Flo would say to me. Honest to Jesus, Billy, I don't wear the pants in my household any more. I don't even ever get a decently cooked meal. And I only get a hunk of tail once a month, and sometimes she doesn't even want to give it to me then. And that lousy bitch of a mother of hers is always there rapping me behind my back and putting things in Flo's head that don't belong there. You know, I think that Flo would be all right if she wasn't so easily influenced by her mother. But she insists that she has to have her mother there because she's nervous. Nervous, my ass hole! But, honest, Billy, I don't know what to do. And then, too, Billy boy, that mother-in-law is always trying to work up that son of hers who never did an honest day's work in his life to fight me. For the sake of peace in the family, you know how it is, I don't do nothing to him. But if he ever gets tough, why, if that rat ever gets tough, I'll paste that goddamn mush of his all over the sidewalk. I ain't afraid of him."

"Kick them all in their teeth," said Billy.

"You know, Billy, a man goes along trying to hold up his end of the game and plays ball square, and then he has to have all these difficulties bothering him. It ain't right, that's all. I can't hardly work any more with worry. Why, when I go home from work all fagged out, I can't get no rest or relaxation. They won't even let me read my newspaper in peace, with their goddamn jawing and fighting and nagging. And when they go to bed, if I want to stay up and read with everything quiet, I have to be running around getting things and carrying glasses of water to Flo and that damn bitch, and when I do finally get settled down to read, Flo starts yelling down from the bedroom that I ought to be in bed and not be wasting electricity. Billy, I just lead the life of a dog."

"Well, Mulroy, if I were you I'd give them all the go-by," said Billy.

"How can I?" Porky asked pathetically. "If I do, she'll hook me for alimony."

Porky suddenly frowned and was silent. Billy O'Brien whistled. Then Porky said:

"Billy boy, you're my friend, my pal, aren't you?"

"Of course I am."

"Then do me a favor. Please, please, Billy boy, don't tell them other Inspectors what I told you. They'd laugh at me."

"Hell, I've forgotten it already," Billy said, keeping a straight face but remembering how Porky had told others this same story. He wanted to laugh at Porky, but at the same time he felt sorry for him.

"Say, Milly's real stuff, ain't she?" Porky said.

"She's been well laid, you can see that," Billy said.

"I'd like to lay her—just once," Porky said.

They walked on. Porky thought that if he could only get some dame like Milly, just once, only once, maybe then he wouldn't care.

He chewed his fingernails nervously.

A Day at the Zoo

IRENE WAITED for Alex on a bench along a gravel path in Lincoln Park. When she saw him approaching in the distance, her pretty but tired face lit up. But as he came closer she noticed his slow gait and guessed he was dejected. She knew that he had failed again. She waited for him, sad. They embraced, and he kissed her almost fiercely.

"I'm sorry. But I know, dear, I know you'll find something very soon," Irene said, patting his hand.

"A man at the Consolidated told me to come back in two weeks. He said he couldn't promise me anything, but from the way he talked I'm sure there'll be a job for me there."

They slowly walked along the path. Her hand timidly found his. The day was muggy, but as they walked the sun made one of its fitful appearances, and the grass and the leaves of the trees shone brightly for a moment.

"I know from the way that man at the Consolidated talked that I'll get something there in the next couple of weeks," Alex said.

"My darling boy," she said, squeezing his hand.

The sun sank behind darkish clouds, and the park again deepened into a solid green that seemed even darker against the grayness of the day. They walked on, filling empty minutes with trivial words of affection and hope. After they had walked for a while, they sat on a bench and were silent. They looked absently through a frame of trees and up at the dark, low sky.

"I like it here," he said.

"I don't care even if you haven't got any job. I'm happy," she said with feeling.

"People sometimes get like that—happy, when there's no reason to," he said cynically.

They kissed, and then they sat listening to the chirping of the many sparrows, and to the birds singing behind them in the trees. A bluebird hopped from under their bench and darted perkily and sleekly across the path. They watched it disappear around some bushes on the other side of the path.

"I wish we could go away and not have to worry about work, or just be alone in New York, or some other place, any place," she said, wistfully.

He wished so, too. He wished he could get a job. He looked at his shoes. They were old: the heels run down, the soles almost worn through.

"But I don't care. I love you, and I'm happy. I know that something will happen," she said.

The sun broke through the clouds again, dispelling shadows of the trees that had crossed their faces.

"It would be just wonderful to have a little money and go away and not be bothered by anything or anybody," she said.

"We never get over being bothered by something," he said.

"But if we could, I just wouldn't care. I wouldn't care what happened, and I wouldn't care if I had your baby then."

"Maybe you'd change your mind."

"I wouldn't," she said earnestly.

She asked him what name he wanted to give the baby, but he showed no interest in this. She pouted.

Pigeons were waddling about on the gravel and grass like corpulent, sloppy housewives until they suddenly would take off into short flights with a noisy flapping of wings. From the distance, they heard the joyful echoes of children playing. An odd-looking couple passed them, the woman's stomach swollen in pregnancy, her face large and coarse. The man was short and untidy, and his insignificant personality seemed concentrated in his small but cocky mustache. They were quarreling, and the man was telling her that what she needed was a good punch on the nose. She answered loudly that she would just like to see him laying as much as a little finger on her, and if he did, she would show him, and show him plenty. In reply, he seemed to attempt a complete expression of his strength of character in the single word, "Yeah!" They passed from hearing.

"We won't ever fight like that, will we?"

"No, darling."

"If we did, there wouldn't be any use of us going on."

He nodded his head and lit a cigarette. She began to cry.

"I don't want to swell and be ugly like her. I don't want to swell like that and have you not care for me any more."

He patted her, and she smiled.

"I don't care. I'm glad I'm going to have your baby," she said.

He grimly said that his luck would change and that he'd surely get a job. Then everything would be all right. And they'd get along and be able to take care of themselves and their baby.

An old woman, weighing no more than eighty or ninety pounds, limped along the path. Her skin was sallow and wrinkled, and she wore a tattered blue coat and an antique hat with ruined artificial flowers dangling from the brim.

"I'm never going to grow old like that," she said.

"Everybody grows old," he answered.

"I won't. We won't get old like that. And after I have your baby, I'll be thin again, and you'll have a job and be able to buy me some nice dresses," she said insistently.

He leaned toward her and kissed her.

A gray-haired man with a gray mustache and a patch over his right eye moved aimlessly by. His fat body seemed to have been sucked of its energy. A squirrel shied toward them, but, receiving no food, it skirted away and hopped up an oak tree.

"I love you," she said with a kind of hurt fierceness in her voice.

"I just feel I'm going to land something pretty good, soon. I feel it's stacked in the cards. Today I tried, but it was just a bad day. Every day can't be bad. There's a law of averages. Even if times are hard, I'll get something. I got to. And old Small hadn't any right laying me off. I always did my work for him. But maybe it was for the better, because this proposition at the Consolidated looks better than anything I had working for Small. I would have just rotted away there, anyway," he said.

"I know it, dear."

She brushed aside a tear and sang the chorus of a popular song. From a distance, they heard the hum of automobiles and the swish of their tires. These noises seemed like distractions from another world, a world where people struggled, fought, starved, died. For the present, they felt themselves away from that world. They smiled at each other. They heard a grinding of ungreased brakes, and she shuddered, and then there was no noise except the summer wind.

"Dear, we never had a honeymoon. I want to go away and have a honeymoon, away from everything," she said.

"Well, if I get this job at the Consolidated, and we are careful and save, maybe next year on my vacation, if I get one, we can go away for a few days."

"But I want to go away before that and have just *us*, and not our baby, and be happy just alone with you."

"It would be jake. . . . But, well, some day we will. I'm not dumb, and somebody will have to give me a job. This depression can't go on forever," he said.

"We wouldn't care about anything then because we'd be happy, wouldn't we?"

A nursemaid came by, dragging along a crying baby. A mother followed, and the child at her side was describing an Uncle Joe as a saphead. The mother slapped the child, and he bawled loudly.

"We won't raise our baby like that. She's horrid."

"Yeah," he said abstractedly.

"And on Sundays you'll take it out, and we'll have a carriage and you'll wheel it?"

He nodded.

"It's going to be part of *us*, and we'll be good to it, and you'll make the formula for its milk all the time?"

He said nothing. He kept looking at the people as they passed. She chattered on. Some boys carrying fishing poles went by. And clean little girls beside bored stout mothers or nursemaids. Old men hobbling and shouting political commonplaces into mutually deaf ears. Lonely-looking middle-aged men and women. Loud-talking, gesticulative foreigners. Louder Americans. They continued sitting. Then, growing oppressed and worried, she began to cry again. He looked away, clenching and unclenching his fists, tightening his lips, telling himself silently, that Jesus, Jesus Christ, something had to happen.

"Let's walk on," he suggested.

They wandered on toward the Lincoln Park Zoo. A husky young fellow with an opened shirt collar and a gaudy girl chewing gum passed them; as they went by, the girl was saying, "He's chump. Chump! He took me to the Kit Kat, and you know, Charlie, the sap spent ten bucks on me. He's chump. And then, comin' home, he thought he was going to get fresh with me, so I just pushed his hands away and looked at him, and I sez, 'Listen, whatchuh think I am? Huh?' I tol' him to keep his hands where they wouldn't get him into no trouble, because, Charlie, I'm true to you."

They walked slowly, passing an overdressed stout woman who cooed at the pigeons and fed them peanuts. Approaching the zoo, they got whiffs of manure and the odors of the animals. Their first sight at the zoo was of a white peacock with a long, magnificent fan. It crouched in the corner of a rectangular, sandy-floored outdoor cage, surrounded by a harem of three other peacocks. A child was feeding Cracker Jack to some other peacocks and a turkey in the cage, who squatted in its pride and disdained eating.

"We'll have to take our baby, when it's old enough, to see the peacock," she said as they moved along.

"Yes, and, you know, I was just thinking, I might go back and see Small. Maybe he can take me back in the fall if business picks up."

A flat-footed and tired mother walked by, her son pulling her forward like a healthy puppy straining at the leash. He was shouting for her to hurry so he could see the elephant.

"Our baby isn't going to grow up like that brat," she said.

"No," he said, but with no interest.

"Ours is going to be different."

"Some people don't train their kids right," he said.

They watched the bears, housed in an open cage, stone-walled on three sides, with iron spikes to prevent them from climbing out. The fourth side was barred, and they stood looking between the bars. A path, parallel to the one they had taken, and elevated on the other side of the cages, enabled people to look down at the animals. People there were watching a group of boys tease a grizzly bear. The boys made repeated motions to throw peanuts. The grizzly rose on its haunches and spun around, slowly waving its paws, waiting, begging. When the boys finally moved on, the grizzly circled the cage, moving at a slow but steady pace. Someone began throwing peanuts to him, and again he performed his trick of spinning around and waving his paws.

The odors were not too strong because of the open air and an increased wind that had sprung up from the nearby lake. Irene and Alex moved along the line of cages. In the last bear cage there were some polars. The cage was sprayed from a pipe that was elevated about seven feet. One of the polar bears was bathing. It walked backward through the spray of water, swaying its shoulders, setting its paws down flat-footedly on the stone floor. Then it lumbered forward with the same movements and repeated its walk backward through the spray. Its mate squatted and watched the people from above, waving its right paw every time it perceived anyone making the gesture of throwing it a peanut.

"Darling, let's feed it some peanuts," she said.

"We hadn't better waste any money. We only got about eight dollars to last us until I get a job."

"But it's so cute, the way it begs for peanuts."

"It has enough to eat."

"It would only be a nickel, and I know you'll get a job tomorrow."

They hurried to a nearby stand for peanuts, returned, and fed them to one of the polar bears. The other bear continued to walk backward through the spray until the monotonous repetition bored them. They moved on.

Catching a whiff of a different animal odor, they noticed some sleeping red foxes and a gray and graceful timber wolf running light-footedly about in a circle. Then they came to the domed, shaded cage where the alligators lazed in a dark green pool and on the cool, damp stone island in its center. Several boys were watching, excitedly betting pennies as to which of the alligators would move first.

They went to see the elephant. It was quartered in a barred and extensive stone square, and strong odors of straw, feed, and manure emanated from its cage. The elephant stood under an iron shed in a corner, tossing straw on its back, swinging its trunk evenly and rhythmically. They called, and it jogged toward the fence. They dropped peanuts outside the bars, and it gathered them in its trunk and swung two or three at a time into its mouth. When they began dropping empty shells, it turned away, jogged back under the iron shed, and again tossed straw over its back.

They walked on. The sun had reappeared. They moved by the red-brick structure that housed lions, and they heard a steady succession of roars. Opposite this building a lone seal was perched on a rocky elevation, crying out with such monotony that they became terror stricken.

They crossed a driveway and stood debating whether or not they should spend money for a bite to eat. She thought not, but he was impelled by a mood of sudden recklessness and insisted that he would get a good job any one of these days.

They entered the refectory and found seats by a window.

"It's nice here," she said.

He nodded. They lit cigarettes.

"But sometime we'll be old like the people in the park, and we'll die."

"Yes."

"We'll die and be buried in a coffin, and it'll be cold under the ground."

"I think that by fall things ought to be better, and Small might take me back if I don't get that Consolidated job. But I kind of feel I'll be getting that, or something better, in the next week or two. Something has got to be around the corner, something. I feel it in my bones. Today was just a bad day."

"Darling, if I die having your baby, you'll take care of it, and be good to it, and give it things?"

"Honey, please . . ."

"But you will. Tell me you will!" she persisted.

He nodded and then gazed out the window. He turned and watched an old man lifting a glass of Coca-Cola with a palsied hand.

"I know I'll get something," he said.

When they had finished eating, they got up, and he paid at the desk, regretting the money he had so foolishly wasted. He took her arm to cross the driveway and walk toward a park exit.

"I'll get something. You see if I don't. I'll get a better job, and everything is going to be all right."

"I know you will. I have faith in you," she said, turning aside to hide a sudden tear.

They left the park and took a streetcar back to their two-roomed apartment. He thought of the animals he'd seen at the zoo. He was as trapped as they were. He might as well be in a cage. He gritted his teeth. He told himself that, depression or not, he would fight on and not give up, and he'd land a job and work hard, for himself, for Irene, for their baby that was coming. He told himself that that was what you did if you were a man instead of a monkey in a cage. You just didn't give up, because, if you did, the whole world might just as well be a zoo. He squeezed her hand. She edged nearer to him in the crowded car. Yes, goddamn it, he wouldn't give up, because, goddamn it, he was going to be a man and not a monkey in a zoo.

He held her hand, hurt but coldly determined.

A Romantic Interlude
in the Life of Willie Collins

I

WILLIE COLLINS decided to go to the Happy Expressmen's
Club monthly dinner. After all, he was Chief Dispatcher in
the Wagon Call Department, and that was a very important
and responsible position, wasn't it? He should know important men in the Company, have personal contacts with them,
and he'd be able to do this by meeting them at the dinner.
Gas-House McGinty often went to these dinners, and once
that Big Windbag had even spoken at one of them. Wasn't he
a better man than McGinty?

After he got used to attending these affairs, he might even
give an instructive talk on how he picked up the special gascar freight that would make an impression on the bigwigs and
the high muckety-mucks of the Company.

Willie dressed up in his Sunday clothes for the affair and
put on a fire-sale broadcloth shirt he had just bought and
a recently purchased polka-dot jazzbo tie. Walking to
the hotel during the evening rush hour, he imagined how he
would impress the big shots, and then how he would lord it
over McGinty and the Route Inspectors as he had a right to.
McGinty would be there, but catch him eating at the same
table as Mac!

He laughed aloud, and passers-by gazed at him curiously,
but he didn't notice them.

Mac would probably spill soup on his vest. Mac was just the

kind of guy who would show off by trying to eat fancy. Well, he wouldn't pull none of that fancy stuff. He would just eat. He had a natural way of eating that was okay. He knew he had a natural refinement about himself that fellows like Mac tried to get by being fancy but couldn't. He didn't have to worry about them things. He laughed at how he'd tell the boys tomorrow about how Mac had spilled soup on his vest.

"Where's the Expressmen's meetin'?" asked Collins, blushing, trying to feel perfectly at ease as he faced a bellboy in the Shrifton Hotel.

"Blue Circle Room, sir," the bellboy replied.

"Huh?" asked Collins.

Collins asked again, very confused.

"Blue Circle Room, across the lobby and to your left, sir," the bellboy answered.

Collins strutted across the lobby and turned into the ornate Blue Circle Room; it was decorated in blue and gray. Long tables were ranged about it. A headwaiter bowed Willie in, asked him if he was at the officials' table, the speakers' table, or one of the other tables.

"I'm Chief Wagon Dispatcher," he said, thinking how far he had come along since the days when he'd been a boy out on the wagons. Yes, he was a self-made man.

He was ushered to a table in the center of the room. He saw McGinty at what he guessed to be a table for officials. Mac was wearing a new suit, and he looked as though he'd had the Jesus Christ barbered out of his face. McGinty was smiling at something said by the fellow next to him, a bald-headed man with a full face, with gray hair at the sides of his head. Mac, the dirty fourflusher!

"My name is Dowling, I'm over in the Main Office," a darkish, square-faced man next to him said.

"Mr. Dowling—oh, say, how do you do? I'm Mr. Collins, Chief Dispatcher up in the Wagon Department."

The two men shook hands.

"I do business with you all the time. I generally speak to one of the clerks, usually McGillicuddy or else to Mueller."

"Yeah," said Willie.

"Is this the first time you've come to one of our Happy Expressmen's meetings?" asked Dowling.

"Yeah, Mr. Dowling."

"We're trying to make their appeal broad. They're a fine thing for the Company, you know. It gets the men together, and the men in various departments, like you and I, can get to know each other."

"Yeah, sure, sure," Collins said.

He was thinking that he didn't have to take no odds off this fellow, and, also, he was wondering what he could say that would be big and impressive.

"I see that one of your confreres is here: McGinty," Dowling said.

"Oh, yeah, Mac."

"That tractor board system he runs—it's a marvelous idea."

"Yeah, it's a good idea," said Collins.

But what about his own work? McGinty, the fourflusher, stealing all the praise for himself. Where would McGinty be if he, the Chief, didn't go and get the freight? Where would he be? Huh? High and dry, that's where. McGinty only transferred freight. That came after the business of getting it picked up. Mac wasn't in the front-line trenches. He, Willie Collins, was a captain in the front-line trenches, and, then, this bastard Mac, stealing all the thunder.

"It's going to be a jolly dinner here tonight. They serve excellent food," said Dowling.

"Yeah, yeah, so I heard."

Collins fingered his menu. The waiter was serving now.

A fruit cocktail was laid in front of Collins. He looked up and down the table. He didn't know anybody, except those he had just met, Dowling, Scoggins, or Coggins, or Moggins, or something like that, from the Accounting Department, and Julius from the Lost and Found, who was sitting opposite him. He suddenly felt lost, timid. He wasn't sure how he should go about eating his fruit cocktail, served in a thin, low glass dish, something like a dish used for sundaes in ice-cream parlors.

There were several spoons, knives, and forks in front of him, and, observing the others take up spoons, he imitated them.

He ate cautiously. Well, these Main Office bastards didn't need to think he wouldn't know how to eat. He imitated them. There was desultory conversation.

"You guys think you can bowl," Julius flaunted.

"Yeah, well, wait until next week. Don't be so damn certain of yourselves just because you beat us once," a voice down the table flung back.

"You know, fellows," Julius said boisterously, "the Supply Department down there really thinks it's got some bowlers. I'll tell you somethin' funny about them. You know, we're afraid to bowl them, because it's so hard to get any nigger kid to set up. Them damn fools think the legs of a nigger kid is bowling pins, and they try to hit them instead of the real pins. I tell you, I'm afraid even to bowl with them guys. They're dangerous."

There were some laughs and smiles.

The dinner progressed. Consommé was brought to Collins. He had not been sure just what this would be, and while he waited he had been almost afraid of it, but when he discovered it was only soup, he was greatly relieved.

"At these meetings, everybody is like a happy family. You'll see as you get to coming to more of them, Mr. Collins," Dowling remarked.

Collins was beginning to like it, and to like the soup, too. Only that bastard McGinty, over at a table full of big shots, showing off, the goddamn Bag of Crap. Wait till tomorrow when he gave the fourflusher away.

II

The time for coffee and speeches had come. Mr. Barton, a Chief Clerk in the Main Office, and Secretary of the Happy Expressmen's Club, was chairman. He rose and floridly introduced Mr. Staley, a vice-president from another district, who was visiting Chicago, and Mr. Staley cleared his throat. He said in a booming voice:

"*Boys!*"

He paused. He cleared his throat again.

"*We, all of us, remember how the express service was mustered to the aid of the nation during the still recent Great War against the Kaiser, and we all, all of us who were then in the service, remember how each and every one of us did our bit. There was a lesson to be learned from that patriotic experience —the lesson of service. Service, I say. The express business is founded on service.*

"*Boys, it is not only founded on service. It has in back of it a tradition of service, a glorious tradition, which we of today must carry on, which we of today must make our contribution to.*

"*Boys, fellow expressmen, now realizing this, when I was asked to say a few words to you here this evening, I thought that I would remind you of a chapter in that glorious tradition of service which has been carried down and bequeathed to us, the expressmen of today.*

"*I thought I would tell you of one of the most glorious and inspiring chapters in the noble history of the express business in the building of this greatest and grandest of all nations on earth, and I bar none, when I make that statement.*

"*I thought that if I took this chapter in the history of the express business, and reminded you of it, it would serve to inspire you in your daily work, just as it inspires me. I know, friends and fellow expressmen, when things get blackest for me, and when difficulties look like they are insurmountable, I draw my inspiration from such chapters of express history as the one I will tell you all about. I think of the pony express, and I realize that my own difficulties are not even the proverbial drop in the bucket compared with the difficulties that were met and overcome by those who served in the pony express.*

"*Now, you all heard of the pony express. It existed for only sixteen short and exciting months, and then it was supplanted by the transcontinental telegraph. Yet it was of tremendous importance in sewing together the East and the West at a dark time of Civil War, when this nation was fighting to justify and achieve the motto of that great, that greatest of presidents, that noblest of martyrs, the Great Emancipator himself, who had so wisely said: 'The Union must be preserved.'*

"During the Civil War, and just prior to that calamitous struggle, there was some Confederate sympathy in California. The majority of Californians were loyal to the Union, however, but there was an active minority strongly in favor and strongly determined to sever California from the Union. Communications were bad, and some means of communication was needed to bring California closer to the East. The pony express was that means, and the messages, swiftly conveyed to California, by the pony express, played no small part in saving California for the Union Cause. To us, a nine-day trip to the coast seems no wonder. But in those days, by reducing the distance to nine or ten days, as the pony express did, was a veritable miracle, a thing as truly astounding and miraculous to the people of those times as the new radio of these last few years is to us now.

"And in order to achieve this, much greater hardship was demanded of those involved than any of us need face nowadays. The pony express rider was a hero, a brave man. If he wasn't, he never could have made the contribution he did to our great nation. And he was served by that faithful animal, that even still serves us somewhat in the express business today, the horse; although in five or ten years we will have practically all or nearly all of our service motorized, and the faithful horse, having done his noblest bit, will be given a vacation, so to speak. For although the pony express was so called, it was not merely ponies that were used but also horses.

"The pony express was established by the firm of Russell, Majors, and Waddell, a firm long known for honesty and integrity, and it was a success only through their courage, honesty, and farsightedness. But they never made money out of it. In fact, they suffered a loss of about two hundred thousand dollars, but they were patriotic businessmen, and that loss was

nothing in comparison with the service they knew they were rendering to the nation. It cost these gentlemen one hundred thousand dollars a month to maintain it, not to mention the additional cost of fighting Indians. They bought the best horses that money could buy, and they figured on relays every twelve or so miles. They hired eighty drivers and kept the pony express going at all hazards.

"But I know that you men are not as much interested in the details of the organization of the pony express as you are in the thrill, the romance, the color, the adventurous aspects of this venture. For the pony express was an adventure.

"It was inaugurated on April 3, 1860. On that day, a great crowd was assembled in the streets of St. Joseph, Missouri; flags were flying, and there was a jubilant brass band. The Hannibal and St. Joseph Railroad special train rumbled into the station, on time, with mails from connecting points eastward. Mail pouches were rushed to the post office, and the express mail was arranged. The people crowded and surged and milled around the old Pikes Peak Livery Stables, hushed and subdued and expectant. The moment of departure is at hand. The doors open. A spirited horse is brought out. A wiry little man, Johnnie Frey, who is barely twenty years old, inspects the horse. There is a pause, and in the distance a cannon booms, giving the signal. The rider is off and at the post office in about a minute. The pouches are thrown over the saddle, and he is off again, soon reaching the wharf at the Missouri River, where a steaming ferry awaits him. The horse thunders onto the boat, and off at the other side, and is away, started on the first leg of this journey over boundless America, a journey over mountains and deserts, a journey of two thousand miles, which clips ten days off the old mail distances and forms a closer tie between the East and West.

"In all, there were about eighty drivers kept employed by Russell, Majors, and Waddell in the pony express. These were all men of tested nerve and courage, men who could ride and who were brave and fearless. They were paid from fifty to one hundred and fifty dollars a month, the highest salaries paid

outside of the supervision. On entering the service of the Central Overland California and Pikes Peak Express Company, they were compelled to take this oath of fidelity:

" 'I, John Doe, do hereby swear, before the Great and Living God, that during my engagement, and while I am an employee of Russell, Majors, and Waddell, I will under no circumstances use profane language; that I will drink no intoxicating liquors; that I will not quarrel or fight with any other employee of the firm, and that in every respect I will conduct myself honestly, be faithful in my duties, and so direct all my acts as to win the confidence of my employers.'

"It's not as bad as that now in the Continental. Of course, every pony express driver didn't fulfill and keep the letter of this oath. They were no saints. They were rough and ready men, who wouldn't be judged religious by the standards which some of us hold. They were men of the West, hardy and rough and tough, and some of them were bad men, too. But they were faithful. They traveled hundreds of thousands of miles, fighting aaginst storms and rains and nature and Indians, and they did not lose one single mail. Only one of their number was killed on duty, but others were killed in scrapes and quarrels when they were off duty. Keeping the schedule with them was a religion. And, gentlemen, let me say that, bad as some of these pony express riders were, and some of them were even hanged for murder, if we could devote ourselves to keeping our schedule as well as they devoted themselves to keeping their much more difficult and hazardous schedule, we would be doing a lot. Gentlemen, none of us has to ride on horseback through the wilderness, without sleep, perhaps even without food and water, not knownig when he will be attacked and scalped by Indians. And the station agents along the pony express route—their lives were even in greater danger, because they were stationary. The pony express rider always had the chance of outracing the Indians if they attacked him, as many a rider did, and, riding on mounts that were the pick of the West, this was often not a too difficult task. But many a faithful station master has been the martyr to his country.

"Gentlemen, the knowledge of these things should fortify us in our daily work, and when we have to give ourselves and put forth our best effort, we should do it without any stinting of ourselves, without any petty little worrying, without any attempt to make martyrs out of ourselves. We should remember these men, our forbears in the express business, who gave their lives and their all.

"It was in the pony express that many of the greatest and most famous frontiersmen of the sixties and seventies were trained. One was Buffalo Bill. William F. Cody was the best known of the pony riders. He had a very dangerous route, which followed the bed of a rocky canyon and had to be crossed three times within a space of sixty yards. The water of this stream came down from the mountains, and it was icy, and the current was swift, tricky, dangerous, treacherous. At any time rider and horse were liable to be plunged into a whirlpool. He had another stream to ford that was tricky and dangerous because of quicksands. He had a region to pass that was dangerous because of Indians and also because of desperate men. I believe they were called road men. And, mind you, he had to travel at an average of fifteen miles an hour.

) "Cody's run ended at a place called Three Crossings. Once, when he came into Three Crossings, his relay had been killed the previous night, and there was no one to carry the mail on. But young Cody was undaunted. He went off on a fresh horse immediately to cover an additional eighty-five miles. He finished this trip, turned around, and took the return mail over that route and his own, making a run of three hundred and twenty-two miles. This was probably the record run by any pony express rider.

"How many of you who are drivers out there kick and complain if you get an additional call to make, or if you have to do a little extra work? If there are any of you who do—and I admit it is only human to kick and complain now and then— the next time you are in that mood, just think of the ride young Cody made. Think of what he did, not only uncomplainingly but eagerly and willingly. Remember this, also! The

express service is as important to the nation today as the pony express was in its day. Working as an expressman today, even though it may not be as hazardous as pony-express work was, is every bit as much working for this great nation as was that work. We are all contributing our bit now, as they were then. They helped to make America a going and growing concern then. We are carrying on now.

"Gentlemen, I should like to recount more of the deeds and adventures of those enrolled under the banner of Russell, Majors, and Waddell, but I shall not take up too much of your time. I should like to tell you of the role of honor of pony-express riders, of men like Bob Haslam. And also of men like Jack Slade, a Division Agent. He was a good servant of the company, though a bad man, one of the toughest customers of the West, who was eventually hanged by vigilantes. But, as I said, my time is limited, and I think I have told you enough to give you an idea of the richness of the tradition which has been willed to us, and which it is our duty to carry on in accordance with the needs and the conditions of our own times. We all should learn and keep with us the lessons to be derived from this part of history. It should be knowledge fortifying us to do our own tasks in an ever more acceptable way. It is to us to prove that all this heroism and sacrifice was not in vain."

Willie Collins applauded long and vigorously; the light of inspiration shone in his eye. The speech had lifted him completely out of himself, and he had been thinking of how he worked in a great tradition, and of how what he did today carried on that same tradition. With his eyes still shining, he told himself:

—Goddamn it, what I do is history, even if it ain't that dangerous. I'm carrying on, too.

III

The galloping hoofs of pony-express riders were in Willie's mind as he rode home on the Van Buren-Street car. He was just about the size to have been a pony-express rider, too, and he knew he would have been a damned good one. He was glad to be living now, but he thought how swell it would be if people could live two lives, and if he could have lived before as a pony-express rider. The mere mention of Jack Slade, the bad man, had fascinated him, and he thought of himself as a Jack Slade. He drew an imaginary gun, and it barked at Indians, cowboys, the world. Willie Collins jumped on his thorough-bred and was off with the pony-express mail, the pouch slung over his saddle. Away, away the horse clattered, hoofs ring-ing over the prairie in a steady echo. Indians hovered behind trees, but on and on rode Willie Collins, through a curtain of poisoned arrows, one of them sticking out through his wide sombrero. Out he whipped his pistol, and another redskin bit the dust. And another. Desperadoes chased him, but none could catch fleet Willie Collins. He rode into his station, but the next rider had been killed, and on and on he rode, on and on, covering the whole two-thousand-mile route without a stop. The galloping hoofs of pony-express riders clattered and echoed in Willie Collins's brain, and guns barked out sure and straight death to the echoing clatter of these hoofs.

IV

Willie walked rapidly along a lonely street in Cicero. On either side were wooden houses, most of them dark. He was always a little fearful coming home late at night along this street. After all, Cicero was a place full of bad men. Nothing had ever happened to him, but nonetheless he was nervous and anxious. Of course, if some thug did try to hold him up, he'd say that he was a friend of Eddie Chance and that they went to the same church. He heard footsteps behind and hurried more rapidly.

Turning the corner, he felt relieved. His home was only a few doors down. He climbed the porch of the wooden house and unlocked the door. Once inside, he heard footsteps passing. Might have been a narrow escape. He sighed gratefully.

"Is that you, Willie?" his wife called.

"Yes, dear," he said obsequiously.

"You're late."

"It was the meeting. Wonderful meeting, dear," he said, entering their darkened bedroom.

While he undressed, the galloping hoofs rang in his head. Ah, to have been a pony-express rider. How romantic the express business had been then as compared with what it was now. Still, he was carrying on. He got into bed with those hoofs ringing more loudly in his head, and he fell asleep imagining himself to have been Jack Slade.

Johnny's Old Man

JOHNNY WALKED HOME quickly, carrying the can of foaming beer. In his mind there was a confused picture of the Wentworth Avenue saloon: the sawdust floor, the men, big men, at the bar with the brass railing, one of the men drunk and calling Heinie Zimmerman of the Chicago Cubs a thick-headed Dutchman, the smiling Irish bartender who had told him to help himself at the free lunch counter, and the small man who had said, "So you're Jack Collins's kid, huh?", and had given him a nickel. Something about the saloon, about the language, the tough voices, the size of the big men at the bar made him awfully afraid, and he was always glad to get out of it, even though the bartender was nice to him. He hurried home, because his old man usually cursed him and gave him a sock on the ear when he didn't come straight back from the store, especially when he had been sent for a can of beer. He walked fast, but he was careful, so as not to spill any of the beer. He remembered once how his old man kicked the living hell out of him when he had spilled a can of beer.

The Collinses lived on Forty-fifth Street, just off Wentworth Avenue, in a rambling old wooden house with five dirty rooms, a leaky roof, an outhouse, a weedy back yard, and a damp, unusable cellar. The rent was ten dollars a month, but his old man was always cursing and complaining that the landlord was a lousy robber.

Johnny's mother was a fat, slovenly woman, the mother of eight children, all of whom were living. Johnny, thirteen, was the oldest. His mother always insisted that she could not take good care of the children and the house at the same time. When Johnny's old man was in a good-natured mood, he would tell her to let the house go and watch the kids, but when he was drunk, he'd tell her she was a goddamn old hag and clip her one on the jaw. When he punched her, she always retired to her dark, musty bedroom, to cry and to pray.

Johnny came home with the can of beer. His old man was taking it easy in his favorite chair, his back to the kerosene lamp; his feet, perspiring, with the toes sticking through the holes of stiff socks, lay comfortably on a crumbling davenport. Johnny gave his father the can. The father angrily complained it had taken him long enough. Johnny said that they were busy at the saloon and that he'd had to wait. The father said "yes" sarcastically; then he said he did not want his own son crapping him like that. Johnny retreated into a corner and cowered.

The mother screamed at the father, demanding that he stop abusing her son. He told her to shut up and take better care of her brats and of his house. She told him to earn more money. He told her to pray, because then St. Anthony or some other saint might leave some gold in the back yard. She told him not to be blasphemous. He told her to clean herself up, take care of the house, and not to go around always looking worse than a two-bit whore in a waterfront town. She told him he couldn't call her a whore and get away with it. He said she had better shut her goddamn trap. She picked up a stick from the woodpile in the corner and said that no sonofabitching, lousy, nonproviding husband was going to call her names. She waved the stick and called on God to testify that she was a good woman, who had protected her virtue by lawful wedlock. She reminded him that he'd married her because she had been good and had refused all of his dirty advances before he had put a ring on her finger. And then, turning up her nose, she said: "Maybe you wanted a whore?"

He said "Yeh" sarcastically.

She screamed and cursed.

Johnny still cowered in a corner of the room. He loved neither his father nor his mother. He became terribly afraid when they began to yell and fight, as they were now. He was afraid the old man might knock the mother out and someone would call the police, and then they would all be disgraced, and all the kids in the block would look down on him even more than they did already. He called out, "Please, papa," and "Please, stop, mama," but his appeals were lost in the shrill contest.

The father punched the mother in the ear, and she slumped into a praying heap in a corner. She moaned and sighed, called on Jesus, Mary, and Joseph, blessed herself innumerable times, and threatened to go out and get Father Corbett, the pastor of St. Martha's. He told her to go ahead, and that if the priest came around, sticking his long nose in Jack Collins's family affairs, Jack Collins would bust his nose, too. Then the father drank his beer and wiped the suds off his mouth with the opened cuff of his dirty, blue working shirt. The youngest baby woke up and started bawling. The mother hastened to feed it some milk. Then two other youngsters started bawling, and the father had to sing them to sleep for his own peace of mind. In about fifteen minutes, the house was calm; all the children were asleep except Johnny. He sat quietly by the parlor window, unnoticed. The mother and the father acted as if nothing had happened; he finished his beer. In a little while they went to bed. Johnny, tiptoeing past their closed room, heard the bed shaking, as if people were wrestling on it. Johnny knew what was happening.

He returned and looked out the window, where the black night was so beautiful and hid all the dirt and ugliness of the street. He cried, and he dreamed of what he would do when he grew up, of how he would go away and become a great man and never have nothing to do with his old man and his old lady. He knew that God commanded you to honor your father and your mother, but Sister Maria at school said that God also wanted your parents to be good to you. He thought of how, when he grew up, he would have all the things he wanted.

He would have ice cream, and cake, and all the mashed potatoes he could eat, at every meal. He would have a season box
at the White Sox games, and a chauffeur would drive him from
his home on Grand Boulevard and call for him after the game.
He would wear a new suit every day. He was going to get
even, all right. He thought of how he would come back to the
old neighborhood and scorn everybody. He would be a Rich
Gentleman with a cane, like the men he saw in the movies
two weeks ago. Everybody would look at him and try to be
friendly, and he wouldn't have nothing to do with them. No,
sir, he would fix them all, and especially the McNulty kids,
who always laughed at him because his old man drank and his
old lady was dirty. Two days ago Billy McNulty had said
that his mother said he shouldn't play with Johnny Collins,
because in the Collins's house they were always blaspheming,
and scandalizing, and drinking and cursing, and that old man
Collins was always beating the old lady. Johnny knew it was
all true, but he didn't like people saying so, and it hurt a whole
lot when they did. But he would get even.

He kept looking outside at the dark. The dark was mysterious, and houses, posts, blocks of wood, holes in the street that
Johnny knew so well now looked so strange and different. He
looked out the window, his eyes full of terror. He tried to
imagine good things, but he was too afraid. Footsteps and
other street noises menaced him. Every time he heard them, he
grew afraid and wondered if they signaled the approach of a
robber come to kidnap him and who would kill him because
there would be no ransom money. He sat, and his eyes were
fastened on the awesome street. He shuddered. He did not
like his father, but it was warm-like and comfortable to know
that his old man was in the house when he got afraid like he was
now. But someday he was going to be big and brave. Then the
husky, strange men who passed with loud footsteps would not
make him timid and afraid. But now he was afraid, and not a
big great man.

His father came out of the bedroom to go outside to the

toilet. He saw Johnny. Johnny was relieved from his fear. He could not be hurt by robbers now.

The old man looked at him.

"Jesus Christ, ain't you in bed yet?" he said, giving Johnny a kick.

Johnny scurried into his bedroom. It was filthy, with dirty, unopened windows, and smelly and air fouled from the unwashed, perspiring bodies of his three younger brothers. He curled up without removing his clothes, and cried. He cried until he fell asleep and dreamed of a big man with a cane, who wasn't afraid of anything.

I Want to Go Home

CLIFF SAT in the inside of the Café de Flore, thinking of Chicago. He was small, thin, and nervous. His eyes kept darting about; his mind went blank, and the sound of loud, noisy conversation drummed on it. The café was jammed. There wasn't a vacant table. Cliff was sitting in a corner. He wore a shabby suit and an old khaki shirt without a tie. Next to him there was a stout little Frenchman with a gray beard, who was talking volubly in French to a stout woman. Cliff wondered—was this Frenchman an artist? Last night he had seen Picasso pass on the sidewalk and had scowled at him. Picasso was now *passé*. When Cliff thought of the word *passé*, the image of a dust heap rose in his mind, and he would silently use the words *dust heap*. His mind went blank again. He scarcely knew a word of French, and he became confused when he heard so much of it spoken. Alone, as he was now, he would have thoughts and feelings he would never dare to mention to anyone in the Quarter.

Cliff was twenty-five and had been in Paris for four months. He was living in a small hotel in the Montparnasse, paying three hundred francs a week rent, and he was planning to become a student at the Sorbonne and to live in France on the money he would get through the G.I. Bill of Rights. During the War he had been a mechanic in the Army but had never been shipped overseas. He had liked the Army very much, and now he often found himself wishing the War weren't over, so that he could still be in the Army, tinkering with motors, working on engines, getting dirty as he would lie under a car with a wrench or some other tool in his hand. Sometimes, when he stood before a canvas in his cramped little room, holding a brush, he would have a profoundly nostalgic feeling for the Army and for a monkey wrench. He would look at his brush, and he would go blank. He would sit on his bed, and his mind would remain in a state of consoling emptiness.

His mind was consolingly empty now. Margie was late for her date with him, but, then, he didn't care about that. Margie was always late, but she came around sooner or later. She had to come tonight because she knew he needed money. He sometimes thought that she would rather give him money than sleep with him.

Cliff glanced around the café again. The sight still was strange to him. So many Frenchmen and French dames. So much French. So much noise. But he liked the noise. Even as a boy he couldn't bear to have everything quiet, and almost the only time he had ever enjoyed quiet was when he would be working on a motor in the Army, or now, when he would think of those days.

He could scarcely separate the sounds he heard into separate syllables or words. When he heard the word *garçon*, he knew what it meant, and there were several others that he could recognize, too. He even could speak a few French words. He knew the word *merde* and used it a lot, and *combien, d'argent* and a few other words. He could recognize still others, like *alors* and *didons*, when he heard them, and he kept meaning to ask Margie what they meant, but he always forgot.

He took a sip of his Vermouth and lit a Gaulloise. Tonight, when Margie forked over some dough, he'd buy a pack of Luckies. Luckies cost two hundred francs a pack. And, boy, the French sure went for American cigarettes, just the same as they went for jazz.

Continuing to sit alone, Cliff seemed out of place in this

café. There were a number of bearded young men in the crowd and many sloppily dressed young Americans. Cliff knew some of them. He nodded to three American boys, one of them from the North Side of Chicago. He had nothing against these lads, but he could just imagine what the boys around Fifty-fifth and Halsted would say if they knew Cliff Burns was here in Paris and seeing a lot of these three lads.

The crowd in the café continued to talk loudly. These people acted very important, and they gave the impression that their talk was significant. This gave Cliff a quiet laugh, because, now that he was an artist, he knew that art was not at all the high-flown thing you might think it was. At Chez Américains around the corner, a picture of his was hung now, along with pictures by some of the most famous artists in the world. It was the best painting he had done so far, but then, he'd only done six pictures. This was the one he'd called "Still Shades." Whenever anyone asked him why he'd put a button right in the center of the canvas, he told them that the form of the picture demanded a button right in the center beween the white and black curved lines, but to himself he would quietly remark:

—Ass hole.

The bearded Frenchman on his left was still talking. The thin, blond fag from the North Side of Chicago was twisting and squirming his shoulders like a girl, and then he and the two other fags laughed. People kept coming and going. The waiters moved about among the crowded tables. The small inner room of the café was thick with smoke, and the noisy talk didn't let up for an instant. It soothed Cliff. It brought that feeling of consoling blankness into his mind. It was about as nice to sit here and listen to all the important noise as it was to listen to jazz at the Club.

But suddenly he looked at his watch. Margie was three quarters of an hour late. He pulled out his last one-hundred-franc note and left it on the table and rose. He went over to the fairies and told them to tell Margie he would be back, and then he left. The tables on the sidewalk in front of the café were filled, and Cliff strutted and shoved his way through the crowd and walked past the Deux Magots.

If Margie waited for him, she would worry and get sore. That was the way she had to be treated.

II

Ever since he had arrived here in Paris, Cliff had been planning to take a long walk, but he just hadn't gotten around to it. Every time he decided to go, he would change his mind. There would be plenty of time for walks. He would be here a long time yet because he would be going to the Sorbonne on the G.I. Bill of Rights. That was something—him going to a university in France. He'd never expected that to happen to him. But almost everything that had happened to him was the same. He'd never expected it.

Passing the Abbey of Saint-Germain-des-Prés, he remembered how—it must have been six, seven, eight years ago, he couldn't remember exactly when it was, because he couldn't remember time—he and some of the boys had been standing on the street corner, doing nothing, with nothing to do, and they'd been talking about how sweet and nice it would be to meet some rich young babe and have her take care of you, and, think of it, here he was in Paris, and Margie was taking care of him, and she even spoke French for him.

As he walked on, he decided not to take that long walk tonight. Hell, he couldn't speak French, and he didn't know the streets, and if he got lost he'd have a heck of a time finding his way back to the Café de Flore. And he'd keep Margie waiting too long. He'd just mosey on down to the Boulevard Saint-Michel, because he knew his way that far and had walked it before, and because it was in a straight line, and all he had to do to find his way back was to turn around and walk back along this same sidewalk.

He had to laugh to himself. Because here he was in Paris,

surrounded by foreigners, and he was an artist. Some day he would be a famous man, and people would look at him on the street the same way they looked at Picasso. But Picasso was passé now. Just think of it—some day he would be as famous as Picasso. How come he had the gift to be an artist? In grammar school and in high school he'd never been much interested in drawing, and he hadn't looked at many pictures. He'd been to the Art Institute twice alone, as far as he could remember, and then Margie had taken him a couple of times. Margie was the one who'd discovered that he had this talent, and he was thankful to her for that much. She was probably sitting in the Flore waiting for him now. She'd said last week that she wouldn't wait like this, but she'd wait for him because—why? Why would she wait for him?

He thought about this question for a few moments, and he decided that the answer was that she would just wait, and that was that. She knew he had to depend on her, and that without her over here in Paris he was lost and couldn't pay his rent or eat. And then, when he became a great artist, she'd bask in his glory.

He strolled on. He guessed it would be best for him to stay over here and not return to Chicago until he was established, and then he could go back. He remembered how lost and lonely he had been in Chicago right after he'd been demobilized. He'd take long walks and he'd see all those people on the streets, and he'd think how they didn't know him and didn't care about him. He couldn't go back to that. Over here, people noticed him and said to themselves that he was an American. And he wasn't afraid here walking alone, but he guessed he would be if he got off the beaten path and got lost in some other part of Paris. He'd hate to get lost on a dark street and run into one of those Algerians he'd been hearing about. But, knock on wood, he hadn't had any trouble in France, except the time he'd got drunk and wandered off when Margie hadn't been with him and he'd gotten beat up and been rolled for all his seven hundred francs.

That was why Margie would wait for him. Because she felt

responsible for him and would feel she was to blame if anything happened to him.

He felt light and easy inside now, and he guessed he'd go
back to the Flore and pick up Margie.

III

Margie was twenty-four, tall and slender, and she had brilliant, shining, golden-red hair. She had blue eyes, but they
usually seemed not to focus on anything, and there was a lost,
vacant look in them. Her face, with her soft skin, her even
features, her rich full lips, was usually expressionless. She
talked in a low, even tone of voice, with little inflection and
little range in it. She rarely smiled, and when she did, her
smile was cold and false, a frozen smile.

Her father was a rich Chicago real estate dealer, and she
was his only daughter. She had run away from home at the
age of seventeen and had married a college boy who drank
heavily and was a 4F. She had enjoyed all the turmoil and
excitement her elopement had caused, but she hadn't known
why she had eloped. She had seen Frank—that was his name—
at a party in Evanston, and she had gone over and sat down
beside him, as though she were in a trance, and then, when he
had asked her to go outside on the back porch with him, she
had, and she had scarcely known what was happening to her
until suddenly she was hurt, and what he was doing to her
hurt her, and she then felt so good because she was being hurt,
and she had to be hurt because she just had to be. And three
weeks later she had run away with him, and they'd been
married at Crown Point, Indiana, and lived in a rooming
house on the Near North Side. What she had liked best about
her elopement and marriage was the sense of excitement and
commotion and confusion, and her feeling that now her
mother and father would understand and be sorry, because

when a girl was no longer a virgin and went off and married, it was like being dead for her father.

Margie's marriage had broken up, and she had gone home. Her father, instead of being angry with her, as she had imagined he would be, had been very quiet and kind, and he had seemed hurt. At first, this had made her feel bad, but then, as she had watched him very carefully and very closely, one day she told herself that he didn't care, he didn't care. It was at this time that she began to write more. She had always written, ever since she had been eight years old. Thoughts came to her, and she would put them down in poems. Often she would write in a trancelike state, and then she would be surprised to read what she had written. On her return home after her marriage had broken up, she decided that it was her destiny to be a poetess.

Margie told her father about this decision one night after dinner when they happened to be sitting alone in the parlor. He was a quiet and reserved little man at home, inclined to be formal with his wife and daughter. With business associates he was jolly and talkative, but once he was with his family, all his good fellowship vanished. He was especially formal and matter-of-fact when he spoke with Margie. He would ask her commonplace questions about herself, and as she answered them she would often tell herself that he didn't care, he didn't care, he wasn't really interested in her. She noticed the fathers of girls she knew, and they all seemed different from her father. Other girls, she believed, had fathers who were more interested in them than her father was in her. He had never been really interested in her, she would tell herself. And sometimes she would think he had never even wanted her. As a small girl she had often had this feeling very strongly, and she used to want to sit on his lap and have him pet her and kiss her, and he would never give her all the petting and kissing she wanted. Now, though she was grown up, she still liked to be petted and kissed, and she found boys who would pet her and kiss her. She liked this more than she liked the rest of it, but she let the boys do what they wanted, because that was the way petting and kissing ended. But she liked the petting and the kissing best of all.

Margie's poems were usually written in prose, and almost all of them were about love. Many expressed the thought that there was hatred in loving. And after she had been with boys, she would frequently tell herself that she hated them. She hated her former husband. She knew that she hated him. Again and again, she had told him she hated him.

Margie met Cliff at a small club she went to because she could hear swing music there and could meet colored people. She liked colored people because they seemed to her to be more like herself than white people, and because they seemed to her to be kind and nice. She liked to be petted by colored boys, and she took a particular fancy to a gifted young Negro saxophone player. When he made love to her, something would seem to happen to her that didn't when so many other boys made love to her. His name was Howie, and he was short and had creamy brown skin, and she thought she looked so pretty when she was with him because her skin seemed even lighter than it was. She liked being taller than he was, too, but she didn't know why she liked to be with a boy who was shorter than she. Howie was simple and gay. He enjoyed his work, and when she would sit and listen to him play, she would sometimes even become jealous of his saxophone because of the way he handled it and because of the expression she sometimes saw on his face and in his eyes when he looked at it.

And swing music did things to her. She listened to it, and she would be farther away from home and from so many things in the world than she had ever been at any other time, even when she was being kissed and petted. She would sometimes seem farther away and happier while listening to this music than she would ever be when she was in Howie's arms and would feel him pressing on her and would feel his brown skin right against her.

Howie had been separated from his wife. Suddenly he was

reconciled with her, and he told Margie they could no longer go together. Margie thought of committing suicide. For three straight days she went to the beach off Lincoln Park and sat in her swimming suit, looking off at the blue and calm water and thinking of how she could drown herself if she wanted to. But if she did commit suicide, she knew that wasn't the way she wanted to do it. And she stood in the hallway at home, right near the bathroom door, while her father was shaving. She thought of getting his razor and cutting herself. She would cut her wrists, and her breasts, and her belly, and maybe her throat, and the razor would slash her and hurt her, and the pain would be sharp and it would hurt, hurt her as she had never been hurt, and she would sink down on the floor in pools of her own blood, and she would die. But instead she went to her room and wrote some poems.

And she would walk and walk, not knowing exactly where she was walking, and she wouldn't care if anything happened to her or not, because she didn't care, and what did it matter if anything happened to her or she got hurt? Nobody cared. She didn't care, and nobody cared, and if you were hurt it wouldn't be as bad as the way she was hurt, because Howie had left her, and, anyway, nobody cared.

When she saw Cliff sitting near her in the smoky, crowded, noisy little room, she smiled. He was listening to the music and slapping his thighs, and he wasn't paying any attention to her. Yet she was certain he saw her and that he knew she was smiling at him. He looked poor and sad. His clothes were old and unpressed, and he needed a haircut. She felt sorry for him and thought he was a person to be pitied, just as she was a girl that somebody ought to feel sorry for. She thought of herself and of this ragged-looking lad. She had so many things, and what did they mean? He must have almost nothing. And she could tell from the way he tried to show he was interested in the music and in all these people that he must be a lonely person. He was a lonely boy. She was a very lonely girl. Sometimes she felt as though she really didn't have a father or a mother, and she didn't really care that she had none. She listened to the music for a while and kept looking back at Cliff. Finally he turned toward her when she was smiling at him, returned her smile, and brought his chair to her table.

Within a week she and Cliff became lovers. And when she convinced her father to send her to Paris so that she could become a writer, she managed to take Cliff with her.

IV

"Where were you?" Cliff aggressively asked Margie, finding her at a table with two young Frenchmen in the Café de Flore.

"I was right here," she said defensively.

"I waited a long time for you, and you weren't here," he said, sitting down.

"I looked all over the Quarter for you."

"Didn't you get my message that I'd be back? I took a walk for some inspiration. I was in the mood and took a walk."

"I didn't know what happened to you," she told him.

"Were you worried?" he quickly asked her.

"No," she said almost tonelessly.

He didn't believe her. She had worried. He'd bet his last cent that she'd worried about him. But he'd let that pass for now.

Margie introduced him to the two young Frenchmen. Cliff didn't get their names, but it didn't matter. Anyway, he hoped she'd tell them he was an American artist.

"You are a painter?" one of the Frenchmen asked him in English.

"Yes. I'm an abstract painter. I have my theory. Only abstract painting is pure painting," Cliff said, talking as though he were reciting something he had learned by rote. "I feel the same way about writing. Just as painting should be pure form, so writing should be pure sound. Writing should be like music. It should approach pure sound."

The young Frenchman, who was tall and well built, interrupted slyly:

"I'm a writer."

While he and Cliff were talking, Margie spoke in French with the other young Frenchman, a short, thin fellow with dark hair.

"I won't be ready to publish for about four years," the young Frenchman said to Cliff.

"I'm not quite ready myself. But I have a picture at Chez Américains. Do you know Chez Américains?"

"Oh, yes."

"How come I haven't met you there?" Cliff asked him.

"What is it that you said?" the young Frenchman asked.

"Oh, I was saying, that is, I was asking how it happened that I hadn't met you around here."

The young Frenchman remarked that it was merely one of those things that they hadn't met.

"I got a deal at the Club—I get in free every night," Cliff bragged. "I organized that, all right."

Then Cliff theorized about painting. He said that painting was only painting when it was abstract. Images had been all right in the past, but that was another age. Even surrealism was passé, and the surrealists hadn't painted pure forms, abstractions. The young Frenchman cut in to explain himself. He would be ready to publish in about four years, he said. He believed in experimenting with words in order to find new associations in them and in sounds.

"Maybe you'll write like I paint," Cliff said.

"The older generation is afraid of me. They are afraid of my generation," the young Frenchman said, ignoring Cliff's remark.

These words caught Cliff's interest, and he listened attentively.

"They're corrupt, and they revolt my moral sense. And they do not know what I—what my generation—will do. They are afraid of us."

"I guess it's the same in painting," Cliff said, and he thought

of how his paintings might shock people he knew in Chicago
—in fact, his paintings would probably shock the whole city
of Chicago.

v

Chez Américains looked out of place on the Rue Saint-Benoit,
which was a narrow, typical old street off the Boulevard Saint-
Germain. Chez Américains was new and shiny, with a modern
front. There was a glass case with books at the entrance. Inside, there was indirect lighting, and the light seemed soft
and bluish because of the soft, light-blue walls. There was a
small bar, and many pictures were hung on the walls. In another room, which was larger, there were small tables and
modern chairs, and many more pictures, including some by
famous artists.

When Cliff and Margie—who wore a long, dark mink coat
—entered, a few young people were standing near the bar.
Two tall, thin young Americans looked at Cliff and Margie.

"Hi," they both said, as though they were performing a
ritual.

"Hi," Cliff said.

The two young men looked at Cliff blandly.

"My picture's on the wall," Cliff said. He pointed to the
left of the bar. "See."

They slowly turned their heads and looked at the painting
with noncommittal expressions.

"Like it?" Cliff asked eagerly.

They nodded.

"It wasn't hung in a good place. It's all by itself and not
in there where they have all the pictures by the big shots."

The painting was done in line and wash, with large areas
of white divided by black lines in the shape of carelessly
drawn buttocks, and at the bottom there were blobs of red.
The black paint had been put on badly and was smudged on
the canvas. And in the exact center of the whole composition

there was a black button that Cliff had ripped off his suit coat. Looking at the two Americans and then at his picture, Cliff said:

"It's my best to date. I've only done six. This is my sixth picture, my best one. But they got another good one of mine here. Want to see it?"

"All right," one of the Americans said.

Cliff led them to the side of the room and picked up a canvas in the corner. The picture was divided into sections of brown and red by black lines. The paint had been applied thickly, and the two large colored areas looked corrugated. The brown section at the left seemed almost like corduroy trousers.

"Why did you put the button in the other picture?" one of the Americans asked.

"I wanted to," Cliff said.

He set the picture back. They came back to the center of the small entrance room.

"Still playing?" Cliff asked one of the Americans.

The American said he was. He played two nights a week, to help out financially. They spoke for a few minutes about swing music, and then Cliff and Margie turned to go into the other room. They met two Negroes at the entrance and spoke with them for a moment about Cliff's picture and swing, and then they sat in a corner.

There were about twenty people in the room. Cliff heard French spoken in low voices and wished he didn't. For Chez Américains was like something you might find in America or in a movie, and it gave him a homelike feeling. If he didn't hear this jabbering in French, he could forget he was in France. He liked being in France, and he knew he liked being here, but, even so, he sometimes enjoyed forgetting he was in Paris instead of being back home in Chicago, Illinois. He looked around the room blankly. Then he recognized some faces and saw two Americans he knew, one with straggly blond hair and the other with a beard. He usually spoke to these lads, but he didn't know their names. He thought they were artists.

Well, they didn't have a picture hung here. He wondered how many of the persons in the place had seen his picture and liked it. He examined the people more carefully, though with a hasty glance, wondering if any of them might be rich collectors who came down here to look at the paintings and might buy one, might buy his picture. No one in the place looked rich, but you could never tell in Paris. Look at the old buildings and stores. Nearly all the buildings looked old, and you couldn't get used to the idea that these old places weren't like slums inside. Paris was different from Chicago, and the French must be different. It was easier to spot a rich American than a rich Frenchman. And he didn't see any rich Americans sitting here now.

"I haven't any money," Cliff said, turning back to Margie, who had been sitting with a frozen look on her expressionless face, looking off toward the other room so she could be seen in profile.

Margie pulled out several thousand francs from her coat pocket and handed them to Cliff. Cliff accepted the money casually, as though it were his due. He didn't even say thank you to her, but casually shoved the bills into his trousers pocket.

The waiter came over. Cliff ordered a cognac in English, and Margie asked for a fruit juice.

"I'll get some cigarettes," Cliff said.

He signaled to a pretty girl who stood at the small checkroom near their table, and she came over with a tray of cigarettes.

"Lucky Strikes," he said.

He pulled out the money Margie had just given him and handed the girl a thousand-franc note. She gave him back eight hundred francs, and he tipped her fifty francs. Turning to Margie and opening his package of cigarettes, Cliff said with feigned casualness:

"I owe myself a treat like this. I haven't smoked an American cigarette in five days."

Margie said nothing.

"Well, don't you think I earned myself a pack of American cigarettes?"

Margie shrugged her shoulders.

"Is something eating you?"

"No. I have no opinion on what you said."

"What did I say?"

"Something about American cigarettes."

"Oh . . . they only cost two hundred francs."

"Why should I be bothered for sixty cents?"

"That's what I mean. I'm an artist." Then, as though giving expression to an afterthought, "We're both artists."

Margie raised her brows in an expression that might have been either defensive or critical. Often, when she was annoyed or disturbed, she would act this way. She believed that some-times silence was a weapon, and, also, that silence could make a girl seem interesting or strange. And as she sat with Cliff she was thinking that she didn't want to be with him always, and that she didn't really love him. And she knew he was in one of his moods when he wanted to pick a fight with her. When he was in that kind of mood, she knew she hated him, she hated him just the way she often hated him after getting out of bed with him and starting to dress. And he must hate her now. That was one reason why she stayed with him, be-cause they both just didn't love each other, they hated each other.

"What do you really think of my picture?"

"I like it," she answered in a noncommittal tone.

"You don't. You believe in tradition. Your own writing is traditional. It's not sound, not form in sound. So how can you like my picture?" Cliff went on, speaking in a sharp, aggressive tone of voice.

"I do. I like your picture. It paints your dreams and your unconscious."

"I don't know anything about that stuff—Freud. But I do paint myself. I mean my emotions. And the artist must have pure emotions. And I say pure emotion is pure form."

The waiter brought their drinks. Cliff paid, and he tipped

the waiter seventy-five francs. He took a sip of the cognac
and forgot that a few moments ago he had been sore at Margie.
He wasn't sore at all now. He felt very good, and this was
good cognac, and his picture was hanging here with pictures
of the greatest and most famous artists in the world, and here
he was in Paris, and he could do what he wanted, with no
pressure on him, no job to go to, no boss, no old man and
no old lady to worry about, and Margie was a pretty piece,
if he only was more interested in her that way, but, anyway,
everybody in the Quarter here thought that he was, and many
of them looked at him in his shabby clothes when he walked
along with Margie, and she wearing her mink coat, and he
was just sitting pretty.

He took another sip of his cognac.

Margie sat with her face expressionless, trying to appear
strange and interesting and important to whoever might
notice her.

VI

A fat, gross-looking man, with his soiled shirt open,
sat at a table in the small entranceway to the Club.
Cliff took Margie's arm and strutted up to him, smiled, and
said he guessed he'd come in tonight. He had made a deal to
bring Americans here, and he didn't have to pay any fee
himself. A couple of other Americans had made the same kind
of deal. They went in and walked down a few steps to a
cellar. It was a jazz joint that had been running for a little
more than a year. The cellar was crowded and noisy. At one
side there was a bar, and opposite it, a hat-check stand with a
blond French girl behind it. Swing music was being played,
and the club was noisy. There was a crowd at the bar, another
crowd in a huddle near the hat-check stand, and other groups
stood by the entrance to the part of the cellar where there
were tables, a small dance floor, and a dais for the orchestra.

Cliff liked this joint. It was pretty much like a place in
America, and sometimes when he was here he had to remind

himself that he was in Paris instead of in Chicago. And he felt more important here and more like strutting than he did anywhere else in Paris, because this place was really American, and the French were coming here and acting like Americans, listening to swing and dancing, and if you were an American here, you were one of the ones being imitated.

A young Negro approached Margie and asked her to dance, and she handed Cliff her coat to hold. He stood holding it and looking very important. He could dance, but he usually didn't feel like it, and he wasn't jealous of Margie dancing, because if he let her dance with other fellows and didn't show too much interest in her or in dancing, he would be hard to get, and you had to be hard to get when it came to girls.

He liked it, just hearing the noise and the music, and having a crowd around, and letting the noise and the music and its rhythm take the place of thoughts, and knowing he was around a lot of people and that he knew them and they knew him.

He stood watching the dancers. The floor was becoming so crowded that the couples were all wedged into one moving mass. Most of them were French, and they talked a great deal as they danced. Cliff thought about this. Americans didn't talk so much when they danced as the French. But, then, Americans didn't talk as much as the French, anyway. Margie paused, clinging to the colored boy. There was a traumatic look on her face. She didn't smile at Cliff, but he didn't care. In fact, he was glad he didn't have to dance with her. He was willing to take her here and let her dance all night with anyone who asked her.

A couple got up from a table in a corner. Cliff went right over to it. The tables were set closely together, and he had to move the table to get into the chair by the wall. The dance ended, and Margie came to the table.

"What do you want to drink?" he asked casually.

She didn't know. He didn't, either. So he said they ought to have whisky, and Margie ordered two whiskies, speaking French to the *garçon*. As soon as he was seated, Cliff wanted to be moving about, talking to fellows he knew who were out in the other room. He liked to bounce around, to see and to be seen, but he guessed that he ought to sit with Margie for a few minutes.

"Sandy is here again tonight," Margie said.

"Where is he? I didn't see him."

"He was dancing."

They spoke of Sandy, almost with an air of gravity. Then they dropped that discussion and sat silent. Cliff noticed Sandy, a medium-sized, blond young American. He called "Hi" to him, and Sandy called back "Hi."

A lanky, young American sat down with them. He was blond, good looking, and self-consciously lazy and casual in his gestures, manners, and movements.

"Well, I see we're all back here at the same stand, and it's the end of another day," he said.

"Did you see my picture?" Cliff asked.

"Yes."

"Did you like it?"

"Yes. . . . Yes, I liked it."

"It isn't hanging in a good place," Cliff said.

"It's hanging where everybody can see it."

"Yes, I got to admit that much. I'm going to do better pictures. You know, you have to get settled in a place before you can paint. I'm settled in Paris now, and I feel I know Paris. So now I'm going to do some real work. It takes a little time to get settled and know the place you're living in."

"Yes—I've been living in Paris a year, and I'm not getting anything written. I'll have to go to the south of France to get going on my book. There are too many distractions here. You get lazy with all the distractions. There's always something to do, someone to see—and there are certainly plenty of girls. I've been trying to make up my mind which girls I go for the most—French or American."

"Yeh?" asked Cliff, as though he were interested, but he wasn't interested in what the lanky young American was saying.

"Yes, I'm just lazy," the lanky young American went on.
"I think I could write if I set myself down to it. But how
can anybody write in Paris? Paris just stimulates me to lazi-
ness. Hell, I come here every night, and so I can't get up
early. Then, I do have to go to the Sorbonne in order to stay
over here, and that takes more time. And then there's girls."
He shrugged his shoulders, stretched out his feet, leaned on
the table, and added, "I guess I like the French ones best."

An American, pale and effete, and wearing a long black
beard, asked Margie to dance. She got up and danced.

Cliff and the lanky American sat listening to the music,
and now and then they leaned toward each other to comment
on it.

It was very noisy.

VII

"You can't say I'm jealous," Cliff said to Margie in a sharp
voice.

"I didn't say you were."

"But I don't see why you're always late and keep me waiting for you."

"I waited for you," she told him.

"Only after I waited for you. I'm always waiting for you.
You never can meet me on time. It makes me nervous."

"Clifford, let's not repeat all that."

"If I spoke French and you didn't, and if you had to rely
on me the way I do on you, I wouldn't treat you like you
treat me."

"How do I treat you?"

"If I get nervous, it's not good for me as an artist. I don't
have to be an artist. I could go back home and get a job in
a garage. I'm a good mechanic."

"Clifford, I'm the only one who helped you to become an
artist."

The music started again. They leaned across the table to
hear each other in the noise.

"Well, you could help me more if you didn't treat me the way you do. After all, if this was America, I wouldn't be in the fix I'm in. The only thing I can do over here is paint."

"That's what you ought to do."

"Well, it's not easy if I don't have peace of mind, is it? Picasso has peace of mind, doesn't he?"

"I do take care of you."

"But you make me worry."

"Clifford, you're jealous. You're jealous because you're not free. I wanted you to come to France to learn to be free, because the French are free."

"You hate me, don't you?"

"Everybody who loves, hates."

"I don't hate you."

"But you do. Didn't you . . . what did you say and do to me the other night?"

"That . . . that's sex!" he said.

"Clifford, I won't quarrel with you."

"Who said I wanted to scrap with you?"

"But you do."

"I do not."

"Then don't talk this way to me."

Cliff looked at her with an expression of bewilderment that didn't correspond to his feelings at all.

"Why, I'm only talking to you the way I always do," he protested.

Margie didn't answer him. She casually lit a cigarette. She was not going to let him pick a fight with her.

Another young Negro asked her to dance, and Cliff got up and went out to the bar to talk with some of his friends.

VIII

Cliff lay awake in the dark hotel room. Margie was sleeping beside him. He thought of her poem about two people sleeping together and then hating each other. He opened his eyes and stared at the darkness. These poems were about himself and Margie. But he didn't hate her. Or did he? He was disgusted, and he felt dirty. He had tried, tried to love her and to think that it was beautiful, as beautiful as he guessed art and romance should be. And he had tried, he had tried to feel that he was feeling and knowing all that he wanted to feel and know when he heard good swing music, and he just couldn't feel and know what he wanted to feel and know. And Margie beside him, breathing, he could hear her breathing, and he could feel and sense and smell her beside him. He didn't want to be sleeping with her. He wanted to be alone.

He had been alone in Chicago. Gosh, Chicago was so far away. What was happening there now, at this very moment? What was his mother doing? What was his father doing?

He turned away from Margie and edged over to the side of the bed. He wanted to be as far away from her as he could.

He felt lost here in the darkness of this hotel bedroom. This darkness covered all that was home to him. How small it was. He wasn't happy or satisfied with it, and sometimes when he was alone here in this room, he was afraid. If he wasn't exactly afraid, he was almost afraid.

He was thinking only to himself, and nobody need ever know what he was thinking. He could tell himself that he was afraid. He was. He was afraid. And sometimes, a hell of a lot of the time, he knew that he didn't want to be here, and he wasn't at all sure that he was going to be the great artist he pretended he was going to become.

He guessed he was just full of it, full of crap. But he was fooling them over here, the goddamn fools, and he was even fooling the frogs, too.

What did he want to do? What did he want to happen?
And Chicago?

He was afraid, and he lay in the darkness, thinking of Chicago. He found himself wishing he were back there. He imagined himself walking along North Michigan Avenue, and he began to drowse off into sleep. Chicago became like some vague and pleasing dream, and his fears vanished.

He feel asleep dreaming of Chicago, and of himself back there at home, working as a garage mechanic.

Yellow Streak

EDDIE HYNES was a chunky, light-haired lad with a lantern jaw. As a student he was low average, but he looked as if he would become a good athlete. His father was a motorman working on the streetcars, and Eddie was being sent to Saint Stanislaus at some sacrifice on the part of his parents. He usually was well dressed and had spending money, but he didn't waste it. Among the students of his class he even had the reputation of being tight. But, then, Eddie had a reputation for being many things in school. He was sullen and also hot tempered. At times he would be rough with younger boys, and then he would be surprisingly friendly with them. There were few lads in school who were razzed and laughed at as much as Eddie. After being subjected to this ragging, he would as likely as not suddenly become friendly with those who had been most cruel in what they had said to him. His main interest was sports, and he wanted to be on every team. In his sophomore year, he played on the junior baseball team. Eddie had played center field, and though he had not distinguished himself, neither had he been a failure. When he stepped out in a baseball suit he looked like a player. It was the same in his later years in school when he went out for basketball and football.

Quite often during the luncheon period, there would be scrambling for a basketball. Anywhere from ten to fifty or more lads would get into the scramble, passing the ball, chasing it, wrestling for it. It was mostly the freshmen who got into

these scrambles. But Eddie was almost always in them. He
would shove and fight and push for the ball, sometimes going
down with a group piled on top of him. When the bell would
ring for the students to line up by class and to tramp upstairs
to afternoon classes, Eddie would be dirty, perspiring, and
sometimes winded. He'd stand in line with his class, nervously
mopping his sweating face, and as he did this, he would tell
one or another classmate about what a scramble it had been. A
couple of times he ripped his pants in these scrambles, and it
seemed as if he took pride in doing this. Most third- and
fourth-year students, and especially upper-class students who
played on one of the school basketball teams, disdained getting
into these scrambles for the ball. But Eddie would fling himself into a shoving, pushing group, baring his teeth, jostling
and shoving, until he would be in the center of the melee,
fighting as though for dear life to keep his hands on the ball.
In these moments he seemed to forget himself. He would
knock down, rough up smaller boys, push them aside. Whenever a scramble for the ball was going on and Eddie was in it,
a number of the students in the yard who had nothing to do
and weren't in the scramble would watch him, watch and
laugh at him. Eddie had a habit of getting himself looked at a
lot, and also laughed at.

In sports, Eddie showed plenty of form in practice. This
was especially so in basketball. He had so much form in basketball that he was slow, especially in getting the ball away when
he was shooting at the basket. He had this same exaggerated
form when he ran. He walked and moved and gestured differently when he was in an athletic uniform than when he
wasn't, and his movements on the basketball floor were different from what they were in the schoolyard when he would
be scrambling for the ball. In a game, he would never cling to
the ball or fight for it the way he would in the schoolyard
scrambles. In fact, it was easy to take the ball away from him,
though in the schoolyard it looked as if he would fight to the
death for possession of the ball.

In the games, he would often show his sulky streak, too. If

he tried to dribble and the ball were taken away from him, he would sulk and ignore the game for several moments while he stood peevishly by himself. For those few moments he would be useless to his team. In one game he took the ball in a sulky, angry mood and slammed it down on the floor.

His play was very erratic and uneven, and he was a wholly unpredictable player. He would do peculiar things on the floor. No one playing with him knew when some strange pass might be tried as a trick, a trick so surprising that it would fool his teammates. Or his attention would suddenly wander, and a pass thrown him would be intercepted because he was not playing as he should. He could not think with his teammates, something a good basketball player must do. When a team is welded together, the players grow to know what to expect from one another, almost as if they were all acting by instinct, sometimes as if by a common instinct. But Eddie Hynes couldn't play this way. It was not merely because he was a show-off. More important than that, he would often fail to sense a situation on the floor. He just wouldn't know what to do. He couldn't sense the next step in the changing and ever fluid situation when a game was in progress. He might be in the right place at the right time, and he might not be. He might muff an easy pass, or occasionally he might do something sensational and spectacular.

Eddie's lack of a sense of his teammates during a game was matched by his lack of a sense of those with whom he associated at school. When some of the boys would be talking, he would occasionally come out with some remark utterly irrelevant to what was being said. One minute he would be threatening to bust someone in the nose, and the next he'd be smiling and laughing, with his arm around the lad. He had no real friends in school. He was close to no one. He rarely ever talked about himself. If he were with others, and nothing were being said, he would try to needle someone, but his needling was heavy handed and unimaginative and would usually be turned back on him. Then, when he became the butt of the jokes, he would get angry and curse and threaten, although he

never carried out his threats. After this, he would go off and
sulk for a few moments. Then he would rejoin the group,
smiling broadly, as though nothing out of the way had happened.

He didn't like to be by himself. Whenever there was any
kind of group around, he would join it. And in the group, he
would be smiling until his anger and sulkiness were aroused.
His smile, however, was false. He would smile as if he meant it
for anyone who might be watching him. He would smile
when there was no reason for smiling, just as he would sometimes laugh at the wrong time.

In his second year, Eddie went out for basketball and made
the lightweights. It was a poor team. Eddie played in all the
games, and in most of them he was on the floor for at least a
half. When he was in, he played forward. He made a few
baskets and looked very well for short periods. In most of the
games, he would have at least one streak in which he looked
good and played almost up to his form. But suddenly, in
the midst of this streak, a ball would be passed to him and he
would muff it. Or else he would get an easy, open shot right up
by the basket and miss the mark. He had a habit of sticking
his tongue out and licking his lips and face, and he always, or
nearly always, did this when he pulled some bonehead play or
missed a pass. Yet he had enough streaks in that second year to
be a promising player. And he tried. No one on any of the
teams tried harder than Eddie. He never missed practice, and
he kept playing and trying every moment of practice, except
for those sudden periods when he would sulk. Once those
passed, he was trying again, and it looked as if he were trying
with everything in him. He tried, of course, with a lot of
motion. He had good form, but it slowed up his play. He
seemed rigid both physically and mentally.

In Eddie's third year he made the lightweight basketball
team again. He was a regular during the early practice games,
before the Catholic League season opened. In these games he
played better than he had the year before. It looked as though
Eddie had definitely improved and were really developing now.

But his playing was not so good when the League games started. His eye became poorer. He slowed up. He had looked much faster on the floor in those early practice games than he did in the League games. By the end of the season he was playing indifferently.

In his last year, the school resumed football, after not having had a team for a long time. Eddie, of course, tried out. He looked very good in the first days of practice, for he had all the movements of a fine athlete in baseball, football, and basketball. Clad in his football, basketball, or baseball suit, he looked like an athlete. In those first days of practice, Eddie seemed one of the most promising players on the squad. The school was starting from scratch in football, and many of the boys had to be taught from the ground up. They did not know even the simplest fundamentals about blocking, running interference, tackling, running with the ball, kicking, or passing. In contrast to a number of the candidates for the team, Eddie looked like a finished player. On the first day the candidates practiced falling on the ball, for instance, Eddie was one of the few who knew how to do this correctly. And to an unpracticed eye he looked very good in running signals, when he would take the ball and run with it as though he were carrying it in a game. And he looked equally good catching passes.

However, he would muff more than he should have. When he caught or tried to catch a pass, he would stick out his tongue, and some of the other students even teased him about it and told him he would bite it off or get hurt in a game some day if he didn't keep his tongue in. One of the first of those to comment on Eddie's playing was Danny O'Neill, who was then a junior. He had played with Eddie the year before on the lightweight basketball team, and even before the end of the season had become dissatisfied with the way Eddie played, with the sudden moments when Eddie's mind would seem not to function, and with the way Eddie sometimes would muff passes. Danny noticed that Eddie muffed too many passes thrown to him in practice, and he would some-

times tell Eddie that he had butter fingers. Eddie would get
sore at this. In fact, whenever he made some misplay or muff,
even in practice, he would get angry with his teammates. Joe,
the coach, who had played halfback in an Eastern college, and
also was playing professional football, picked Eddie as left
halfback when he first put a team together to run signals. It
looked as though Eddie were slated to be a regular. In the first
scrimmages, Eddie was usually left halfback for the team
Joe had tentatively selected as the regular team. In these scrimmages, most of the candidates were still too much concerned
with their own play to notice Eddie's. But he was slow in
getting off with the ball, and, although he was heavier than
most of the boys, he wasn't very effective in running interference, especially when he was supposed to take an end out of
the play by cutting the end down. And when he was called
on to hit the line, he would often turn a little sidewise as he
came to the line, and would not drive with his full power. Also,
it developed that he would fumble fairly frequently when he
carried the ball through guard or off tackle. He couldn't put
his head down and plunge with all his power. But this was discovered only gradually. And during the first days of practice
he did seem one of the most promising candidates for the team.
It was expected that he would be a regular halfback.

II

Eddie's father used to come to watch the basketball games
whenever they were played at night. Many of the boys envied
Eddie because of this. Few of the other boys' fathers ever came
to any of the games. Eddie's father was tall and rather thin.
He would wear a black or a dark blue suit, and his clothes never
seemed to belong on him. Like many workingmen of that time,
he looked dressed up, dressed up and almost out of place in his
Sunday suit. He was dark haired and had a dark, full mustache, and he rarely said anything to the boys other than

"hello" or "good-by." He and Eddie would come together, both of them silent. Eddie dressed in the style of the times, but without extravagance. In those days, cake-eaters were wearing bell-bottom trousers. Eddie's trousers were a bit wide at the cuffs, but weren't cake-eater trousers. One of his suits was green, and of an inexpensive material. It faded rather quickly, and then it looked shabby. Another was gray, with a belted jacket. And after he had won his school letters, he liked to wear a sweater with the letters sewn on it.

When Eddie and his father would show up on the night of a basketball game, they could be seen walking silently along the street, side by side. The father was the taller of the two, but by the time Eddie was in fourth year, he was broader than his father. There seemed to be some kind of understanding between the boy and his father, but they rarely spoke when they were together.

Mr. Hynes would sit and watch the game very attentively, rarely smiling, and saying little to anyone. Then, while Eddie took a shower and dressed after the game was over, he would wait, usually standing by himself, with an air of seeming embarrassment. When Eddie showed up, dressed and carrying his basketball gear in a small bag, the two of them would walk off.

But on two occasions something went wrong between Eddie and his father. Eddie sulked and spoke sharply and went off by himself. The father merely looked sternly at him, said something in a low, quiet voice, and followed Eddie along the street, walking at a slow, even pace. Eddie stayed ahead of his father for a few minutes. Then he stopped and waited. When Mr. Hynes caught up with Eddie, they walked along together, silent. But Mr. Hynes would come to the next night game following these blowups, and he acted just as he usually did.

Eddie's father never came to the football games. When the season started, Eddie was a regular halfback. He played in part of the first games the team played, but he was rarely given the ball to carry. After the first game, Eddie was used only in the first quarter. He was too erratic. He made a couple of fumbles, and when he had a perfect opportunity to intercept a pass with a clean field he muffed the ball.

By the middle of the season Eddie was no longer a regular, although he had played in every game until that time. During the first week of November, the team played a scrimmage game against the Park High lightweight football team. The team played sloppily and without enthusiasm, and the coach was both angered and disappointed. Eddie was kept in the line-up for the entire scrimmage. He played worse than he had played at any time during the season. He wouldn't hit the line, but, instead, when he came up to the line of scrimmage with the ball he would turn sidewise, lift his head, and check his own driving power.

The scrimmage lasted about twenty minutes. It was still light out. The players were all dispirited, and they started walking off the Jackson Park football field. The players all expected to be released from practice for the day.

In an angry voice, the coach called them together. Heretofore he had been very gentle with the boys. Now he talked sharply and in a cutting voice. Then he lined them up in two lines facing one another. The players in one line were ordered to run head on. Those in the other line were ordered to tackle. Both the runner and the tackler were told not to avoid each other. The coach stood watching. He called out the signals. A player from each line ran. There was a head-on clash. The lad who was tackled picked himself up, dazed. The coach called out again. Two more ran. Another head-on tackle.

After each tackle, the players who had run and tackled took places at the end of the line opposite one they had been in so that everyone would have both to tackle and to be tackled. Thus the lines kept changing. The coach stood by himself, hands on hips, a burly, barrel-shaped man, bawling out his signals, and one after another the players sprang forward. One after another was tackled head on. There was thud after thud as one tackler after another would pile into the runner. Lad after lad slowly rose from the ground, shaking his head, clearing his mind, recapturing his wind after these head-on collisions. And in each line the lads were tense and silent. They knew they were being tested for their guts. They were grim. They waited, tense and taut, grim. Then the signal. The run. The smack into a teammate coming straight at the tackler. Then the boys slowly getting up from the ground, some of them holding their stomachs, others shaking dazed heads, and a slow walk on to the end of the opposite line.

When Eddie ran, he stopped dead in his tracks and half turned as he came close to the teammate who was rushing at him for the tackle. He went down like a felled log. He rose and, with his head down, walked slowly to the opposite line. He waited in line with his eyes on the ground, shamefaced.

And the tackling went on. Eddie's turn to tackle came. He stood poised. His form looked good. The coach barked the signal. Eddie ran forward. He stopped. He made a half-hearted attempt to tackle. He missed.

A moment later, the coach called the team to him. Tired, bruised, dirty, dispirited, they formed a circle around him. He talked in an angry but sincere voice, telling them they had been soldiering on him. The lads respected and admired him because of his usual gentleness and friendliness. They were ashamed of having played so badly for him. He gave them a tongue-lashing that they accepted meekly. Then he said curtly:

"Hynes, turn in your uniform."

After telling Eddie to turn in his uniform, the coach released the team for the day. The players started trooping slowly off the field to walk back to the school, where they would change their clothes and take showers.

It was dark now. A warm November night was setting in. Singly and in groups they walked off. They were silent. They moved tiredly and slowly. Some of them were bruised.

Eddie walked alone, carrying his helmet. He kept his head lowered. Back at school, he said nothing as he took his shower. He left his suit in the locker room and went off alone, carrying his books.

III

The next day, Eddie smiled very apologetically at his team-mates. He had little to say. Everyone in school had heard how he had been thrown off the football team for being yellow. No one mentioned the subject to him. He was not razzed. In fact, many of the students were silently sympathetic. At noon the next day, he didn't pitch in when there was a mass scramble for the basketball. He stood by the wall alone, watching, his face rather taut and his expression strained.

But in about two days he was again acting as he always had. He laughed, scrambled violently for the basketball during the lunch-hour mix-up, razzed other students, and blew up angrily when he was razzed. Yet he did not show so much spirit as he had formerly shown. He had been disgraced before his teammates, disgraced in the eyes of all the students in school. He didn't discuss this. Others also avoided the subject, even when they would be razzing and teasing him.

The football season ended, and basketball practice was begun immediately. Eddie surprised the entire school by showing up for basketball practice. He was treated as a veteran and given a school uniform immediately. He was now a little too heavy to be a lightweight. He was scheduled for the heavy-weights.

During the first days of basketball practice, Eddie looked better than ever. It seemed as though he were putting his heart and soul into the effort of erasing the stigma of being yellow. He joked a lot and was in very good spirits. During practice sessions he was always the first in uniform and on the floor. Whenever he had a chance he would practice shooting baskets and free throws in order to sharpen his eyes.

Eddie was the only senior on the heavyweight team, and he was also the only player who had already won his letter in basketball for two years. Almost automatically, he was elected captain of the team. This took place the day before the first practice game in early December. Father Theo, athletic director of the school, managed it.

Eddie's teammates all wanted him to have a good season. They felt that if he did he would erase the stigma of having been yellow. And in practice Eddie gave more promise than he had ever given in the past.

The heavyweights won their first practice game easily, by a score of twenty-one to ten. Eddie scored four baskets and one free throw. This was the largest number of points he had ever scored in one game in his entire career at Saint Stanislaus.

But Eddie's old habits asserted themselves, for at this point in his high-school career he had very fixed habits in his athletic performances. By the time the Catholic League season opened, Eddie's playing was erratic and moody. He was once again having sulky periods during games. He showed fine team spirit in practice, but in games he often had no team spirit at all. After the first League games he was not kept in the games for long periods. Since he was captain, he was put in the starting line-up, but he was usually on the side lines before the end of the first half. By the end of the season, with the heavyweight team in last place, Eddie was a substitute, even though he was captain. He failed once again as miserably as he had in every other season.

The students began to talk about him, and even to show some scorn of him. They talked of him as being yellow. But Eddie usually acted as though he were utterly unaware of this talk. He smiled in the same old way. He reported for practice during the latter part of the basketball season with the same old pep and enthusiasm he had shown in practice sessions all during his high-school athletic career. His fellow students couldn't understand him.

Eddie went out for the baseball team during his fourth year. This would be his last chance in sports. Like most of the other teams on which he had played, this one was weak. Eddie played second base, and then was made a sub, because of his hitting. He put his foot in the bucket, and sometimes he would swing at the ball in a spiritless and lackadaisical fashion. As had happened again and again in the past, he gave up easily.

Early in May, the coach quit, and Joe, the football coach, took over. He gave Eddie a chance. The team was demoralized and lost two games by over twenty runs. In these games Eddie played his best. He was full of pep, and he kept up a running chatter of talk, trying to encourage the other players. The more runs the other teams scored, the more peppy and talkative Eddie became. The other players felt hopeless. They were humiliated and wanted the games finished. But Eddie kept talking and chattering, patting them on the back. He made hits in both games and fielded perfectly. He kept up his peppy talk until the last man was out. Joe congratulated him for his spirit in front of all the players. Eddie beamed. It was as though this public congratulation by Joe had wiped away the stigmata of Eddie's being considered yellow. The other players, in the face of their humiliating defeats, were too dispirited to care what happened. But Eddie remained full of pep until the end of the season. He kept reporting for practice every day and went through these practice sessions as though they were important. He ran, slid, and kept doing something every moment. He was so peppy and talked so much that his teammates resented him. They decided he must be goofy. But the colder they were to him, the friendlier Eddie became. He talked of the team as though it might be a championship outfit. He kept speaking of going down fighting. When they lost one game, twenty-six to one, he spoke of their indomitable fighting spirit.

After the last game, he had very little to say. There were only a few school days remaining for the senior class, and during these last days, he remained moody and quiet. But once he did speak with his classmates about what a wonderful time they all had had together, and about how he hated to be graduating. And he also said that he wished he could have one more year, especially so that he could play on the teams.

After graduation, Eddie rarely saw his old classmates. Then

he became a motorman on the streetcars. Now and then a former schoolmate would recognize him. Standing up and running the car, he would talk of the good old days at Saint Stanislaus, and about the swell teams they had had. And he seemed very happy in his work as a motorman. And when he saw former students on the cars, he told them that he was doing what he was cut out to do and that he wouldn't change jobs with anyone for love or money.

An American Dream Girl

Most of the passengers in the club car were middle aged, and some of them were gray. They looked at the girl with interest when she entered and passed them to take a seat between me and a rigid young man who had an absent look in his eyes. I smelled the perfume she was wearing. She was pretty, but her face was like a mask. There was little expression on it. It was carefully powdered, and her eyebrows were thinly penciled. She had very light hair. Her dress was black, stylish, and expensive. She was slender and on the tall side. She sat erect, and there was no change in her expression, as though it were a firm defense against the world and herself. I noticed that the book she had was a novel by John P. Marquand which had been published just recently and had received considerable attention. She ordered a Scotch and soda, and seemed to read very slowly, judging by the number of pages she turned. I guessed that she was not particularly interested in the book. After paying for her drink, she left a twenty-cent tip on the tray. She sipped her drink and continued to read at her slow pace.

The stiff young man became very conscious of her. Before she had sat down, he had tried to get into conversation with various passengers. He had mentioned the mine strike which was then in the news. No one had been interested in his remark that it was bad for the country. No one was any more interested in his comment on the gloominess of the weather. Apparently ill-at-ease, he talked compulsively, and in order to attract attention to himself. He kept turning toward the girl, glancing down at her book, watching her out of the corner of his eye, and then he would sit rigidly and look down the car with an absent expression and a peculiarly fixed stare. He rang for the steward and then ordered a glass of ginger ale. But drinking the ginger ale didn't distract and put him at ease for long. He continued to pay obvious attention to the girl.

After she had read a few pages, she put down the book, sipped her drink, and sat straight, with no change in her mask-like expression. The young man asked her if she liked the novel. In a very low voice she said she did.

"I like to read. There's nothing I like like a good book. Good books are good," he told her.

His words seemed peculiarly hollow and insincere. He spoke so loudly that everyone could hear him. And yet his voice was as characterless as hers, which was so low that I, sitting at her left, could scarcely hear what she said to the young man. He was making conversation, and she gave him little help. He told her that he read a lot of books. She said she read books whenever she had the time. He said he liked books to be realistic. She said she liked them to have romance. He told her he didn't like books to be realistic but to be romantic. She took a drink. The young man continued to sit rigidly. He gazed ahead fixedly. He held his head as stiff as a board. His lips were pressed together in that tight way that reveals inner tension.

"Books are educational," he told her.

"Oh," she said in her low, monotonous voice, "I just like to read something that's exciting and romantic."

"What's life without excitement and romance?" he asked her, laughing strangely.

"I like excitement," she said monotonously.

The young man became conscious of me and brought me into the conversation. Merely to draw him out, I asked:

"What's the use of being excited?"

He laughed again. It was an inward, self-conscious laugh.

"Yes, what's the use? Excitement only . . . excites," he said.

"Too much excitement is exciting," I said dryly.

"I like to have fun," she said in such a dead voice that one could only wonder what the word *fun* might really mean to her.

"Yes, we have got to have our fun. I'll bet you have fun. Tell me about fun," he said to the girl.

When he looked at her, a tremor of fear crossed her face. She drew her elbows in against her sides for a moment. Then she turned to me, and, with her lips pressed together, she gave me a restrained, self-conscious, and pleading little half smile. It was the first change I noticed in her expression since she had sat down.

"Do you live in Chicago?" I asked.

"Yes. But I come from Minnesota. I live in Chicago and work there. I'm going to New York for three days," she said in the same monotonous and characterless voice.

"The Big City," the young man said. "I like big cities. They're more exciting. More things to do. Do you like to do things?"

"What do you want to do things for?" I asked.

"I don't. The best kind of life is the quiet life. Yes, the quiet life."

"It's quiet, isn't it? The quiet life is quiet," I remarked dryly.

"No . . . I mean yes." He turned to the girl. "What kind of life do you like, the quiet life?"

"Yes, I like it quiet."

The young man began to speak to her more aggressively. I asked him questions that led him to contradict what he had just said. He talked of books again, and of Chicago and New York. Finally I had asked him enough questions to confuse him, and he became silent. I sat there and casually talked with the girl.

"I need this to pick me up," she said, lifting her glass for another drink.

She had been out late the evening before, at the Club Alabam in Chicago, and she had had too many drinks. She was hungry, but it was too early to eat. The drink made her feel better. She told me what she did—she was a model. She spoke in the same colorless, low voice, and as she talked I had to lean forward repeatedly in order to hear her.

"Is it easy work?" I asked her.

"Oh, yes. Of course, some days you are on your feet a lot, and you have to go out on dates. I like to go to different places than the ones I'm taken to on dates. I like to go to places on the South Side where there are colored people. They're just as good as we are. Some of the men I have to have dates with don't like them. But everybody is as good as everybody else. I have no race prejudice."

She worked at least three or four days a week and was paid twenty-five dollars a day when she worked.

"How did you happen to become a model?" I asked her.

"I went to a charm school. I learned a lot. I can meet any kind of person and be interesting. And I learned how to sit correctly, and what to say, and how to walk and talk, and I learned how to make up, and to wear clothes, and to fix my hair. I fix my hair and dress and make up different than I used to. I was a teacher in the charm school, too. The school got me my first job as a model. Now jobs come to me. I'm going to a party in New York. Mr. Cuno is giving it."

I didn't know who Mr. Cuno was.

"Haven't you heard of Mr. Cuno? He's rich. I model for pictures for his company. He's rich. He's giving a party at his country home, a house party. I was going to take a plane. I like airplanes, but I wanted rest and quiet so I took the train. I'm going to fly back to Chicago."

I waited for her to go on.

"I took the train because I won't get much sleep in New York. I don't sleep good. I didn't get to bed until four o'clock last night. I don't like to sleep alone. I get afraid if I have to sleep by myself."

She sat there, her face unchanging and masklike. She continued to talk in the same low, monotonous tone of voice.

She spoke only of herself. She had gone to work in a factory when she was seventeen, but she hadn't liked the work. It was too hard for her. Then she had landed a job as a secretary in a real estate office, and from there she had gone to charm school. She spoke of her girlhood and childhood.

"I never could give enough love to my mother and father. They gave me everything I wanted. They were good to me. I never could give them enough love. They both wanted me to love them a lot . . . I have to love everybody in my own way. I loved my brother. He was not my brother. My mother and father adopted him to give me a brother. I loved him so much. They were worried about it, my father and mother. I never loved anybody the way I loved him. He loved me, too, just like I loved him. I had a car when I was fifteen. My mother and father let me drive it. They gave me everything to make me happy. My adopted brother had a jalopy. One day he drove across the field. If he was driving in my car, he never would have driven so fast across a field. He would not have wanted to, because my car was new. He had an old jalopy, and it didn't matter what happened to it. He was killed. I saw him. Oh, he was mangled. And I loved him. I loved him, and he loved me, like no brother and sister, nobody ever loved anyone else. That's maybe why I can't sleep. Since then I keep thinking of him all bloody and mangled, and sometimes I get up and take a taxicab at two and three o'clock in the morning and go to be with a friend. Friday night the taxicab driver said a girl like me should not be out alone so late. My friend held my hand."

She was physically uncomfortable sitting so erect. Now and then she would twist, but she wouldn't sit in any other posture than what she had been taught at charm school. And her voice continued to grow softer and softer.

"I talk too loud, and it does something to my ears. I can't stand loud noises. They do something to me. When I hear loud noises, except music, I get nervous. I go to a doctor. He is a nice old man, and he talks to me and holds my hand, and I feel better. I know all about psychiatry and psychoanalysis. I could read you like a book."

I smiled at her and listened.

She had been married but had not loved her husband. She had left him. Her boy friend was married and had two children. She sometimes visited the wife and played with the children. The wife did not like her too well.

"My boy friend is jealous. He wouldn't come to see me off on the train. He was jealous. I don't care. I'm going to Mr. Cuno's party. It's going to be a big party, for business. I have to go to parties and go out on dates. The other models do. I like dates with my boy friend better. Some of my dates . . . the men get mad at me. If you don't like them, and if you don't let them, they get very mean and they say mean things."

"What do you talk about on these dates?"

"Oh, I don't know. Jokes. They talk about themselves, and they tell me I'm gorgeous, and jokes. They like jokes."

A picture of her life began to unfold. Sitting before me, she was a re-made girl. In a way, she was two girls: the girl from Minnesota and the Chicago artist model. Her posture might have suggested this. She was so uncomfortable that she would wiggle and twist, but she would not permit herself to fall back into a relaxed posture. She had been told that to sit erect was the only correct posture, and she was doing what she had been told. And the expression on her face didn't change any more than did her voice. I thought of the characterless expression I had often seen on the faces of models, a kind of mask that now and then opens into an artificial smile. This dehumanized quality in her face could also be sensed in the way she talked, the lack of emphasis in her speech. She spoke of the details of her work, the jealousy of other girls, her dates, and an abortion she had had which had left her incapable of bearing children. She told me of her fears and her sleeplessness, of her parents, of her dead adopted brother, of her experiences in the factory, and in a real estate office, of the parties she went to, and of the party she was going to in New York—and all in the same tone of voice.

We went to dinner. She continued to tell me about herself.

She confessed that the other young man had frightened her. She was glad he wasn't near her in the diner. She said she'd go to bed early, about seven-thirty, because she hoped to get a little sleep then. She knew she would wake up and would lie awake and afraid all night in the Pullman. She became increasingly uncomfortable sitting erect and eating. When we had coffee, the cups rattled. This noise seemed very loud to her. She was disturbed. She now talked so low that I couldn't hear her, and when I mentioned this, she was surprised. She thought she had been talking very loudly.

After eating, we returned to the club car. She was relieved to see that the rigid young man had left. She wanted to hear music. The steward turned on the radio. A band was playing swing music. She didn't listen to it. She told me more about her dates. Most of the men who took her out became very abusive if she refused to go to bed with them. They were all successful and respected men in Chicago. They had money and spent it on her freely, but they wouldn't take her out twice if she said no to them.

Such was her life. Work, senseless dates, fears, terrors, with near breakdowns every six months or so, a visit to this old doctor she mentioned, the doctor holding her hand and telling her that she was not a bad girl, and then a repetition of the same thing. And she lived on her illusions of her own charm. If she sat up in such discomfort, she was sitting the way a girl should sit. She was contributing to her charm. If she made her face over into a mask, she was beautiful. If she wore a girdle which pinched in her waist, as she apparently did, she had a beautiful figure. And after this work, after modeling and posing in shows and for national magazine ads, after dates, after her night or two a week with her lover, she would go to bed and there lie in terror of something unreal and unseen, and she would get up at all hours and take taxicabs just to be with anyone who would hold her hand, would lie with her and hold her, give her the security of human warmth, tell her she was a good girl and that she wasn't alone. This was her life.

As we talked, I occasionally noticed some of the middle-aged passengers. They had continued to watch us, and now and then I would catch a glance of envy in their eyes. About seven-thirty, she said she was going to bed. I walked out of the club car with her, followed by these envious glances. The bored businessmen, the middle-aged men, the fat men, the bald-headed old man all looked at me with their thoughts obvious on their faces. I walked as far as the dining car with her, in order to get a glass of milk, said good night to her, and watched her walk down the long, narrow corridor of a car of roomettes. She didn't look back. She walked slowly along, carrying her book. I wondered where this road of hers was leading to. Where would she end? What could life hold for her in a few years, when younger girls would take her place as models and as dates?

She disappeared. I sat drinking my milk and thinking about her. There, I thought, is an ordinary American Dream Girl. I kept thinking of her walking along the long corridor of the Pullman car, and pondering about what might be the end of the road for her.

The Renegade

IN HIS FRESHMAN YEAR, Hal Walters met Ethel Corbin and believed that he loved her. She was quiet and very pretty; she was dainty, dark-eyed, and had a neat, appealing figure. Her father owned a large furniture store in upper Manhattan, and as Hal and she came to know each other better, he began to think she was planning to marry him and to have him go into the furniture store. Hal had vague ambitions to write. Sometimes he would look ahead and imagine that the relative prosperity of the Corbin family could serve him well in getting launched on a literary career, and he would wonder, if he and Ethel did marry, would she be able to get an income from her family that would permit him to do his own writing without having to be a huck or to sacrifice his integrity. But he had no intention of going into the furniture store.

Hal was slightly undersized, thin, homely, and nervous. He was quite precocious, and although only in his freshman year, he already had acquired a smattering of generalities about life, sex, literature, and politics. He spoke to his instructors, to fellow students, and to Ethel with an arrogant air of confidence. One of his instructors characterized him as a young man incapable of either listening or learning.

Hal thought of his own future only in the vaguest terms. He believed that as a young man with intelligence and honesty he had two strikes on him and that the cards were stacked against him, and against everyone in his own generation who was smart. At times he would think, and also de-clare, that it was impossible to become an honest success in the corrupt and dangerous times in which he lived. At other times he would boast that any dope could be a success. He made few efforts to write, and when he did, he was arrogant and presumptuous. But when he spoke of his future literary plans, he would often mention the names of contemporary American writers, and would then remark that if they could become successful, so could he.

Hal and Ethel began to go out on dates. Soon they were seeing each other every day. They would embrace ardently, and they petted in a feverish manner, but they both shied away from any consummation. When Hal would leave her after such embraces, he would feel both frustrated and relieved. He was fearful that if she sacrificed her virginity to him, she would destroy him with her love, rob him of his own individuality, and tie him down to a dull, bourgeois life. But at the same time he would also imagine that Ethel did not respect him because he did not take her, even take her almost violently. And he wished that in a moment of passion she would beg him to take her. He indulged in many fantasies in which, in such a frenzy of passion, she would beg him to have her.

With Ethel he talked a great deal, and she would rarely disagree with him. They liked the same writers, especially Flaubert and Cabell, and he assumed both for himself and for Ethel a superiority to others of their own generation. Whenever she would show signs of disagreement with him, he would either sulk or become sharp. He sometimes accused her of not understanding him, and he told her over and over again that she was not a completely free spirit. They rarely talked of sex in a personal way. When they would embrace, they would be silent and serious. Their embraces were almost grim.

Early in his sophomore year, Hal began to see clearly that he had to go farther with Ethel. They were both becoming excessively nervous. If he did not take her now, he feared she would not respect him. But he couldn't make himself do what he wanted to. It was just at this time that he began to take a more active interest in radical politics. He often gave the impression of being intelligent, and the young Communists on the campus started to cultivate him. After he had spoken with some of them a couple of times, he realized that he had been thinking about the problems of the world in a vague and only semiconscious manner, and he became guilty in his own eyes. He saw that one must become an antifascist. After reading a few articles, he became a convinced and determined enemy of Hitler, Mussolini, Hirohito, and Franco. He believed that he ought even to go to Spain and fight and die in the fight against fascism. It was at this point in his development that he and Ethel broke up. He began to talk to her about fascism instead of about literature, and he said they both ought to do something to help save the world. He frightened her. When she tried in a quiet way to switch him away from politics, she failed. They broke up.

Hal's vanity was wounded by his split with Ethel. He saw this in the light of a sacrifice, his first sacrifice in a career which he now thought he ought to dedicate to his fellow men and the workers. At the same time he saw himself as a young man gloomily making a dangerous decision. His father, a small merchant in the Bronx, had stinted and saved in order to educate Hal. Hal had lived for years with a feeling of pressure because his parents had made sacrifices for him, and he resented them for having done this. He lacked the will and the confidence to become what his parents wanted him to be— some kind of successful professional man. He regarded his father with both pity and resentment. His father didn't understand him. Hal now told himself that he'd decided that Ethel couldn't understand him because she was petit bourgeois. When he had begun to voice his real self, the idealist in his nature, she had shown him her true colors. At the same time he would also berate himself for not having possessed her. He knew he had been sexually timid with her. But whenever these thoughts came to mind, he would quickly sidetrack them and think about politics.

When Hal had begun to tell Ethel of his newly found

political convictions and opinions, he would talk in an increasingly aggressive spirit. He spoke almost as if his criticisms were directed at her, and as though she might even be one of the fascists whom he feared and whom he so urgently wanted to prevent from taking control of the entire world. This was why he had frightened her. She was not interested in politics and read the newspapers only intermittently. She didn't like men like Hitler and Mussolini, but she knew nothing about their political careers. To her, fascism was a word that denoted something evil. More than anything else, Hal's tone and manner had caused her to change. She had reached the point where she was beginning to believe she was in love with him, and she began to imagine that they some day would be married and have a home of their own and be very happy. But when Hal suddenly began to exhibit such vehemence about fascism and about dedicating himself to politics, she was startled. And he immediately sensed that he was frightening her. This gave him a feeling of exaltation. One night they were sitting on a bench, looking out at the Hudson River. They had gone there to sit and hold each other and to kiss and pet. It had become one of their favorite spots. The sky, the black shrubbery, the play of moonlight and starlight on the dark water, the electric lights and darkened shapes across the river, the wide sky— all this was part of what they considered a romantic setting. And as they had sat looking out at the river and kissing and holding each other, their ardent feelings had become so intense that they had been fearful they would go farther than they dared with each other. And going too far had become a kind of unspoken fear with them. It lurked behind their recurrent moments of embarrassed silence. At first after Hal had kissed Ethel, he had voiced endearing little sentiments, had called her endearing names. But then he would kiss her silently and with fearful determination. As they kissed, they would ache with frustration because they dared not do what their bodies and their entire beings told them to do.

They had gone to their bench on this night, feeling

the same embarrassment, knowing they would arouse each other to a pitch that would be agonizing, and that then they would not take the final, fatal step. And after Hal had held and touched and kissed Ethel passionately, he had unexpectedly launched forth on a political diatribe, speaking in sharp and bitter tones. He knew he was hurting her, and this brought him a kind of happiness that bordered on pain. This was the last time they kissed each other.

He hadn't been surprised when, the next day, Ethel had told him that they had better not see each other again. But then he began to brood, to see himself as shamed, lonely, and beaten. He washed his own cruelty out of his memory and blamed her for having rejected him. He found justification for his feelings in his new political attitudes. And after a period of brooding, of chaotic and self-pitying moods, he decided to become a Communist. But just as he was ready to join, he had a meeting with the Communist student group, and he asked them a number of questions in as aggressive a manner as he had used with Ethel. Then he burst out in a violent and unprepared speech that was ultrarevolutionary. He mocked the bewildered young Communists as compromisers. Swept on by his own rhetoric, and happily discovering that he knew a little more about radical politics than he had been aware of, he stigmatized them as cowardly reformists without principles. This action gave him a sense of gratification that seemed deeper and richer than any he had known with Ethel. He was very proud of himself.

These experiences constituted the basic training for his chosen career as a professional revolutionary. He had sacrificed his girl, and he had stood on principle and not become a young Communist. He saw a dialectic in these two episodes. His break with Ethel was the negation, and his refusal to join the Communists was the negation of the negation. And then he decided to join a dissident group that styled itself the one true and only revolutionary party. This was the positive synthesis. He had said yes. He had passed through the process of the negation.

II

The Party Hal joined numbered about a thousand members. It prided itself on being truly Bolshevik and on standing for the real principles of the Russian Revolution. It declared that it, and not the bureaucratic Stalinists, were the true Communists. There was more intellectual appeal in its press than there was in the Communist papers, and it published brilliant articles by the great revolutionary leader who was now in exile. The Party was supported by its membership and was poor, but its very poverty and smallness appealed to Hal.

After joining this Party, Hal was filled with dreams. The smallness of the group, the hardness of the road ahead only served to intensify his elation. His daydreams became ever more grandiose. He saw himself as one of a small and almost unknown band that was scorned and opposed on all sides, but which would nonetheless one day change the entire history of the world. As he walked the streets of New York or moved about at school, he kept thinking of how he was different from almost everyone he saw. He was one of the small band of people who would lead the world out of its abyss of barbarism. And he liked to think of how he, young and unnoticed, already belonged to history. He lost all interest in his studies. He became smirkingly hypercritical. Sitting in his classes, he would listen only to try to discover where his professor might be either ignorant or antirevolutionary. He now saw his teachers as merely the cowardly purveyors of a decadent bourgeois culture. And he had broken forever with that culture.

One of his new comrades—he was deeply moved by the word *comrade*—was Joseph Zinnzer. Zinnzer's Party name was Benton. Comrade Benton was spoken of in Party circles as the coming theoretician. One day Hal heard another comrade describe Benton as the Riazanov of America. Hal didn't know who Riazanov was, and he dared not ask for fear of revealing his ignorance. Benton took an interest in Hal and explained many things to him. He was a youthful-looking, slim, tall, mild-mannered young man with a cultivated voice.

"It's infected," Benton said to Hal as they sat having a glass of beer near Party headquarters in the Union Square area. "All of bourgeois life is infected, poisoned. It's filthy."

Benton spoke with intensity and anger. Hal, hearing him, was more frightened than roused.

"Take my father," Hal remarked after Benton had gone on speaking bitterly of the infection and filth in the life of the bourgeoisie. "He doesn't understand nothing from nothing. I can't make him understand. And where is he? His hair is gray. He gets along. But what does he get out of life? Just a little comfort."

Benton rapped the table and said with angry authority:

"In five years the entire world will be a hotbed of revolution. And then what will comfort mean? What did comfort mean to Lenin and Trotsky in 1917? Comfort!"

Benton tried to sneer, but he produced more of a smirk than a sneer. Hal wanted to like Benton, and it seemed that he had some bond or kinship of feeling with him. Benton obviously was of middle-class origin. And he impressed Hal as being tough minded. He had already heard the phrase "Bolshevik hardness," and Benton seemed to Hal to be hard. Benton had traveled the spiritual road Hal knew he must travel. But at the same time Hal was uneasy, unsure of himself in Benton's presence. Benton, raising his voice, using words of denunciation and vituperation, appeared fearless, a person who would never relent, nor betray, nor weaken in a moment of danger. The world was now full of Hal's enemies, the enemies of the working class and of the world revolution. And was there anything in the world that the rotten bourgeoisie, and the Communists, too, feared as much as the world revolution? But to be a leader of the world revolution you yourself had to be fearless. Was he? He didn't know. He was afraid he might not be hard enough for his historic role.

"Stalin," Benton told him, "is more afraid of us than of any other force in the world."

It was very strange to Hal to think that he, collectively with his new comrades, could be one of the most feared persons in the world. And when he would smirk at his professors, or at other students, he would remind himself that he was more to be feared than was realized. And he found confirmation in this unsure sense of himself as a dangerous person when he argued with his father. For when he mentioned socialism or revolution, he angered his father. They had noisy arguments. His father would become red-faced, and he would talk loudly and gesticulate constantly as he yelled:

"I work all my life to make a successful American out of you. You become a radical, a revolutionist, a renegade to me."

"Do you want me to defend a rotten system?" Hal shot back at his father.

"It's rotten? My hard-earned dollars are rotten? My business is rotten? But you, no, you aren't rotten! Is that what they teach you in school?"

"They're rotten, too."

"Everything is rotten; everything but you. All alone, you will save the world?"

Hal's father was a short, stout, gray-haired man. With his shirt sleeves rolled up and his brown vest opened, he somehow seemed comical to Hal, standing in their dining room and arguing. But this quarrel was not merely funny. It was part of his preparation for the final struggle. This was part of his training to become a professional revolutionist. He argued back, speaking hotly and cruelly, and as he spoke he thought of Benton.

From the very beginning of his probation as a Party member, Hal heard constant praise of the leadership. Benton told him that he himself had joined the Party only after studying all the radical and revolutionary groups and parties and discovering that the leadership of their Party was the most honest and most revolutionary in the world.

"Bruno," Benton said to Hal, addressing him by his Party name, "our leadership is intransigent. We're not flattered by the so-called great. We're not seduced by power. We know, and our leadership knows its superiority to the leadership of the bourgeoisie and of the Stalinists. Our leaders, Bruno, are the advance guard of humanity. They carry the burden of the future of the human race on their shoulders."

Hal was awed. He wanted Benton's words to be the truth. He was committed, and, having become thus committed, he wanted to think that his Party leaders were the greatest and most daring men in the world. This would reflect on him. It would make him more important in his own eyes. And he, too, might one day become a Party functionary, a leader.

Hal heard much of Patrick A. Nolan, the General Secretary of the Party. Nolan was called "the Lenin of America," and he was also spoken of as the greatest trade union *spets* in the country. At first Hal didn't know what *spets* meant, but the word impressed him. Then he learned that it meant specialist, and he remained impressed. Before he met Nolan, Hal was properly awed. He was told that Nolan was the ambassador of the workers in world politics, but that he was human nonetheless, and that when you came to know Comrade Nolan you were impressed with how he so nobly represented the human element in the class struggle. Over and over again he heard adulatory and awe-inspiring descriptions of Nolan the Leader.

Hal met Comrade Nolan at Party headquarters, which were located over a bar near Union Square. It was in an old building of six stories, and the Party occupied the two middle floors. The quarters were crowded and disorderly, with papers and pamphlets all about. There were pictures and banners on the walls, and Nolan had a private office in the front. The door was often closed, and when it was, Hal would be told that the Old Man was inside, working and thinking.

Pat Nolan was a big, stocky man with a benign red face, a lazy and graceless manner, and a mop of jet black hair that was turning gray. His eyes were puffy. He would often stand or sit silently among his comrades, and they would wait tensely for him to speak. He treated them all in a patriarchal manner, and the comrades deferred to him in an almost reverential way. If he began to speak, they listened and looked at him in respectful silence. They spoke to impress him. They would even become hushed in his presence.

Benton and two other comrades were almost ceremonial in their manner when they brought Hal up to Pat Nolan. Nolan shook hands with him and stood for a moment as though in meditation.

"Bruno," Nolan said pompously, "you're new in the Movement. I've been in the Movement a long, long time."

Hal was uncomfortable. As it was, he was on probation in the Party, and he felt doubly uneasy in the Leader's presence. He was under inspection. When he talked, he suspected that what he was saying was being considered a test of himself. And that the eyes of these comrades were testing eyes directed at him.

"Comrade Corbin is a promising young revolutionist," Benton said.

Pat Nolan was silent and seemed lost in thought. Then he spoke, and he seemed to weigh every word he used.

"Fine. Fine. We can use every promising revolutionist we can find. There aren't enough of them for our needs. And we need them for the hard days ahead. . . . Yes, I've been in this Movement a long time, a long time, and, if I say it, I've learned a few things in it. Do you know what I have learned more than anything else, Corbin?"

"What?" Hal asked in awe.

"Integrity and principles, integrity and principles count for everything. They are among the abc's of revolutionary politics. That's what you've got to start with—that's what the workers want their leaders to have. If you haven't got these, you won't be of any use to us. Brains, we admire brains. We're not anti-intellectual like the Stalinists. Young fellow, I've seen a lot in my days as a revolutionist. Yes, I've seen plenty. And I've seen what's happened to the opportunists, the betrayers, the renegades. . . ." A look of hate crossed

Nolan's face. "And all this happened because they didn't have integrity and principles. And this is what we tell young comrades when they come to us. We don't fool them or mislead them. We tell them just what I'm telling you."

Hal was now so trapped in awe that he couldn't speak.

Nolan gave him a pat on the shoulder and with casual majesty turned to go into his office.

Hal saw that the other comrades were still hushed. And he felt that he had just had the greatest experience of his life.

III

At first Hal was given routine tasks to perform. He was sent out to sell the Party's weekly paper, *The Socialist Future*. He had been told of the great tasks that awaited him and his comrades, of the excitement, the joy, the sense of fulfillment that was to be found in Party life, but in these first days he found none of this fulfillment.

He doggedly performed these routine tasks. He would leave Party headquarters carrying his small bundle of papers under his arm, feeling shy and ill at ease. He didn't like this kind of work. Certainly he could do something more important than this. He couldn't throw himself into the job of selling papers for the Cause with energy and enthusiasm. He couldn't shout out to passers-by with conviction. When he raised his voice he somehow felt he was making a fool of himself. And the coldness, the lack of attention, the disregard of people on the streets merely dampened his enthusiasm all the more.

Streams of people would pass, but he would make very few sales. Policemen would eye him with hostility. Now and then someone would speak to him with unfriendliness or with anger. Stalinists would curse him. One pretty girl spat in his face and called him a fascist enemy of the people. These insults and the cold disinterest of the great mass of pedestrians on Fourteenth Street troubled him. When he did sell a paper, he would be very proud of himself. Often he would think of

how alone he and his comrades were, of how many there were
either against the revolution or else who just didn't care. He
would feel lonely, and he would become afraid. How could a
small band like this, which couldn't even sell its weekly paper
in respectable quantities, how could it think of ever leading
the world revolution? This question would recur to him again
and again as he stood on Fourteenth Street near Union Square,
now and then self-consciously calling out or else just holding
up a paper for the passers-by to see.

But one day he sold twenty copies and returned to Party
headquarters full of enthusiasm. Benton and some of the others
who were in the leadership or close to it were almost as happy
as children.

"It's no accident that your sales increased," Benton said,
ostentatiously pointing his index finger as he spoke.

"It's a straw in the wind. A small straw, but it's a straw in
the wind," another comrade said.

"You know the story about Trotsky and the soup?" a third
comrade asked.

"What story is that?" Hal asked.

"During the 1917 revolution, when Trotsky was Chairman
of the Soviets, one day he noticed that the waiter would give
him warmer soup than he did Don or the other Mensheviks.
Trotsky knew how to interpret that. He knew that the masses
were going over to the Bolsheviks.

"You have to have revolutionary insight to interpret these
little incidents and details. But with revolutionary insight
you can interpret them. That's why I say, Bruno, it's no accident. We're gaining. Good work. Good work you're doing."

Benton was moved by Hal's success. He put his arm around
Hal's shoulder for a moment. They all seemed like gay children. Hal was thrilled. He had contributed something. He had
done good work. But then a question framed itself in his
mind. Wasn't this all strange? Wasn't it strange that these
older and more experienced comrades should act like this?
They knew so much, and they wrote and talked with such
knowledge and such contempt, too, for the leaders of the world,

and here they were like happy children merely because he had sold twenty copies of the weekly paper on a street corner. He didn't like his own question, and he let it go unanswered. He pumped up an enthusiasm for his sales and tried to share the mood of his comrades. And he realized he had won recognition from important Party persons. This was a gain for him. He had impressed them. He was closer now to acceptance. Also, during these first days, Hal discovered that he would always win praise for good work, for good sales, for managing to distribute a large number of leaflets, or for performing other simple Party tasks. He would get the same kind of reception and response he had received when he had sold twenty copies of the paper. But when he asked questions or made suggestions, his comrades acted differently. They never replied to a question unless it happened to be one that could be answered readily in terms of the Party line. When he made a suggestion, they were always cautious about what they said. They were cold to enthusiasm or curiosity. If he talked about some ideas he had about Party work, or about books, or if he asked questions, he would meet with this strange cautiousness that made him feel almost as though he were receiving silent, unspoken disapproval. In the face of such reactions he would sometimes think he was in error. His sense of himself would dwindle. He would become apologetic and immediately would say something in affirmation of the Party program so that the others would know he was loyal.

These were hard days for Hal. He was constantly told that the individual was not important but that the Movement was everything. The Party came first, and each member must subordinate himself or herself to it and to its needs. No sacrifice was too great for the Party. He wanted to believe this, wanted to submerge himself. But the conditions of his life up to the time he had joined the Party had not prepared him for such a total submergence of self. Suddenly, after joining, he had to learn that his own wishes, moods, feelings, and ideas weren't important. These had to be sacrificed whenever they came into conflict with the needs and aims of the Party. The process of submerging and dedicating himself produced constant inner strains. He began to think that he wasn't important in himself, and that, at the same time, he hadn't as yet turned himself into an instrument of the Party and of history. He had heard Pat Nolan say that one must be a Party man above all else and that it was fundamental that you learn to wear the Party harness. The harness of the Party, Pat had added, was freedom, disciplined freedom, and teaching this disciplined freedom was part of the training of the cadres to be the leaders of the revolution. This life of preparation, Pat had also said, was the only moral and free life to be found in the present era of capitalist decay and barbarism. No human beings, Hal had been told again and again, bore the same responsibilities to humanity and to the future as did Nolan and the other Party leaders. At times, this talk threatened to overwhelm Hal.

But Hal was trying to assimilate this attitude toward the Party. He had tried to burn his bridges behind him, and yet he was only walking on a new and temporary bridge. He had not as yet been accepted. He had not as yet fully proven himself. He dreamed of proving himself by some grand and daring action, by risking his life in some class struggle. He wanted to prove himself by brave deeds. But he was given more routine chores. He helped with the mailing of the paper and the monthly theoretical magazine. He handed out more leaflets. He continued to sell papers. He did some door-to-door canvassing on the East Side. He knocked on doors and would hold up the weekly edition of *The Socialist Future* and say that he wanted to talk about this paper because it was dedicated to the interests of the workers. Sometimes doors were slammed in his face. Often he would meet with indifference. A few old men looked at him with fear. He gained no recruits and got very few subscriptions.

At school he was equally unsuccessful. He had arguments with Stalinists, and the result was that he was quickly scorned. Whispering campaigns were started against him. He was told by his comrades that in the face of this reaction he must have patience, that patience was one of the greatest virtues a revolutionist could have. He was also told that he must keep working among the young Stalinists. They were misled, but they offered the best raw material for the revolutionists. Part of his necessary discipline was to withstand the insults of the Stalinists without retaliating in kind. But insults hurt him and contributed further toward the subtle changes developing in his own feelings toward himself. His training period was one in which he was losing a sense of his own importance. He was suspended between his old world and this new one that was small and intense. Now he belonged to neither world. He looked at outsiders, those who were not in the Party, with smug disdain. And yet he wasn't truly accepted as an insider. All this intensified his craving for action. With some bold and brave heroic action he would prove himself. He would test his bravery and his loyalty, and then the forging of his character would have been achieved. He would have nothing to worry about, and he could become like the Party leaders.

But still he was kept at routine Party chores. His feelings became more and more quenched. His language became more violent. He borrowed the contempt for the bourgeois world which the Party leaders always exhibited. He began to use adjectives of disgust, sickness, death in his references to the bourgeois world. He saw this world in the image of his father and mother, and of the students and professors at school. His contempt for his home, his school, and for knowledge, which had been associated in his mind with his school, grew with this steady and subtle stifling of his feelings.

IV

The life and activity of the Party was largely internal. Party members saw one another constantly, and when they were together they talked and bragged about the Party and Party life. The politics of every other political group and tendency were treated as conspiracies. Every political statement made by anyone who didn't belong to the Party was treated as if it had a

double meaning. Nothing was taken at face value. Thus the
conversations he heard were ones in which the innuendoes and
suspicion of conspiracy were endlessly voiced, either directly
or else in many indirect ways. Distrust crept into the very
pores of Hal's mind. In time, he began to sense somewhat
vaguely that this distrust was to be found among his own comrades. They didn't trust one another. They were very watchful
whenever Pat Nolan's name was mentioned. But this only impelled Hal to want to belong all the more.

An opportunity to impress the leadership with his loyalty
and reliability came after he had been on probation for about
four months. A rank-and-filer named Grady Jones, who had
been to sea, was dissatisfied with the policy of the Party concerning the seamen. He had wanted to ship out to the Far East
but had been ordered to take a ship to France in order to es-
tablish contacts and to act as a courier. He said that he had had
to bring over literature that could just as easily have been
mailed, but the Party had insisted it be taken by courier. Grady
even said that most of the documents he had taken had consisted of papers, the theoretical magazine, and pamphlets which
were sold openly on street corners in New York. But the Party
had told him that he must accept this task as a duty. He was
disgruntled. He voiced his dissatisfaction to various members.

He and Hal had become casually friendly. One night, after
a meeting, they sat together drinking beer. Grady unburdened
himself. He condemned Pat Nolan, who he said had built a
small clique which ran the Party and which was stifling internal Party independence. Hal was shocked and uneasy, but he
remained noncommittal. As Grady went on talking, Hal,
against his will, found that he was believing what Grady said.
And though he realized that he was being treated in the same
way as others who were no longer on probation, he didn't dare
to commit himself to Grady. He was confused.

The next day Benton got in touch with him, and they had
dinner together. Benton began by talking about the Movement
and its glorious future.

"One day millions of workers will come to us and honor

us," Benton said over a roast-beef sandwich in a dingy restaurant near Fourteenth Street. Hal was awed, but he still was disturbed as a result of what Grady had told him the night before.

"We're small today, but we are firm and intact," Benton went on. "And we have experience. The entire experience of the socialist revolutionary movement is ours. That is more precious than numbers, than mass support without principles. We'll win mass support. In this conjunction of history we can't be a mass party. But we're finding avenues to the masses, and even though these are small now, they'll open up wide some day. They'll be revolutionary boulevards leading to decisive actions. But this is our crucial period, our period of testing. And during this period we have to be hard. Our motto is 'Bolshevik hardness.' "

Benton's talk sent a chill down Hal's spine. He was afraid he would never attain this Bolshevik hardness. He looked at his comrade with both fear and admiration. And he wondered what Benton had done to harden himself. He wanted to ask this question, but he didn't dare. He already had learned to be very reticent about asking questions.

After continuing his preamble in praise of the Party for several more minutes, Benton spoke of Grady.

"He's disgruntled. And Pat Nolan says, rightly, that the Party has no place for the disgruntled. Grady is a fine fellow, and everybody in the Party who knows him likes him. But he's disgruntled. And that weakens the fiber of the cadres. Disgruntlement is the beginning of an infection. We know this on the basis of our experience. In politics if you say A, you have to say B. And when A is an expression of abused and disgruntled feeling, B and C will be very dangerous. Disgruntlement is the road to betrayal."

"Of course, I didn't agree with him," Hal said quickly.

"What did he say?" Benton asked eagerly.

Hal smothered his resentment. He saw that he had been trapped. He didn't know what to do but to tell Benton what Grady had said to him. Benton listened attentively, and from

time to time, as Hal struggled to remember and to tell more
accurately what Grady had said, a pious smirk would cross
Benton's face.

"Yes, Grady is an infection," Benton said again after Hal
had finished recounting the conversation he had had with
Grady.

Two days later, at Party headquarters, Nolan patted Hal on
the back. In a week he was put on the paper. His days of
peddling literature were over. He was also given a salary of
twenty dollars a week. For of late the Party had been more
successful in its fund-raising and could put one more functionary on the payroll.

V

Benton, who was an editor of the weekly paper, took Hal
under his wing. He gave Hal a syllabus on dialectical materialism which Benton himself had prepared as the text of a course
he had given in the Party school. The syllabus confused Hal,
but he conscientiously tried to study it. He saw himself as
becoming a dialectician and a theoretician. Again and again he
had heard the Party leaders and functionaries talk of their
theory, and the word theoretician was one used with great
respect in Party circles.

At first Hal didn't have much confidence in his abilities, and
he therefore came to lean heavily on Benton. Benton helped
him with his first articles. These were general in scope and
were based on items in the capitalist press. With Benton's help
and in his first three weeks as a Party journalist, Hal wrote
articles on Spain, France, China, and Indo-China. These articles, however, were as much Benton's as his own.

Hal was praised for the articles, and after a few weeks he
began to be very hopeful about his future in the Movement.
He now was glad he had performed the routine chores. He
thought he understood why he should have been assigned such
tasks. These assignments revealed the wisdom and the experience of the Party. In order to wear Party harness, you had to

become a new person, and you couldn't do that by starting right off as a functionary. You had to do the routine rank-and-file work of the Party. He had done that. It had been a school of experience. And, having proven himself, he was now a professional. What more important work could anyone do than that of a Party functionary? And he was a functionary.

Pat Nolan often said that nothing could be too good for the leaders of the Party, and he also asserted that the Party rank-and-file wanted the leaders to receive proper treatment and salaries that were good in terms of the resources of the Party. In return, the functionaries and leadership gave direction to the Party line, guarded the priceless heritage of the Party, and worked devotedly. Hal decided that he would work devotedly. He labored long over his articles. He spent much time with Benton, listening to Benton talk, learning.

After he had been on the paper for two months, Benton brought him into Nolan's office for an interview.

"Well, how do you like our Party?" Nolan asked, swinging back in his chair.

"Comrade Nolan, it's changed my life."

Nolan sat back, looked at the ceiling, crossed his hands behind his graying head, and after a period of silence he said in a slow and somewhat drawling voice:

"We've been watching you, Bruno. Yes, we've been watching you. Watching you and nursing you along. You look like good material to us. Yes, you look like good material."

"Thank you, Comrade Nolan, I . . ."

Hal didn't know what to say. He gazed at the leader with sudden devotion. Here was a man he could trust. This man seemed so human. His face was so kindly. He spoke so simply, without any pretensions. Yes, here was a real leader to follow.

"I told you right after you joined us that in this Movement integrity and principles count. We think you have shown you have both. But now you've got to make up your mind."

Nolan came forward in his chair and looked at Hal seriously and intently.

"There's another thing I want to tell you, lad. You can't live in two worlds. It's one world or the other. We learned that long ago. And we don't live in two worlds. Our Party is our world. It's the world of the future. Out there," Nolan made a sweeping gesture toward the window, "is the dead world. It's that world or this world. We think you belong in this world. Here, that's where we think you belong."

"Yes . . . yes. I want to," Hal said, almost stuttering.

"That's what you have to choose. You're doing fine work on the paper here. We think you ought to stay on the paper, get training from older comrades, associate with them, learn from them, absorb their experiences. But you can't do that and be a college boy. What education can you get in college compared to the education we can give you?"

Nolan opened up the question which had been framing itself vaguely in Hal's mind. He knew now that he had to quit college. And at the same time he thought that he was being given consideration here such as he had never received in college. Nolan was thinking about him. He was sure that Nolan was interested in him and wanted to see him develop. He filled almost with love for this man, whom he saw as a benign and kindly leader watching over all the comrades as a fond father, looking out here from this small and dingy office as a kind of patient and loving father of the workers of America and of the whole world.

"Yes, I ought to quit college. I wanted to bring up this question with the comrades."

Benton proudly smirked.

"You'll never regret your decision," he told Hal.

"Trust us, lad, and we'll train you as a Bolshevik fighter," Pat Nolan said.

"Thank you, Comrade Nolan. I want you to know how much I appreciate your fatherly talk to me."

"That's what the comrades put me here to do. We're comrades, lad. Comrade is the finest word in our language."

When they left Nolan's office, Benton was so moved that he was inarticulate. He was like a little boy trying to say some-

thing he lacked the capacity to frame in words. Finally he was
able to say:

"Pat Nolan is the finest man I ever met."

Hal, too, was deeply touched. But he hid his feelings. The
recognition and the sympathy he had just received pleased him,
and he took it as a justification of his political decision. He
belonged here now. And he had been asked, asked to give up
his college career and to devote himself to full-time Party
work. Pat Nolan himself had been the man who had asked him.
Yes, he agreed with Benton about Pat Nolan.

Hal quit college.

VI

The haze through which Hal saw the Party was only gradually dissipated. The Party was almost like a foreign nation that
preserved its own rights of extraterritoriality within New
York. A number of the members gave it both devotion and an
intensity of concentration; they lived in and for the Party. The
wives of many leaders and members worked at jobs and supported their husbands, thus permitting them to give full time
to the Party. Some of these girls and women worked eight
hours a day in offices or in the needles trades, and at night they
would give their time and energy to Party tasks. Some of them
could not find enough to do. They performed all kinds of
volunteer work. They typed documents until late into the
night. They knocked on doors and rang doorbells, recruiting
and soliciting subscriptions for the paper and the monthly
theoretical magazine. They stood at a table for hours, after
having worked all day, getting out mailings. They swept the
office and cleaned it. They stood on corners, even in the cold
and rain, selling publications and handing out leaflets. Before
the meetings of other groups started, they would stand outside
the halls, trying to give away their own Party literature. At
times they risked physical assault from the Stalinists because
they would try to distribute their own Party literature in

front of Stalinist meetings. They would be beaten up, spat on, kicked, and their papers and pamphlets would be snatched out of their hands and torn up. They would loyally perform any task assigned to them, and they did this with dull, unflinching, unimaginative, but courageous devotion.

Within the Party, the comrades revealed attitudes both of contempt and superiority or else of submission. The majority of them never questioned any of the statements of the leadership. They piously accepted what they were told and what was written in the Party publications. And at the same time they met outsiders with contempt and a sense of their own superiority. Most outsiders were enemies or potential enemies. Non-Party members were met with suspicion. Party members had endless little unconscious habits that could repel people. They were full of hostility to the outside world. The distrust they felt for so many of their own comrades was directed with much greater intensity toward the non-Party world. Non-Party members could be enemies. They were people who didn't know what the life of the Party could do for a comrade, and they didn't understand the great mission of the Party. They didn't have faith. They went on living their own individual lives, living for pleasure, not caring about the workers or about performing a historic role. And along with the Party workers' suspicion and sense of difference there was their faith in the Word. The words of the leadership, the words printed in the publications, the words expressing the Party line or program were always correct. All that needed to be done was to spread the Word. If the Word were spread to the workers, the workers would flock to the Party. But the whole bourgeois world was organized in conspiracy with the Stalinists and the labor fakers to prevent the workers from hearing the true Word. Still, the true Word would be heard. It would be accepted. And then there would be growth, the masses would go into motion, and America would come upon great and glorious days like those of November, 1917, in Russia. All this was believed as absolute, and it inspired many acts of courage and sacrifice.

Hal had not been a Party journalist for long when he came
to see that he was different from the rank-and-filers. He developed the habit of using the pronoun "our" when he spoke
of the rank-and-filers. He developed the same possessive feeling toward them that Pat and the top leaders showed. And at
the same time there was a faction in the Party which assumed
that a rank-and-filer was a worker. Actually, there were few
proletarians in the Party. Most of the members came from the
lower middle class, and there was a high percentage of high-
school graduates and college students, and even of college
graduates, among them. Nolan was the leading *spets* on the
workers, and a fantastic and unreal notion of the workers was
held by most of the Party membership. Hal became submis-
sive, respectful, and even sentimental whenever he met a real
worker. He spoke to such a man in tones of awe.

Hal gradually became adapted to the attitudes of the Party
without being fully aware of what was happening to him. He
slid into the habit of assuming that the Party was always right,
and that critics and questioners were enemies or potential
enemies. Grady was expelled about nine months after Hal had
been given a job on the paper, and when Benton explained that
Grady had to be expelled because the Party had to cut out all
cancers, he accepted this explanation. And the changes in Hal
were not merely in his mental and emotional attitudes. His
voice changed. He spoke with a kind of slick and authoritative
tone, and often a sneer would automatically come into his
voice. He would attempt to strengthen his condemnations by
raising his voice, by slurring his words, by sneers, and even by
derisive sounds when he mentioned the names of those whom
he denounced. But in defending or affirming positions of the
Party, he would talk in tones and accents of borrowed authority, and his words would be accompanied by gestures that he
imagined conveyed force, power, and conviction. He would
pound his fist on the table. He acquired a whole new series
of grimaces. And when he was faced with a question or issue
that did not easily permit a Party-line answer, he would remain in smirking silence. As though by instinct, he developed

the habit of always finding out what he ought to say by making comments or asking questions in such a way as to get the correct answer from his older comrades. In brief, he had been broken in so that he was able to live in the Party harness.

VII

Hal now needed the association of his comrades. When he was away from the Party environment, he felt out of place. At times, when he was alone, he would be threatened with a loss of his sureness and his convictions. If he met old friends, he would meet them with a smirk, and he would let go at them, attacking their convictions, exposing the infected character of their lives and their values to his own satisfaction. He quarreled, denounced, and threatened people with the verdict of history. Walking about the streets of New York, he alternated between moods of contempt and fear. He could feel no common bond with these crowds of people. He saw them coming and going, and merely by looking at them he could know that they were not politicalized, that they didn't care, and that they didn't believe in the Revolution. Often he would see them as enemies, enemies who would support the other side. There were times when he would walk on upper Fifth Avenue, on upper Madison, or on Park Avenue merely to sneer and glare at the well-dressed women. They were walking infections who merely looked like human beings. But they weren't human. They were bourgeois. They were living off the blood and sweat of the workers whom he and his comrades would save. And after these walks he would sink into moods of depression and would hasten to Party headquarters, where he could find his own kind. These walks stimulated him in his writing, and when he got back to headquarters he would dash off denunciatory articles. His pieces were filled with adjectives and metaphors suggesting disease and infection, decay and death. And as he pounded them out, he would sometimes look up from the typewriter and let his eyes wander about the shabby and disorderly Party quarters, noticing comrades, observing some of the unattractive girls who worked in the office, and he would think that this office was the real center of health of the country and that Park Avenue and Fifth Avenue and Madison Avenue were the moral germ centers of the nation.

Hal's reputation in the Party rose fast. He won recognition as a leading Party journalist. And as this took place, his manners toward his own comrades changed further. He was rude and overbearing to many of them. He was curt and demanding with the girls in the office. He was pompous with rank-and-filers. At meetings he would sit with his head tilted at an angle, his arms folded pompously in front of him, and his expression one of smug conceit. He spoke often at meetings, and in his speeches he imitated Pat Nolan, who was considered a great orator. His tone of voice became like Pat's. He imitated Pat's gestures. He shouted. In fact, he was now consciously working away at the task of remaking himself into a leader of the revolution.

Finally, Hal won recognition as a member of the clique or group of special friends of Pat Nolan. He was invited to Pat's house for a small celebration of the fall of Mussolini.

Pat lived in a modest but comfortable apartment near Party headquarters. The rent for this flat came from Party funds. About twelve comrades were gathered around Pat. He was sitting in an easy chair, with his shoes off and his collar open, and he held a glass of beer in his hand and recited the poetry of Shelley and Byron, which he had read in his youth. They were all gay. The Party was better off financially because of war prosperity. The occasion was festive.

"Drink again, comrades. This is a great occasion," Pat said, after having recited a snatch of a poem by Shelley.

The comrades all drank.

"The historic turn has come," Pat said after they all had more beer.

"Yes, that's so. Just as Pat said, the turn has come. Our day is near."

"Mussolini, that rat. Where is he now? What is power and

glory? The day of the power of the rats is over. Now our day is coming," Pat proclaimed.

"It's coming sooner than many think," Hal said.

"Did you hear what Bruno said? He's one of my boys. Bruno, we're proud of you. We trained you. We made you. We picked you up, a confused bourgeois youth, and we trained you. Stick with us, boy, and you'll be a revolutionary made of steel."

"I'll try always to devote myself."

"Stay with us and you'll have a future. We know enough, we know all we need to know to make the revolution. And now it has started, it's going to spread just like a forest fire. It's roaring now in Rome and all over Italy. And they laughed at us. They scorned us. Some of our own comrades left us, the traitors. Now what can they say? Now events are on our side, and all the traitors can crawl in the mud at our feet. They will. They'll try to crawl back to us, and when they do, they can shine our shoes, they can be our bootblacks."

They all listened. More beer was drunk. Pat spoke with deeply felt venom. And his talk unloosed the tongues of his admiring comrades. They fed his hatred and mentioned names that he would pick up and curse. And with each malediction he would add:

"And that rat, too, can shine our shoes."

They had a good time. They left Pat's house feeling happy. They were convinced the revolution had started.

VIII

After the night at Pat's, Hal found himself becoming increasingly uneasy. He had left the apartment in a mood approaching elation. His mind had been filled with anticipation of events to come. He had envisioned the workers marching to power along the streets of New York. He had fancied himself making speeches to incite the workers, and he had lain in bed that night composing a great and historic revolutionary oration. But slowly, gradually, and insidiously some uneasy doubt crept into his mind. He feared he didn't really believe the Revolution had started. He feared he didn't believe the fall of Mussolini would lead to the world revolution and the coming to power of his Party. And as days passed into weeks, this doubt deepened and grew. While he was in the throes of these secret doubts, he wrote articles which contradicted his inner feelings. His writings revealed only the shallowest optimism.

During the last days of the war, he became more doubting than ever. And then, after the end of the war, he woke up one day and discovered he didn't believe what he was writing. He continued to function as a Party journalist. He continued to write as though he had undergone no change in his convictions. But he began to have attacks of colitis. Pat sent him away for a vacation after a particularly severe attack. He returned, tanned and healthy, eager to pitch into his work again, and to try to believe. But he couldn't believe. He couldn't believe that this shabby headquarters was the office of the future of mankind. He couldn't believe that Pat Nolan was the greatest man of the age. And he began to discover that others were in the same state he was in. Innuendoes, gossip, asides in conversations, hints on all sides gave him the feeling that other comrades felt more or less as he did.

A factional fight concerning the Russian question developed in the Party. The dissatisfaction, doubt, and frustration of many comrades was elevated to a plane of principles, but along with erudite and recondite arguments and theses there were bitter denunciations. Hal wavered between the factions. He suddenly joined the opposition to Pat. He thought they were going to win. He became the most violently antagonistic of the opposition and wrote their most important documents. He even debated with Pat at one branch meeting. Pat fought back by a series of sly and careful maneuvers. When the convention was held to decide the struggle, Pat was in control. The opposition was repudiated, and Hal was given the opportunity to confess his errors or face expulsion. He admitted his errors. But nevertheless he was ordered to stand charges before the

Party Control Commission, a Party institution of leading members which investigated and judged erring comrades.

Hal suffered a recurrence of colitis. He now felt utterly lost.
He didn't know what the future held for him. He didn't know
how he could go back into the world he had deserted. And he
knew he was washed up in the Party. But at the same time Pat
kept him on the Party payroll, and under instruction he was
required to write and assert everything with which he had
disagreed during the faction fight. He was appointed one of
the journalists who had to write the articles that advanced the
Party program most concretely. Then he faced the Control
Commission. It was composed of the same comrades
he met regularly in the office and whom he had met
at Pat's house at parties and gatherings before the factional fight. Benton was chairman of the meeting, and the
members of the Commission all looked at Hal with cold,
cruel, insolent faces, as if they had never seen him before.
He couldn't believe these were the same comrades with whom
he had worked for a number of years. Their very voices had
changed. They spoke to him with merciless contempt. And
other comrades testified against him. He discovered he had
even been shadowed, and that chance remarks of his had been
reported and records of them made. Accusation after accusation was hurled at him. When he rose to defend himself, he
faced comrades who stared at him as though he were both a
criminal and a stranger. As he spoke, trying to defend himself,
their cruel faces seemed immobile. When he concluded, he
was met with silent contempt. He was expelled from the Party.
Benton delivered the verdict, speaking with a contemptuous
hatred, and yelling and shrieking when he concluded by calling
Hal an enemy of the workers and a renegade counterrevolu-
tionary.

Hal walked out of the Party headquarters, alone and
shaken. It was a cold night. He wandered about the city, dazed
and hurt. He didn't know what to do, where to go. He felt
that he was friendless and lost. There was no world to which

he belonged. He returned to his little East Side room late, but he couldn't sleep.

In a few days Hal went back to live at home. His parents received him with friendliness. Through his father he got a job. He managed to work his way up to a successful position in the real estate business, and he married a well-to-do girl from his neighborhood. He was well off financially within two years, but he was now a young man who had been permanently scarred by the scalpel of hatred.